About the Authors

Lynne Marshall used to worry she had a serious problem with daydreaming, then she discovered she was supposed to write those stories! An RN for twenty-six years, she came to fiction writing later than most. Now she writes romance, which usually includes medicine, but always comes straight from her heart. She is happily married, a Southern California native,

addition to travelling, Tina loves to cuddle with her pug, Alex, spend time with her family, and hit the trails on her horse. Learn more about Tina from her website, or friend her on Facebook.

The Hot Docs on Call

COLLECTION

July 2019

August 2019

September 2019

October 2019

November 2019

December 2019

Hot Docs on Call: Tinseltown Cinderella

LYNNE MARSHALL

AMALIE BERLIN

TINA BECKETT

MILLS & BOON

First Published in Great Britain 2019
By Mills & Boon, an imprint of HarperCollins *Publishers*
1 London Bridge Street, London, SE1 9GF

HOT DOCS ON CALL: TINSELTOWN CINDERELLA
© 2019 Harlequin Books S.A.

His Pregnant Sleeping Beauty © Harlequin Books S.A. 2016
Taming Hollywood's Ultimate Playboy
© Harlequin Books S.A.2016
Winning Back His Doctor Bride © Harlequin Books S.A. 2016

Special thanks and acknowledgement are given to
Lynne Marshall, Amalie Berlin and Tina Beckett *for
their contribution to* The Hollywood Hills Clinic *series*

ISBN: 978-0-263-27670-1

1019

MIX
Paper from
responsible sources
FSC™ C007454

This book is produced from independently certified FSC™ paper
to ensure responsible forest management.

For more information visit: www.harpercollins.co.uk/green

Printed and bound in Spain
by CPI, Barcelona

HIS PREGNANT SLEEPING BEAUTY

LYNNE MARSHALL

This book is dedicated to the two paramedics who helped me make my character, Joe, a true hero. Thank you John-Philip Maarschalk and Rick Ochocki for your expert input and help. What would the world be without our first responders?

CHAPTER ONE

CAREY SPENCER HAD never felt more alone in her life than when she got off the bus in Hollywood.

Joseph Matthews, on that night's shift for the prestigious Hollywood Hills Clinic, had just delivered one of the industry's favorite character actresses to the exclusive twenty-bed extended recovery hotel. It was tucked between Children's Hospital and a smaller private hospital on Sunset Boulevard, and the common eye would never guess its function. Joe had agreed to make the Wednesday night run because James Rothsberg himself had asked. After all, the lady *had* won an award for Best Supporting Actress the year before last.

As the lead paramedic for the ambulance line he owned, Joe had attended the not-to-be-named-aloud patient during the uneventful ride to the recovery hotel. She'd been heavily sedated, her IV was in place, her vitals, including oxygen saturation, were fine, but she'd had so much work done on her face, breasts and hands she looked like a mummy. When they'd arrived, you'd have thought he'd delivered the President to Walter Reed National Military Medical Center the way the abundant staff rushed to the ambulance and took over the transfer.

Now, at nine p.m., back sitting in the front of the private ambulance, Joe switched on some music. Jazz, his favorite station. Yeah, he owned this bus—hell, he owned all six of them—so he could play whatever music he wanted. But that also kept him thinking about work a lot. It was the first of the month and he'd have to make copies of the June shift schedule for the EMTs and paramedics on his team before they showed up for work tomorrow morning.

"I'm hungry," Benny, his EMT, said from behind the wheel.

Why was Joe not surprised? The kid had barely turned twenty and seemed to have hollow legs.

Restless and out of sorts, a state that was nothing new these days, Joe nodded. "How about that Mexican grill?" They'd just made their last run on Friday night, without plans for later, so why not?

"You read my mind." Benny tossed him a cockeyed grin, his oversized Afro flopping with the quick movement.

He turned off Hollywood Boulevard and up N. Cahuenga to the fast-food place by the cross-country bus depot, where a bus had just arrived from Who Knew Where, USA. Benny had to wait to pull into a larger-than-average parking space. Joe mindlessly watched a handful of people trickle off the bus.

A damn fine-looking young woman wearing oversized sunglasses got off. Sunglasses at night. What was up with that? She was slender and her high-heeled boots made her look on the tall side. She wore jeans and a dark blue top, or was it a sweater? Her thick hair was layered and long with waves and under the bus depot lights looked brown. Reddish? He wondered what her story was. Probably because of the shades at night. But he didn't bother to think about ladies these days. Yet, still, dang, she was hot. And stood out like a rose in a thorn patch.

Benny backed the private ambulance into the space at the farthest end of the restaurant lot, and Joe got out the passenger side, immediately getting hit by the mouthwatering aroma of spicy beans and chipotle chicken. He stretched, eager to chow down. A sudden movement in his peripheral vision drew his attention. Someone sprang from behind a pillar and snagged a lady's purse strap and wrist, pulling her out of the crowd and toward the nearby alley. It was the woman he'd just been gawking at! The other travelers had mostly dispersed. She put up a fight, too, and squealed, yet the few people left lingering didn't seem to notice...but he did.

Joe ran to the mouth of the alley. "Hey!" Then sprinted toward the young woman, who was still fighting to hold on to her purse.

The tall but skinny, straggly-haired dude dragged her by the shoulder strap and wrist deeper down the alley. *Why doesn't she just let go? Ah, wait, it's one of those over-the-torso jobs.*

"Hey!"

This time the guy turned and whacked her with his fist, knocking the young woman to the ground. Her head hit with a thud. He ripped off the purse, hitting her head on the pavement again, then stepped over her to get to Joe with a wild swing.

Joe blocked the first punch with little effort—the dumb punk didn't know what he was dealing with as he boxed for his workouts—but the guy pulled a knife and lashed out. Joe threw another punch and landed it, even while feeling a hot lightning-quick slice across his ribs. Now he was really ticked. The guy ran deeper into the alley with Joe in pursuit, soon disappearing over a large trash bin and tall crumbling brick wall. Joe skidded to a brief stop and watched in disbelief. For a scumbag the man was agile. Probably from a lot of practice in assaulting innocent people.

The girl! Holding his side, he sprinted back to where she lay. Out cold.

Benny met up with him. "I called the police. You okay?"

"Just a superficial wound." Still, he checked it briefly since an adrenaline rush could mask pain. The last thing he wanted to find out was that the cut was deep enough to cause evisceration and he hadn't noticed. Fortunately the only thing he saw was oozing blood, nothing gushing. He'd throw a thick absorbent pad over his middle as soon as Benny got back with the trauma kit, oxygen bag and backboard. He didn't want to bleed all over the poor lady. "Bring our equipment, okay?" He grabbed a pair of gloves from Benny's belt, and knelt in front of the young woman as Benny took off for the ambulance. "I'm a paramedic, miss. Are you okay?" he said loudly and clearly. She didn't respond.

She'd hit her head hard when she'd fallen—correct that, had been punched to the ground. He tried to rouse her with a firm hand on her shoulder. "Hello? You okay, you awake, miss?"

He watched the rise and fall of her chest. At least she was breathing normally. He felt her neck for the carotid pulse and found it. Rate and strength normal. Good. He scanned her body for bleeding or other signs of obvious injury. Maybe the scumbag had stabbed her too. Then he used the palms of his gloved hands to sweep the underside of her arms and legs to check for bleeding, and did the same beneath both sides of her back. So far so good.

There was a fifty-cent-sized pool of blood behind her head, but he didn't move her neck, not before he and Benny had placed a cervical collar on her. Her assailant had run off with her purse and she didn't appear to have any other form of ID. He checked her wrist and then her neck to see if she wore any emergency alert jewelry. No such luck. They'd have to wait until she regained consciousness to find out who she was.

Even under the dim lights in the alley she had an obvious black eye, and because the dirtbag had yanked off her torso-anchored purse strap the sweater she'd been wearing had been pulled halfway down her left arm… which was covered in bruises. She'd just been mugged, but these marks weren't fresh. Anger surged through him. She'd been beaten up long before today.

What kind of guy treated a woman like that?

He shook his head. Of all the lousy luck. She hadn't stepped off the bus five minutes ago and had already gotten mugged and knocked unconscious. The only thing she had going for her on this nightmare of a Friday night was him. He shuddered for the young stranger over what might have played out if he hadn't been here.

Maybe it was those thick eyelashes that seemed to glue her eyes shut, or her complete vulnerability, being unconscious in an alley, or maybe it was the obvious signs of abuse, but for whatever reason Joe was suddenly struck with an uncompromising need to protect her.

From this moment on tonight he vowed to take responsibility for the out-of-luck Jane Doe. Hell, if anyone had ever needed a guardian angel, she did.

Benny had moved the ambulance closer, and brought the backboard and equipment. Joe let Benny apply a large sloppy dressing around his middle as he checked her airway again, noting she had good air exchange. He worried, with the head injury, that she might vomit and wanted to be near if she did to prevent aspiration.

"We're going to give you some oxygen and put a collar round your neck," Joe said calmly, hoping she might already be regaining consciousness and hear him explain everything they did to her. They worked together and soon had Jane on the backboard for stability. Joe secured her with the straps, never taking his eyes off her. She had definitely been knocked out cold, yet still breathed evenly. A good thing. But he knew when unconscious people woke up they could often be combative and try to take off the oxygen and cervical collar. Hell, after what she'd just been through, could he blame her if she woke up fighting?

With her long dark auburn hair spread over her shoulders and her hands strapped to the transport board, she made the strangest image.

An urban Sleeping Beauty.

"Ready for transfer?" Joe said, breaking his own thoughts.

"Don't you want to wait for the police?"

"If they're not here by the time we get her in the back of the van, you call them again and tell them to meet us at the clinic. She might have a skull fracture or subdural bleed for all we know, and needs medical attention ASAP." He knew the next forty-five minutes were all she had remaining in the golden hour for traumatic head injury. "I'm going to call Dr. Rothsberg and let him know what we've got."

He jumped into the back of the van first to guide the head of the gurney on which they'd placed the long spine board and patient as Benny pushed from the back, then he rolled the gurney forward and locked it in place with sprung locks on the ambulance floor.

He'd ride in the back with her. If she woke up, confused and possibly combative, he wanted to be there. Plus it would be his chance to do a more thorough examination.

Joe did another assessment of Sleeping Beauty's condition. Unchanged. Then he made the call. Unexpectedly, Dr. Rothsberg said to bring her to the clinic instead of county. Which was a good thing, because Joe would have taken her home before he'd consider delivering a Jane Doe to county hospital to potentially slip through every conceivable crack due to their overstretched system.

He stripped off the makeshift dressing and his shirt to assess his own wound, which was long and jagged, still wept blood and would definitely need stitches. Now that he was looking at it, it burned like hell. Benny had a short conversation with the police, who'd just arrived. Great timing! He showed them where they'd found her and where the attacker had fled over the wall then left them to look for witnesses as Joe cleaned and dressed his own wound. Damn, the disinfectant smarted! One of the policemen took a quick look inside the ambulance, saw the victim and Joe with his injury, nodded and took off toward the alley.

Benny closed the back doors of the van, got into the driver's seat then started the ambulance. "They'll take our statements at the clinic later."

"Good," Joe said, taping his dressing, constantly checking his patient as he did so.

As Benny drove, with their lights flashing, Joe checked her vital signs again, this time using a blood-pressure cuff then a stethoscope to listen to her lungs.

He opened her eyes, opening the blackened eye more gingerly, and used his penlight to make sure she hadn't blown a pupil. Fortunately she hadn't, but unfortunately he'd had to move a clump of her hair away from her face in order to do so. It was thick and wavy, and, well, somehow it felt too intimate, touching it. It'd been a while since he'd run his fingers through a woman's hair, which he definitely wasn't doing right now, but the thought of wanting to bothered him.

By the status of her black eye, it'd been there a few days and definitely looked ugly and intentional. Someone had punched her. That was a fact. There was that anger again, flaming out of nowhere for a woman he knew zero about.

He decided to insert a hep-lock into her antecubital fossa so the clinic would have a line ready to go on arrival. A head injury could increase cranial pressure and so could IV fluid. He didn't want to add to that, and so far her blood pressure was within normal limits. While he performed the tasks he thought about everything that had happened to his patient prior to winding up in that alley.

She'd gotten off the bus and hadn't waited to collect a suitcase, which meant all she'd carried with her was in that large shoulder bag. And that was long gone with the punk who'd knocked her cold and jumped the wall. He tightened his fists. What he'd give to deck that guy and leave him in some alley.

If Joe added up the clues he'd guess that the lovely Sleeping Jane was running from whoever had bruised her arms and blackened her eye. She'd probably grabbed whatever she could and snuck away from...

"Who are you?" Joe asked quietly, wondering if she could hear him, knowing that unconscious people sometimes still heard what went on around them. "Where did you come from?"

He lifted one of her hands, that fierce sense of protectiveness returning, and held it in his, noticing the long thin fingers with carefully manicured but unpainted nails, and made another silent vow. *Don't worry, I'll look out for you. You don't have to be afraid where I'm taking you.*

They arrived at The Hollywood Hills Clinic, nestled far beneath the Hollywood sign at the end of narrow winding roads with occasional hairpin turns. The swanky private clinic that hugged the hillside always reminded him of something Frank Lloyd Wright might have designed for the twenty-first century, if he were still alive. The stacked boxy levels of the modern stone architecture, nearly half of it made of special earthquake-resistant glass, looked like a diamond in the night on the hillside. Warm golden light glowed from every oversized window, assuring the private clinic was open twenty-four hours. For security and privacy purposes, there were tall fences out front, and a gate every vehicle had to clear, except for ambulances. They breezed through as soon as the gate opened completely.

Benny headed toward the private patient loading area at the back of the building. Joe put his shirt back on and gingerly buttoned it over his bandaged and stinging rib cage.

He still couldn't believe his good fortune over landing the bid as the private ambulance company for James Rothsberg's clinic only two short years after starting his own business. He'd been an enterprising twenty-three-year-old paramedic with a plan back then, thanks to a good mind for business instilled in him by his hard-working father. James must have seen something about him he liked when he'd interviewed him and Joe had tendered his bid. Or maybe it had had more to do with the nasty info leak the previous ambulance company had been responsible for, exposing several of the A-list actors in the biz on a TV gossip show, making Joe's timing impeccable. He used to think of it as fate.

James's parents—Michael Rothsberg and Aubrey St. Claire—had had enough info leaks in their lives to fill volumes. Everyone, even Joe, remembered the scandal, and he'd only been in his early teens at the time. Their stories had made headlines on every supermarket rag and cable TV talk show. Everyone knew about their private affairs. After all, James's parents had been Hollywood royalty, and had been two of the highest-paid actors in the business. Watching them fall from grace had become a national pastime after a nasty kiss-and-tell book by an ex-lover had outed them as phonies. Their marriage had been a sham, and their teenage children, James and Freya, had suffered most.

James had told Joe on the day he'd hired him that loyalty to the clinic and the patients was the number-one rule, he wouldn't tolerate anything less, and Joe had lived up to that pledge every single day he'd shown up to work. He'd walked out of James's office that day thinking fate was on his side and he was the luckiest man on earth, but he too would soon experience his own fall. Like James, it hadn't been of his own making but that didn't mean it had hurt any less.

These days Joe didn't believe in fate or luck. No, he'd changed his thinking on that and now, for him, everything happened for a reason. Even his damned infertility, which he was still trying to figure out. He glanced at the hand where his wedding ring had once been but didn't let himself go there, instead focusing on the positive. The here and now. The new contract. His job security.

The clinic had opened its doors six years ago, and two years later, right around the time James's sister Freya had joined the endeavor, Joe's private ambulance service had been the Rothsbergs' choice for replacement. Having just signed a new five-year contract with the clinic, Joe almost thought of himself as another Hollywood success story. Hell, he was only twenty-eight, owned his own business, and worked for the most revered clinic in town.

But how could he call it true success when the rest of his life was such a mess?

James Rothsberg himself met the ambulance, along with another doctor and a couple of nurses, and Joe prepared to transfer his sleeping beauty.

A little bit taller than Joe, James's strong and well-built frame matched Joe's on the fitness scale. Where they parted ways was in the looks department. The son of A-list actors, James was what the gossip magazines called "an Adonis in scrubs". Yeah, he was classy, smooth and slick. He was the man every woman dreamed of and every man wanted to be, and Joe wasn't afraid to admit he had a man crush on the guy. Strictly platonic, of course, based on pure admiration. The doctor ran the lavish clinic for the mind-numbingly affluent, who flocked to him, eager to pay the price for his plastic surgery services. Well, someone had to support the outrageously luxurious clinic and the well-paid staff. In fact, someone on staff had recently commented after a big awards ceremony that half of the stars in attendance had been through the clinic's doors. A statement that wasn't far from the truth.

"James, what are you still doing here?"

"You piqued my interest," James said. "I had to see Jane Doe for myself."

Joe pushed the gurney out of the back of the ambulance, and Rick, one of the evening nurses, pulled from the other end.

James studied Jane Doe as she rolled by. "She didn't get that shiner tonight."

"Nope," Joe said. "There's a whole other story that went down before she got mugged."

James nodded agreement. "That reminds me, I got a call from the police department. They'll be here shortly to take your statement." He tugged Joe by the arm. "Let's take a look at your injury before they get here, okay?"

Joe was torn between looking after Sleeping Beauty or himself, but knew the clinic staff would give her the utmost medical attention. Besides, it wasn't every day the head of the clinic offered to give one-to-one patient care to an employee.

"Thanks, Doc. I really appreciate it."

"It's totally selfish. I've got to look out for my lead paramedic, right?" James said in a typically self-deprecating manner. That was another thing he liked so much about the guy. He never flaunted his wealth or his status.

Joe glanced across the room at the star patient of the night, Ms. Jane Doe, still unconscious but breathing steadily, and felt a little tug in his chest, then followed James into an examination room.

After the nursing assistant removed Joe's dressing, James studied it. "So what happened here?"

Joe explained what had transpired in the alley as the doctor applied pressure to one area that continued to bleed.

"Oh, you're definitely getting a tetanus shot. Who knows what was on that guy's blade."

"Well, he *was* a scumbag."

"Good thing you've got a trained plastic surgeon to stitch you up. I'd hate to ruin those perfect washboard abs."

Joe laughed, knowing his rigorous workout sessions plus boxing kept him fit. Boxing had been the one thing he could do to keep sane and not beat the hell out of his best friend during his divorce. "Ouch," he said, surprised by how sensitive his wound was as the nursing assistant cleaned the skin.

"Ouch!" he repeated, when the first topical anesthetic was injected by James.

The doctor chuckled. "Man up, dude. I'm just getting started."

That got an ironic laugh out of Joe. *Yeah, sterile dude, man up!*

"You won't be feeling much in a couple of minutes."

Joe knew the drill, he'd sutured his share of patients in his field training days, but this was the first time in his entire life he'd been the patient in need of stitches. Hell, he'd never even needed a butterfly bandage before.

"So, about the girl with the black eye," James said, donning sterile gloves while preparing the small sterile minor operations tray. "I wonder if she may have had any prior intracranial injuries that might have contributed to her immediately falling unconscious."

"I was wondering the same thing, but she hit that pavement really hard. I hope she doesn't have a subdural hematoma."

"We're doing a complete head trauma workup on her."

"Thanks. I know this probably sounds weird, but

I feel personally responsible for her, having seen the whole thing go down, not getting there fast enough, and being the first to treat her and all. Especially since she doesn't have any ID."

"You broke a rule, right? Got involved with your patient?"

"Didn't mean to, but I guess you could say that. I know it's foolish—"

James turned back toward him. "And this might be foolish too, but when the police come we'll tell them we'll be treating *and* letting our Jane Doe recover right here."

Touched beyond words, as the cost for staying at this exclusive clinic would be astronomical, Joe wanted to shake the good doctor's hand but he wore sterile gloves. "Thank you. I really—" He was about to say "appreciate that" but quickly went quiet, not used to being the patient as the first stitch was placed, using a nasty-looking hooked needle, and though he didn't feel anything, he still didn't want to move.

"If I stitch this up just so, there'll hardly be a scar. On the other hand, I could make you look like you've got a seven pack."

As the saying went, it only hurt when he laughed.

A couple of hours later, the police had taken a thorough report, and also told Joe they hadn't found anyone matching the description a couple of witnesses had given for the suspect, they also said they hadn't recovered Jane Doe's purse.

Joe sighed and shook his head. She'd continue to be Madam X until she came to. Which hopefully would be soon.

"We do have one lead, though."

He glanced up, hopeful whatever that lead was it might point to Jane's identity.

"The clinic staff found a bus-ticket stub in her sweater pocket. If she used a credit card to purchase the ticket, we might be able to trace it back and identify her."

"That's great. But what if she paid cash?"

"That might imply she didn't want to be traced."

"Probably explain those bruises, too."

The cop nodded. "The most we could possibly find out is the origin of the ticket. Which city she boarded in, but she's bound to wake up soon, right?"

Joe glanced across the room. Jane was now in one of the clinic's fancy hospital gowns and hooked up to an IV, still looking as peaceful as a sleeping child. "It's hard to say with concussion and potential brain swelling. The doctors may determine she needs surgery for a subdural hematoma or something, for all I know."

The young cop looked grim as he considered that possibility, and Joe was grateful for his concern. "Well, we'll be in touch." He gave Joe his card. "If she wakes up, or if there's anything you remember or want to talk about, give me a call. Likewise, I'll let you know if we find anything out."

"Thanks."

An orderly and RN rolled Jane by Joe. "Where's she going?"

"To her room in the DOU. She's in Seventeen A."

The definitive observation unit was for the patients who needed extra care. Dr. Di Williams ran the unit like a well-oiled machine. Jane would be well looked after, but… He made a snap decision—he wasn't going home tonight. If James and Di would let him, he'd wait things out right here.

Fifteen minutes later, Sleeping Beauty was tucked into a high-end single bed in a room that looked more like one in a luxury spa hotel than a hospital. The only thing giving it away were the bedside handrails and the stack of monitors camouflaged in the corner with huge vases and flower arrangements. The tasteful beige, white and cream decor was relaxing, but Joe couldn't sleep. Instead, he sat in the super-comfy bedside chair resting his head in the palm of his right hand, watching *her* sleep. Wondering what her story was, and pondering why he felt so responsible for her. He decided it was because she was completely vulnerable. He knew the feeling. Someone besides a staff nurse had to look out for her until they found out who she was and could locate her family.

Sporting that black eye and those healing bruises on her arms, it was likely she had been in an abusive relationship. Most likely she'd been beaten up by the man she'd thought she loved.

His left thumb flicked the inside of his vacant ring finger, reminding him, on a much more personal level, how deeply love could hurt.

CHAPTER TWO

A FIRM HAND sent Joe out of a half dreaming, half awake state. He'd been smiling, floating around somewhere, smiling. The grip on his shoulder made a burst of adrenaline mainline straight to his heart, making his pulse ragged and shaky. He sat bolt upright, his eyes popping open. In less than a second he remembered where he was, turned his head toward the claw still grabbing him, and stared up at the elderly night nurse.

Cecelia, was it?

"What's up?" he said, trying to sound awake, then glancing toward the hospital bed and the patient he'd let down by falling asleep. Some guardian he'd turned out to be. She'd been placed on her side, either sound asleep or still unconscious, with pillows behind her back and between her knees, and he hadn't even woken up.

"Your services are needed," Cecelia said with a grainy voice. "We have a helicopter transfer to Santa Barbara."

"Got it. Take care of her."

"What I'm paid for," Cecelia mumbled, fiddling with the blanket covering her patient.

Joe stood, took one last look at Jane, who still looked peaceful, and walked to the nearest men's room to freshen up, then reported for duty in the patient transitioning room.

Rick, the RN from last night, was at the end of his shift and gave Joe his report. "The fifty-four-year-old patient is status post breast reduction, liposuction and lower face lift. Surgery and overnight recovery were uneventful. She's being transferred to Santa Barbara Cottage Hotel for the remainder of her recovery. IV in right forearm. Last medicated for pain an hour ago with seventy-five milligrams of Demerol. Dressings and drainage tubes in place, no excess bleeding noted. She's been released by Dr. R. for transfer." The male RN, fit and overly tanned, making his blue eyes blaze, gave Joe a deadpan stare. "All systems go. She's all yours." Then, when out of earshot of the patient, Rick whispered, "I didn't vote for her husband."

Joe accompanied the patient and gurney to the waiting helicopter on the roof and loaded the sleeping patient onto the air ambulance. He did a quick head-to-toe assessment before strapping her down and locking the special hydraulic gurney into place. He then made sure any and all emergency equipment was stocked and ready for use. After he hooked up the patient to the heart and BP monitor, he put headphones on his patient first and then himself and took his seat, buckling in, preparing for the noisy helicopter blades to whir to life then takeoff.

After delivering the patient to the Santa Barbara airport and transferring the politician's wife, who would not be named, to the awaiting recovery hotel team, he hoped to grab some coffee and maybe a quick breakfast while they waited for the okay to take off for the return trip.

Two hours later, back at the clinic, Joe's only goal

was to check in on Jane Doe. He hoped she'd come to and by now maybe everyone knew her name, and he wondered what it might be. Alexis? Belle? Collette? Excitedly he dashed into her room and found her as he'd left her…unconscious. Disappointment buttoned around him like a too-tight jacket.

The day shift nurse was at her side, preparing to give her a bed bath. A basin of water sat on the bedside table with steam rising from the surface. Several towels and cloths and a new patient gown were neatly stacked beside it. A thick, luxurious patient bath blanket was draped across her chest, Sleeping Beauty obviously naked underneath it. He felt the need to look away until the nurse pulled the privacy curtain around the bed.

"No change?" he asked, already knowing and hating the answer.

"No. But her lab results were a bit of a surprise."

"Everything okay with her skull?"

"Oh, yeah, the CT cranial scan and MRI were both normal except for the fact she's got one hell of a concussion with brain swelling. Well, along with still being unconscious and a slow-wave EEG to prove it."

Joe knew the hospital privacy policy, and this nurse wasn't about to tell him Jane Doe's lab results. Theoretically it wasn't any of his business. Except he'd made a vow last night, and had made it his business to look after her. As he hadn't signed off on his paramedic admission notes for Jane last night, he suddenly needed to access her computer chart to do so.

He headed to the intake department to find a vacant computer, but not before running into James, who looked rested and ready to take on the day. Joe, on the other hand, had gotten a glimpse of himself in the mirror when he'd made a quick pit stop on arriving back at the clinic a few minutes earlier. Dark circles beneath his eyes, a day's growth of beard... Yeah, he was a mess.

"What are you still doing here?" James asked.

"Just got back from a helicopter run to Santa Barbara for one of your patients."

"Cecelia told me you stayed here last night."

Damn that night nurse. "Yeah, well, I wanted to be around if Jane Doe woke up."

He didn't look amused. "This is an order, Joe. Go home and get some sleep. Don't come back until your usual evening shift. Got it?"

"Got it. Just have to sign off my charting first."

Several staff members approached James with questions, giving Joe the chance to sneak off to the computer. He logged on and quickly accessed Jane Doe's folder. First he read her CT scan results and the MRI, which were positive for concussion and brain swelling, but without fractures or bleeding, then he took a look at her labs. So far so good. Her drug panel was negative. Good. Her electrolytes, blood glucose, liver and kidney function tests were all within normal limits. Good. Then his gaze settled on a crazy little test result that nearly knocked him out of the chair.

A positive *pregnancy* test.

His suddenly dry-as-paper tongue made it difficult to swallow. His pulse thumped harder and his mind took a quick spin, gathering questions as it did. Did the mystery lady know she was pregnant? He wondered if the father had been worried out of his mind about her since she'd gone missing. Or was the guy who beat her up the father...because she was pregnant?

Had she been running away? Most likely.

Shifting thoughts made bittersweet memories roll through his mind over another most important pregnancy test. One that had changed his life. He wanted more than anything to make those thoughts stop, knowing they never led to a good place, but right now he was too tired to fight them off.

He'd once been on that pregnancy roller-coaster ride, one day ecstatic about the prospect of becoming a father. Another day further down the line getting a different lab test irrefutably stating there was no way in hell he could have gotten his wife pregnant. Any hope of becoming a father had been ripped away. The questions. The confrontations. The ugly answers that had finally torn his marriage apart.

Hell.

He needed to leave the clinic. James had been right. He should go home and get some sleep because if he didn't he might do something he still wanted to do desperately. Give his best—strike that—*ex*-best friend the beating he deserved.

On the third day Joe sat in his now favorite chair at the mystery lady's bedside, thumbing through a fitness magazine. Di Williams, the middle-aged, hardworking head of DOU, had shaken him up earlier when she'd explained Sleeping Beauty's condition as brain trauma—or, in her case, swelling of the brain—that had disconnected the cerebral cortex circuits, kind of like a car idling but not firing up the engine. She'd also said that if she didn't come around soon, they'd have to consider her in a coma and would need to move her to a hospital that could best meet her longer-term needs.

The thought of losing track of the woman he'd vowed to look after made his stomach knot. The doctor had also said she'd be getting transferred to a specialist coma unit later that afternoon for an enhanced CT scan that would test for blood flow and metabolic activity and they'd have to go from there, which kept Joe's stomach feeling tangled and queasy.

Time was running out, and it seemed so unfair for the girl from the bus. What about her baby?

Jane moved and Joe went on alert. It was the first time he'd witnessed what the nurses had said she often did. He'd admitted, when no one had been around, to flicking her cheek with his finger from time to time to get some kind of reaction out of her, but nothing had ever happened. The lady definitely wasn't faking it. She moved again, this time quicker, as though restless. A dry sound emitted from her throat. He held his breath and felt his heart pump faster as he pushed the call light for the attending nurse.

Jane Doe was waking up.

Tiny sputtering electrical fuses seemed to turn on and off inside him as his anticipation grew. He stood, leaned over the hospital bed and watched the sleeping beauty's lids flutter. Instinctively, he turned off the overhead lamp to help decrease the shock of harsh light to her vision as her eyes slowly opened.

They were dark green. And beautiful, like her.

But they'd barely opened before they snapped shut again as her features contorted with fear.

Carey fought for her life, flailing her arms, kicking her feet. Someone wanted to hurt her. It wasn't Ross. Not this time. She ran, but her feet wouldn't move. She tried to scream, but the sound didn't leave her throat. Fear like she'd never felt before consumed her, but she couldn't give up, she had to protect herself in order to protect her baby.

Someone shouted and ran toward her. She knew he

wanted to help. Broad shoulders, and legs moving in a powerful sprint. "Hey!" His voice cut through the night. That face. Strong. Determined. Filled with anger over the man trying to take her purse. She fought more. She had to break away from the smelly man's grip.

"Hey!"

Fight. Fight. Get away.

"Hold on, everything's okay. You're safe." Did she recognize the man's voice? "I've got you." Hands gripped her shoulders, kept her still. She held her breath.

More hands smoothed back her hair. "It's okay, hon." A woman's voice. "Calm down. You're in the hospital."

Hospital? Had she heard right?

Carey shook her head. It hurt. She was hit by a wave of vertigo that made her quit squirming. She lay still, waiting for the hands to release her. It felt like she was in an extremely comfortable bed. She relaxed her tight, squinting eyes and slowly opened first one then the other. She turned her head to a shadow looming above her. It had features. The face she remembered from her dreams. Strong. Brave. Was this *still* a dream?

She stared at him, her breathing rapid, waiting for her eyes to adjust to the light. He was the man who'd taken on her attacker. She scanned his face. Kind brown eyes. Short dark hair. A square jaw. Good looking.

"You're in the hospital and you're safe," he said in a low, comforting voice.

She looked beyond him to a gorgeous room. A hospital? It looked more like an expensive hotel with muted colors and modern furniture, chic, classy, a room she'd never been able to afford in her life. Was she still dreaming? Since she'd stopped protesting, it was quiet. Oh, and there was an IV in her arm. Being an RN herself, she recognized that right off. A catheter between her legs? And she wore a hospital gown. But this one was silky and smooth, not one of those worn-out overstarched jobs at the hospital where she worked.

Everything was so strange. Surreal. As she gathered her senses she couldn't remember where she was other than being in a hospital. She couldn't figure out why she'd be here. Wait. Someone had attacked her. She'd been pushed down. *Oh, no!* Her hand flew to her stomach, and she gasped.

"My baby!" Her voice sounded muffled and strange, as if her ears were plugged.

"Your baby's fine," the woman said. "So you remember you're pregnant."

Her hearing improved. She nodded, and it hurt, but she smiled anyway because her baby was fine.

The attractive young man smiled back at her, and the concern in his eyes was surprising. Did she know him?

"My baby's fine," she whispered to him, and a rush of feelings overcame her until she cried.

Then the strangest thing happened. The man that she wasn't sure if she knew or not, the man with the kind brown eyes…his welled up, too. "Your baby's fine." His voice sounded raspy.

She cried softly for a few moments, his eyes misty and glistening as he gave a caring smile, and it felt so good.

"Where am I?"

"You're in the hospital, hon," the nearby nurse said.

"But *where* am I?"

"Hollywood," he said. "You're in California."

She thought hard, vaguely remembering getting on a bus. Getting off a bus. It was all too much to straighten out right now. She was exhausted.

"What's your name, honey?" The nurse continued.

"Carey Spencer." At least she remembered her name. But she needed to rest. To close her eyes and...

"She's out again." The kind man's voice sounded far, far away.

"That's what happens sometimes with head injuries," the nurse replied.

Dr. Williams cancelled the plan to transfer her to a coma unit since it was clear Carey Spencer was waking up. Joe assigned another paramedic to cover his shift and stayed by her bedside, hoping to be there when she woke up again. The next time, hopefully, would be permanently. He had dozed off for a second.

"Where am I?" Her voice.

Had he slept a few minutes?

He forced open his eyes and faced Carey as she sat up in the bed, propped by several pillows. Her hair fell in a tangle of waves over her shoulders. Those dark green eyes flashed at him. She'd already figured out how to use the hand-held bed adjuster. "Where am I?" she asked more forcefully.

He'd told her earlier, but she'd suffered a head trauma, her brain was all jumbled up inside. Because of the concussion she might forget things for a long time to come. She deserved the facts.

"You're in the hospital in Hollywood, California. You got off a cross-country bus the other night. Do you remember where you came from?"

"I don't want anyone contacting my family."

He rang for the nurse. "We won't contact anyone unless you tell us to."

"I'm from Montclare, Illinois. It's on the outskirts of Chicago."

"Okay. Are you married?"

She shook her head, then looked at him tentatively. "I'm pregnant." Her eyes captured his and he could tell she remembered they'd gotten emotional together earlier when she'd woken up before. "And my baby's okay." She gave a gentle smile and odd protective sensations rippled over him. Those green eyes and the dark auburn hair. Wow. Her blackened eye may have been healing, but even with the shiner she was breathtaking. In his opinion anyway.

"Yes. Everything is okay in that department. How far along are you? Do you know?"

"Three months."

"And you came here on the bus for...?"

She hesitated. "Not for. To get away." She lifted her arms, covered in fading bruises. "I needed to get away."

"I understand." The uncompromising need to protect her welled up full force again. "Are you in trouble?"

She shook her head, then looked like it hurt to do so and immediately stopped.

The nurse came in, and asked Joe to leave so she could assess her patient and attend to her personal needs. He headed toward the door.

"Wait!" she said.

He turned.

"What's your name?"

"I'm Joseph Matthews. I'm the paramedic who brought you here."

"Thank you, Joseph. I owe you my life. And my baby's," she said from behind the privacy curtain.

He stared at his work boots, an uncertain smile creasing his lips. She certainly didn't owe him her life, but he was awfully glad to have been on scene the night she'd needed him.

The police were notified, and Joe didn't want to stick

around where he had no business, though in his heart he felt he deserved to know the whole story, so he went back to work. Around ten p.m., nearing the end of his shift, James approached. "Did you know she's a nurse?"

"I didn't. Interesting."

"She won't tell us how she got all banged up, but the fact she doesn't want us to contact the father of the baby explains that, doesn't it."

"Sadly, true."

"So, since she's recovering, if all goes well after tonight, I'm going to have to discharge her."

Startled by the news, Joe wondered why it hadn't occurred to him before. Of course she couldn't live here at the clinic. Her identity had been stolen along with her purse and any money she may have had in it. She was pregnant and alone in a strange city, and he couldn't very well let her become homeless, too. Hell, tomorrow was Sunday! "I've got an extra room. I could put her up until she gets back on her feet."

Joe almost did a second take, hearing himself make the offer, but when he thought more about it, he'd meant it. Every word. Even hoped she'd take him up on it.

"That's great," James said. "Though she may feel more comfortable staying with one of our nurses."

"True. Dumb idea, I guess."

"Not dumb. Pretty damn noble if you ask me. I'll vouch for you being a gentleman." James cast him a knowing smile and walked away.

Joe fought the urge to rush to Carey's room. She'd been through a lot today, waking up after a three-day sleep and all, and probably had a lot of thinking and sorting out to do. The social worker would be pestering her about her lost identification and credit cards and helping straighten out that mess. The poor woman's already bruised brain was probably spinning.

He needed to give her space, not make her worry he was some kind of weird stalker or something. But he wanted to tell her good night so he hiked over to the DOU and room Seventeen A, knocked on the wall outside the door, and when she told him to come in, he poked his head around the corner.

"Just wanted to say good night."

She seemed much less tense now and her smile came easily. She was so pretty, the smile nearly stopped him in his tracks. "Good night. Thanks for everything you've done for me."

"Glad to be of service, Carey."

"They're going to let me go tomorrow."

"Do you have a place to stay?"

"Not yet. Social Services is looking into something."

He walked closer to her bed and sat on the edge of his favorite chair. "I…uh… I have a two-bedroom house in West Hollywood. It's on a cul-de-sac, and it's really safe. Uh, the thing is, if you don't have any place to go, you can use my spare room. It's even got a private bathroom."

"You've done so much for me already. I couldn't—"

"Just until you get back on your feet. Uh, you know. If you want. That is." Why did he sound like a stammering, yammering teenager asking a girl on a date? That wasn't what he'd had in mind. He just wanted to help her. That was all.

She was the vision of a woman trying to make up her mind. Judging him on whether she could trust him or not, and from her recent experience Joe could understand why she might doubt herself. "Um, Dr. Rothsberg will vouch for me."

"I'll vouch for who?" James walked in on their awkward moment.

"I was just inviting Carey to stay in my spare room, if she needs a place to stay for a while."

James nailed Carey with his stare. "He's a good man. You can trust him." Then he turned and faced Joe and looked questioning. "I think."

That got a laugh out of Carey, and Joe shook his head. Guys loved to mess with each other.

"Okay, then," she said, surprising the heck out of Joe. "Okay?"

"Yes. Thank you." The woman truly knew how to be gracious, and for that he was grateful.

He smiled. "You're welcome. I'll see you tomorrow, then." It was his day off, but he'd be back here in a heartbeat when she was ready for discharge.

He turned to leave, unusually happy and suddenly finding the need to rush home and clean the house.

CHAPTER THREE

JOE HAD WORKED like a fiend to clean his house that morning before he went to the clinic to bring Carey back. He'd gotten her room prepared and put his best towels into the guest bathroom, wanting her to feel at home. He'd stocked the bathroom with everything he thought she might need from shampoo to gentle facial soap, scented body wash, and of course a toothbrush and toothpaste. Oh, and a brush for that beautiful auburn hair.

Aware that Carey only had the clothes on her back, he'd pegged her to be around his middle sister Lori's size and had borrowed a couple pairs of jeans and tops. Boy, he'd had a lot of explaining to do when he'd asked, too, since Lori was a typical nosy sister, especially since his divorce.

Once, while Carey had been sleeping in the clinic, he'd checked the size of her shoes and now he hoped she wouldn't mind that he'd bought her a pair of practical ladies' slip-on rubber-soled shoes and some flip-flops, because she couldn't exactly walk around in those sexy boots all the time. Plus, flip-flops were acceptable just about everywhere in Southern California. He was grateful some of the nurses had bought her a package of underwear and another bra—he'd heard that through the grapevine, thanks to Stephanie, the gossipy receptionist at The Hollywood Hills Clinic, who'd said she'd gone in on the collection of money for said items.

Now he waited in the foyer for the nurse or orderly to bring Carey around for discharge, having parked his car in the circular driveway. Careful not to say anything to Stephanie about the living arrangements, knowing that if he did so the whole clinic would soon find out, he smiled, assured her that Social Services had arranged for something, and with crossed arms tapped his fingers on his elbows, waiting.

She rounded the corner, being pushed in a wheelchair—clinic policy for discharges, regardless of how well the patient felt, but most especially for someone status post-head injury like her. She was dressed the way he'd first seen her last Wednesday night, and she trained her apprehensive glance straight at him. Even from this distance he noticed those dark green eyes, and right now they were filled with questions. Yeah, it would be weird to bring a strange lady into his home, especially one who continuously made his nerve endings and synapses react as if she waved some invisible magnetic wand.

He wanted to make her feel comfortable, so he smiled and walked to pick up the few things she had stuffed into a clinic tote bag, a classier version of the usual plastic discharge bags from other hospitals he'd worked at. It was one of the perks of choosing The Hollywood Hills Clinic for medical care, though in her case she hadn't had a choice.

It was nothing short of a pure leap of faith, going home with a complete stranger like this, Carey knew, but her options were nil and, well, the guy *had* cried with her that first day in the hospital when she'd woken up. The only thing that had mattered to her after the mugging was her baby, and when she'd been reassured it was all right, she'd been unable to hold back the tears. Joseph Matthews was either the easiest guy crier she'd ever met or the most empathetic man on the planet. Either way, it made him special. She had to remember that. Plus he'd saved her life. She'd *never* forget that.

When Dr. Rothsberg had vouched for him, and she'd already noticed how everyone around the clinic seemed to like the guy, she'd made a snap decision to take the paramedic up on his offer. But, really, where else did she have to go, a homeless shelter? She'd been out of touch with her parents for years and Ross was the reason she'd run away. She had zero intention of contacting any of them.

Recent history proved she couldn't necessarily trust her instincts, but she still had a good feeling about the paramedic.

When they first left the clinic parking lot Joseph slowed down so she could look back and up toward the hillside to the huge Hollywood sign. Somehow it didn't seem nearly as exciting as she'd thought it would be. Maybe because it hurt to turn her head. Or maybe because, being that close, it was just some big old white letters, with some parts in need of a paint touch-up. Now she sat in his car, her head aching, nerves jangled, driving down a street called Highland. Having passed the Hollywood Bowl and going into the thick of Hollywood, she admitted to feeling disappointed. Where was the magic? To her it was just another place with crowded streets in need of a thorough cleaning.

It was probably her lousy mood. She'd never planned on visiting California. She'd been perfectly happy in

Montclare. She'd loved her RN job, loved owning her car, being independent for the first time in her life. She still remembered the monumental day she'd gotten the key to her first apartment and had moved out once and for all from her parents' house. Life had been all she'd dreamed it would be, why would she ever need to go to Hollywood?

Then she'd met Ross Wilson and had thought she'd fallen in love, until she'd realized too late what kind of man he really was.

Nope. She'd come to Hollywood only because it had been the first bus destination she'd found out of Chicago. For her it hadn't been a matter of choice, but a matter of life and death.

Back at his house, Joe gave Carey space to do whatever she needed to do to make herself at home in her room. She'd been so quiet on the ride over, he was worried she was scared of him. He'd probably need to tread lightly until she got more comfortable around him. He thought about taking off for the afternoon, giving her time to herself, but, honestly, he worried she might bolt. Truth was, he didn't know what she might do, and his list of questions was getting longer and longer. All he really knew for sure was that he wanted to keep her safe.

The first thing he heard after she'd gone to her room had been the shower being turned on, and the image that planted in his head needed to be erased. Fast. So he decided to work out with his hanging punchbag in his screened-in patio, which he used as a makeshift gym. He changed clothes and headed to the back of the house, turned on a John Coltrane set, his favorite music to hit the bag with, and got down to working out.

With his hands up, chin tucked in, he first moved in

and out around the bag, utilizing his footwork, warming up, moving the bag, pushing it and dancing around, getting his balance. With bare hands he threw his first warm-up punches, *slap, slap, slap*, working the bag, punching more. The stitches across his rib cage pulled and stung a little, but probably wouldn't tear through his skin. Though after the first few punches he checked to make sure. They were healing and held the skin taut that was all.

As his session heated up, so did the wild saxophone music. He pulled off his T-shirt and got more intense, beating the hell out of the innocent bag where he mentally pasted every wrong the world had ever laid at his feet. His wife sleeping with his best friend, the lies about her baby being his. The divorce. He worked through the usual warm-up, heating up quickly. Then he pounded that bag for women abused by boyfriends and innocent victims who got mugged after getting off buses. *Wham*. He hit that bag over and over, pummeling it, his breath huffing, sweat flying. *Thump, bam, whump!*

"Excuse me, Joseph?"

Jolted, he halted in mid-punch, first stabilizing the punchbag so it wouldn't swing back and hit him, then shifted his gaze toward Carey. She had on different jeans, and one of his sister's bright pink cotton tops, and her wet hair was pulled up into a ponytail, giving her a wholesome look. Which he thought was sexy.

"Oh. Hey. Call me Joe. Everything okay?" he asked, out of breath.

"That music sounds like fighting." She had to raise her voice to be heard over the jazz.

"Oh, sorry, let me turn it off." That's why he liked

to work out with Coltrane, it got wild and crazy, often the way he felt.

Her gaze darted between his naked torso and his sweaty face. "I was just wondering if I could make a sandwich."

"Of course. Help yourself to anything. I've got cold cuts in the fridge. There's some fruit, too."

"Thanks." Her eyes stayed on his abdomen and he felt the need to suck it in, even though he didn't have a gut. "You know you're bleeding?"

He glanced down. Sure enough, he'd tugged a stitch too hard and torn a little portion of his skin. "Oh. Didn't realize." He grabbed his towel and blotted it quickly.

"Did you get hurt when you helped me?"

"Yeah, the jerk sliced me with his knife." Still blotting, he looked up.

Her eyes had gone wide. "You risked your life for me? I'm so sorry."

"Hey, I didn't risk my life." Had he? "I was just doing my job."

"Do paramedics usually fight guys with blades in their hands?"

"Well, maybe not every day, but it could happen." He flashed a sheepish grin over the bravado. "At least, it has now."

Her expression looked so sad he wanted to hug her, but they hardly knew each other.

"Thank you." He sensed she also meant she was sorry.

"Not a problem. Glad to do it." He waited to capture her eyes then nodded, wanting to make sure she understood she deserved nothing less than someone saving her from an alley attacker. They stood staring at each other for a moment or two too long, and since he was the one who always got caught up in the magic of her eyes, she looked away first. Standing in his boxing shorts, shirtless, he felt like he'd been caught naked winning that staring match.

"So… I'm going to make that sandwich." She pointed toward the door then led into the small kitchen, just around the corner from the dining area and his patio, while he assessed his stitches again. Yeah, he'd taken a knife for her, but the alternative, her getting stabbed by a sleazebag and maybe left to die, had been unacceptable.

The woman had a way of drumming up forgotten protective feelings and a whole lot more. Suddenly the house felt way too small for both of them. How was he going to deal with that while she stayed here?

Maybe one last punch to the bag then he promised to stop. *Thump!* The stitches tugged more and smarted. He hated feeling uncomfortable in his own house and blamed it on the size. He'd thought about selling it after Angela had agreed to leave, but the truth was he liked the neighborhood, it was close enough to work, and most of his family lived within a ten-mile radius. And why should he have to change his life completely because his wife had been unfaithful? Okay, one last one-two punch. *Whump, thump. Ouch, my side.* He grabbed his towel again and rubbed it over his wringing-wet hair.

One odd thought occurred to him as he dried himself off. When was the last time a woman had seen him shirtless? His ex-wife Angela had left a year ago, and was a new mother now. Good luck with that. He hadn't brought anyone home since she'd left, choosing to throw himself into his expanding business and demanding job rather than get involved with any poor unsuspecting women. He was angry at the world for being ster-

ile, and angrier at the two people he'd trusted most, his
wife and his best friend. Where was a guy supposed to
go from there? Ah, what the hell. He punched the bag
again. *Wham thud wham.*

"Would you like a sandwich?"

Not used to hearing a female voice in his house,
it startled him from his down spiraling thoughts. A
woman, a complete stranger no less, was going to be
staying here for an indeterminate amount of time. Had
he been crazy to offer? Two strangers in an eleven-
hundred-square-foot house. That was too damn close,
with hardly a way to avoid each other. Hell, their bedrooms were only separated by a narrow hallway and
the bathrooms. What had he been thinking? His stomach growled. On the upside, she'd just offered to make
him a sandwich.

Besides everything he was feeling—the awkwardness, the getting used to a stranger—he could only
imagine she felt the same. Except for the unwanted attraction on his part, he was quite sure that wasn't an
issue for her—considering her situation, she must feel
a hell of a lot more vulnerable. He needed to be on his
best behavior for Carey. She deserved no less.

"Yes, thanks, a sandwich sounds great." Since the
bleeding had stopped, he tossed on his T-shirt after
wiping his chest and underarms, then joined her in the
kitchen.

"Do you like lettuce and tomato?"

"Whatever you're having is fine. I'm easy." His hands
hung on to both sides of the towel around his neck.

"I never got morning sickness, like most women do.
I've been ravenous from the beginning, so you're getting the works."

She was tallish and slender, without any sign of being

pregnant, and somehow he found it hard to believe she ate too much. "Sounds good. Hey, I thought I'd barbecue some chicken tonight. You up for that?"

She turned and shared a shy smile. "Like I said, I'm always hungry, so it sounds good to me."

He got stuck on the smile that delivered a mini sucker punch and didn't answer right away. "Okay. It looks like it'll be nice out, so I thought we could eat outdoors on the deck." He needed to put some space between them, and it wouldn't feel as close or intimate out there. *Just keep telling yourself she's wearing your sister's clothes. Your sister's clothes.*

He'd done a lot with his backyard, putting in a garden and lots of shrubbery for privacy's sake from his neighbors, plus he'd built his own cedar-plank deck and was proud of how it'd turned out. It had been one of the therapeutic projects he'd worked on during the divorce.

The houses had been built close together in this neighborhood back in the nineteen-forties. He liked to refer to it as his start-up house, had once planned to start his family in it, too. Too bad it had been someone else's family that had gotten started here.

Fortunately, Carey interrupted his negative thoughts again jabbing a plate with a sandwich into his side. He took the supremely well-stacked sandwich and grabbed some cold water from the refrigerator, raised the bottle to see if she'd like one. Without a word she nodded, and put her equally well-stacked sandwich on a second plate. As he walked to the dining table with the bottles in one hand and his sandwich in the other, he called out, "Chips are on the counter."

"Already found them," she said, appearing at the table, hands full with food and potato-chips bag, knocking him over the head with her smile—how much could a lonely man take? Obviously she was ready to eat.

It occurred to him they had some natural communication skills going on, and the thought made him uneasy. Beyond uneasy to downright uncomfortable. He clenched his jaw. He didn't want to communicate with a woman ever again. At least not yet, anyway, but since he'd just had a good workout and he was hungry, starved, in fact, he'd let his concerns slide. For now. Carey proved to be a woman of her word, too, matching him bite for bite. Yeah, she could put it away.

After they'd eaten, Carey asked to use his phone to make some calls.

"What'd I say earlier? *Mi casa es su casa.* It's a California rule. Make yourself at home, okay?" Though he said it, he wasn't anywhere near ready to meaning it.

"But it's long distance."

"I know you've got a lot of things to work out. All your important documents were stolen." This, helping her get her life back in order, he could do. The part of living with a woman again? Damn, it was hard. Sometimes, just catching the scent of her shampoo when she walked past seemed more than he could take.

"The clinic social worker has been helping me, and my credit cards have been cancelled now. But I couldn't even order new ones because I didn't have an address to send them to."

"You've got one now." He looked her in the eyes, didn't let her glance away. He'd made a promise to himself on her behalf that he'd watch over her, take care of her. It had to do with finding her completely helpless in that alley and the fierce sense of protectiveness he'd felt. "You can stay here as long as you need to. I'm serious."

She sent him a disbelieving look. In it Joe glimpsed

how deeply some creep back in Illinois had messed her up and it made him want to deck the faceless dude. But he also sensed something else behind her disbelief. "Thank you."

"Sure. You're welcome." Though she only whispered the reply, he knew without a doubt she was really grateful to be here, and that made the nearly constant awkward feelings about living with a complete stranger, a woman more appealing than he cared to admit, worth it.

Later, over dinner on the deck in the backyard, Joe sipped a beer and Carey lemonade. Her hair was down now, and she'd put on the sweater she'd worn that first night over his sister's top. In early June, the evenings were still cool, and many mornings were overcast with what they called "June gloom" in Southern California. She'd spent the entire dinner asking about his backyard and job, which were safe topics, so it was fine with him. Since she'd been asking so many questions, he got up the nerve to ask her one of the several questions he had for her. Also within the safe realm of topics—work.

"I heard at the clinic that you're a nurse?"

She looked surprised. "Yes. That was the call I made earlier, to the hospital where I worked. I guess you could say I'm now officially on a leave of absence."

"So you'll probably go back there when you feel better?" Why did this question, and her possible answer, make him feel both relief and dread? He clenched his jaw, something he'd started doing again since Carey had moved in.

She grimaced. "I can't. I'll have to quit at some point, but for now I'm using the sick leave and vacation time I've saved up and, I hope you don't mind, I gave them your address so they could mail my next check to me here."

"Remember. *Mi casa es tuya.*" He took another drag on his longneck, meaning every word in the entire extent of his Spanish speaking, but covering for the load of mixed-up feelings that kept dropping into his lap. What was it about this girl that made him feel so damn uncomfortable?

His practiced reply got a relieved smile out of her, and he allowed himself to enjoy how her eyes slanted upward whenever she did. It was dangerous to notice things like that and, really, what was the point? But having the beer had loosened him up and he snuck more looks than usual at her during dinner. "The clinic is always looking for good nurses. What's your specialty?"

"I work, or I should say worked, in a medical-surgical unit. I loved it, too."

"See…" he pointed her way "…that would fit right in. When you feel better, maybe you should look into it. I can talk to James about it if you'd like." *Yeah, keep these interactions all about helping her, and maybe she'll skip the part about asking you about yourself.*

"James?"

"Dr. Rothsberg."

"First I have to get my RN license reissued from Illinois since it was stolen along with everything else."

So maybe she did have plans to stay here and seek employment. Now he could get confused again and try to ignore that flicker of hope he'd kept feeling since she'd walked into his life. He ground his molars. "Would your license be accepted in California?"

"I did some research on the bus ride out and I'll have to apply here in California. That'll take some time, I suspect."

"Well, I'm working days tomorrow, so you can spend the whole day using my computer and phone and maybe start straightening out everything you need to."

She nodded. "I do have some people I owe a call." Deep in thought, she probably went straight to the gazillion things she'd have to do to re-create herself and begin a new life for her and her baby in a new state. He wouldn't want to be in her shoes, and wished he could somehow help even more. Would that go beyond his promise to watch over her?

At least the social worker and the police department had started the ball rolling on a few things. But, man, what a mess she had to clean up, especially since she hadn't wanted her family notified of her whereabouts. Why was that?

Joe wanted to ask her about her living situation back home, but suspected she'd shut down on him like a trapdoor if he did this soon, so he tucked those questions into his "bring up later" file. With an ironic inward laugh, he supposed they had a lot in common, not wanting to bring up the past and all. "You feel like watching a little TV?" He figured she could use something to distract her from all the things she'd have to tackle tomorrow.

"I'd like that but only after you let me clean up from dinner."

"Only if you'll let me help." Hell, could they get any more polite?

She smiled. "So after we do the dishes, what would you like to watch?"

"You choose." Yeah, he'd let his guest make all the decisions tonight. It was the right thing to do.

"I like that show about zombies."

"Seriously?" He never would have pegged her as a

horror fan. "It's my favorite, too, but I didn't think it would be good for your bambino."

"Ha," she said, picking up the dishes from the bench table on the outdoor deck. "After what this little one has been through already, a pretend TV show should be a walk in the park." She glanced down at her stomach while heading inside and toward the kitchen. "Isn't that right, sweetie pie."

There he went grinding his molars again. He followed her in and watched her put the dishes on the counter and unconsciously pat her abdomen then smile. That simple act sent a flurry of quick memories about Angela and how excited they'd once been when she'd first found out she'd gotten pregnant. They'd been about to give up trying since it had been over a year, had even had fertility tests done. They'd rationalized that because they were both paramedics and under a lot of stress, and he worked extended hours trying to make a good impression with Dr. Rothsberg, that was the reason she'd been unable to get pregnant.

So they'd taken a quickie vacation. Then one day, wham, she magically announced she was expecting. Joe had practically jumped over the moon that night, he'd been so happy. They'd finally start their own version of a big happy family. Since Angela's body had gotten the hang of getting pregnant, he'd planned to talk her into having a few more kids after this one. He'd walked on air for a couple of months…until his fertility report had dropped into the mailbox. Late. Very, very late.

What a fool he'd been.

Trying to give his overworked jaw a break, Joe went to town scrubbing the grill from the barbecue as if it was a matter of life and death. By the time they'd finished with the cleanup, he didn't know about Carey any more, but he definitely needed the distraction of some mindless TV viewing.

She sat on the small couch, passing him along the way, and he caught the scent of her shampoo again. It was a fresh, fruity summer kind of smell with a touch of coconut, which when he'd bought it for her had never planned for it to be a minor form of torture.

Mixed up about his feelings for the smart and easy-going nurse from Illinois, he intentionally sat on the chair opposite the couch, not ready to get too close to her again tonight. It brought up too many bad memories, and he so did not want to go there. There was only so much boxing a guy could do in a day. Torture sounded better than reliving his failed marriage. He clicked on the TV right on time for the show they both liked to escape to. If zombies couldn't make him forget how attracted he was to the lovely stranger living in his house, nothing could.

Carey put her head on the pillow of the surprisingly comfortable guest bed, thinking it was the first time she could remember feeling safe in ages. Things had gotten super-tense living with Ross those last few weeks, and, talk about the worst timing in the world, she'd gotten pregnant right around the time she'd known she had to leave him.

She didn't want to think about that now, because it would keep her awake, and she was really tired. It'd felt so normal and relaxing to sit and watch TV with Joe. He'd made the best barbecue chicken she'd ever eaten and she'd made a pig out of herself over the baked potato with all the toppings, but she chalked it up to his making her feel so welcome. The only problem was she couldn't get the vision of him in his boxing shorts, working out with the punchbag, out of her mind. Wow, his lean body had showcased every muscle in his arms and across his back as he'd punched. His movements had been fluid and nothing short of perfection. Not to mention his washboard stomach and powerful legs. The guy didn't have an ounce of fat on him.

What on earth was she thinking? Her life was in a shambles. She had an unborn baby to take care of. The last thing she should be thinking about was a man.

A naturally sexy man with kind brown eyes and a voice soothing enough to give her chills. She squeezed her eyes tight and shook her head on the pillow.

When she finally settled down and began to drift off to sleep she realized this was the first day she'd ever felt positive about her and the baby's future in three months. Things would work out for her, she just knew it. Because she, with the help of Joe, would make sure they did.

A slight smile crossed her lips as a curtain of sleep inched its way down until all was dark and she peacefully crossed into sweet dreams. Thanks to Joe.

CHAPTER FOUR

On Monday, after working all day, Joe insisted Carey come out with him for dinner, which was fine with her because she'd felt kind of cooped up. They ate at a little diner, then he showed her around Santa Monica, like the perfect host. She got the distinct impression it was to get them, and keep them, out of the house, because sometimes things felt too close there.

At least, that's how it felt for her, and sometimes she sensed it was the same for him. The guy seemed to bite down on his jaw a lot! But she soon ignored her worries about him not wanting her around and went straight to loving seeing the beach and the Pacific Ocean, and especially the Santa Monica pier.

On Tuesday Joe had the day off, and he dutifully took her shopping for more clothes at a place called the Beverly Center. They checked the directory and he guided her to the few stores she'd shown interest in, then he stood outside in the mall area, giving her space to shop. Clearly he wanted nothing to do with helping her choose clothes, rather he just did what he thought he should do out of courtesy to her situation. She protested all the way when he insisted on paying for everything. She sensed his generosity was based on some sense of charitable obligation, and she only accepted his offer when he'd agreed to let her repay him once she was back on her feet. She'd be sure to keep a tally because things were quickly adding up!

Wednesday morning, before he started an afternoon shift, he chauffeured her around to the Department of Motor Vehicles for a temporary driving license, and since she'd received a check from her old job he also helped her open a bank account. She decided the guy was totally committed to helping her, like he'd signed some paper or made some pact to do it. And she certainly appreciated everything he'd done for her, but...

Even though he was easy enough to be around, she felt it was out of total obligation to treat people right in life. Far too often she sensed a disconnect between his courtesy and that safe distance he insisted on keeping between them. Well, if that's what he wanted, she knew exactly how to live that way. Her parents had, sadly, been perfect role models in that regard.

Joe got home on Wednesday night to a quiet house. Carey had said hello, but now kept mostly to herself in her room. It made him wonder if he'd done something to offend her. He'd been trying his best to make her feel at home, though admittedly he may have been going about it robotically. But that seemed the only way he could deal with having a woman in his life again. Since he worked the a.m. shift the next day, he didn't get a chance to ask Carey if he'd put her off or if her withdrawal had nothing to do with him. Something was definitely on her mind, and under the circumstances, being battered, bruised, mugged, homeless, and completely vulnerable, not to mention living with a stranger, he could understand why.

Maybe he'd come off aloof or unapproachable at

times. But she had no idea how nearly unbearable it was to fix meals with her when it reminded him how much he missed being married. And having Carey there twenty-four seven, with her friendly smile and naturally sweet ways, was nearly making him come unhinged. She deserved someone to share things with, to talk to, but it couldn't be him. Nope. He was nowhere near ready or able to be her sounding board. All he'd signed up for was offering her a place to live.

Maybe he could arrange for some follow-up visits with the social worker at the clinic. That way she could get what she wanted and needed and he wouldn't have to be the person listening. Because when a woman vented, from his past experience with Angela, he knew she always expected something in return. Nope, no way would he unload his lousy past on Carey, no matter how much she might think she wanted him to. The lady had far too much on her plate as it was, and, truthfully, re-living such pain was the last thing he ever wanted to do. The social worker was definitely the right person to step in, and he planned to ask Helena to follow up the next day.

On Thursday evening, Joe came home to find Carey scrubbing the kitchen floor. From the looks of the rest of the house, she'd been cleaning all day.

"What's up?" he asked.

She was so focused on the floor-scrubbing she didn't notice him. He stepped closer but not onto the wet kitchen tiles.

"Am I that much of a slob?" he tried to joke, but she didn't laugh. Something was definitely eating at her. "Carey?"

Finally she heard him and shook her head as if she'd

been in a trance and looked at him. "Hi." Not sounding the least bit enthusiastic.

"Everything okay?"

She stopped pushing the mop handle. "Just trying to pay you back for all you're doing for me."

Damn. She may as well have sliced him with a knife. "You don't have to be my house cleaner, you know."

"What else can I do?" The obvious "else" *not* being to sleep together.

Why was that the first thought to come to his mind? Cripes, she had him mixed up. He used her clear frustration as a springboard to what his latest mission on Carey's behalf had been. "I, uh, spoke to the social worker today—the one who helped you while you were in the hospital—and she said she'd love to keep in touch." He'd totally reworded their true conversation, trying to make it sound casual, not necessary, but the truth was he'd talked at great length with Helena at work about Carey's precarious situation. The social worker wanted to keep connected with Carey and promised to call her right away.

"Yes. Thanks. She called earlier today. I'm going to have a phone appointment with her on Monday."

"That's great." He almost said, *I hope it helps you snap out of your funk,* but kept that thought to himself because a sneaky part of him worried he'd put her there. He knew too well how unhelpful being told to snap out of it could be, especially when a person was nowhere near ready. He would protect Carey in any way he could, and felt she shouldn't be nervous all the time. But he'd never been in her shoes, and…

Then it dawned on him. Why hadn't he thought of it before? The woman was a nurse. Nurses were always busy on the job. She was used to helping people, not the other way around. She was probably going crazy with so much time on her hands and nothing to do but watch TV or read while he was away every day. But she'd had a head trauma and needed to heal. "Do you feel ready to go back to work?"

She shifted from being intent on cleaning to suddenly looking deflated. "That's the thing, I can't until the California RN license comes through. Plus I still feel foggy-headed from the concussion. At this point I'd worry I might hurt some poor unsuspecting patient or something. But on another level my energy is coming back, and I'm feeling really restless."

That damn mugger had not only stolen her identity and money but also her confidence. He thought quickly. It was early summer, people went on vacations. "I think there might be some temporary slots to fill in while people go on vacation. Jobs that don't require a nursing license."

She stopped mopping and looked at him, definite interest in her eyes.

"For instance, I know of a ward clerk on the second floor who's getting ready to visit her family back east for two weeks. Maybe you could fill in on something like that. Sort of keep your hand in medicine but in a safer position until you feel back to your old self."

She rested her chin on the mop handle. "How can I just walk in off the street and expect to get a job in a hospital like The Hollywood Hills Clinic?"

He flashed an overconfident grin he hadn't used in a long time. "By knowing a guy like me? I could put in a good word to Dr. Rothsberg for you. What do you say?"

The fingers of one hand flew to her mouth as she thought. "That would be great. But it would also mean

I'd have to quit my job back home." Worry returned to her brow.

Joe was sure he was missing out on another story, probably something huge. Like, who she was running away from, and would they come after her? If only he could get her to open up. This was stuff he needed to know if he expected to protect her. Rather than press her right then, he let her finish her task and went to his room. Besides, he needed time to figure things out for himself, like the fact that he both totally looked forward to seeing her each day but dreaded how it made him feel afterwards.

After he changed into workout clothes, he headed to the back porch for some boxing, since it was the one sure way to help him blow off steam. Well into his usual routine, while she was in the other room, watching TV, he wondered if, in fact, the guy who'd given Carey her shiner might come after her, and an idea popped into his head. "Hey, Carey, come out here a minute, would you?"

Within seconds she showed up looking perplexed, and maybe like she'd rather be watching TV. Yeah, she'd probably already had it with living with him.

"Since you were mugged recently, and I'm sure you never want to go through that again, would you like me to show you a couple of moves?"

She looked hesitant, like learning a few self-defense maneuvers might bring back too many bad memories.

"Maybe it's too soon," he quickly.

"No, I can't keep hiding out at your house. I know there's a bus stop right down at the end of your street, and I shouldn't be afraid to use it." She nodded, a flicker of fight in her eyes. "Yeah, show me how I could have kept that creep from dragging me into the alley that night."

"That's the attitude," Joe said with a victorious smile. She smiled back, that spirited flash intensifying.

"Okay." He clapped his hands once. "I saw the guy grab you by the wrist and pull you away that night. So, first off, a lot of the information that's on the internet for ladies' self-defense is bogus. Here's something that works. When that guy grabbed your wrist, you could have used your other hand to push into his eyes, or, if he wore glasses, you could have gone for his throat. With either move you also could have included a knee to the groin. That stuff hurts the attacker and surprises them. Knocks them off balance. Let me show you."

He grabbed Carey's right wrist and immediately felt her tense, making him think maybe he was right and it was too early to do this lesson with her. But he was committed now and pressed on, and she had enough anger in her eyes to put it to good use.

"Okay, use your left hand and go for my face," He showed her how to make an open, claw-like spread with the fingers and how to jab it at a person's face to do the most damage. "Get those fingers on my eyes and press with all your might."

She followed his instructions and went for his eyes.

"Ow!" He reacted and pushed her hand back to keep her from injuring him.

"Sorry!"

"Don't be sorry, fight for your life. It's up to me to keep you from hurting me. You just caught me off guard. Got it?"

She gave one firm and committed nod.

"That's the spirit. If the guy foils that move with his other hand, like I just did, make sure you put your knee to his groin at the same time." He flashed a charming grin. "Don't actually do that one now, okay?"

She laughed, and it felt good to get her to relax a little.

"Just knee him in the groin area and later you can practice kneeing the heck out of that boxing bag."

"Got it, boss." Yes, she was really into this now.

He said, "Go!" and grabbed her left wrist this time, and she moved like lightning for his face and eyes, driving her knee into his groin at the same time. Being prepared for the move, in case she got overzealous, which she obviously had, he brought his own knee up and across to protect himself, letting her full force hit his thigh. If he hadn't, he'd have been on his hands and knees, riding out the pain, right now.

He didn't want to discourage her efforts but, damn, that could have hurt! "Good." Up close, their eyes locked. He could hear her breathing hard and felt the pulse in her wrist quicken. The fire in her green-eyed stare made him take notice. He stepped back, releasing her wrist. "That was good."

She rubbed her wrist and searched the floor with her gaze, making a quick recovery. This wasn't easy to relive, he understood that, but keeping the same thing from ever happening again was more important than her current comfort zone.

"Now do the same thing, going for my throat." He showed her the wide V of his hand between the thumb and index finger and demonstrated how to drive it into the Adam's apple area of the attacker's neck. "Since most guys, like that scumbag the other night, will be taller than you, force your hand upward with all you've got. Okay?"

Carey agreed and he immediately grabbed her hand, trying to catch her off guard. Something clicked, like she'd gone back in time. She went into attack mode and because he wasn't ready for it she got him good in the throat. He coughed and sputtered and backed away to recover, and only then did she realize she'd shifted from demonstration to true life.

"I'm sorry!" she squealed, grabbing her face with her hands, as if just snapping out of a bad dream.

He swallowed, trying to get his voice back. "That's the way. See how it works? I dropped your hand, and that means you could have run off screaming for help at that point."

"Oh, Joe." Carey rushed to him. "I'm so sorry I hurt you." She touched his shoulder and, without thinking, he reacted by opening his arms. Carey threw her arms around him and squeezed. "Can I get you some water? Anything?"

"Maybe a new throat," he teased, though he really liked having her arms around him, the realization nearly making him lose his balance. She smelled a hell of a lot better than he did, and up close, like this, her eyes were by far the prettiest he'd ever seen in his life, though fear seemed to have the best of them right now.

Surprised, no, more like stunned by how moved she'd been when grappling with Joe, Carey held him perhaps a second too long. Fear still pounded in her chest. At first the lesson had brought out all the bad memories she'd been trying to force down a few months before leaving home and definitely since coming to Hollywood. Ross had changed from attentive boyfriend to jealous predator. He had frightened her. He'd also grabbed her by the wrist like that on several occasions, each time scaring her into submission. Then the creep at the bus station must have seen her as an easy mark, sensed her fear, and grabbed her the same way, pulling her into the alley.

She hated feeling like a victim!

Anger had erupted as horrible memories had collided with Joe's grip on her wrist. She'd never be a victim again, damn it. Never. Suddenly fighting for her life all over again, she'd switched to kill mode and had practically pushed his larynx out the back of his neck. Darn it! She hadn't meant to hurt him, not the man who'd saved her and taken her in, but she clearly had.

Now, being skin to skin with her incredibly fit and appealing roommate had changed the topic foremost in her mind. Being in Joe's arms wiped out her fear and she shifted from fighting for her life to being completely turned on. What was it about Joe?

So confusing. It wasn't right.

Obviously her concussion was still messing with her judgment.

In a moment of clarity she broke away and strode to the kitchen to get him a glass of water, trying to recover before she brought it to him.

"What about pepper spray?" She schooled her voice to sound casual, completely avoiding his eyes, as if she hadn't just survived a flashback and had flung herself into Joe's arms. There was nothing wrong with a decoy topic to throw him off the scent, right? The man had turned her on simply by touching her. Pitiful. Blame it on the head injury.

"First you have to get it out of your purse, right?"

She nodded, quickly realizing the fault in her premise. He stood shirtless, damp from his workout, skin shiny and all his muscles on display. Cut and ripped. A work of art. She handed him the glass. Thought about handing him his T-shirt so he'd cover up and make her life a little safer for the moment, or less tempting anyway. At least it seemed easier for him to swallow now and that made her grateful she hadn't caused any permanent damage. Could she have? If so, he'd just given her a huge gift of self-protection. No way would she let herself be a victim. By God, she'd never let anyone hurt her again.

"Plus, I've heard about guys who've been sprayed and didn't even react," he continued. "Also, when you're scared or nervous, you might spray all over the place and not hit the eyes."

She kept nodding, watching him, completely distracted by his physique, unable to really listen, wishing she'd brought herself a cool drink too. Surely her head injury had left her brain unbalanced, taking her back to the worst moments in her life one second and then the next rushing into the realm of all things sensual.

"Your hands and your knees are your best defense. Want to practice again?"

She sucked in a breath and shook her head quickly. This was all too confusing. "I think that's enough for tonight."

He put down his glass on the nearby table, folded an arm across his middle, rested the other elbow on it and held his chin with his thumb and bent fingers, biting his lower lip and nailing her with a sexy, playful gaze. "Chicken, eh?"

Joe had saved her life. He'd also just given her a great gift of learning self-defense. And there *was* that sexy sparkle in his eyes right now…

"Are you challenging me?" Suddenly awash with tiny prickles of excitement again, she moved toward him and grabbed his wrist with all her might. "Let's see you fight your way out of this one, buddy." She knew she didn't have a chance in hell of keeping hold but enjoyed the moment, and especially grappling with the hunk. When was the last time she'd had fun horsing around with a man and not felt the least bit afraid or vulnerable?

She trusted Joe not to hurt her.

He swung his free arm around behind her and pulled her close, pretending to get her in a head lock but quickly moving into a backward hug. "I don't suggest you ever let your attacker get you in this position," he said playfully over the shell of her ear.

"There won't be any more attackers," she said through gritted teeth. "Because I'll kick their asses first."

He tightened his hold, but in a good way, a sexy way. She went limp in his arms, feeling his closeness in every cell and nerve ending, confused by the total attraction she had for him. This was the worst time in the world to fall for someone. She was pregnant with another man's baby, for crying out loud. He must have felt the shift of her mood from fight to flight, or in this case to catatonic, and he quickly backed off. They'd gotten too close. Too soon. That sexy, challenging gaze in his eyes from a second before disappeared and he reached for his water to take another drink as a distraction.

"So," he started again, sounding nonchalant, "another good idea, if a bad guy only wants your wallet, is to reach into your purse, grab your wallet and throw it as far away as you can. He probably wants your money, not you, and will go after it. Then scream like hell and run for your life. Of course, if he has a gun you may want to reconsider that move."

She gave the required light laugh over his obvious smart-aleck attempt to change the focus of what had just gone down. But their eyes met again, his honey brown and inviting as all hell, and it seemed they both knew some line had just been crossed. Though she couldn't tell from Joe's steely stare how he felt, and wasn't about to guess because the thought made her get all jittery inside, she hoped he couldn't tell how shaken she was.

She watched him with a mixture of shame and longing, but mostly confusion. Damn that concussion. "Thanks for the lesson," she whispered. "I'd better get some rest now."

They'd gotten too close, that was a fact.

She turned to head for her room, but a sense of duty stopped her. The man had saved her life then offered to share his home with her. Where did a guy like that come from? The least she could do was tell him what she'd been through, why she'd run away from home. He deserved to know how she'd ended up smack in the middle of his life. And if she shared, maybe she'd find out something about him, too.

"Joe?" She circled back to face him.

"Yeah?" He'd gone back to throwing punches at his punchbag and stopped.

"I ran away from a man who wanted to possess me. Completely. Little by little he clipped away at my life. Half the time I didn't even notice, until one day I realized he'd isolated me from everything I liked and loved other than him." She picked at a broken fingernail. "He wanted to control my life, and when I got pregnant he acted like that would ruin everything and got abusive with me." Carey stared at her feet rather than risk seeing any judgment on Joe's face. "I ran away the night he handed me a wad of money and told me to take care of 'it', as if my baby was a problem that needed fixing. He didn't want to share me with anyone, not even our kid."

She finally glanced up to find nothing but empathy in Joe's eyes. "I fought him and he roughed me up. So when he gave me the money I grabbed whatever I could without being obvious, acted like I was going to do what he wanted, then ran for my life."

Joe stepped toward her but she backed up, needing the distance and to tell him her entire story.

"I came to California because it was the next bus out of Montclare, and I didn't have time to pick or choose. I must have looked like a sitting duck because I stepped off the bus and immediately got dragged into that alley." Frightened to relive that night, and frustrated by the emotion rolling through her, she dug her fingers into her hair. "At first I thought maybe Ross had somehow found me and he was taking me back home. Then I realized I was getting mugged, but it was too late. I didn't know how to protect myself." She removed her hands from her hair and held them waist high, palms upward, beseeching Joe to understand. "If it wasn't for you I don't know where I'd be.

"I owe my life to you, and I've got to be honest and say it's strange to feel that way." She sat on the edge of the nearby dining table chair. "Yet here you are day after day watching over me, making my life better. I'm grateful, I am, but please understand that I'm confused and scared and..." Her voice broke with the words. "And I don't know what the future holds for me. Whether I stay here or go somewhere else, I just don't know, but the only thing that matters right now is my baby." Her forearm folded across her stomach and she blinked.

"I get it," Joe said. "Believe me, I understand how life-changing a baby can be."

"You do? Are you a father?"

"Uh, no." He immediately withdrew.

"So how do you know, then?"

"Look, forget I said that. Right now, all I want is for you to be healthy and safe." He came to her and crouched to be eye level with her. "I'm sorry if I've made you uncomfortable. I can't help but find you attractive, so there, I've said it, and I know that's not acceptable."

How was she supposed to answer him? "It may not be acceptable but I feel the same way." Oh, God, she'd put her secret thoughts into words. "It's just the worst timing in the world, you know?"

"I know. Like I said, I get it." He made the wise decision not to touch her but instead to stand and step back.

"Thank you for understanding."

"Of course."

She stood and started walking, this time without looking back, and headed on wobbly legs to her room. Had she just admitted she found Joe Matthews as attractive as he'd just confirmed he found her?

This was nuts! So she'd blame it on the head trauma.

Joe stood perfectly still, watching Carey make her exit. He half expected to hear her lock the door to the bedroom. He hoped he hadn't made her feel creepy about him. It hadn't been his intention to get her in a hug, but he'd been showing her ways to get out of predatory attacks and had inadvertently become a predator himself.

Great going, Joe. You made your house guest think you wanted to crawl into her bed.

He went back to the porch and punched the bag. "Ouch!" He hadn't prepared his fist and it hurt like hell. And what had gotten into him to let slip that he'd known how it felt to be an expectant parent? That wouldn't happen again. He wound up, wanting to punch the bag again, this time even harder, but stopped himself.

Regardless of how awkward he may have made Carey feel, she'd just opened up to him. Man, she'd had it tough back in Chicago. He couldn't remember the name of the suburb she'd come from, and right now that didn't matter. What mattered was that she shouldn't feel like she'd run all the way across country only to find herself in the same situation again.

She needed to get out of the house. To begin something. To get that job and start some money rolling in before she got so pregnant she wouldn't be able to. His head started spinning with everything that needed to be done for her. He needed to help her get her independence back.

From personal experience he knew about a special class at The Hollywood Hills Clinic. A class that would be perfect for where she was right now in her life. He knew the right people to talk to about it, too. And he'd move ahead with her getting that job, so if she wanted, in time, she could move out.

Maybe he couldn't erase what had happened between them just now, but he sure as hell could make some changes for the better happen, starting tomorrow.

He flipped off the light and headed to his room to take a cold shower and hopefully catch a little sleep.

On Friday afternoon Carey sat on the backyard deck in the shade of the huge jacaranda tree, the flowers falling into piles of light purple and scattering across the wood planks like pressed flowers in a painting. She'd been reading an article about early pregnancy on the internet on Joe's tablet when she heard his hybrid SUV pull into the garage and shortly after he came through the gate in the backyard.

Did he know she was out here? Or, more likely after last night, maybe he wanted to avoid her by coming through the back way, hoping she'd be inside.

"Hey," he said, all smiles, as if nothing monumental had occurred between them last night.

"Hi. You're home early."

He came toward the deck but didn't come up, keeping a safe distance between them, placing a foot on the second step and leaning a forearm over his knee. "One of the perks of owning your own business is that I call the shots. It was a slow day, so I took off early."

"Lucky you." His smile was wide, giving her the impression he had some good news. Maybe he had found somewhere for her to move to? If she was honest, that would give her mixed feelings, though the social worker Helena had said she'd look into housing for her, too, and she'd agreed to it at the time. "But I know you've worked hard to get where you are and at the ripe old age of twenty-eight you deserve your afternoon off. Twenty-eight, that's right isn't it?"

He nodded proudly. Yeah, he'd made something out of himself and he wasn't even thirty yet. "And you are?"

"Twenty-five."

"A mere child." He smiled, pretending to be the worldly-wise older man, but his gaze quickly danced away from hers. Yeah, he was still mixed up about last night, too. "So, listen, about you feeling isolated and stuck here and everything…"

"I didn't say that."

"You didn't have to. I figured it out after you went to your room last night. But let's not rehash that, because I've got some good news."

She shut down the tablet and leaned forward in the outdoor lounger. "Good news? They found my stuff?"

He wrinkled his nose and shook his head. "Sorry, I wish. But here's the deal—the clinic has this prenatal class, they call it Parentcraft and it's starting a new session tomorrow. I hope you don't mind, but I put your name in, and Dr. Rothsberg gave me the okay. I thought you could ride into work with me in the morning, and check it out."

"You signed me up? Isn't there a fee? I…uh…can't—"

"Like I said, James took care of everything. He's a generous man. There's a spot for you and the first session starts tomorrow at ten."

"Joe, I'm really grateful for you doing this, but you're helping so much, I don't think I'll ever be able to repay you."

"Carey, I'm not doing any of this to make you feel indebted to me. Please, don't feel that way. My parents taught me a lot of stuff, and helping folks was big in our family. When you're back on your feet you'll find a way to help someone else in need. That's all. No debt to me, just pay it forward."

"Joe…" She stared at him, trying her hardest to figure him out. Was he a freak of nature or her personal knight in shining armor? She leaned back in the lounger and looked into the blue sky dotted with its few wispy clouds. "It's just hard to take in all this goodness after the way my life had been going this past year." She heard him step up the stairs and walk toward her.

"Well, get used to it." He sat on the adjacent lounger then reached out to touch her hand. "That man you ran away from is ancient history. It may not have been your plan, but Hollywood is your new beginning. Just go with the flow, as my yoga-brained sister likes to say."

Carey laughed, wondering about Joe's family. They must be some special people to produce a gem like him. "Okay. Thanks. I'm excited about the class tomorrow."

"Great, and while you're at the hospital you can fill out the papers for the temporary ward clerk job, too."

"What?"

"I know, too much goodness, right?" He laughed, and she thought she could easily get used to watching his handsome face. "James, uh, Dr. Rothsberg, has taken care of everything. Hey, not every clinic can boast their very own Jane Doe. We just want to help get you back on your feet."

"This is all too much to take in."

"Then don't waste your time." He stood. "Come on, I'll take you to my favorite deli on Fairfax. You like roast beef on rye? They make their sandwiches this thick." He used his thumb and index finger to measure a good four inches.

Well, come to think of it, she was hungry. Again! And what better way to keep her mind off the whirlwind of feelings gathering inside her about that man than stuffing her face with a sandwich. Otherwise she'd have to deal with her growing awareness of Joe, the prince of a guy who had literally come out of nowhere, protecting her, saving her, taking her in, changing her life in a positive way, and, maybe the most interesting part, forcing her to remember pure and simple attraction for the opposite sex.

Saturday morning Carey was up and dressed in one of the new outfits Joe had bought her, a simple summer dress with a lightweight pastel-green sweater that covered the tiny baby bump just starting to appear. She was nervous about applying for a job, though she knew she really needed to get out among the living again, to prove to herself she was getting back on her feet. Also, having something to do after a week of lying low since being discharged from the clinic was a major reason she looked forward to applying for the job. As for the parenting class, with her huge desire to be a good mother she was eager to start.

Joe had dressed for work, his light blue polo shirt with The Hollywood Hills Clinic logo above the pocket fit his healthy frame perfectly and highlighted those gorgeous deltoids, biceps and triceps. The cargo pants, though loose and loaded with useful pockets, filled with EMS stuff no doubt, still managed to showcase his fine derriere. She felt a little guilty checking him out as he walked ahead to open the door to the employee entrance. How much longer would she be able to blame her concussion for this irrational behavior? In her defense, there was just something so masculine about a guy wearing those serious-as-hell EMS boots!

He glanced at his watch. "You should have enough time to get your paperwork done for the job application first. I'll walk you over to HR."

"HR?"

"Human Resources."

"Ah, we call it Employee Relations back home."

"Yeah, same thing, but first I'm going to show you where your parenting class will be so you'll know where to go when you're through. Follow me."

Carey did as she was told, clutching her small purse with her new identification cards and temporary driving license, while walking and looking around the exquisite halls and corridors with vague memories of having been there before. Though the place seemed more like a high-end hotel than a hospital. And this time she had money from her last pay check from the hospital back home, instead of being completely vulnerable, like before. Ten days ago she'd arrived on a stretcher, and today she was applying for a job and starting a new parenting class. She was definitely getting back on her feet. Who said life wasn't filled with miracles?

"Oh, Gabriella," Joe said, to a pretty woman walking past, "I'd like to introduce you to Carey Spencer. She'll be starting your class later." He turned to Carey. "Gabriella is the head midwife and runs the prenatal classes."

The woman, who looked to be around Joe's age, with strawberry-blonde hair and a slim and healthy figure, smiled at Carey, her light brown eyes sparkling when she did so. They briefly shook hands, then all continued walking together, as the midwife was obviously heading somewhere in the same direction. As Gabriella was just about Carey's height, their eyes met when she spoke. "Oh, lovely to have you. How far along are you?"

"A little over three months."

"Perfect. We're beginning the class with pregnancy meal planning trimester by trimester, plus exercises for early pregnancy."

This was exactly what Carey needed. Just because she was a nurse it didn't mean she knew squat about becoming a mother or going through a pregnancy. "Sounds great." Her hopes soared with the lucky direction her life had taken. Thanks to Joe and Dr. Rothsberg.

"Yes, I think you'll love it." Gabriella cut off into another hallway. "Be sure to bring your partner," she said over her shoulder. "It's always good to have that reinforcement."

And Carey's heart dropped to her stomach, pulling her pulse down with it. Was having a partner a requirement? Obviously, Gabriella didn't know her circumstances.

Joe gave her an anxious glance. "That won't be a problem. Trust me, okay?"

Surely, Carey hoped, in this day and age there were

bound to be other women in the class without partners. Joe was probably right about it not being a problem. But, please, God, she wouldn't be the only one, would she?

Forty-five minutes later, after submitting her job application for the temporary third-floor medical/surgical ward clerk in HR and feeling very positive about it, Carey had found her way back to the modern and pristine classroom and took a seat. Several hand-outs had been placed on the tables. A dozen couples were already there, and more drifted in as the minutes ticked on. She glanced around the room, seeing a sea of couples. Oh, no, she really was going to be the only one on her own. How awkward would that be?

Fighting off feeling overwhelmed but refusing to be embarrassed, she glanced at the clock on the wall—three minutes to ten—and thought about sneaking out before the class began. She could learn this stuff online, and wouldn't have to come here feeling the odd man out every week. But Joe had gone out of his way to get her enrolled, and Dr. Rothsberg was footing the bill. She went back and forth in her mind about staying or going, then Gabriella entered and started her welcome speech.

She'd sat close to the back of the room, and it would still be easy to sneak out if she wanted or needed to. But, wait, she wasn't that person anymore, the one who let life throw her a curveball and immediately fell down. Nope, she'd turned in her victim badge, and Joe had helped her. She could do this. She forced her focus on the front of the class to Gabriella, who smiled and brightened the room with her lovely personality. The last thing Carey wanted to do was insult anyone, especially after Joe and Dr. Rothsberg had made special arrangements to get her here. But, oh, she felt weird about being the only single mom in the class.

"Why don't we go around the room and introduce ourselves?" Gabriella said.

Soon everyone else would notice, too.

The door at the back of the class opened again. Feeling nervous and easily distracted, Carey glanced over her shoulder then did a double take. In came Joe, his heavy booted steps drawing attention from several people in the vicinity.

"Sorry I'm late," he said to Gabriella, then walked directly to Carey and took the empty chair next to her. "If you don't mind," he whispered close to her ear, "I'll pretend to be your partner today." For all anyone else knew in the class, he could have told her he loved her. The guy knew how to be discreet, and from the way her heart pattered from his entrance he may as well have just run down a list of sweet nothings.

He'd obviously picked up on her anxiety the instant Gabriella had told her back in that hallway to be sure to bring her partner. He was here solely to spare her feelings.

Joseph Matthews truly was a knight in shining armor! Or in his case cargo pants and work boots.

As he settled in next to her his larger-than-life maleness quickly filled up the space between them. Warmth suffused her entire body. Being this close to Joe, having access to gaze into those rich brown eyes, would definitely make it difficult to concentrate on today's lesson.

"You're next, Carey. Introduce yourself and your partner," Gabriella said, emphasizing the *partner* part.

Joe hadn't meant to put Carey on the spot, but after seeing the panic in her eyes earlier, when Gabriella had told her to be sure to bring her partner, he couldn't let her go through this alone. At first he'd wanted to run like hell when he'd shown her the classroom. Coming here had brought back more awful memories. He and Angela had actually started this class before she'd moved out.

Feeling uneasy as hell when he'd dropped Carey off earlier, he'd gone back to his work station, but had soon found he'd been unable to concentrate on the job. His mind had kept drifting to Carey sitting here alone, feeling completely out of place, and he couldn't stand for that to happen. Besides, wasn't it time for him to move on? Determined to put his bad memories aside once and for all—his divorce hadn't been his fault—he'd made a decision. She shouldn't have to attend this class alone. If offering her support could ease her discomfort, he'd take the bullet for her and be her partner. The woman had been through enough on her own lately.

"Oh," she said, as if she'd never expected to have to introduce herself, even though everyone else just had. "Um, I'm Carey Spencer, I'm a little over three months pregnant, I, uh, recently moved to California." She swallowed nervously around the stretching of the truth. Joe reached for her hand beneath the table and squeezed it to give her confidence a boost. "I'm a nurse by profession, a first-time mother, and…" She looked at Joe, the earlier panic returning to those shimmering green eyes. He squeezed her hand again.

"I'm Joe Matthews," he stepped in. "Carey's friend. *Good* friend." He glanced at her, seeing her squirm, letting it rub off on him a tiny bit. "A really close friend." Overkill? He gazed around the room, having fudged the situation somewhat, and all the other couples watched expectantly. "We've been through a lot together, and we're both really looking forward to taking this class and learning how to be good parents."

Okay, let them think whatever they wanted. His

statement was mostly true—in fact, it was ninety-nine per cent true, except for the bit about being "really close" friends, though they had been through a lot together already. Oh, and the part about him ever getting to be a parent. Yeah, that would never happen. The reality hit like a sucker punch and he nearly winced with pain. Why the hell had he willingly walked into this room again? Carey's cool, thin fingers clasped his hand beneath the table, just as he'd done to support her a few seconds ago. The gesture helped him past the stutter in thought.

He'd come here today for Carey. She needed to catch a break, and he'd promised the night he'd found her in the alley that he'd look out for her. If she needed a partner for the parenting class then, damn it, he'd be here.

"I'm a paramedic here at the clinic, so if I ever need to deliver a baby on a run, I figure this class will be good for that, too." He got the laugh he was hoping for to relieve his mounting tension as the room reacted. "It's a win-win situation, right?"

He shifted his eyes to the woman to his left. If taking this class together meant having to really open up about themselves, well, he was bound to let her down because he was far, far from ready to talk about it.

Carey didn't know squat about his past, and if he had his way, she never would. Why humiliate himself again, this time in front of a woman he was quickly growing attached to, when once had already been enough for a lifetime?

CHAPTER FIVE

ON THE SATURDAY after the next Parentcraft class, Carey stood in the kitchen, using her second-trimester menu planner for dinner preparation. She'd had to stretch her usual eating routine to include items she'd never have been caught dead eating before. Like anchovies! Why was Gabriella so big on anchovies? Obviously they were high in calcium and other important minerals, plus loaded with omega three and six fatty acids, but Carey didn't think they tasted so great and smelled really bad. Carey practically had to hold her nose to eat them.

Fortunately this Saturday-night menu included salmon—yay, more omega fats—which Joe was dutifully grilling outside on a cedar plank. Dutiful, yeah, that was the right word for Joe. Everything he did for her seemed to be done out of duty. Sure, he was nice and considerate, but she never sensed he was completely relaxed around her.

She diligently steamed the broccoli and zucchini, and in another pot boiled some new red potatoes, grateful that Joe seemed okay to eat whatever she did. So far she'd managed to keep her occasional junk-food binges to herself. Nothing major, just items that had definitely been left off the Gabriella-approved dietary plan for a pregnant lady, like sea salt and malt vinegar potato chips, or blue corn chips, or, well, actually, any kind of chip that she could get her hands on. She rationalized that if occasionally she only bought the small luncheon-sized bags she wouldn't do the baby any harm. Or her hips.

Her weight gain was right on target, and when she'd seen Gabriella in clinic for a prenatal checkup, thanks to Dr. Rothsberg, she'd complimented her on how well she was carrying the baby. The ultrasound had been the most beautiful thing she'd ever seen, and the first person she'd wanted to share it with had been Joe, and since he'd brought her to the appointment, once she'd dressed she'd invited him back into the examination room. He'd oohed and aahed right along with her, but she'd sensed a part of him had remained safely detached. She could understand why—he was a guy and it wasn't his baby.

It made sense…yet he'd gotten all watery-eyed that day in the clinic when she'd found out her baby was okay, and he'd made that remark that one time about knowing how life-changing a baby could be. She'd asked him point blank if he was a father, but he'd said no and had powered right on. What had that been about? Heck, she'd only just recently found out how old he was, and the only thing she knew beyond that, besides he had a big, kind family, was that he was divorced.

The thing that kept eating away at her thoughts was that Joe didn't seem like the kind of guy who'd give up on a marriage.

Carey popped the top from another beer can and carried it outside to Joe. Being so involved together in the parenting class had definitely changed their relationship for the better, yet she knew Joe held back. She'd opened up about Ross in the hope of getting Joe to share whatever it was that kept him frequently tense and withdrawn.

At first she'd written off that always-present slow simmer just beneath the surface as being due to his demanding job as a paramedic, and also the fact he ran the business. But he clearly thrived on being in charge. It was obvious he loved the challenge. No, that wasn't the problem, it was when they were in the house together, her occasionally indulging in baby talk to her stomach, or discussing the latest information from the Parentcraft classes that she noticed him mentally slip into another time and place. Granted, another person's pregnancy wasn't exactly riveting to the average person, but Joe had volunteered to attend the class with her. If it was an issue, why had he signed on?

Now outside, she smiled and handed him a second beer. "Ready for another?"

His brows rose. "Sure. Thanks." As he took it, their eyes met and held, and a little zing shot through her. The usual whenever they looked straight at each other.

She turned and headed back toward the kitchen, feeling distracted and desperately trying to stay on task.

"You trying to get me drunk?"

"Maybe." She playfully tossed the word over her shoulder then ducked inside before he could respond.

Tonight was the night she hoped to get him to open up. If she had to ply him with beer to do it, she would.

Later over dinner… "Mmm, this is delicious," Carey said, tasting the cedar-infused salmon. "That lime juice brings out a completely different flavor." They sat at the small picnic table on the deck under a waxing June moon.

"Not bad, I must say. What kind of crazy food do we have to prepare tomorrow?"

"Watercress soup with anchovies, what else?" She laughed. "That's lunch, but for dinner we get chicken teriyaki with shredded veggies, oh, and cheese rolls. Can't wait for the bread!" She leveled him with her stare. "I have to thank you for putting up with this crazy diet."

His gaze didn't waver. "I've enjoyed everything so far." He reached across the table and covered her hand with his. "Since I'm your prenatal partner, the least I should do is help you stay on the diet. Your baby will thank me one day."

Sometimes he said the sweetest things and she just wanted to throw her arms around him. But she'd made that mistake once already during the self-defense training and it had mixed up everything between them for days afterwards. Since then he seemed to have shut down like a spring snare, and she'd carefully kept her distance. But he'd just planted a thought she couldn't drop. Would her baby ever know him?

Right now his hand was on top of hers, and she couldn't for the life of her understand why such a wonderful man wasn't still happily married with his own assortment of kids.

She lifted her lids and caught him still watching her, both totally aware of their hands touching, so she smiled but it felt lopsided and wiggly. She stopped immediately, not wanting him to think she was goofy looking or anything. Things felt too close, it nagged at her, and she knew how to break up that uncomfortable feeling pronto. "You mentioned once that you were divorced." She decided to get right to the heart of the conversation she'd planned to start tonight.

He removed his hand from hers and sat taller as ice seemed to set into his normally kind eyes. "Yeah." He dug into his vegetables and served himself more fish, suddenly very busy with eating. "My wife left me."

Why would any woman in her right mind leave Joe? "That must have hurt like hell."

"It was not a good time." He clipped out the words, with an emphasis that communicated it would be the end of this conversation. And why did she know without a doubt that he wasn't telling her anywhere near the whole story? Because he'd hinted at "getting it" and knowing how babies changed lives. Things didn't add up. Had he lost a child?

So she pressed on, hoping that talking about herself some more might help him to open up. "Sometimes people *should* get divorced." She pushed her empty plate away and sipped from her large glass of iced water.

"For instance, my parents were a train wreck. My dad was out of work most of the time, and my mother was always taking on whatever odd jobs she could to make up for it. Instead of being grateful, my typically belligerent father went the macho route, accusing her of thinking him not good enough to take care of the family. Occasionally he'd haul off and hit her, too. I swore I'd never, *never* put myself in the same position."

Joe protested, shaking his head. "You didn't."

"Didn't I? After working my whole life to be independent, I fell for the exact same kind of guy as my dad. A man so insecure about his masculinity that he kept me isolated, insisting it was because he loved me so much. Then he turned violent whenever I stood up to him, and especially when I told him we were going to have a baby. What a fool I was. I didn't learn a thing from my parents' lousy marriage." If she hadn't already finished eating she wouldn't have been able to take another bite, with her stomach suddenly churning and contorting with emotion.

"He must have had a lot going for him to get you interested at first, though. I'm sure he hid his insecurities really well." His hand came back to hers. "Don't call yourself stupid. You have a big heart. You just didn't see the changes coming."

"You give me a lot of credit." She squeezed his hand. "I'm still mad at myself for winding up in this position."

"As crazy as it sounds, I'm kind of glad you did." He squeezed back then let go completely, keeping things safe and distant. "You're better off here."

With you? She wanted to add, *I am better off here but where do we go from here?* "What are we, Joe?"

He screwed up his face in mock confusion. "What do you mean?"

"Are we friends? You can't call me a tenant because I'm not paying you rent." She tried to make an ironic expression, but fell far short because the next pressing question was already demanding she ask it. "Am I one huge charity case that you, in your kindness, the way your parents taught you, just can't bring yourself to send away?"

"God, no. Carey, come on." He wadded up his napkin and tossed it on the table. "You're overthinking things, making problems where there aren't any. We're friends." He shrugged.

"We can't call ourselves friends if you won't open up to me." She stood and started clearing the table. "Friends share things."

Joe shot up and helped to pick up dishes, as usual, and they headed to the kitchen and washed the plates in silence. A muscle in his jaw bunched over and over. Not only had she *not* gotten Joe to open up, she'd made sure he'd keep his distance and would probably never let her close. Major fail.

But what should she expect, being pregnant with another man's baby?

Early on Monday morning the phone rang. Sunday evening had been strained but tolerable between them, and Joe had withdrawn more from Carey by working during the day and later by working out while listening to that aggressive jazz saxophone music while he did so. It made her want to put on headphones. Carey didn't know if she could take much more of him distancing himself from her, but under the circumstances she felt trapped for now. Which felt far too familiar, considering her past.

Joe had the day off and answered, then quickly handed the phone to Carey.

"This is Mrs. Adams from social services. The police department told us about your current situation, and Helena from The Hollywood Hills Clinic Social Services also contacted us. Sorry it took so long, but there is quite a backlog. Anyway, we have found a temporary apartment in Hollywood where you can stay for now."

"Well, that's wonderful. When can I have a look?"

"You can move in this weekend, if you'd like. Or today if you need to. We have a voucher worth a month's rent and this unit has just become available. Would you like me to bring the voucher by?"

"Yes. Of course. Thanks so much."

Carey hung up having made arrangements with Mrs. Adams, glancing up to see Joe watching her skeptically. She owed him an explanation and told him exactly what Mrs. Adams had just said.

"So, if all works out, I'll be out of your hair, maybe as soon as tonight."

"Where is this place? Will you be safe?" There went that jaw muscle again.

"I don't know anything, but would social services send me somewhere unsafe?"

"They're just trying to put a roof over your head." His fingers planted on and dug into his hips, his body tensed. He wore an expression of great concern, making his normally handsome face look ominous. "Safety might not be their number-one goal. I'm going with you."

Every once in a while, thanks to her recent experience with Ross, Joe seemed too overbearing. Yeah, she'd messed up lately, but she was a big girl, a mother-to-be! And she would be in charge of her life from here on. "I can take care of myself. Thanks."

His demeanor immediately apologetic, he came closer. "I didn't mean to come off like that, dictating what I intended to do, but please let me come with you. I'd like to see where you'll be living. I know all the areas around here."

Since he sounded more reasonable, she changed her mind. "Okay, but I make the decision. Got that?"

"Got it. But first off you've got to know that you don't have to move out. You're welcome to stay here as long as you need to."

"Thank you, but as a future single mother I've got to prove to myself I can take care of things. I got myself into this situation, I should get myself out. Besides, I'll be starting the temporary job next Monday, and—"

"Your salary won't be enough to rent an apartment in any decent neighborhood. I'm not trying to throw a wet blanket on your plans, I'm just being honest."

She refused to lose hope. "I'm going to go see that apartment with Mrs. Adams and then I'll decide."

"Can you at least call her back and tell her I'll drive you over there?"

"Okay, but only because it will be more convenient for her."

"Fine."

That afternoon Joe parked on North Edgemont in front of an old redbrick apartment building that was dark, dank and seedy-looking as hell. He clamped his jaw and ground his molars rather than let Carey know what he thought. She'd made it clear it would be her decision, and he'd honor that. The only thing the area had going for it was a huge hospital a couple of blocks down on Sunset Boulevard.

If they'd offered the rent voucher the first week she'd moved in, he would have encouraged her to jump on it. Having a woman in his house again, especially a pregnant woman, brought back a hundred different and all equally awful memories. Having to do things together, like shopping for groceries and fixing meals, was nearly more than he could bear. Plus, with Carey living with him, it seemed Angela had moved back in, just in a different form. So he'd concentrated on Carey being a victim and he was her protector. Keeping it clinical and obligatory had been the key.

Best-laid plans and all, he'd gotten involved with her anyway. Why had he taken it on himself to teach her self-defense, and why in hell had he volunteered to be her prenatal class partner? The problem was there was too much to like about Carey. So he glanced at the dreary apartment building and felt a little sick.

If she decided to take this place, he'd have to find her

a car. Which wouldn't be a problem with his father's business. No way did he want her walking these streets at night, coming home from work and getting off the bus. Pressure built in his temples just thinking about it.

He stood back and let Carey introduce herself to Mrs. Adams, who showed her inside. The term *flophouse* came to mind, but Joe kept his trap shut. Damn, it was hard.

The single room had a tiny alcove with a half-refrigerator, a small microwave and a hot plate. How would she be able to continue with the nutritious meals from Gabriella's class? He'd throw out the mattress from the pullout bed and burn it rather sleep on it, and the rusty toilet in the so-called bathroom made his stomach churn. Not to mention that the constant dripping from the kitchen sink would keep her awake at night.

Caution was as plain as day on Carey's face as she glanced around the place. But he already knew her well enough to know she'd try to make the best out of a lousy situation. Hell, she'd been putting up with him withdrawing every time they'd gotten too close. Probably walked on eggshells around him. But was living with him so bad that she'd choose a dump like this just to get away?

Last night she'd said a real zinger, not realizing it, of course, but nevertheless her comment had hit hard. When she'd talked about her ex being insecure about his masculinity to the point of taking over her life, it had made Joe cringe. He could relate, especially since getting the lab results about him being sterile, and following up later with a urologist as to the reasons why. Was that part of him wanting to protect Carey? Was it some twisted way of making himself feel like a complete man again?

"And you said you have a voucher for the rent here for the next month?" Carey asked.

Mrs. Adams, a tiny African-American woman with short tight curls and wearing a bright red blouse, looked serious. "Yes, we can also provide food stamps and you can move in now or this weekend if you'd like."

Carey was about to say something, and damn it to hell if it meant he was waving around his insecure masculinity or whatever, Joe couldn't let this fiasco continue another second. "What's the crime rate in this neighborhood?" he butted in.

An eyebrow shot up on Mrs. Adams's forehead. Was she not used to being asked that question by people desperate enough to need county social services assistance? "I honestly don't know. It's a busy neighborhood. There's a church right up the street, a hospital down on Sunset. There's a small family-run market on Hollywood Boulevard and the apartment building is really well situated for all of her needs."

Carey stood still, only her eyes moved to watch him. Was it trust or fear he saw there? Was his being concerned coming off as overbearing? He hoped she saw it a different way, the way he'd intended, that he was worried for her safety. He subtly shook his head but she quickly glanced back at Mrs. Adams. "Thank you so much for showing me this place. Do I have to sign anything?"

Joe understood she'd been trying to be a good soldier, stiffening her lip and all, but all it had done was turn her to cardboard. She obviously wanted to make the offer from social services work out, but Joe strongly suspected that in her heart she was scared. And he was pretty sure he saw it in her eyes, too. Those lush meadow-green eyes seemed ready for a storm. How could she not be afraid? Now that he'd identified what was going on with her, he could practically smell that fear. He just hoped it wasn't directed toward him.

She didn't belong here. She belonged with him. Safe. Protected. That's all there was to it. Was he being crazy, like Ross? With all his heart he hoped not, but right at this moment it was hard to evaluate his motives because the lines had blurred and there was no way in hell he'd let this happen.

Joe stepped forward, unable to let the scene play out another moment. He reached for and gently held Carey's upper arm, pleading with his eyes, hoping she wouldn't see a crazed, insecure man. He fought to keep every ounce of emotion out of his voice. "Stay with me." Making the comment a simple suggestion. Then he stumbled, letting a drop of intensity slip back in. "Please."

Carey hadn't given in, though she'd wanted to. Mrs. Adams had gone on alert when Joe had taken her arm in his hand. The poor woman had probably thought he was the guy she needed to get away from. Carey had made sure she knew otherwise. No, Joe wasn't scary, but he had a rescue complex and she needed to help him get over it.

They drove back toward West Hollywood mostly in silence. True, the last thing she wanted was to move into such a depressing place, but rather than cave just because Joe wanted her to she'd asked Mrs. Adams to give her twenty-four hours to make her decision. It had also seemed to calm the woman's sudden uneasy demeanor over the battle of wills between Carey and Joe about moving.

And this had been where Joe had proved he was nothing like Ultimatum Ross. Trusting her decision, he'd agreed that was a smart idea, and Mrs. Adams had smiled again. Inside, so had Carey.

The man was too good to be true, and she couldn't trust her instinct to believe he was what he was, a great guy! She'd thought she'd fallen for a great guy back home, a man who'd gone out of his way to charm her and make her laugh, and above all who'd wanted to take care of her. Look where that had led. But the last two weeks of living with Joe had been little short of perfection. He was patient and friendly, didn't have mood swings, like Ross, had just mostly kept his distance. Sometimes that had been maddening. Joe was tidy and helpful and—oh, she'd tried long enough to avoid the next thought—sexy as hell! The male pheromones buzzing through that house had awakened something she'd tried to put on hold since long before she'd gotten pregnant. Desire.

When she'd taken off her blindfold and finally seen who Ross truly was, she hadn't wanted to be engaged to him anymore. But he was such a manipulating and suspicious guy that she'd pretended to be sexually interested just enough to keep him off the scent. She'd intended to leave him. Had made plans for it, too. Then the unthinkable had happened and she'd gotten pregnant. The only thing she could figure was she'd missed a birth-control pill. Ross had hated hearing that excuse, and he'd accused her of wanting to ruin everything they'd had together. He'd even accused her of being unfaithful.

And he'd gotten violent.

How could she ever trust her instinct where men were concerned?

She needed Joe to open up to make sure he wasn't hiding something awful. Maybe she could use him wanting to rescue her all the time as a bargaining chip to get him to share something personal. She'd been kind of forced to tell him about Ross, what with her bruises and black eye and being pregnant and running away. But her attempt to get him to tell her about his failed marriage Saturday night had fallen flat. Maybe his divorce still hurt too much.

"If you expect me to continue to live with you, we have to actually be friends, not just say we are."

"Of course we're friends." He kept his eyes on the road.

"No, we're not. I've shared some very personal stuff with you, and yet you're nothing but a mystery to me. Friends know things about each other."

"What do you want to know?" He sounded frustrated.

"Why did your wife leave you? What happened? What broke up your marriage?"

He braked a little too hard for the red light, then stared straight ahead for a couple of moments. "If you're thinking I was a player you'd be wrong. In our case it was the other way around."

Carey nearly gulped in her shock. What woman in her right mind would be unfaithful to a guy like Joe? What in the world was she supposed to say to that? "She left you for another man?" She admitted she sounded a little dumbstruck.

"As opposed to a woman?" He gave an ironic laugh and glanced at her with challenge in his eyes. "I guess that might have hurt even more, but yes to your question. It was another man." He could have been testifying in court by his businesslike manner. Just the facts, ma'am.

So Joe was one of the walking wounded, like her.

"I'm so sorry." It was probably a lot easier for him to assign himself the role of protector than to open the door to getting involved with another woman. Especially a vulnerable person like her. Joe had proved to be wise on top of all his other wonderful assets.

Though she knew without a doubt what had gone down today, looking at the apartment, was on a completely different level. Joe had asked her to stay. She'd seen from that touch of desperation in his eyes that he'd meant it, too. She didn't have a clue if once upon a time he'd asked his wife to stay and she'd left anyway, but right at this instant Carey made a decision.

No way would she be another woman walking out on Joseph Matthews. "May I borrow your cell phone?"

While driving, he fished in his pocket and handed it to her. She looked in her purse for the business card. "Hello, Mrs. Adams? This is Carey Spencer. Yes, hi. About that apartment, I am so grateful for the rent voucher and the offer of food stamps, but I have decided to stay where I am."

Not another word was spoken on the drive home, but Carey could have sworn the built-up tension in the car had instantly dissipated as if she'd rolled down the window and let the Santa Ana winds blow it all away.

The following Monday Carey started her new job as a substitute ward clerk and couldn't hide her elation over working again. More importantly, the California Board of Registered Nurses assured her she'd get her RN license in a couple more weeks, just in time to apply for another job, this one as an RN, after the vacationing ward clerk came back. Life was definitely looking up.

The evening shift on the medical/surgical unit was nonstop with admissions and discharges, and she was grateful she'd spent a couple of afternoons learning the computer software and clinic routine with the current ward clerk the week before she'd left.

Joe had offered to rent her a car, but she didn't feel ready to drive the streets of Los Angeles, especially those winding roads in the Hollywood Hills, just yet, so Joe had reworked things and scheduled himself on evening shifts so he could bring her to work and back.

She sat transfixed before the computer at the nurses' station, deciphering the admitting orders from Dr. Rothsberg for a twenty-eight-year-old starlet who'd been intermittently starving and binging herself then herbal detoxing for the last several years, until now her liver showed signs of giving out. She'd been admitted with a general diagnosis of fever, malaise and abdominal tenderness. Though bone thin everywhere else, her abdomen looked to be the same size as Carey's, but the actress wasn't pregnant.

Carey had arranged for the ultrasound and CT studies for the next day, and had moved on to requesting a low-sodium diet from the hospital dietary department, which had a master chef. She could vouch for the great food with a couple of memorable meals she'd had during her stay. The patient would probably never notice the lack of salt amidst a perfect blend of fresh herbs and spices. Then she reminded the admitting nurse that her patient was on total bed rest. She went ahead and read Dr. Rothsberg's analysis and realized therapeutic paracentesis was likely in the petite Hollywood personality's future.

Deep in her work, she glanced up to find Joe smiling at her. "I brought you something," he said, then handed her a brown bag with something inside that smelled out of this world.

She stood to take the bag over the countertop, inhaled and couldn't resist. "Mmm, what is it?"

"Your dinner. I was on a call in the vicinity of Fairfax, so I got you one of those deli sandwiches you gobbled down the last time we were there."

"Turkey salad, cranberries and walnuts with bread dressing?"

"Yup."

"Including the pickle?"

He nodded, as if offended she'd even suggest such an oversight.

"Well, thank you. I'll be starving by the time my dinner break rolls around."

"You're welcome." He got serious and leaned on his forearm, making sure to hold her gaze. "I've been thinking. We'll have to get more organized now that you're working and pack a lunch for you every day. We can still use Gabriella's guidelines."

"Sounds good." Totally touched by his concern for her well-being, she fought that frequent urge to give him a hug. Fortunately the nurses' station counter prevented it this time. "But please let me splurge on things like this once in a while." She held up the deli bag.

He winked, and it seemed a dozen butterflies had forced their way into her chest and now attempted to fly off with her heart. Since she'd decided to keep living with him, he'd changed. He'd become easier to talk to, and though he still hadn't opened up he'd quit grinding his teeth so much. Truth was, the man could only suppress his wonderful nature for so long. Now she was the lucky recipient of his thoughtfulness and loving every second of it.

"See you later," he said, making a U-turn and heading off the ward. The perfectly fitting light blue polo shirt showed off his broad shoulders, accentuating his trim waist, the multi-purpose khaki cargo pants still managing to hug his buns just right, and those sexy-as-hell black paramedic utility boots… She guiltily watched his every move until he was out of sight. Wow, it looked like she didn't have to worry about her sick relationship with Ross at the end before she'd run away, and ruining her natural sex drive. She'd faked interest and excitement with him for her safety. Now, with Joe, without even trying, the most natural thoughts of all had awakened some super-hot fantasies. Like the desire to make love and really mean it. What would that be like with Joe?

"Uh-huh. Nice." One of the other nurses in the area had joined her in staring at the masculine work of art as he'd swaggered out the door. How could a guy *not* swagger, wearing those boots?

Getting caught ogling Joe made Carey's cheeks heat up, especially after what she'd just been thinking, so she tossed a sheepish look at the nurse then delved back into the admission packet for the actress.

Joe went straight to the clinic's paramedic station just off the ER to check on the EMT staff. He knew the emergency nurses sometimes got upset if the guys didn't help out when things got busy. Joe was always prepared to intervene and explain that wasn't their job, and the RNs didn't need to get all worked up about the EMS guys sitting for half a minute, waiting for the next call. On the other hand, he'd insisted to his guys that if a nurse said she needed more muscle, and they weren't doing anything at the time, they should jump to it and help out with lifts and transfers. Keeping RNs happy was always a good idea. He'd also taken to suggesting the guys hang out in their truck on downtime rather than at the tiny desk with two computers designated as their work station, so as not to complicate things in the ER.

Not taking his own advice, he took a seat and brought up the evening's schedule, and in the process sat in the vicinity of James, who was conferring on the phone about a patient he'd just admitted to Carey's floor with liver issues. James nodded and smiled at Joe, and Joe returned the courtesy.

Soon James hung up. "How's that scar doing? Any more tearing with your workouts, you beast?"

Joe laughed. "I'm all healed. Thanks." Joe saw James's sister, Freya, appear across the ER, obviously looking for someone.

"There you are," she said over the other heads, immediately making her way toward James.

James ducked down in an obvious fashion. "Oh, boy. Here we go," he said jokingly in an aside to Joe. "What does she want this time?" He raised his voice to tease his younger sister.

Knowing from their rocky history that the brother and sister's relationship had never been better since Freya had come to The Hollywood Hills Clinic as a sought-after public relations guru, Joe chuckled at James's wisecrack.

"There you are," Freya said, her dark blue eyes sparkling under the fluorescent ER lights. "I know you've been avoiding me, but I need a firm date for when you'll visit the Bright Hope Clinic. Here's my calendar, I've highlighted the best days and times for me and them. What works for you?" She shoved her small internet tablet calendar in front of James, making it impossible for him not to pick a day and time.

Her long brown hair was pulled back into a simple

ponytail that waved down her back, nearly to her waist, yet she still looked like she could be royalty. Hollywood royalty, that was. Joe had heard rumors about her once having had to go to rehab for anorexia, but from the healthy, happy-looking pregnant woman standing before him he'd have never guessed.

James took a deep inhale and scrolled through his smartphone calendar, matching day for day, saying, "No. Nope. Not that one either. Hmm, maybe this one? September the first or the second?"

"Let's take the first." Freya quickly highlighted that day. "It is now written in stone. Do you hear me? There's no getting out of it. You'll show up and do those publicity photos in the clinic in South Central and smile like you mean it."

"Of course I'll mean it. I'm going for the children."

"I know, but you know." They passed a secret brother-sister glance, telling an entirely different story than the simple making of plans for publicity shots. Joe deduced that since Dr. Mila Brightman ran Bright Hope, she was the issue. She happened to be Freya's best friend, and also the woman James had stood up on their wedding day. Or, at least, that was the scuttlebutt Stephanie the receptionist had told Joe one day on a break over coffee in the cafeteria. It had happened before Joe had started working there, she'd said, so all he could do was take Stephanie's word for it. The woman really was a gossip. But, damn, if that was the case, no wonder James hesitated about going. How could he face her after dumping her on the day of her dream wedding?

Having achieved her purpose, Freya rushed off, no doubt wanting to end her day and get home to her husband Zack.

"The last thing I want to do is upset a pregnant lady,"

James said to Joe in passing, "but, hey, you know all about that, right?"

The casual comment took Joe by surprise. At first he thought James was referring to his ex, Angela, but then realized he must have been referring to Jane Doe, aka Carey, who lived with him and happened to be just shy of four months pregnant.

"Tell me about it," Joe said, hoping he'd recovered quickly enough not to seem like a bonehead, and pretending that pregnant ladies were indeed unpredictable and demanding, while knowing for a fact Carey was anything but.

On Friday night, at the end of the first week on the job for Carey, Joe insisted they stop for a fast-food burger on the way home. How could she have been in California for three weeks and not tried one? They didn't even bother to wait to get home but devoured them immediately on the drive. Even though it definitely wasn't on her second-trimester diet list, she'd never tasted a better cheeseburger in her life.

"My parents are having a barbecue on the Fourth of July," Joe said, his mouth half-full, one hand on the steering wheel, the other clutching a double cheeseburger.

A national holiday had been the last thing on her mind lately. Plans seemed incomprehensible. She thought of that dreary apartment she'd almost taken and shivered at the thought of being on her own there, especially on the Fourth of July, grateful to have Joe's sweet house and lovely garden in the back to look at. She'd be just fine.

"Do you want to come? They'd love to have you."

What? He was inviting her to his parents' home?

Why? Out of his usual sense of obligation? "Oh, you don't have to—"

"I want to, and my whole family's going to be there so you can meet my sisters and brothers, too."

"Do they know about me?" Why was he pushing to take her?

"I have a prying mother and a loose-lipped sister. Mom's got this sixth sense about changes in my life, no doubt recently fueled by Lori loaning out some clothes."

"The whole story?" She really didn't want her personal failures shared, especially with Joe's family.

He shook his head and took another bite of his burger. "I wouldn't do that. You know better. But you said you wanted to be friends, and I take my friends to family barbecues."

She'd put her foot down when she'd decided to stay with him. He'd agreed to consider her a friend. If this was his way of proving it, as confusing as it would be for her, not to mention nerve-racking, she really shouldn't refuse to meet his family. It might set things back if she didn't.

"Then I guess I'll have to go." She played coy, but cautious contentment she hadn't felt in ages settled in a warm place behind her breastbone. This was more proof that Joe was *nothing* like Ross. He pushed her to get out and do things, got her a job, and now he wanted her to meet his family on Independence Day no less. Wow, what did it all mean?

Joe finished his hamburger as they neared his house. It'd tasted great, as always, but now his stomach felt a little unsettled. He'd tried not to think about the ramifications of what he'd just done, but couldn't avoid it. Trust, or lack thereof, in women in general and Carey, by reason of her gender, made him have second thoughts about the invitation. The gift of Angela's infidelity just kept on giving.

Maybe he'd jumped the gun in asking her to his parents' Fourth of July party. It was too soon. She might get the wrong impression and he wasn't anywhere ready to get close to her. He pulled into the driveway and rather than pull into the garage he parked under the small carport instead. It wasn't like he could change the date of Independence Day, and for the record he wondered if he'd ever be in a place to trust a woman again, whether next week or two years from now.

But the damage had been done. He'd asked Carey to go along, and he couldn't very well take the invitation back. He'd just have to live with it.

Once home, Carey went directly to her room to change her clothes, planning to watch a little TV to unwind after another busy evening shift at the end of her first week. But not without noticing a shift in his mood since he'd issued, and she'd accepted, the invitation to his parents' Fourth of July barbecue. When she came back, Joe was already working out on the patio, hitting his punching bag like it was a full-out enemy. For someone who'd just wolfed down a double-double cheeseburger, French fries and a large soda, he looked the picture of health.

Feeling a bit guilt-ridden, she wandered into the dining room to have a better look, wondering if he'd taken his T-shirt off for her benefit. She particularly loved watching the muscles on his back ripple whenever he landed a good punch. She stood quietly, taking in the whole workout, admiring every inch of him.

Before she'd run away, she'd worried about ever having normal desire for a man again. Faking love with Ross had scarred her more than she'd ever dreamed.

But it hadn't stopped there. Ross had dominated her entire existence to the point of making her fear for her life. How could she ever desire a man who'd treated her like that?

Yet Joe, without even trying, brought out her most basic feelings. He turned her on. So confusing. Maybe she could blame that on the concussion or the pregnancy. Yet what a relief to know she was still a red-blooded woman with a normal sex drive.

With his back to her, he grunted and huffed as he punched the bag, and she could swear the muscles on his shoulders and arms grew more cut by the moment. Needing to either bite her knuckle to keep from groaning or do something to cool herself off, she chose to head to the kitchen for a bottle of water. When she opened the refrigerator, she grabbed one for Joe, too.

This time making her presence known, she went out onto the patio, setting his water near him. "You're making me feel very guilty about having that burger and not intending to do my preggers exercises tonight, you know."

Joe laughed, and because of it messed up his timing and the punch nearly missed the bag altogether. He went for the bottle. "Thanks." Carey enjoyed watching his Adam's apple move up and down his throat while he gulped the water. A few drops dribbled down his chest. Yeah, she noticed that, too.

Her eyes drifted to the jagged scar running across his ribs, still red and tender-looking. He'd been stabbed rescuing her. The thought seemed surreal and sent a barrage of intense feelings ranging from gratitude to lust to guilt rushing through her. On impulse she walked toward him, reached out and gingerly ran her fingers across the scar. His skin was damp, smooth and...

She slowly lifted her gaze from the fit washboard abs to his chest and the pumped pecs lightly dusted in dark hair, then onward to his strong chin and inviting mouth and last to his intensely brown, almost black with desire, eyes.

The moment, when they were up close and locked into each other's stare like that, shuddered through her.

Feeling absurdly out of character in general, and especially because she was four months pregnant, she ignored her insecurities, focusing only on the consuming pull between them, making a trail with her fingertips across the expanse of his muscled torso, along the broad rim of his shoulder, then upward to his jaw.

She swallowed lightly in edgy anticipation.

He didn't move, just kept willing her into the depth of his eyes, and she knew without a doubt he was as into this moment as she was. So she edged closer, lifted her chin and, though feeling breathy from nerves, she went for it, covering his mouth with a full-on kiss.

CHAPTER SIX

IF JOE LET Carey's kiss continue, he'd have to take her all the way and probably scare her half to death with his need. The mere touch of her lips had unleashed pure desire, like a lightning bolt straight down his spine.

But he knew Carey well enough now, and the woman was trying to show her gratitude for his saving her and taking her in. He didn't want gratitude, or, if she knew his whole story, pity, or anything else. All he wanted was to get lost in her body, to make love.

He broke off the kiss to get things straight. "I don't expect anything from you. You don't have to—"

She didn't listen or give him a chance to call her out, she just kissed him again, and, damn it, those lips he'd so often admired on the sly felt better kissing him than he could ever have imagined. He quit fighting his need and pulled her near, devouring her mouth, half hoping she'd get scared and back off so that what was otherwise inevitable wouldn't happen. But the hard and desperate kiss only seemed to fan her need as much as his as she pressed her body flush with his.

He could handle this, wouldn't lose control. They'd just make out for a while then call it quits. But then there was the feel of her lips, smooth, plump, that inviting-as-all-hell tongue, and the touch of her fingertips at the back of his neck and on his shoulders. The sound of her deep breathing, the scent of coconut in her hair, and especially those little turned-on sounds escaping her throat made it so hard to not completely let go. And, damn, that wasn't the only thing that was hard. Yeah, he was pumped, horny, and making out with a woman who seemed to want him as badly as he needed her.

This was about sex. Against a wall. He needed to look into her eyes, to see if she really was as into this as he was, because he wouldn't take her if she wasn't. Electricity seemed to run through his veins, maybe partly because he was worked up from boxing, but most definitely from holding and kissing her. Surely she felt that electricity too. If she was just looking for some comforting necking, she'd come on way too strong, so it was best to check things out. Figure out where she was at before he let loose. He placed his thumbs in front of her ears, his fingers digging into that thick and gorgeous auburn hair, and though hating to separate their mouths he moved her head back.

Carey seemed dazed and was breathless, so it took a moment for her to connect with his stare. Her eyelids fluttered open and maybe Joe's interpretation was skewed from wanting her so much, but her eyes were on fire. For him.

Her nostrils flared and she breathed quickly. "Please don't stop," she whispered. "This has nothing to do with gratitude, believe me." She kissed him again, and the dam of unspoken longing, secret desire, and flat-out need totally broke.

She wanted him. He wanted her. Tonight he'd have her.

He walked her backwards, reached under the back of

her thighs and lifted her as he did so. She wrapped her legs around his waist, and soon her back was against a well-secluded wall in the corner of the patio. She'd already pulled her top over her head by the time they'd gotten there, and once at the wall, just as quickly, she released her full breasts from the constraints of the bra.

He looked down. The view of their chests mashed together exhilarated him, the hot, soft feel of her breasts even better. But she was hungry for his mouth and wanted all his attention there. So he obliged. He wedged her tight against the wall, sitting her on the edge of a book case, leaning into her, weaving his fingers with hers and lifting her arms flush to the plaster so he could be closer still. She moaned, enjoying the full body contact every bit as much as he did. He inhaled her sweet-scented neck and nuzzled it deep with kisses. She liked it, moaning again and bucking her hips just above his full erection, causing more lightning bolts along his spine.

Soon Carey wiggled off his hips, standing just long enough to tug down his boxing shorts and her yoga pants. She took the time to run her hand along his glutes and give them an appreciative squeeze as she stepped up close and hugged him again.

His erection landed between their bodies and the surge of sensation from her skin to his nearly sent him over the top. God, he wanted her. And she obviously wanted him. Right then.

He may be sterile and she pregnant, but he still knew the purpose of protected sex, and it wasn't all about birth control. Any guy his age had a stash of condoms, even though lately he hadn't been in the least bit interested in getting involved enough with a woman to use them…until Carey.

Living with Carey these past few weeks had made him very much aware of where those condoms were, too. "One second." He stopped pressing her to the wall, and regretfully removed himself from between her gorgeous thighs. "Don't move." He stepped back and his eyes took her in, in all her lush splendor. God, he wanted her.

Joe zipped around the wall to his bedroom and returned in record time, afraid she might have already changed her mind.

She wasn't there. His heart sank.

"I'm in the bathroom. I'll be right there!"

The wall was looking less and less appealing so he went into his bedroom and pulled back the covers on his king-sized bed, finding it hard to believe he'd soon be making love to Carey.

Carey never had expected to be having sex with Joe tonight, but now that she'd started it, and sex was definitely on the table, or nearly against the wall in their case, she wanted to freshen up. Ross may have scarred her but Joe could heal her. She didn't expect anything more than tonight, just the chance to find out she could let go and be with him, someone new, different, better than toxic Ross. If she didn't take this opportunity, she might never get over her past or feel normal again.

She stepped into the hall to find Joe waiting for her, having made the mistake of glancing at her pregnant abdomen just before she did. A wave of insecurity nearly made her back out, but the instant she saw his Adonis-like form, and the unadulterated desire in his eyes, every insecure thought left her mind. She wanted Joe more than she'd ever wanted to be with any man.

She rushed to him and he picked her up again, her

cooler skin crashing with his hot damp flesh. She inhaled his musky scent and grew hungrier for him. He carried her to his bed and, probably because she was pregnant, laid her down gently. Frantic for him, she'd have none of that, pulling him firmly toward her, and impatiently bucked under him.

He had other plans, though, and took his time exploring her body, figuring out what excited her and what drove her wild. Just about everything at this point! On his side, facing her, he rested on one arm, lowering and lifting his head to kiss her mouth, her neck, her breasts, while his free hand cupped her and explored her most intimate area. Breathless with longing, sensations zinging every which way through her body, she never wanted the intensified make-out session to end. Until, very soon, the mounting desire was too much and she needed him, all of him, inside her.

She rolled onto her side, throwing her leg over his hip, straddled him and pushed him back onto the mattress. From his firm feel she had zero worries whether he was ready or not. She slid her awakened center, thanks to his earlier attentions, along his length, thrilling at the feel of it and the thought of him soon being inside her. He'd already made her wet so she skimmed along his smooth ridge with ease, several times, stimulating herself more than she thought she could take. He definitely liked it.

But stopping her in mid-skim, as if he might lose control, he sheathed himself in record time then, taking control, placed her on her side with her back to his chest. One arm was underneath her and that hand cupped her breast while the other dipped between her thighs and opened her, rubbing the amazingly sensitive area, and she was soon straining at the onslaught of arousal. She moaned in bliss and Joe, being definitely ready, tilted her hips back, making her swaybacked, then entered her.

The culmination of sensations as he pressed into her took her breath away. She rolled with him, taking in every electrifying thrust. His hands remained attentive in those other strategic places as friction built deep inside, knotting behind her navel and lower. Heat lapped up the base of her spine, across her hips and over her breasts, flooding the skin on her chest and cheeks. She could feel the fully ignited body flush nearly burning her skin. If possible, he felt even harder now and an absurd thought occurred to her. She was making love with him, Joe! It wasn't a wish or a fantasy or a secret dream anymore. It was really happening.

Maybe it was the added hormones of pregnancy, and more probably it was the undivided attention from Joe, but she'd never, *ever* been this turned on in her life. With her entire body tingling and covered in goose bumps, running hot with sensations—not to mention the involuntary sounds escaping her throat—there would be no guessing on his part about how he made her feel. *Freaking amazing.*

She couldn't take more than a few minutes of the intense sensory overload without completely giving in to it. His pumping into her, slowing down and drawing out every last response, then speeding up at the perfect moment to drive her near the flashpoint soon became her undoing. She turned her head and found his mouth. They kissed wildly, wet and deep.

When she came, her center seemed to explode with nerve endings lighting up, zinging and zipping everywhere as they relayed their ecstatic message deep throughout her body. She gasped and writhed against him, riding the incredible wave for all it was worth, while sensing his time was near. Soon his low, elongated moan became the sweetest music she'd ever heard.

It had taken several minutes for things to settle down between Joe and Carey. He'd briefly jumped out of bed for the bathroom to take care of business, returning to find she'd probably done the same. He smiled when she came back with the fresh flush of lovemaking on her face and across her chest. Though she'd run a brush through her hair, it was still wildly appealing. He continued floating on the post-sex euphoric cloud when she crawled back into bed beside him. He'd just had mind-blowing sex with an amazing lady and he felt great. Beyond great. He pulled her close, delivered a sweetheart kiss then snuggled in, savoring the afterglow between them. But it was late and they'd worn each other out.

Within a few short minutes Carey fell asleep. She'd gone still, wrapped in his arms, then her breathing shifted to a slower, deeper rhythm. It felt right, holding her, breathing in her scented hair, touching her soft skin and womanly body. But sleep wasn't ready to come to Joe.

His hand dropped over her abdomen and the noticeable early second-trimester bump. It jolted him. His mind raced with comparisons with another woman and another time. He'd avoided the thought long enough, now it wouldn't let him go.

What the hell had he just done? He'd ruined everything.

The battle in his mind continued with rival thoughts. He had to be honest, he'd wanted this more than anything, and being with Carey had been on his mind for longer than he cared to admit. She'd knocked every sensible thought out of his head just by being the wonderfully appealing, sweet woman she was. The sexy-as-hell—and who'd just proved it beyond a doubt—mother-to-be.

Yes, she was pregnant with another man's baby, and though the circumstances were totally different, the scenario seemed too damn familiar.

Also, Joe worried that Carey was confusing gratitude with desire. She'd denied it when he'd bluntly asked her, but they were both obviously under some voodoo spell when it came to each other. He wouldn't dare call it love. Hell, she'd just escaped a toxic, abusive relationship. Any decent guy, and Joe considered himself one of the good guys, would be an improvement.

Back and forth he silently argued, feeding his confusion rather than solving anything. He'd essentially been acting like a partner to Carey in all but name—how had he not seen that before? It'd started with the staggering need to protect her and moved on to bringing her home. They'd lived together for almost a month, sharing the little everyday things that true couples did. He was the first person other than the midwife to see Baby Spencer in the ultrasound. He'd secretly teared up, seeing how the fetus already sucked its thumb and had a tiny turned-up nose in the profile. She'd even asked him to go to the next doctor's appointment with her, too, joking she was worried she'd forget something, and he'd been following her pregnancy like an auditor.

Just like he'd done with Angela at the beginning of her pregnancy.

What had possessed him to step into the role of being Carey's partner in the parenting class? He squeezed his eyes tight, avoiding the answer, holding her a little tighter than before. It wasn't out of pity for her being the only one enrolled without a significant other—no, he had to be honest. It was because he'd wanted to. Maybe even needed to.

Did he enjoy getting kicked in the teeth?

Damn it, for one of the good guys he was really screwed up. Losing Angela had nearly done him in, along with getting hit by the hardest dose of reality in his life. He was sterile. He'd never be a father. And Angela had cheated on him, taking the task of getting pregnant to his best friend, Rico.

In time he'd lose Carey and her baby, too, once she got back on her own two feet again. Just like he'd lost Angela and the baby he'd once thought was his for a brief but ecstatic period of time.

He slipped out of bed, unable to stay close another second to the woman who'd just thrown his entire world on its head. He pulled on his boxing trunks, went to the kitchen and drank a full glass of water, then walked to the couch and sat. Being away from her spell helped his body settle down. His mind was another story altogether, though. He folded his arms across his chest, plopped his feet on the coffee table and, using the TV controller, turned to an old black and white movie with the sound muted. Fortunately it dulled his thoughts and little by little, as the dark drama unfolded and minutes passed, he finally drifted off to sleep.

"Joe? What are you doing out here?"

Sunshine slipped through the cracks in the living-room window blinds on Saturday morning. Joe eased open one eye from where his face was mashed against the armrest cushion on the couch. "Huh? Oh, I couldn't sleep and I didn't want to wake you so I came out here."

"I was worried I'd snored or something." She'd obviously tried to lighten the mood, so he laughed easily, as if nothing was wrong at all. She looked nearly angelic, standing with the window behind her, her silhouette outlined by bright morning light. She was wearing an oversized T-shirt with those long, slender legs completely bare. It made him want her all over again, but that was the last thing he should ever do.

"No." He scrubbed his face, trying to wake up, realizing she hadn't bought his explanation, and he needed to be straight with her. "You didn't snore." Yeah, he had to nip this in the bud and, though it might sting today, she'd thank him later for sparing her more pain.

"What's up, Joe? I don't have a good feeling about us having sex and then you sneaking off to the couch."

He wasn't ready to look at her, and when he told her his thoughts she deserved his undivided attention. "I need some coffee." He stood and she followed him into the kitchen. He glanced at her before he got on the job of filling the coffeemaker and saw the frightened and forlorn woman he'd first seen at the bus station. It made him feel sick to do that to her so he stopped avoiding the moment and grabbed one of her hands. "Look." He shook his head. "I'm sorry we crossed the line last night. It was fantastic, amazing, and a huge mistake."

"No. It was totally okay with me. Couldn't you tell?" She searched his eyes, looking for answers. It made him look down at the hand he held. "In fact, it was an incredible night. I never dreamed making love with you could be so wonderful."

He glanced upward, finding those eyes…greener in the morning light. "It was great, but things are too confused between us. You need time to heal from your lousy relationship with Ross, and the most important thing in your life right now should be your baby. Focus on the baby, instead of getting all involved with me. Not that I didn't love what we did in there last night, it's just that we're dangerous for each other right now. I shouldn't take time and energy away from you focusing on what you want to do with your life. I'll just interfere, and you need to think what's best for you, not anyone else."

Who was he kidding, laying all the excuses at Carey's feet? He still wasn't ready to trust another woman, to open up about the pain of his wife's infidelity. And that's what he'd need to do in order to be with someone new. Her. It was why he'd been living like a workaholic hermit all this time. What would she think of him if she knew how scared he was to tell her the truth, and if he wasn't ready to be completely honest, what was the point of being with her?

He pulled her close and held her, and it hurt to feel her stiffen when he wanted to love her. But now he had to push her away because she deserved better. She deserved a future of her own making. All he'd do was mess things up. "We both have a lot going on in our lives right now and it isn't a good time to confuse things even more with sex." He pulled back to engage with her eyes, but she was now the one avoiding eye contact. "And, believe me, that was incredibly hard to say, because I wanted you like I've never wanted anyone else last night."

It seemed she'd stopped breathing, a dejected expression changing her beauty to sadness. He felt queasy, like he'd already finished the pot of coffee and the acid lapped the inside of his stomach. But he forged on because he had to.

"It's not right for us to be together now. Our timing

is off. We just have to face that. And no one is sorrier than me."

Something clicked behind those beautiful eyes. Her demeanor shifted from tender and hurting to world-weary chick. "Yeah, you're right. It really was stupid." She pecked his cheek with a near air kiss. "Now I need to shower."

He watched her walk away, her head high and shoulders stiff. In that moment he hated more than anything having given her a reality check, and the thought of drinking a cup of coffee made him want to puke.

CHAPTER SEVEN

CAREY STOOD UNDER the shower, hiding her tears. Joe's rejection had stung her to the core. She'd given him everything she had last night yet this morning he had closed the door.

She lifted her head and let the water run over her face. He'd made her remember her shameful past, and she wanted to kick herself for trying to forget. If there was one lesson she should have learned by now it was not to ever let herself get close to any man again. Yet here she was a month after running away from Ross, opening her heart to Joe. Could she have been more stupid?

Joe wasn't out to hurt her. It had just turned out that way, and it was her fault. She'd suspected from the beginning that he carried heavy baggage. It may have taken a near stranglehold to get him to reveal one small fact—the tip of the iceberg—that his wife had screwed him royally, and what the rest of the story was, Carey could only guess. One thing was certain, he was hurting and afraid of getting involved again.

Truth was she wasn't the only one with a past not to be proud of. Joe belonged in her league. All the more reason the two of them were a horrible match.

Yet she'd trudged on, defying the truth, letting his

kindness and charming personality, not to mention his great looks, win her over little by little. She'd let him take care of her and he'd quickly earned her trust. She still trusted him. But she couldn't let herself fall any deeper in love with him. Something in her chest sank when she inadvertently admitted she'd fallen for him. No. That couldn't be. She needed to stomp out any feelings she already had for Joe beyond the practical, and she needed to do it now. She lived here because she couldn't afford her own place. Yet. In time she'd be free of him, wouldn't have to be reminded daily how wonderful he'd been at first. Then how tightly he'd shut her out. Yet how much she still cared for him fanned the ache in her chest.

She diligently lathered her body, aware of more tears and that sad, sad feeling nearly overtaking her will to go on. Then her hands smoothed over her growing tummy and she knew she couldn't let anything keep her from the joy of becoming a mother. Her baby deserved nothing less than her full attention. Wasn't that what Joe had said, too?

From now on she'd concentrate on getting her life together and becoming a mother, and forget about how being around him made her feel as a woman. Really, how stupid was it, anyway, that fluttering heart business. It never paid off.

After showering and hair-drying and dressing, with her mental armor fully in place, she marched into the kitchen where she heard Joe puttering around. "I've decided to take you up on that offer to rent a car for me."

"Sure, we can do that this afternoon since my dad owns a rental franchise." He responded in the same businesslike tone she'd just used on him.

"Thanks. In the meantime, may I borrow *your* car? If I don't leave now I'll be late for the Parentcraft class."

He was dressed. He stopped drying the coffee carafe, turned and looked at her dead on. "I'm going too, but you can drive if you want."

He tossed her the keys, and in her profound surprise she still managed to catch them. "Uh, I don't think so."

"Well, I know so, because you forget things. And two sets of ears are better than one, especially since you're probably already distracted from everything I pulled on you this morning."

"It would be totally awkward for both of us. You know that."

"No, I don't because I've never done this before. Besides, no one else needs to know."

He was making her crazy with this line of thinking, and so, so confused. "I can't just give myself to someone then forget about it. What's wrong with you?"

"You're right, I'm totally screwed up, I admit it, but I started this class with you, and I intend to be there for you all the way to the end."

Why was he being so unreasonable? But, honestly, how could she hold against him what he'd just acknowledged? He was the first guy in her life who insisted on sticking something out with her. It seemed a very unselfish thing to do.

Now her head was spinning, and it wasn't because of the recent concussion. "This is all too complicated. I'd rather just go myself." He'd hurt her enough for one day. She couldn't possibly sit next to him in a class for two hours and not think about what had happened. Surely he knew that. What was wrong with the man?

He touched her arm and she went still. Something told her he was about to convince her to let him go, and right this minute—*thanks a million, armor, for abandoning me*—she felt too confused to argue.

"Carey, I know how it feels to be let down by someone. I know you've been let down a helluva lot lately, and I respect you too much to do that with this class on top of everything else I've already fouled up."

She felt like grabbing her head and running away. "Let's just drop this. I'm going now." She turned to leave, but he stopped her again.

"Listen, I may have totally screwed up by letting my body do the thinking instead of my brain last night, but long before that… I'll be honest and say I made a promise to myself about you. That first night I promised I'd look after you. And once I found out you were pregnant, I vowed to be there for the baby, too."

He took her by the shoulders, leveling his gaze on hers, delving into her eyes. She couldn't bring herself to look away. "This class is important. You need to know what Gabriella has to say. I signed on to be your partner, and I intend to stay on. We may have made a huge mistake, sleeping together so soon, but in this one thing I'm going to be the only person in your life right now who won't bail on you. Please let me go with you."

Damn her eyes, they welled up and she had to blink. The man was too blasted honorable, and she hated him for it. Hated him. "I won't be able to concentrate with you there." It came out squeaky, like she needed to swallow.

"You wouldn't be able to concentrate if I didn't go either. All the more reason for me to be there." He patted her stomach. "Little baby Spencer needs us to pay attention. Now, let's go."

He gently turned her by her shoulders then nudged her in the small of her back through the door, and because she couldn't stop the stupid mixed-up tears she handed back the keys. "You'd better drive."

Carey finished the temporary job as ward clerk just in time to interview for a staff RN position in the same ward at the clinic. Having seen her work ethic already, and now that she had her RN license straightened out, they hired her on the spot. Carey was thrilled! Life was looking up. Except for that messy bit of being crazy about Joe Matthews and him being adamant about living by some code of honor. He was so damn maddening!

Ever since they'd made love, and especially after he'd explained how he'd made a promise to look after her, she'd thought she'd figured him out. Basically, he was the guy of her dreams but didn't know it yet. The next big test was to get him to realize that. The guy followed the rules, maybe hid behind them, too. She could live with that for now, but it sure was hard! No deep, dark Joe secret would scare her away. Nothing he exposed could deter her. He was a good man, and she didn't want to lose him, no matter how stubborn he was. But she had to be careful not to let on about her continued and growing feelings for him or she'd blow it. The big guy needed to be handled with the utmost care. For his own good.

Things had been very strained at the West Hollywood house since they had "faced the facts" a little over a week ago. It seemed they'd both bent over backwards to be polite and easy to get along with since then, taking the art of being accommodating to a new extreme, but simmering just beneath the surface was the tension. Always the tension. There was nothing like confusing love with kindness and one spectacular "crossing the line" event to create that special brew. Now she'd clearly seen the error of her ways.

He thought he'd convinced her to only look out for herself and the baby, and she was! But she was also letting her heart tiptoe into the realm of love, the kind she'd never experienced before. The problem was, she couldn't let her champion paramedic know or he'd run. So the question remained, was she being the world's biggest fool or the wisest of wise women?

Only time would tell.

The nursing recruiter spent the entire first day on the new job orienting Carey and preparing her for the transition to the floor. From this day forward she'd remember July the first as her personal almost-Independence Day in California. But first she had to get through the holiday weekend, which included meeting Joe's family at their annual barbecue celebration. Why? Because he was the kind of guy who would never retract an invitation once made. Hadn't he proved that already by continuing with the prenatal classes?

Man, he irked her…in a good way.

Another reason was that purely out of curiosity she wanted to meet the family that had spawned such a unique guy as Joe. If she played her cards right, she might find out a lot more about him. As she'd predicted, so far he'd yet to renege on the invitation, but she thought she'd test the waters anyway.

"Listen," she said, on the night of July third, "I think I'll skip the barbecue tomorrow." Her heart wasn't into the excuse by a long shot. After his incredibly lame but amazingly touching reason for continuing with the parenting classes, she was curious to see how compelling he could be over Independence Day.

"But you've got to come. Mom will hound me for weeks if I back out now."

"You don't have to back out. I'm just not sure I'll go."

"If you don't go, I won't either."

"You can't play me like that."

"Play you? I just gave us both a way out. I'll tell her you don't want to come."

"So I get blamed? Oh, no. It's not that I don't want to go, it's our weird relationship I'm worried about. How would we hide that?"

"By acting like friends. We are still friends, right?"

"In some crazy bizarro-universe sort of way, yes, I guess we are. Besides, your mother would be horribly disappointed if you didn't go."

"Exactly my point."

Darn it, his logic had outsmarted hers once again. "You are so frustrating!"

"So you're saying you want to spend your first Fourth of July in California by yourself? Really?"

She couldn't argue with that line of thinking. He'd invited her into his family, an honor for sure but one that wouldn't come without questions. Probably most of the questions would come from his mother. Did she want to open herself up to that? And, more importantly, why did he? But, on the other hand, did she really want to spend the holiday by herself? "Honestly, I'd rather not be alone, but I don't want to feel on the spot either."

"Trust me, I know how to handle my family, and I promise you'll have a good time. You'll like them."

That's what she was afraid of.

"My parents live close enough to the Hollywood Bowl to see the fireworks there," he said, driving to his boyhood home. "When I was a kid I used to lie flat on my back in the yard so I wouldn't miss a thing."

Carey wasn't sure she'd be able to handle anything about today, but she smiled and pretended to be interested in his story and happy he felt like talking about it. No way would she let on to Joe how tough each and every minute spent with him was for her. She did it to hold out for a bigger reward, but so far he wasn't showing any signs of opening up or changing. Holiday Joe was still By-the-Book Joe.

Carey sat in the car, wearing red board shorts with a string-tie waist to accommodate her growing tummy, a white collared extra-long polo shirt and a blue bandana in her hair. Joe wore khaki shorts and a dark gray T-shirt with an American flag on the chest in shades of gray instead of in color. Still, the point was made. They were celebrating the Fourth of July. With his big family. Oh, joy. Cue butterflies in stomach.

Although they'd made love and had opened up to each other that one night, Carey hadn't learned one bit more about Joe's broken marriage. Evidently he was determined not to ever let her know the whole story. Because of that, she felt stuck in a holding pattern, unable to be a real friend even though he'd insisted they were, definitely not a lover but merely a person who needed a place to stay, biding her time until she could move out. Every agonizing day, since things hadn't changed, it became more evident it was time to make her break.

In the back of her mind she kept assuring herself that with her new RN salary she should be able to save up enough fairly soon to rent a small but decent apartment somewhere and then get out of Joe's hair once and for all. Yet the thought of *not* seeing him every day sent a deep ache straight through her chest. Because she still cared for him.

He glanced at her, taking his eyes off the road briefly and giving a friendly yet empty smile. If only she could read his mind. She returned the favor with a wan smile of her own. What a pitiful pair they'd become. They'd both taken to wearing full mental armor since the morning after their one perfect night. Politeness was killing them. And it hurt like hell.

Joe's parents' home turned out to be in the Hollywood Hills area, not far from Joe's house. He explained while they snaked up the narrow street that he'd grown up in a neighborhood called Hollywood Heights. She could see the Hollywood Bowl to the north and some huge and gorgeous estates to the west, wondering if he might have grown up there and was secretly rich. The thought amused her. Hey, the guy had owned his own business since he'd been in his early twenties. Hadn't he said his father owned a car rental franchise? Maybe his dad was a CEO of one of the major chains. But then they turned into a long-standing middle-class neighborhood instead, and, to be honest, Carey was relieved.

Joe had never mentioned much about his family before, beyond the sister who'd loaned some clothes. Carey thought about that as they pulled into the driveway of a beautifully kept older Spanish Revival home. The front of the one-story, red-tile-roofed house was covered in ivy with cutouts where the living-room windows were and a well-maintained hedge lined the sprawling green yard in front of two classic arches on the porch. The fact that rows of palm trees stood guard on each side of the house made her smile. So Californian.

She had no idea how long his family had lived there,

but he'd just said he'd been a kid here. That made her wonder what it would be like to always have a family home where you went for holiday celebrations.

Joe introduced Carey to his parents, who clearly adored him, and she could see that he'd gotten his soft brown eyes from his mother, Martha, and his broad shoulders and dark hair from his dad, Doug. They both grinned and immediately made Carey feel welcome, though there were questions in their gazes. She wondered if they assumed she and Joe were a couple.

The sister who'd loaned Carey clothes turned out to be named Lori, and she made a point to put it out there right off—Joe was the nice guy he was only because she'd been his middle sister by two years and had often insisted he play dress up and dolls instead of cowboys and Indians. Carey laughed and watched Joe blush, something she'd never seen before. She'd bet a fortune he'd always looked out for his kid sister and younger siblings, too.

Being an only child herself, she'd never experienced the power of a sibling, in this case to put a macho guy like Joe in his place in front of his mysterious new woman friend—who'd once been so desperate as to need to borrow Lori's clothes. Now she was dying to find out who they thought she was and, more importantly, what they thought she was to Joe.

Andrew—Drew to his family and friends—was the taller but younger brother to Joe by four years, and was a fairer version of Joe but had the narrower build of his mother. Where Joe was a muscled boxer, Drew looked more like a long-distance runner. Both looked fit but in different ways.

"We're waiting for Tammy and Todd to arrive before

we begin making ice cream," Martha said, as she gave Carey a quick tour of the house.

Carey soon found out they were the babies of the family at twenty-two, fraternal twins who still seemed to hang out with each other all the time and therefore would be arriving together. Interesting. This family believed in togetherness. Another foreign idea to Carey. Maybe that had something to do with Joe insisting they continue the parenting classes together?

The rest of the four-bedroom house gave the appearance of being lived in but with obvious recent upgrades, like a state-of-the-art kitchen and a family-friendly brick patio and neatly manicured lawn, complete with a small vegetable garden. Now she understood where Joe had probably gotten his idea for his own inviting patio and backyard. He hadn't fallen far from his family tree.

Being in this home, sensing the good people who inhabited it, caused nostalgia for something Carey would never have to sweep through her, pure bittersweet longing. She'd be all the family her baby would ever have. Their home would be each other, small but loving. She vowed her child would always feel loved, no matter where they lived. Seeing good people like Joe's parents with such love in their eyes when they looked at their adult kids gave her hope for her and the baby. She wanted it more than anything for herself, that parent-child relationship.

The moment the twins walked in with a couple of bags of groceries, everything stopped and it was clear they were the wonder kids. The light of their mother's life. Martha made over them as if they were still in their teens, and Joe raised his brows and half rolled his eyes over her ongoing indulgences. *Wow, would you look at that, the babies have just managed to go to the market all by themselves*, he seemed to communicate with that look. Since she and Joe had a strong history of nonverbal communication, she was willing to bet on it. Come to think of it, Lori and Drew had exactly the same expression, and it made Carey smile inwardly. Nothing like a little friendly sibling rivalry, something she couldn't relate to. She also found it interesting that Tammy had dark hair like her father and Todd was nearly a blond—the only one in the family.

"Let's get that ice cream going," Doug said, clapping his hands, reminding Carey of Joe. He grabbed Todd, since his shopping bag contained the essential ingredients, putting him immediately on ice-cream duty. Joe was assigned to grill the burgers on the gorgeous built-in gas stainless-steel barbecue on the patio, and Lori enlisted Carey to help put together some guacamole dip and chips to go along with cold sodas and beers for those partaking, as an appetizer. Except, coming from Illinois, Carey didn't have a clue how to make guacamole, so all she actually wound up doing was mashing the avocados and letting Lori take over from there. With Martha overseeing the condiments and side dishes, already made and waiting in the refrigerator, the early dinner preparation seemed to run like a well-oiled machine.

Carey felt swept up, like a part of the family, and she cautioned herself about enjoying it too much. These were Joe's people, she'd never be a part of them. Today was simply a gathering she'd been invited to take part in rather than be left alone on a huge national holiday. If there was one thing to be sure of in these otherwise confusing days, Joe was way too nice a guy to let that happen. Yet, curiously, no one else had brought a date.

His mother loved to tell tales about her kids, embarrassing or not, she didn't care. It was clearly her privilege to share as their mother. Carey learned a whole history of childhood mess-ups and adventures for all five of the Matthews kids as the afternoon went on. Then Lori took her aside and asked her a dozen questions about what it was like to be unconscious for three days. They wound up having a long conversation, just the two of them, and Carey could see herself making friends with Lori if given the chance. It made her feel special to be taken in so easily, and closer to everyone—a sad thing since she understood there would never be a chance to really be close to any of them beyond today. Unless Joe came to his senses.

Later, as they ate, Carey found out that Drew's lady friend was in the navy and was currently deployed in Hawaii. Poor thing, he'd said with a grin, and just as quickly notified his parents he was planning to take a trip to see her in August if his dad would be willing to give him the time off. Hmm. Carey wondered if anyone else worked for their dad.

Just as Carey prepared to take a bite of her thick and delicious-looking home-grilled cheeseburger, which required both hands to hold the overfilled bun, a gust of wind blew a clump of hair across her face. Before she could put down the burger to fix it, Joe swept in and pulled the hair out of her face, tucking it behind her ear, a kind but cautious glint in his eyes. The simple gesture was enough to give her shivers and make her once again long for that dream she'd had to tuck away. Fact was, the guy couldn't resist coming to her rescue. Plus at his parents' house they couldn't very well hide out in their separate bedrooms, avoiding each other.

Why did things have to be the way they were? Why couldn't they just go for it? She took the bite of seriously delicious burger, Joe having cooked them to perfection, her mind filled with more secret wishes. But even as she wished it she knew that between the two of them, with all the baggage they held on to, the fantasy of being Joe's woman would probably never be.

Lori, a yoga instructor, soon explained that her significant other was a resident at County Hospital and couldn't get the day off. Martha mentioned that Todd and Tammy would be seniors at the University of Arizona and were living at home for the summer. It made Carey feel like a special person to have the entire family to herself. And they all truly seemed to enjoy having her there.

"This is the most delicious peach ice cream I've ever tasted," she said later to Todd when the homemade dessert was served.

"It's my dad's secret recipe. He wants to make sure I carry on the family tradition."

It made Carey wonder if only the men got to learn the peach ice-cream recipe and she glanced at Joe, her unspoken question being, *Do you know how to make it, too?*

Incredibly, he gave a nod. She looked at Lori, who shook her head. Then she glanced at Drew, who'd made eye contact with her and nodded. Cripes, this intuitive communication business must run in the family, and evidently only the guys got the ice-cream recipe.

"Before you call me sexist." Doug spoke up, obviously noticing all of the subtle communication going on. The mental telepathy gift was beginning to creep Carey out! "I have my reasons," Doug continued. "It's to make sure that once a lady tastes this ice cream, she'll love it so much she'll never be able to leave one of my boys." He gave a huge, self-satisfied grin over the explanation that Carey couldn't argue with. Obviously it had worked with Martha. And from the taste of it, she understood perfectly well why. It was also very apparent Joe had never thought to make any for her.

Then it hit her that Joe's wife had left him, peach ice cream or not, and putting her own feelings aside she worried that Doug had inadvertently brought up a touchy subject for Joe. She glanced at him as he studied his bowl of dessert, though he'd stopped eating it. Martha seemed uncomfortable, too, and sent those unhappy feelings Doug's way through a terse look.

The family was well aware of Joe's heartache, and that was probably why they'd been so delighted he'd brought her over today. Oh, if they only knew how disappointed they'd soon be, but that would be nothing near what she already felt. If only...

As the afternoon wore on into evening one by one the siblings made excuses to leave, and soon it was only Joe and Carey hanging out with Doug and Martha.

"Over the years the trees in the neighborhood have grown so high they block out a lot of the view of the Bowl fireworks." Martha seemed compelled to give Carey a reason.

"I thought you said you could watch the fireworks from your backyard?" she said when she had Joe alone at one point.

"The really big ones we still can, but everyone has plans, you know how that goes."

She guessed she understood, but the thought of families, like trees, outgrowing themselves made her feel a little sad. It didn't seem to faze Martha and Doug, though. After all, the twins would be home for the entire summer.

It amazed Carey that after spending only one afternoon with the Matthews clan she already felt she knew more about their open-book world than she did about Joe, having lived with him for over a month.

"We're staying, though, right?" To be honest, Carey looked forward to seeing those famous Hollywood Bowl fireworks from his family's backyard.

"We sure are." His beeper went off and he checked it. "Excuse me." He got up, walked toward some bushes and made a return call.

She figured it was work related and suspected she might not get to see any fireworks at all today. Her sudden disappointment quickly dissipated when Joe smiled at her.

"Guess what? I've just received a special invitation."

"To what?"

Joe winked. "I must be doing really well at the clinic because James himself just invited me and a guest to his private fireworks viewing tonight."

"At his house?" A flash of pride for Joe made the hair on Carey's neck stand on end, further proving she was still far too invested in the guy. "Why so last minute?"

A satisfied smile stretched Joe's lips, the ones Carey had secretly missed kissing. By the way she'd longingly glanced at them just now, she'd probably just given herself away. "Well, apparently someone cancelled, and I was the first person he thought of."

"So you're a replacement?"

"I'd rather not put it like that but, yeah, I guess I am."

She wanted to hug him. "I didn't mean to burst your bubble. It's really a big honor."

"I know. I've heard that every year he invites a handful of employees to share the evening with him. It's sort of his way of giving a pat on the back to his best-performing department heads." Pride made his smile bright, and Carey quickly realized how rarely he grinned. If only she could put a smile like that on his face again. She had, that one special night.

"That's fantastic, Joe." Without thinking, she touched his arm, immediately being reminded of and missing the feel of his strength. "You're a hard worker and it's good that Dr. Rothsberg has noticed."

He covered his pride with a humble shrug. She wanted to throw her arms around him, but he'd made it very clear that he was never going to let her near again. Yet she'd had a wonderful afternoon and evening with his family and really liked every single one of them, feeling closer to him because of them, and a secret dream to be a part of his life rose up, refusing to get brushed aside again. Stupid, stupid girl.

Joe knew better than to push things any further than they already had, after spending the entire afternoon with Carey and his family. But he'd had a great day. Carey had fit right in with everyone, and they all clearly liked her. It made him wonder if he'd made the right decision to never let anything further happen between them. In so many ways she was right for him. It was all the stuff from before that kept both of them hung up. He hated to admit how scared he was, because it seemed so damn wussy, but he was. And Carey had wounds and scars of her own, yet she seemed more willing to move beyond them than he was. Being here with her made him feel confused again. Needing to keep his distance but not wanting to completely let go.

And here she was, in his old backyard, smiling at him. The Tiki torches lining the patio emphasized the red in her beautiful auburn hair and made her eyes look as green as the lawn. He couldn't seem to stop himself

from making another big mistake where Carey was concerned. Knowing he really shouldn't open the door for
more, James had told him to bring Carey along when
he'd mentioned where he was and who he was spending the holiday with. And right now he couldn't think
of a single reason not to.

Letting the moment take control, Joe made a snap
decision. "Will you come with me?"

At a quarter to nine Joe pulled into the designated employee parking lot at The Hollywood Hills Clinic, the
huge, lighted building as alive with activity as ever.
Hospitals never got to take days off, but Carey was
grateful she had this one Monday before she started
her new job.

He directed Carey to a mostly hidden employees-
only elevator by putting his hand at the small of her
back. His touch made her tense with longing. *Stop it!
Don't get your hopes up.*

Soon they were on the top floor, walking down a
long, marble-tiled hallway. Joe opened huge French
doors at the end and they stepped onto a balcony. She
immediately heard music and loud talking coming from
above. In the corner of the small balcony was a spiral
staircase leading to the roof. Joe took her hand to show
the way. Again, touching him like this set off a million
unwanted feelings and emotions with which she wasn't
ready to deal. Fortunately, the spectacle of a group of
highly gorgeous people on the roof quickly took her
mind off that.

Wow! The panoramic view of the entire city of Los
Angeles was spectacular from up there, too.

Dr. Rothsberg, the tall and handsome, blue-eyed
blond, golden boy of medicine, immediately came to

greet Joe. "Hey, great, you could make it." He turned to Carey. "I'm so glad you could come, too."

"Thanks for having me." Carey tried to hide her fascination with the incredible specimen of a man but was worried her dazed stare may have given her away.

Dr. Rothsberg kept smiling as though he was used to people looking at him like that. "Make yourselves at home. There are drinks over there." He glanced at Carey. "No alcohol for you, young lady."

She laughed, perhaps a little too easily, wondering if all women acted this way around the guy, then figuring, *Hell, yeah.*

Joe led her to the bar and got her a root beer, already knowing her weakness for that particular soda, while he grabbed an icy IPA because it wasn't everyday he got a chance to enjoy an imported Indian pale ale.

"See that lady over there?" Joe pointed out a beautiful woman with hair a similar color to Carey's. She nodded. "Her name is Dr. Mila Brightman and she runs a clinic in South Central L.A. It's called Bright Hope. She used to be engaged to James." He'd lowered his voice and moved closer to her ear so she'd better hear him say the last part.

Carey's eyes went wide. It was hard enough being around Joe after only spending one incredibly beautiful night with him, so what must it be like to be on the same rooftop as an ex-fiancé? "What happened?"

"I don't like to spread gossip, but I heard from Stephanie the receptionist that he stood her up at the altar."

Holy moly! Why would she come close to the man if that was true?

"She's best friends with Freya, James's sister," Joe continued.

"Oh, I met Freya one day in the recruiter's office. She's our PR lady, right?"

Joe nodded.

"That should make for some heavy family tension. Wow."

"You've got that right."

He'd moved closer to bring Carey up to date without sharing the info with anyone else, and she'd moved in because of the music and talking, and now they huddled together, sipping their drinks and taking in the incredibly romantic skyline of L.A., and it suddenly overwhelmed her. They'd gotten too close. She couldn't handle it.

"I'm going to get one of those delicious-looking cookies I saw over there." She pointed to a dessert table in a secluded corner that promised to be both a delight and a nightmare for a woman monitoring her baby weight. "Can I bring you one?"

Joe shook his head, a look she couldn't quite make out covering his face. Was he sorry she'd stepped away? Or was he shutting down again? After such a great day, she hoped not.

She crossed to the spread of goodies and wound up having a harder time than she'd thought, making a decision. There was so much to choose from!

On the walk over she'd noticed Dr. Rothsberg surreptitiously watching Mila, who was across the roof, talking to Freya. Then Mila wandered over to the dessert table and stood next to Carey, and though she gave a friendly enough greeting, the woman seemed totally preoccupied with the group where James stood. As Carey continued to decide which two goodies to choose—she'd increased her limit upon seeing all the choices—Dr. Rothsberg also headed for the table.

Not having anything to do with the couple but now knowing their history thanks to Joe via Stephanie,

Carey got nervous for both of them as well as for herself. Yikes. What would happen when they faced each other? She kept her eyes down, studying the huge display of desserts, unable to make a choice or move her feet, willing herself to become invisible.

"Mila," James said, all business, "I'm sure Freya has told you I'll be coming to your clinic for a personal tour in early September."

Carey had wound up being between the two of them but on the other side of the table, and didn't dare move. They didn't seem to notice her anyway, as their eyes had locked onto each other. She chanced a glance upward to see for herself. *Yowza*, she could feel the tension arcing between them, so she distracted herself by first choosing a huge lemon frosted sugar cookie.

"Yes, Freya mentioned it. So thoughtful of you to tear yourself away from your girlfriend to make the trip."

Could the woman have sounded *more* sarcastic? But who could blame her? She'd been stood up on her wedding day. He was lucky she didn't pull a dagger on him! Carey worked to keep her eyes from bugging out and began to slice a large piece of strawberry pie in half so as not to feel too guilty about gobbling it all down. It had whipped cream topping with fresh blueberries sprinkled over it, so it was definitely a patriotic pie. Really, she *should* eat it. For the holiday's sake.

James moved dangerously close to Mila, a woman who looked like she'd claw out his eyes if he got even an inch nearer, and yet he leaned down with total confidence, his mouth right next to her ear. "In case you're interested, I've broken up with her."

Carey couldn't help looking up, but only moved her eyes so they wouldn't see body movement, still praying she was invisible, but the couple didn't seem to see her or care that she could hear their entire conversation. Mila was clearly flustered by his comment. She obviously hadn't known he'd broken up with the other woman. Wow…oh, wow.

Practically impaling Mila with his piercing blue eyes, now that he'd noticed her surprised reaction, he went still. "In the future, why don't you ask me personally how things are going in my life, instead of relying on the gossip pages as your source of information?" The sarcasm was sprinkled over every single word, yet Carey got the distinct impression that a pinch of hurt had been mixed in. She wanted to gasp over their hostile encounter but kept her mouth shut rather than draw attention to herself.

Then she accidentally dropped the knife. They both noticed. "Sorry," she said as she grabbed the pie, put it on the plate with the cookie and rushed away, wondering why Freya hadn't told Mila that James had broken up with his girlfriend, since they were best friends.

She arrived back where Joe stood, casually talking to another employee she'd seen around the clinic over the last couple of weeks. Frank, was it? They said hello and the man seemed friendly enough. Her hands shook as she took the first bite of the cookie. She glanced over her shoulder back to the dessert table but Mila and James had moved away to their respective groups. Even while trying to hide, she'd felt their sexual chemistry.

James may have stood Mila up, an unforgivable thing to do, but Carey could've sworn she'd glimpsed lingering love in his eyes. And though Mila had come off like a hurt and still angry woman toward him, Carey was pretty sure she'd seen relief on her face when James had told her he'd broken up with whoever that other woman was. Then again, Carey did have a huge imagination where love was concerned and may have seen what she'd wanted to see. She glanced at Joe, still chatting with Frank, remnants of her own lost before it ever started love driving home the point.

She promised to keep everything she'd just heard to herself. No way would she want that gossip Stephanie to get hold of this juicy information.

At exactly nine, as if some great force had waved a magic wand, fireworks started popping up all over the valley from the Hollywood Bowl, all the way out to Santa Monica beach. Someone shut off the outdoor lights as the magical display continued. Amazing and mesmerized, having never seen anything as spectacular in her life, Carey stood closer to Joe, and his arm soon circled her waist, and her arm wrapped around his. So natural. And right now there was no fighting her attraction to the man. The constant effort from living with him, plus spending all day long with him today, and especially now with a night filled with sparkles and shimmering colors dripping down the sky, had worn her down. She secretly savored his sturdy, steady build.

Carey gazed up at Joe, who beamed like a kid, nothing like that dutiful mock smile he'd given on the drive to his parents' house earlier today. She offered a bite of the fabulous cookie and was surprised when he took it greedily. Knowing this moment would only complicate things further between them, she ignored caution and leaned into his strength. His fingers gripped her side the tiniest bit tighter and her own version of pyrotechnics exploded in her chest. Yes, this would definitely confuse things. Their eyes locked for an instant. Along with seeing the reflection of fireworks in his darkened gaze, she was pretty sure she saw some regret.

Oh, who was she kidding? She'd just read her own

feelings into those wonderful brown eyes, just like she'd done with Mila and James. She really needed to stop projecting her thoughts and feelings onto everyone else. It would never get her anywhere, just make her feel disappointed. Because no matter how much she might want a second chance with Joe, it didn't matter. He wasn't open to it. But why did he keep glancing at her during the fireworks show? And now his fingertips lightly stroked her side. Funny how holidays could do that to people.

She went back to watching the dazzling and dizzying display of colors across the night sky and became aware of a strange sensation inside her. Had she eaten too much sugar? Or were the gunshot-like sounds of the rainbow-colored rockets popping and crackling through the night causing the reaction?

The feeling was very subtle, yet she couldn't deny it. This had to be *quickening*. She'd learned in her class with Gabriella that primigravida mothers often didn't realize it the first time their babies moved. Who knew? Maybe it had happened before and she'd missed it. But not this time! *Oh. My. God.* Her baby was alive and moving. *Inside. Her.*

"Joe." She nearly had to yell for him to hear her.

Grinning from the bright chaos playing out before them, he glanced down at her. When she knew she had his full attention, she was so excited she could hardly get out the words. "I just felt the baby move for the first time." Her throat tightened with emotion as she admitted it, and the unrelenting firework display went blurry in the background.

His eyes widened and his childlike grin from the fireworks turned to an amazed smile, as if she'd just told him "their" baby had moved. There she went, projecting again. But, in her defense, they had just gone over the information at the last prenatal class. Joe had been there with her, like he'd promised.

He grabbed her full on, pulling her close, then squeezed. "That must feel amazing."

Thankful for his goodness, and her good fortune of feeling her baby move for the first time on the Fourth of July, the blurriness turned to tears. "It did. Oh, my God. How strange and wonderful." She sucked in a breath, feeling like she was floating on air, then pulled away from his shoulder.

His eyes had gone glassy and the dazzling lights sparkled off them as he turned serious. She could have sworn she'd seen a flash of pain, but he quickly covered it up. He shook his head as if amazed and unafraid to show it. Just like the day in the clinic when she'd come to and nearly the first thing she'd asked had been if her baby was all right, and the nurse had assured her it was. She'd cried with joy. So had Joe. The stranger who'd saved her.

He was anything but a stranger tonight. He was the greatest guy she'd ever met.

She hugged him again and promised herself she'd remember the priceless expression on Joe's face for the rest of her life. Then she cried once more as a pang of longing for what she could never have set in deep and wide.

CHAPTER EIGHT

THEY DROVE HOME from the party in silence, still riding the high from the fireworks. Joe kept his confusion to himself. He'd held her in his arms again, and the longing had dug so deep he'd been unable to completely hide it. He was pretty sure she'd noticed his reaction, too. He couldn't continue with Carey like this. She didn't belong to him, her baby wasn't his. She deserved some guy who could love her and give her more children. Not him.

Yet she'd fit in so well with his family, and it had been clear they'd all liked her. It'd made him wonder about possibilities, and he thought he'd given up on those ages ago. Could he actually get over being cheated on by his wife and best friend, or the fact he was sterile? Was he ready, maybe, to finally move on? In his usual rut, the answer came glaring back. No.

Holding her, watching the fireworks together had been a huge mistake. Hell, ever letting her into his life had been a mistake. He'd been the one to point out how much they both had going on personally, and how important it was not to confuse things between them any further. Yet he hadn't had the heart to un-invite her for the Fourth of July celebration with his family. He'd resorted to using the lame excuse of protocol as the reason. Yeah, he was a guy of his word. Besides, his mother wouldn't have let him, and if he hadn't brought Carey, Mom would have spent the entire afternoon badgering him.

Carey's baby had moved, and the truth had knocked him sideways. She had a life to look forward to and she didn't deserve having a guy like him hold her back. Maybe one day he'd be able to forget and move on, but he wasn't there yet, and most days he doubted he ever would be. Their timing sucked. She pregnant. He like one of those zombies on the show they liked to watch together.

If he insisted on continuing to look after her, his job from now on would be making sure she became independent of him. Not to get swept away and continue to confuse and complicate things by grabbing her under the fireworks and holding her like she belonged to him. What the hell had he been thinking? From now on he had to act logically and realistically. It was his only defense for survival. And he really needed to stay out of her way.

Getting her the car from his father's lot had been a start. She could have it as long as she needed it. Now that he knew she'd be working from seven a.m. to three p.m. at the clinic, he'd go in tomorrow and change his schedule to work the evening shift.

The less time he spent near Carey, the better. The alternative was too damn painful.

"Thanks for everything," Carey said once they'd gotten home. She lingered in the living room, a dreamy smile clinging to her face.

He'd been so wrapped up in his thoughts he'd almost forgotten she was there. "Oh. Sure. You're welcome. It was fun." He shoved his hands in his back pockets and kept his distance.

"The best fireworks I've ever seen."

His attempted smile came nowhere near his eyes. "Me too." Empty words. He may as well be talking to a stranger, and she obviously felt his detachment because her expression turned businesslike.

"Well, I'd better get right to bed since tomorrow is my first day on the new job."

He tried a little harder to be part of the human race. "I'm glad you had a good time."

Her eyes brightened. "I loved your family."

That's what he'd been afraid of. "I could tell they really liked you, too." It didn't matter, he needed to step back and let her move on. Without him. "Oh, and good luck tomorrow."

She flashed that genuine killer smile and it took him by surprise. Why did it always do that? Taking every single crumb he offered, she struck him as beautiful and innocent. The sharp pang of longing nearly made him grimace. All he wanted to do was grab her and kiss her, and let his body do the thinking for the rest of the night, so he stayed far across the room, hands shoved in his pockets, and worked on making his smile look halfway real. She noticed his awkwardness and pulled back.

"So good night, then." She turned and headed for her room, her beautiful auburn hair forcing him to watch every step of her departure. That constant ache inside his chest doubled with the inevitable thought.

"'Night," he muttered. *Get used to it, buddy, soon enough she'll be walking right out of your life.*

At the end of the first week of Carey's new job, Joe, after agonizing over how best to handle the situation, told her he had to work on Saturday and would have to miss the next Parentcraft class. His intention was to let her down easily, yet he still dreaded it.

In truth, he'd scheduled the extra shift after he'd talked to Gabriella about helping Carey find a birth coach. He couldn't be the one. The thought of going through labor with her, being there for her at the toughest time, seemed beyond him. He worried he might have an emotional setback because of it, and fall apart on her. Angela and Rico had really done a job on him. He also understood how important it was for a mother-to-be to bond with their birth coach when it wasn't the husband or partner. They'd gone over that very topic the Saturday before. The sooner she found one, the better.

When he got home late that afternoon he saw Carey out on the patio deck, napping on one of the lounging chairs. Though he knew he shouldn't, he tiptoed to the screen door and studied her up close, afraid to breathe so as not to wake her. A real sleeping beauty. It brought back memories of sitting by her hospital bed, watching her, when she'd been unconscious for those three days.

Joe remembered trying to imagine who she was and where she belonged then. Now he knew exactly who she was, how wonderful she was, and how much he wanted her for himself. What a stupid fantasy. He may as well try to sprint to the moon.

She must have felt his presence or she'd been playing possum all along because he turned to leave, then heard her stir.

"Joe?"

"Yeah." He stopped in mid-step. "Didn't want to disturb your nap."

She stretched and yawned, and he didn't dare go out there, just stayed bolted to the floor, wishing things could be different. Knowing they never could be. Yearning to make it so anyway.

"What time is it?"

"Almost five. Want me to get dinner started?"

She swung her legs around and sat, feet on the wooden planks, facing him. "I missed you in class today. We started practicing relaxation techniques and special exercises. She had us work with our partners, but Gabriella worked with me."

"I had to accompany a transfer patient on the helicopter to Laguna Beach today." He'd volunteered. Would he have been able to function getting up close and personal with her in class? He'd definitely made the right decision to work, but he wondered when he'd started becoming a coward.

"The thing is, I talked to Gabriella about our situation, and she said she has access to the local doula registry. Those women love to be birthing coaches, so I asked her to give me some names." She stood and walked toward the screened-in porch door, each standing on opposite sides of the thin barrier. "Bottom line, you don't have to come anymore." With sadly serious eyes, she watched and waited.

He'd wanted to let her down easily because he was a coward. Now she'd beaten him to the task, officially releasing him. He didn't have the right to feel hurt, hell, he'd wanted a way out, but the casual comment—*you don't have to come anymore*—cut to the bone. An ice pick could have done the job just as well.

He resisted reacting, but his skin heated up anyway. He wondered how much she'd told Gabriella about them, if her story fit in any way, shape or form with his. He hadn't expected to feel upset, but he was really bothered, and definitely sad now that she'd come out and said it. Ah, hell, truth was it killed him to stand aside, even though he'd already set the ball in motion to arrange this very thing. He hadn't expected to feel like the air had been kicked out of his lungs and feel a sudden need to sit down. He steadied himself, because he knew one fact that couldn't be denied. "I guess that's for the best."

Clearly feeling let down, if he read her sudden drooping shoulders right, she covered well, too. Just as he had. "Yeah. I guess so, but thanks for being there for me all these weeks."

They'd been reduced to communicating in robotic trivialities.

"You're welcome. It was fun." *While it lasted, which he'd known from the beginning couldn't be long.* He'd just never fathomed the profound pain that would be involved. He'd gotten swept up in emotion and carried away that first Saturday, letting his feelings for Carey blur reality. He couldn't let her be the only one without a partner. He'd let down his usual guard, acted on a whim, and had paid for his mistake every single week since. Sitting beside her, acting like they were a couple, wishing it was so, scaring himself with the depth of desire for it to be so, but knowing, always knowing, it could never be.

His mouth went dry with unexpected disappointment. He needed to get away from her now. "Hey, listen, I'm going to the gym. Don't hold up dinner for me, okay? I'll grab something on the way home."

He left without before he could see her reaction.

The next Friday, Carey admitted a late-afternoon patient. The forty-eight-year-old male had a face everyone who'd ever gone to a movie or watched a TV show might recognize, but no one would know his name. The character actor had been admitted with the diagnosis of severe acute pancreatitis. Basically the guy's pancreas was digesting itself thanks to an overabundance of enzymes, in particular trypsin. His history of alcohol abuse—according to Dr. Williams, the doctor who'd been the attending doctor for Carey, and who she had enormous respect for—had made a major contribution to his current condition. However, according to the doctor's admitting notes, they would do studies to rule out bacterial or viral infection as a possible source as well.

Carey found the computer notes fascinating, and Dr. Williams had left no stone unturned. She'd even commented on the fact the man was almost fifty and still extremely buff. Probably because of his need to stay fit for the action/adventure roles he normally took, Carey decided. But getting back to the doctor's notes, she intended to consider his possible use of steroids as well.

To add another angle, when Carey did the admitting interview, the actor, who also did his own stunts for most movies, told her he'd had an accident on the job and had sustained blunt abdominal trauma. Well, that wasn't how he'd put it—*I got kicked in the gut*—but Carey's notation was worded that way. She put a call in to Dr. Williams to inform her.

Carey often thought how the practice of medicine was like a huge mystery where patients arrived with symptoms and the doctor's job was to gather all the evidence and figure out what was going on. Carey knew the clinic staff's job with this patient would be to watch for fluid and electrolyte imbalance, hypotension, decrease in blood oxygen, and even shock. This guy with the affable smile but pained brow was not to be taken lightly. Like many in the clinic, he was fit and healthy looking on the outside but a mess on the inside. These days, Carey could relate perfectly to that, too.

He'd been complaining of severe abdominal pain for a day or two, and had assumed it was because he'd been kicked in the gut, as he'd described it. Carey noted his abdominal guarding when she made a quick but thorough admitting physical assessment, and found his abdomen to be harder than usual. Of course, that could be due to the fact the man looked like he did hundreds of crunches a day. He'd said his symptoms had gotten worse in the last twenty-four hours, and had told her he felt "sick all over" so he'd come to the clinic's ER. After a few more questions he'd also admitted to going on a drinking binge a few days back. Yet somehow the guy was tanned and youthful looking for his age, until she looked closer. The saying about the eyes seemed true, and they were the mirror to, if not his soul, his health. There she could see the lasting effects of his living extra-large for many years.

His admitting labs showed his amylase and lipase levels were over the top, and that alone could have gotten the guy admitted. Add in the bigger picture, and this actor's next gig turned out to be the role of a hospital patient.

Carey inserted an IV to be used for medications as well as parenteral nutrition since he was on a strict NPO diet. Next she needed to perform a task no patient ever wanted to go through, at least from her experience as an RN. She had to insert a nasogastric tube.

"This is more to help relieve your nausea and vomiting than anything else," she said calmly. "You'll thank me for it later."

He gave her a highly suspicious stare, especially when she gave him a cup of ice chips.

"Suck on these when I tell you," she said as she manipulated the thick nasogastric tube with gloved hands and approximated externally how deep it would need to go to reach his stomach. "Okay, now."

He took a few ice chips and sucked at the exact time she used his nostril to insert the well-lubricated tube and push past the back of his throat and down into his esophagus and all the way to his stomach. His sucking on the ice would prevent her from going into his lungs. He gagged and protested all the way but didn't fight her. He gave no indication of the tubing mistakenly going into his lungs by having shortness of breath or becoming agitated, but she did the routine assessment of the placement anyway. She listened through her stethoscope as she inserted a small amount of air with a big syringe into a side port of the NG tube, hearing the obvious pop of air in his stomach when she did so.

"You did great," she said as she taped the tubing in place on his cheek and attached the external portion to his hospital gown, then connected the end to the bedside suction machine. He gave her the stink eye, but she knew he was playing with her so she crossed her eyes at him. "It's one of the perks of my job. You know most nurses have a tiny sadistic side, right?"

That got a laugh out of him, and she figured she'd tortured the guy enough for now, even though she knew he was lined up for all kinds of extra lab work and additional tests in the next twenty-four hours. So she made sure the side rails on his bed were up and the call light was within his reach, then prepared to leave. "Get some rest."

"Like I can!" he managed to say.

"Carey?" Anne, the ward clerk she'd covered for while she'd gone on vacation called her name just as she exited the patient room.

"Coming." Carey marched to the nurses' station to see what her co-worker needed, only to find a huge vase of gorgeous flowers sitting on the counter. Lavender asters, golden daisies, orange dahlias, and roses, oh, so many perfect roses! "Wow, where'd these come from?"

"They're for you!"

"What?" Joe? What was he trying to do, make up for bailing on the parenting class? Why go back and forth like this, mixing her up even more? Ever since he'd said all those things about not confusing their living situation by getting involved with each other, and especially after the Fourth of July when he'd introduced her to his family, and especially later when they'd shared that significant moment during the fireworks, he'd been avoiding her like crazy. It'd stung and confused her, and she was only just getting her bearings back, thanks mostly to having the new job and not seeing him nearly as often. Was he feeling guilty for leading her on or letting her down? Both? She wanted to pull her hair out over his inconsistency.

Carey searched for a card, but all she found was an unsigned note.

These flowers are as lovely as you.

Sorry, Joe, but that is just inappropriate. Either you want to be involved with me or you don't. You can't have it both ways!

Hadn't he learned in the parenting class that hormones during pregnancy made every emotion ten times stronger? This tug-of-war with her feelings had to stop.

"Do you mind if I take a short break?" she asked one of the other nurses who'd begun to gather around the spectacle of colorful blooms, admiring them. The more she thought about those flowers, the more upset she got.

"Sure. I'll cover for you."

"Thanks." Carey marched to the elevator and pressed the "down" button, got off on the first floor and headed toward the ER. It was after two, and she knew Joe had been avoiding her by working the afternoon shift from two to ten p.m. in case he actually thought he was fooling her. Her eyes darted around the room until she spied him over by the computers, so she trudged on, determined to get some things straight.

"You got a second?" she asked.

"Sure. What's up?" His hair was a mess. Had he not even combed it? Her first thought was how endearing it made him look, but she stomped it out the instant she thought it. There was no point.

She had to admit the guy didn't have the self-satisfied look of a man who knew he'd just surprised a lady with flowers. "Did you send those flowers?"

He pulled in his chin, brows down, nose wrinkled. "What flowers?" He wasn't an actor and, honestly, he couldn't have made up that reaction.

"Are you horsing around with me?" Her frustration growing, she needed to be sure.

He raised his hands, palms up. "Honest. I don't have a clue what you're talking about. It wasn't me." Now he looked curious. "You got flowers and no one signed their name?"

She nodded, racking her brain to figure out who besides Joe would do such a thing.

Now he looked perturbed. "You must have an admirer."

"Oh, come on." Where did he get off, making such crazy statements?

"You don't think guys watch you?"

"I'm *pregnant*, Joe."

"You wear those baggy scrubs, and you're only just now starting to really show."

"You've got to be kidding. I don't encourage anyone. I mean I smile at people, I'm nice, but that's just being polite." If not Joe, then who? And, honestly, she was disappointed they hadn't been from him, and, she wanted to kick herself for even allowing the next thought.

Was that a look of jealousy on his face?

Joe hadn't felt this jealous in a long time. He'd skipped the jealous part with his wife, going directly to fury once he'd found out she'd gotten pregnant with Rico. But this was different. This feeling eating through his gut right now was good old-fashioned jealousy.

Who the hell had sent Carey flowers?

He looked suspiciously around the department. He'd introduced Frank to her at the party on the roof, but surely he could tell Carey and Joe were more than roommates. Plus they hadn't spoken two words to each other beyond, "Hi, how are you?"

It was time to get honest with himself. What could he expect? Carey was stunningly beautiful and he'd noticed admiring glances around the hospital whenever she passed by. At first it had given him great satisfaction to know she was living with him, and no one knew about it. It had been his big, fun secret. The gorgeous woman who'd come in as Jane Doe was his housemate. Now someone had the nerve to make a move on her. And it really ticked him off.

If—no, *when* he found out who it was he'd have an in-your-face moment and straighten out any misunderstanding. Carey was off-limits. Got that? Did he have the right to do that? No. But he felt unreasonable whenever things involved her, and he was being honest with himself. He. Was. Jealous.

"Um, I've got to get back to work. My shift's almost over," she said.

"Sure. Okay. If I find out anything, I'll let you know."

"Thanks."

He watched her leave, her hair high in a ponytail that swayed with each step. When he noticed one of the ER docs also watching her, he wanted to cuff the back of the guy's head. Carey was off limits. Was he being territorial when he had no right to be? Yes. Hell, yes. He folded his arms across his chest, the anger soon turning to self-doubt. How could he honestly expect loyalty from Carey when he wasn't even prepared to come clean with her about the truth of his past?

In a frustrated fit he flung his pencil across the desk. His EMT lifted a single brow at him.

Don't dare ask, if you value your job.

Back home that night, the more Carey thought about it, the more upset she got about the flowers. She tried to remember giving anyone the slightest misconception that she was interested. Beyond Joe, that was. But what bothered her more was that Joe seeming to run hot and cold with her. She still didn't put it past him to send those flowers and pretend he hadn't. Surely he'd noticed how down she'd been lately, since they'd been forced to change their relationship. But wait, they hardly saw each other anymore. Maybe he hadn't noticed anything about her mood swings.

One thing she knew for a fact, she'd gone and ruined everything by kissing him and coming on to him that night. She was a runaway, pregnant with another man's baby. Did she expect Joe to be a saint on top of everything wonderful about him and welcome her into his life with open arms? She should have left well enough alone.

She took the bouquet home and put the vase on the coffee table in the center of the living room. Might as well enjoy them since someone had spent a lot of money on them. She chewed a nail and stared at the flowers. Had their one incredible night together been worth all the confusion and heartache it had caused?

She thought for a couple of seconds and shivered through and through with some incredible memories. Hell, yeah!

Dejected, she went to the bathroom and washed her face and was getting ready for bed when she heard Joe let himself into the house.

There was no way Joe could avoid those flowers when he came in. They may not have been from him, but they sure would be a perfect catalyst to force them to have a long-overdue conversation about a few things.

She needed answers to the question that wouldn't stop circling through her mind, especially since seeing how jealous he'd been earlier: *Where do we stand?*

He'd said he didn't know who had given the flowers to her, and had seemed not to care. He'd even suggested that she'd unknowingly flirted with someone and might have encouraged the gift, which really annoyed her. Like it was her fault. And come on, she was pregnant! Why the hell would she want to get involved with a new guy now?

Precisely! That was what he'd hinted at the night he'd leveled with her. They had no business getting involved.

But she couldn't get Joe's expression out of her mind from when she'd confronted him at work and he'd sworn he hadn't been the one to send the flowers. It had been

LYNNE MARSHALL   153

a look of pure jealousy, until he'd quickly covered it up. He still had feelings for her, as she did for him.

What a mess.

All revved up, she headed straight for the living room and the man who'd just come home. "You know what I don't get?"

"Well, hello to you, too." He looked more tired than he usually did, coming off his shift, like maybe he hadn't been sleeping well. Join the club! Or maybe work had been more stressful than usual.

"If you don't want anything to do with me anymore, why were you jealous?"

"Jealous? What are you talking about?" Now, on top of looking tired, he looked confused.

"I saw your eyes when I told you about those flowers." She didn't need to point them out. He'd obviously seen them the instant he'd walked in. His demeanor shifted, having more to do with her accusation than the flowers.

"I'll admit, it took me by surprise. And I still don't like the idea of some guy hitting on you in such an obvious way."

"But you have no right to." She folded her arms across her chest, having just then remembered she was in her pajamas. "You made it very clear we aren't allowed to have feelings for each other. It's for the best. Remember?"

He went solemn, watching her, and she made it clear she intended to have it out right then and there. Too bad if he was tired or jealous or whatever else. Now was the time. Finally. "If you don't care about me, why were you jealous?"

In an instant he'd covered the distance between them, and his hands were on her shoulders, pulling her toward him. Time seemed to stand still for a moment as they looked deep into each other's eyes and both seemed to know—without the benefit of a single word, just using that damn communication thing they had going on—that once again they were about to do something they'd regret. But it didn't stop Joe from planting a breathtaking kiss on Carey. And it didn't stop Carey from kissing him back like it might be the last kiss she'd ever get in her life. From Joe.

The kiss extended for several seconds, turning into a getting-to-know-you-all-over-again kind of thing. Her breasts tingled and tightened as she felt the tension from Joe's fingers digging into her shoulders while he continued to claim her lips. With them, a kiss was *always* more than just a kiss. She sighed over his mouth, searching with her tongue, soon finding his.

Joe's breathing proved he was as moved as she was, but then just when they were getting to the really good part he stopped. And stared into her eyes, a combination of desire and seething in his.

"Because I *am* jealous. Damn it." He'd finished with her, and now gently pushed her away.

She felt foolish standing there, her breasts peaked and pushing against the thin material of her pajama top, exposing exactly what he'd just done to her. "You can't do this to me, Joe. I don't understand why you act this way. It's not fair to keep me all mixed up like this."

He looked back at her, considering what she'd just said, and then, as if he'd made a huge decision, his expression changed to one of determination. "Then you'd better sit down, because if you want to know why I'm the way I am, it's a long story."

The comment sent a shiver through her. He finally intended to open up to her, and she was suddenly afraid of what she might find out. But she cared about Joe, and if it meant helping her understand him, she'd listen to anything he needed to share. No matter how bad it was or hard to hear.

She took a seat on the edge of the small couch. Joe chose to pace the room.

"How far back do you want me to go?"

"To the beginning, if that helps explain things."

He stopped pacing, stared at his feet for a second or two, as if calculating how far back he needed to go to get his story told once and forever. Then he started. "I met Angela, my ex-wife, when I took my paramedic training in an extension course at UCLA. We started a study group and things heated up pretty fast. Within the year, once we both got our certifications and got jobs, we got married." He glanced up at Carey, who hadn't stopped watching him for an instant. "You know how I love my family." She nodded. "Well, since I was married I wanted to start having kids right off. Like my parents did. I'd launched my business and things were going well, so I figured, let's go for it."

He started moving around the room again, turning his back on her. "After a year she still hadn't gotten pregnant, and we wondered if our stressful jobs might have something to do with it. So we took a two-week vacation to Cancun. Still nothing." He cleared his throat and glanced sheepishly back at Carey. She continued to train her gaze on him, so he turned around and faced her. "We decided to get fertility tests done. But I've got to tell you, things were really tense between us around that time, too." His hand quickly scraped along his jaw. "You know how you hear stories all the time about people who can't have kids, then they adopt a kid and the woman gets pregnant?"

Carey nodded, her heart racing as he came to what she suspected would be a key part of his story.

"Well, Angela got pregnant." He lifted his hands. "Great, huh?"

Somehow she knew it hadn't been great.

"I was thrilled, of course, and we went on our merry way, planning to be parents."

She read anything but happiness in his words, and especially with the tension of his brows and tightening in his jaw she understood he was in pain. Wait a second, she also knew Angela had left him for his best friend. He'd told her that much. But with his baby? Oh, my God, how horrible. And here she'd been dragging him to her parenting classes! If she'd only known.

Making him repeat the entire history for her benefit was cruel. "Joe, you don't have to—"

"Nope. I said I would, and I want you to hear the whole mess. Okay?" He looked pointedly at her, like it was her fault for making him begin and she needed to hear him out.

Carey tried to relax her shoulders but felt the tension fan across her chest instead. "Okay. Go on, then." She could barely breathe in anticipation.

"So we're all thrilled and planning for our baby and five months into the whole thing, out of the blue my fertility results show up in the mail. We'd completely forgotten about them because we were pregnant!" He made a mocking gesture of excitement, and it came off as really angry. "Where they'd been all that time, I didn't have a clue, but, bam, one day the results were there. Angela wasn't home when I opened them." He stopped, needing to swallow again. "And the thing is, it turned out…" He glanced up quickly, if possible looking even more in pain, and then, dipping his head, his eyes darted away. "I'm sterile."

How could that be? He was a healthy, magnificent specimen of a man, but she knew to keep her thoughts to herself.

"I did some research after I got that diagnosis because, honestly, I couldn't believe it. Evidently my sperm ducts are defective from multiple injuries in high-school baseball and from kick boxing. It's the only explanation the doctor could come up with when I finally followed up. Who knew high-school sports could do a guy in?"

Carey stared hard at Joe as she bit her lip, hoping her eyes wouldn't well up. Angela had been pregnant and living a lie under his roof. Of course, now she understood why her being pregnant seemed difficult for Joe. Oh, God, what he'd been through. And she'd rubbed his nose in that memory every single day she'd lived here. She wanted to cross the room and hug him then apologize, but every unspoken message he sent said, *Stay away. Leave me alone. Let me get this out once and for all. You asked for it!* So she stayed right where she was, aching for him and crying on the inside.

"My life stopped right then. All the happy future-parents hoopla came crashing down. My wife was pregnant—but not by me." His words were agitated and the pacing started up again. Carey understood how hard this must be for Joe, but he insisted he needed to tell the entire story. So he paced on, and she waited, nearly holding her breath. "I thought it had to be a mistake. I called the fertility clinic, suggesting they'd mixed things up. They'd obviously lost my results, since it had taken so long to mail them. But, nope, I was one hundred per

cent sterile. Said so right there on that piece of paper."
He flashed her a sad, half-dead excuse for a smile.

"So I had to confront my wife." He'd lowered his
voice as if this part was solemn, or someone had died.
"Angela insisted it was a mistake, because I hadn't
told her I'd already called to make sure. I watched her
squirm and avoid looking at me. I never felt so sick in
my life." Joe gave a pained, ironic laugh. "Oh, she swore
the baby was ours, that it had to be. I listened to her
lie. Then she finally broke down and confessed that if
the baby wasn't ours it was Rico's." Joe's fist smashed
into the palm of his other hand. Carey started to understand the importance of his punching bag. Yet all she
wanted to do was rush to him, hold him and kiss him.
He'd been betrayed by the two most important people
in his life after his family.

"My best freaking friend." A hand shot to his forehead, fingers pinching his temples as if he'd suddenly
gotten a headache, reliving the story. He sucked in a
ragged breath. "Evidently, just before we'd gone to Cancun, when things had gotten really intense here, she'd
gone to him to cry on his shoulder, but a hell of a lot
more than that wound up happening. Turns out my *best*
friend had an unusual way of consoling *my* wife."

Anger and sarcasm mixed as his agitation grew. She
wanted to tell him to stop, not say anything else, but
kept silent, sensing his need to purge the full story at
long last.

"Angela swore she'd been too racked with guilt to
tell me, especially when she didn't know who the real
father was. Can you believe it? If she could have gotten away with it, she would have tried. And I got to
think I was the future father of a beautiful baby for five

months before we were forced to face the facts. What a fool I'd been."

Carey shook her head, feeling responsible for his pain right now. "You don't have to say anything else, Joe."

"But wait, it only gets better! Angela told Rico and he wanted her to get a paternity test! Yeah, he turned out to be a real prince. So there I was looking at this stranger who was supposed to be my wife, and she's telling me about this bastard who was *supposed* to be my best friend, and the only thing I could think of saying was, 'You can leave now. You're welcome to each other.' Yet part of me couldn't bear to kick out a pregnant woman, and I was about to take it back when she got up and called Rico." A look of incredulity covered his face. "Right in front of me she told him I knew everything, and she needed a place to stay."

Joe nailed Carey with his tortured expression. "They've been together ever since. Have a baby girl and seem to be doing fine. Or at least that's what I hear from other people I used to know."

Carey's hand flew to her chest. Joe had lost his wife, child and best friend in a single moment. And to make matters worse, he also knew he'd never be able to have a child of his own. What torture that must have been for a guy who'd wanted a big family. Yet when she glanced at him she saw a man suddenly at peace.

"As you can imagine, relationships have been off-limits for me for a while now. I mean, what's the point? I'm not into one-night stands, and I can't give a woman what she'd want most if we got serious—children of her own. Not unless I send her over to Rico."

"That's not funny, Joe." Carey had heard enough, and she'd realized why Joe was the distant man he was for so many reasons. Why he blew hot and cold. It went against his natural personality to be bitter, though, which had always confused her, but now she understood why. "I'm so sorry this happened to you. Now I see why you overreacted to me getting those flowers. I mean, it makes perfect sense…"

"Nothing *ever* makes perfect sense, Carey." He sounded desperate, tired and defeated. He went into the kitchen and filled a glass with tap water, then drank. She followed him there, wishing she could love away his sadness and anger, yet understanding why he deserved to feel that way. Why he needed to keep her at a distance.

"Then I show up on your doorstep pregnant and homeless, and you're too nice a guy to toss me out. I get it. The last thing I should have done was come on to you, but I believed and still believe that it's mutual attraction. There's something real between us, Joe. You couldn't have faked that night."

He swung around, some of the water slopping out of the glass. "It doesn't matter what happened that night. It can't ever happen again. There's no point. Besides, you're all set up now. You've got a job, an income, you're back on your feet—hell, someone even sent you flowers."

"Joe, that's uncalled for."

"Is it? Ever heard the phrase 'been there done that'? I can't do it again. Won't."

Pain clutched her chest when she realized what he intended to do. Every secret hope she'd held on to was about to get dashed by a guy who'd been beaten up by love and never wanted to open his heart or life to love again.

"Look, Carey, you're a strong woman who knows

what's best for you and the baby." Now he sounded like he was pleading for her to let him go. For her not to torment him by dangling love and sex in front of him by living under his roof. "You'll be an amazing mother. Truth is, you don't need me anymore. You're ready to move on."

"Please don't push us away…" her lip trembled as she spoke from being so racked with emotion "…because you're afraid you'll get pushed first. I'm not that girl. I'm not Angela."

"And I'm not the guy for you. Sorry."

He'd shut down completely, going against every single thing she knew in her soul about him. He wanted to be the scarred guy who could never feel again, but he lied. She'd seen and felt his love firsthand. He hated that his wife had once lied to him, but now he was lying to *her*. He wanted her to leave, and she couldn't argue with a man who'd just turned to stone in front of her eyes.

"Please listen, Joe."

Something snapped. Anguish mixed with fury flashed in his stare. "Don't you get it? Every time I look at you I'm reminded what I can never have for myself. I may be stuck in the Dark Ages, but I can't get past that."

She'd heard his deepest hurt. Joe had pretended, but he really hadn't survived his wife cheating on him with his best friend, on top of finding out he was sterile. That was a total life game changer; he was broken and she couldn't fix it. He'd just said her presence only made the pain worse.

He may as well have stabbed her, and the jolt of reality nearly sent her reeling backwards. Lashing out, he'd wanted to wound her, too, and he'd done a fine job. Her eyes burned and her hands shook.

She'd promised herself she'd never beg a man the

way her mother used to beg her father. And even though her world, the new and improved version of her world since she'd come to California and met Joe, had just been ripped from her, she wouldn't beg.

A sudden surge of anger and pride made her jaw clamp shut and her shoulders straighten. Joe was damaged and wasn't open to reason. There was just no point in trying to get through to him. "I'll be out by the end of the week."

She could scarcely believe her own words, but now that she'd said them she'd have to make sure she'd carry them out. No matter what.

CHAPTER NINE

NEXT WEEK AT WORK, Carey still reeled from her final confrontation with Joe. They'd been avoiding each other like a deadly disease ever since. What a mess. She'd promised to be gone by the end of the week, and had put the word out with the nurses on her floor for any leads on small apartments to rent.

She sat in a corner, scrolling through all of her assigned patients' labs for the day, insisting on giving them her full attention. Afterwards, she'd do her morning patient assessments then pass their meds. Sometimes putting her life on hold for her day job was a relief.

"Carey?" Dr. Di Williams stood behind her.

"Yes? Anything you need, Dr. Williams?"

The middle-aged doctor offered a kind smile. "I hear there's something *you* need."

Carey quirked her brow. "Sorry?"

"An apartment?"

"Oh. Yes, well, something will pan out, I'm sure." She prayed it would because it was Wednesday and she'd promised Joe she'd be out by the weekend at the latest.

"I've got an in-law suite at my house. No one ever

uses it. It's got a private entrance and even a small kitchen. It's yours if you'd like it."

A few people were beginning to realize she was pregnant. Unfortunately, Stephanie had seen her go to the Parentcraft class, so probably the whole clinic knew by now. Obviously, Dr. Williams knew from when Carey had been her patient. "That's very kind of you, but—"

"It's a nice place. My partner and I have a house right here in the Hollywood Hills. Lisa made sure the place was comfortable and inviting, but her parents won't come to visit, and I've given up on mine coming around for years now. So what I'm saying is you're welcome to live there. I know you've had a rough time and I'd like to help you out."

Touched to her core, Carey jumped up and hugged Dr. Williams, who looked both surprised and uncomfortable. "You're a godsend. Thank you."

It was the first time Carey had ever seen the doctor grin. "We thought about adopting once, but our jobs are so demanding we decided it wouldn't be fair to the baby. Plus we're both, well, you know, getting older." She gave a self-deprecating smile. "So we'll enjoy meeting your bambino when the time comes."

She patted Carey's stomach, and Carey fully realized the reality that, yes, her baby would be born, and that after tomorrow, when she'd had another sonogram, maybe she'd even know the sex. Which made ner think how Joe had always called her baby little Spencer. It hit her then. She *really* needed a place to live. She was ready to "nest," as she'd learned the word in her parenting class. She wanted this, and the good doctor had just solved her problem.

"But I have to insist on paying rent."

Dr. Williams tossed her a gaze that perfectly expressed her thoughts—*Please, I'm a rich doctor and do we really have to negotiate money when we're having such a good moment?* "Whatever you want to pay is fine. Money isn't an issue for us. In case you didn't know, Lisa's a doctor, too."

"I'll be in great company." Carey beamed while she talked, never having felt more grateful in her life. Well, after her unending indebtedness to Joe, of course. She gave an amount she felt she could afford, nothing close to what the place would be worth, she was pretty much sure of that. But she was being honest, though, not wanting to insult the doctor by going too low, since she'd have to live on a tight budget. Especially as she'd have to return the rental car soon and would need to find a used car for transportation. *One step at a time, Carey.* Thank goodness she'd banked some unused vacation time at her hospital back in Chicago and they'd sent the final check to Joe's address last week.

"That works for me," Di said. "I'll bring the key tomorrow and you can start moving in right away."

The doctor turned to walk away, but Carey grabbed her hand and shook it, well, over-shook it, because she wanted to make her point. "You and Lisa are lifesavers. Thank you, thank you, thank you."

"Like I said, it'll be fun." Before right this moment fun would never have been a word she would have associated with Dr. Di Williams. Who knew?

Along with the warmth Carey felt for the incredible kindness of others, especially from Joe, and now from a woman Carey hardly knew, she felt new hope for her and her baby. She just might be able to pull this off, start a new life in California and move on from her past once and for all. One sad and nagging point kept her from full elation.

Joe.

She loved the guy. And she'd never get to tell him. But she'd learned her lesson in life well. Just because you wanted something, it didn't mean you'd get it. It would be too much to ask of him to love her and to accept her child, too. Not after everything he'd been through. She understood that now.

She sighed, a bittersweet thought about leaving Joe's sweet little house for her new and as yet unseen place nearly making her cry. She'd gotten so used to living with him she hated thinking about not seeing him every day. Was this really happening? Maybe she was still in a coma and this was one big Alice-in-Wonderland-style dream. The thought amused her briefly.

But she had labs to look at, and one of her assigned patients had just put on their call light.

Thank heavens for the distraction of her day job.

In order to avoid Carey and every disturbing thought she dredged up in him, Joe worked several extra shifts during the last week she lived with him. On Friday he'd even stayed on for an extra night shift so he wouldn't chance seeing her move out. The thought of watching her go would only widen the gaping wound inside him.

He'd finally opened up and told her everything, and she'd seen how messed up he truly was. Even then he'd felt her need to comfort him, but he'd held her off, pushed her away, then, once she'd seen there was just no point, that he'd never let her in, she'd agreed to move out. Whatever they'd once shared had breathed its last breath, and all the CPR in the world couldn't revive it.

It had been a crazy evening on the job with nonstop calls, and truthfully, Joe was grateful for the constant distraction.

James had thought of everything when he'd set up the hospital for his private and exclusive clientele. One perk was an emergency box in every home that went directly to The Hills emergency department instead of the more general Los Angeles system.

At two a.m. another call came through, this one from an affluent area, the Los Feliz Hills, east of The Hollywood Hills Clinic. A woman reported her husband in sudden pain that was shooting down his left arm. The emergency operator sent the message to Joe and he grabbed his team and hit the road within two minutes, siren switched on.

The five-mile distance would take fifteen minutes, thanks to the winding roads in both of the hilly communities. While they drove, the emergency operator stayed on the line and gave instructions to the wife of the patient, in case she needed to begin CPR.

Once in front of the ornate house Joe's team grabbed their emergency kits and EMT Benny rolled in the stretcher. A young housekeeper waited at the front door to the huge several-storied home and directed them up an open stairwell to the master bedroom. Joe couldn't help but notice the largest chandelier he thought he'd ever seen in a home. He quickly recalled the Hills ER operator having mentioned that the patient was the head of one of the movie studios in town.

Joe found the white-haired patient on the floor, unconscious, his wife kneeling over him in near panic.

"He just passed out," she said, fear painting a frightened mask on her face.

"Does he have a history of coronary artery disease?" She nodded.

Joe rushed to the patient's side, finding him unresponsive. He checked his airway and found him to be breathing, then he checked his carotid artery for a pulse.

"Let's get him on the stretcher," Joe directed his team, taking out the portable four-lead ECG machine and hooking up the patient for an initial reading as they applied oxygen and rolled him onto the adjustable stretcher. Then, in an effort to save more precious time, he started the IV as they transported the man down that huge stairwell. Once that IV was in place, he checked the initial four-lead heart strip, which showed possible ST elevation. Once Benny and his partner got the patient in the back of the emergency van, Joe jumped in, immediately switching the man to the twelve-lead EKG for a more thorough reading. Applying the leads, Joe was grateful the old guy wore loose-fitting pajamas, making his job a little easier.

Time was of the essence with MIs and seconds after securing the stretcher in the safety lock in the back of the van Benny and the other EMT shot to the front, turned on the emergency lights but not the siren, as a courtesy not to add stress to the heart patient, and sped down the winding hills.

Now with proof the man was in the midst of a STEMI, thanks to the twelve-lead EKG but still maintaining a decent enough blood pressure—he was even coming around a little bit, giving occasional moans—Joe added a nitroglycerin IV piggyback, gave him morphine through the IV line and aspirin under his tongue. He might not be able to stop the ST elevation myocardial infarction, but he hoped to at least help decrease the patient's pain. All this was done while the ambulance tossed and rolled around the hills, heading for Los Feliz Boulevard and onward toward Hollywood and the clinic.

Without the benefit of lab reports, he couldn't treat the patient more aggressively. And since the definitive treatment for an MI was catheterization, Joe's one job was to keep the guy alive.

The man looked ashen and his breathing had become more difficult. Joe repositioned his head for better airway and increased the oxygen one liter. oxygen sats stank. Then he checked his blood pressure, which was even lower than previously, but assumed it could be due to the nitro and morphine.

The heart monitor started alarming. Damn it, the guy was crashing. At times like these Joe felt frustrated with his role as a gap-filler until the patient got to the ER and could be hit with all the fancy lifesaving drugs. If only the ambulance could get there faster.

When the monitor went to flatline, Joe immediately started CPR, and continued to do so for the last five minutes of the ride to the clinic and the ambulance entrance where the medical big guns waited.

Unfortunately for the patient, medically the future didn't look too bright. In an oddball nonmedical way, Joe could relate.

Joe parked the car in his garage, closed the door, and headed into his house from the backyard entrance on Saturday morning. He hated how the house had felt since Carey had moved out yesterday. Had it only been yesterday? It seemed more like a month or a year even since he'd last seen her. Before, there had been this incredible life force radiating from her room. Today all he felt when he walked near it was his energy getting zapped by pain and regret. Well, he planned to save himself the angst and head right to his room to sleep.

After the stress of that morning, with the Hollywood

movie tycoon who'd wound up dying despite all emergency measures, he felt dejected and needed to sleep. It seemed typical of issues of the heart, and maybe even a metaphor for his own life lately, especially where his relationship with Carey was concerned, and with all the practical training in the world he still couldn't fix his own messed-up heart. Come to think of it, he might tear a page from Carey's story—a short-term coma would be a good thing right about now.

As usual, with any downtime, Carey was foremost on his mind. The word "coma" brought unwanted thoughts about a lady he'd once sat vigil for at her bedside. What had he done? He'd lost her. Sent her away. He unloaded the contents of his cargo pockets onto his dresser top then dug out his cell phone.

Wait a second. He'd worked all night and hadn't turned on his personal phone so he'd missed a text from Carey. He was so tired he squinted to read it.

It's a girl. Latest sonogram. Yes!

The words nearly brought him to his knees. Little Spencer was a girl. Carey didn't have anyone in her life to share the news with but him. A sudden feeling of sadness punched his gut. He'd been so selfishly focused he hadn't considered what moving out had meant for her. She'd volunteered to go and, like a wuss, he'd let her.

She deserved so, so much more. Yet, with all the bad things life had dealt her, she insisted on being upbeat. Yes! she'd written. The text was short but so touching, and all he wanted to do was find her and hold her and tell her how he really felt.

It wasn't going to happen. It wasn't possible.

He should leave well enough alone.

His house had never felt so big or empty since she'd moved out. Only yesterday! Damn, it already felt like a year. How would he go on without her?

"You did the right thing," he said aloud, glancing into the mirror above his dresser. He had to believe it because otherwise he'd go crazy. He was so messed up. Carey and the baby only would have left at some point anyway, so it was better it had happened sooner rather than later, and as *his* idea, not hers. In a childish way he admitted it felt better to have forced the change because he couldn't have survived Carey leaving him. By his spin, sending her away had been the most unselfish thing he'd done in his life.

Besides, she deserved a man with more to offer, someone without baggage like his. Anger, mistrust, suspicion, yeah, he was good at those sorry emotions. She'd had all of that tossed in her face long before she'd met him, beginning with her father and ending with that scumbag Ross. It was Carey's time to catch a break. He'd given it to her by pushing her out the door. Because he knew she was the special kind of woman who would have stuck around, put up with his sorry attitude, and tried to make the best of things if he hadn't made her leave. Beyond a laundry list of the ways she'd be better off without him, the main reason still stood out. He'd come around enough to know that Carey was nothing like Angela. He could trust what she said and did. She was as stable as they came, despite her tough life before coming to L.A. The issue was still with him.

He thought about her ultrasound and the fact her baby was a girl. The crux of the matter was that he would never know what it was like to have a woman he loved carry his baby. A kid who might look like him. And he was too damn messed up to get over it.

Better to set her free now before it got even more difficult because, honestly, he hadn't been prepared for the level of pain her leaving had unleashed. Sometimes he could barely breathe.

He thought about what he'd said to her the other night and cringed. He'd been harsh, insisting he couldn't get past his wife cheating on him, and he'd held it against a completely innocent person. What sense did that make?

He flopped, back first, onto his mattress, hands behind his head, praying sleep would find him and put him out of this torture, if only for a few hours. He'd tried to make peace with his decision about letting Carey go, but deep down something still didn't feel right.

Why, even now—when she'd found a great place to live, from what he'd heard floating around at work, and when she had nothing but good things to look forward to, a solid job, the upcoming arrival of her little baby girl, a bright future—things didn't feel right to him.

Why did he still have the foreboding sense she needed his protection?

He squeezed his eyes tight. *Go to sleep. Just go to sleep. You're getting delusional from lack of rest.*

He was bound to settle down soon because his body was completely drained and his mind so weary he could barely put two coherent thoughts together. Yeah, he'd get some sleep today, he promised himself. But first he needed a glass of water. So he hopped off the bed and headed to the kitchen for a drink.

Carey wanted to scold herself for accidentally taking Lori's clothes along with her when she'd packed the few meager possessions she owned and had moved out. Joe's sister had been nice enough to loan her some jeans and tops when she'd first moved in with zero belongings left to her name. Now she'd have to face him again, as painful as that would be, to return them. Truth was it had hurt to the core when he hadn't even bothered to reply to her text about her baby being a girl. She guessed he'd already moved on. Didn't care. Hadn't he said all she did was remind him of what he'd never have?

An ache burrowed deeply into her chest, not only for herself but for him, too. She still loved the guy. Had she imagined every good thing about Joe, or was this just how it felt to lose him? She was positive she'd never get over him, and had missed him every second since she'd moved out.

Mid-morning, she parked the rental car across the street from his house on the small cul-de-sac, thinking the car was another topic she had to bring up with Joe. As soon as she found a used car she could afford, she'd make sure this one got returned to Mr. Matthews. She wanted to make sure Joe knew she didn't expect to keep this car forever. Just for a little longer. She promised.

She reached around to the backseat and grabbed the tote bag with Lori's clothes inside. Carey had gotten the bag from the clinic the day she'd been discharged and Joe had taken her in. She'd almost slipped up and thought "home" the day when Joe had taken her home. Because that was how it'd felt when she'd walked through that door with him. She glanced at the small sage-green house across the street. Yes, he'd been a stranger then, but he'd saved her life and then kept vigil beside her hospital bed, and she'd never felt more protected or safe in her life than when she'd lived with him.

With the bag in her hand, she got out of the car and battled a feeling of half hope and half fear that Joe would be home. She'd left her house key the night she'd moved out. If he wasn't home now, she'd leave the items on the porch and make a quick getaway. On second thoughts, he'd been working so much it was possible he was sleeping and the last thing she wanted to do was wake him up. Maybe she'd just leave the bag on the lounger on his deck and not even attempt to face him right now. If she snuck off without seeing him, she'd save her lovelorn heart a whole lot of grief.

She started down the driveway, getting halfway to the kitchen-window area when she caught herself. This was cowardly. She was a big girl now. She needed to face him if he was home, though there was no sign of his car so she made a one-eighty-degree turn and headed back toward the front of the house, stunned to find a man she'd never expected to see again only a few feet away.

Ross.

How had he found her? How had he known where she'd been living? A chill zipped down her spine and her stomach felt queasy.

Then it hit her. He was the one who'd sent the flowers. How had he…? Oh, wait, he knew how to manipulate people, especially women, and had probably gotten the work address out of Polly in the employee relations department back in Chicago. Carey had been in touch with her regularly since she'd arrived in Hollywood—first to let the hospital know about her situation and to take a leave of absence, then to set up receiving her backdated pay checks, and eventually to give notice on the job and to collect her unused vacation pay. What a fool she'd been to think he wouldn't find her.

She'd thought she'd been so careful, but nothing seemed to be beyond Ross's reach. The bastard. After the quick flash of fear at seeing him she went directly into anger. The creep had another thought coming if he planned to mess up her life again. She was in control now, in no small part thanks to Joe, and Ross was powerless.

He kept his distance. Even held his hands up, all the while watching her, like a prowling animal waiting to pounce. "I know what you're probably thinking," he said, trying to sound appeasing. "What am I doing here?" He gave a poor excuse for a smile that looked more like an insincere politician's than a former lover's.

"I don't want to see you. Leave. Now."

Quickly his expression changed to that of a mistreated puppy. "I'm sorry. I've come to tell you I'm sorry. I love you. We can still be happy together. Make a life together."

"Ha! That's rich. You wanted me to get rid of my baby. That's not going to happen. There's nothing further to talk about."

She looked at Ross, tall, dark, and had she really used to think he was handsome? All he looked like now was a creep she needed to get rid of. Fast. He'd abused her, both mentally and physically. Had wanted her to have an abortion, had shoved money into her hand to do it, too.

She thought about Ross's polar opposite, Joe, and all he'd tried to do for her. How hard it must have been for him to show up at the prenatal appointments, to be the first one she shared the first sonogram with, when never being able to become a father had still been eating away at him. The moment he'd slid into that chair beside her in the parenting class had nearly made her heart burst with gratitude. He'd acted the part of being a father, even when he'd believed he would lose her and the baby, as if his past was bound to repeat itself. Yet he'd shown up and stuck with it, for her, and had never let on about the pain he must have suffered because of

it. Oh, God, he was her true hero—a man to be wor-
shipped, adored and loved. With all of her heart. And
she did. She loved him.

Facing Ross, right now, she knew without a doubt
what her true feelings were for Joe. Yet Joe had convinced her to walk out on him. And she'd gone because
he'd looked so tortured by her being there.

She stood before Ross, a shadow of a man standing by the driveway hedge, feeling completely alone.
All she wanted to do was go inside Joe's house where
she'd always felt safe, and close and lock the door. Forever. On Ross.

She kept her distance, not trusting him for one second, but Ross took a single step forward.

She'd never let herself be a victim again and he'd
have to hear her out. "You need to know I've finally
experienced a good relationship. I know for a fact there
are good, loving and caring men in the world who put
their partners first. I never learned that from you, but
now I have faith in the world again. In myself." She
touched her heart. "You wanted to control me and tear
me down to keep me under your thumb. I may have let
you before but I never will again." To show how serious
she was, and to prove she wasn't afraid of him anymore,
she took a step forward but still kept safely out of his
reach, then stared him down. "You need to leave L.A.
I'll never go back to you. Never."

Ross's expectant-puppy expression soon turned to
one of defeat. Did he think he could just show up and
everything would be fine again? Was he that out of
touch with reality? Or had it proved once and for all
how he truly had zero respect for her.

Something she'd said must have gotten through to
him because he actually turned to leave. Carey took a

breath for the first time in several seconds. But just as quickly he turned back, lunging toward her with the look of pure rage in his demon eyes.

His first mistake had been showing up uninvited in California. His second mistake was to grab her wrist and clamp down hard enough to cut off her blood supply, then raise his other hand ready to slap her.

Instead of pulling away, fighting mad, Carey growled and steamrolled into him. Catching him off guard, her knee connected full force with his groin, the V of her free hand ramming with all her might smack into his larynx. Everything Joe had taught her about self-defense came rushing back with a vengeance.

Ross doubled over in pain, unable to gasp or shout. And, of course, he'd let go of her wrist. Shocked she'd actually pulled it off, Carey stood there dazed for one second, her body covered in goose bumps, staring at him while he writhed in pain on the driveway.

Well, plan A had worked like a charm. What was she supposed to do next?

Run! Run for the car and get the hell out of there. She turned to make her getaway, but slammed into a brick wall of a man.

CHAPTER TEN

JOE CAME FLYING out of the kitchen door the instant he'd seen the man lunge for Carey. He'd watched the whole encounter between the guy who must be Ross and Carey, the woman he loved and his new superhero, from the window above the kitchen sink.

He'd known Carey needed to face down her demon once and for all, and he'd been ready to pounce if she'd needed him. So, as hard as it had been, he'd stayed on the ready just around the corner and waited. She'd stood up to the man, not wavering for a second. When twisted reasoning hadn't panned out, the guy had lunged at her. Joe had rushed through the back door and flown outside, but she'd beaten him to the punch. Like a pro, she'd taken down her attacker. It had impressed the hell out of Joe, too. Great going.

Pride for Carey mixed with pure fear that she could have been hurt by the bastard from her past made him take her in his arms and hold tight. She didn't fight it either, just leaned into him.

"You okay?"

She nodded, then pulled back to look into his eyes. "Did you see that? I decked him! Thanks to you."

He laughed, all the while watching Ross, who slowly began to get onto his hands and knees.

"Do as Carey says, just stand up and leave. Don't ever come back," he said, with Carey safely tucked under one arm, ready, if necessary to take the matter into his own hands if the guy made so much as a hint of a move in the wrong direction.

Now Ross stood, anger still plainly carved in his face.

"The police will be here shortly," Joe said. "I called when I first saw you. She's also got a restraining order out on you in case you ever get any ideas about coming around again. Consider it your 'go-straight-to-jail' card and this is your final warning."

Ross took one look at Joe, saw the don't-even-think-about-messing-with-me stare and took off, running to the street and back toward Santa Monica Boulevard.

With arms still wrapped around each other, they watched him disappear round the corner.

"I don't have a restraining order out on him," Carey said.

"He doesn't know that."

"And the police, are they coming?"

"Again, he doesn't need to know I was just about to call when I saw you kick his ass, so I hung up to help you." Joe flashed Carey a proud grin. "You were the bomb, babe."

She laughed. "You taught me everything I know."

He pulled her near and hugged her tight. God, he'd missed her. To think he'd almost let her get away sent shivers through his chest. "You're all right? Let me see your wrist, it looked like he had a firm grip." He checked out the area around her thin wrist, which was reddened and showing signs of early bruising. Like a dope, he kissed it because it was the only thing he could think to do, and he wanted more than anything for Carey to understand how precious she was to him. "You need to know something. I said things the other night that were horrible and not true. The only person you remind me of is you, and I never want to lose you. Or your daughter."

She disengaged her wrist from his hands so she could stroke his cheek. Looking into his eyes with her soft green stare, she smiled. He got the distinct message she had a few things to clear up with him, too.

"I never want to lose you either. Standing up to Ross just now made me realize he was the one who should feel ashamed, not me. That dark past I dragged out here needs to stay in Chicago with that loser. It shouldn't have any influence over me or my future. I've started over again. That ugly shadow is gone for good."

He believed her, too. She stood before him a woman of conviction, nothing like the frightened victim he'd first met two months ago.

She went up on her toes and delivered a light kiss. He matched it with a kiss of his own, and damn if it didn't feel like a little piece of heaven had just tiptoed back into his life.

"I meant what I said to him, too," she said, her arms lightly resting around his neck. "You've given me faith again in love. You helped me learn that it's not weak to open myself up to someone and to love again. Even if you didn't want me to." Her eyes dipped down for a second then swept back up. "I couldn't stop myself from loving you. I do, Joe, I love you."

Now he felt like the coward, well, until five minutes ago anyway, when he'd watched Carey confront her biggest fear and kick its ass, and Joe finally knew without a doubt that he loved her, too. No matter how hard he'd tried, he hadn't been able to stop himself from falling in

love with her. He'd pulled out every old and sorry reason
to keep from loving her, but she was meant to be loved,
and he was the guy to do it. And for someone whose
thoughts sounded suspiciously like a caveman's—*Me
Joe. You Carey. We love.*—he had yet to voice the most
important words he'd ever say. He just stood there, staring into her eyes, stroking her hair, loving her in silence.

"It's especially nice when you love someone." She
cleared her throat to draw his attention away from her
eyes and back to noticing all of her. "If that someone
loves you back."

Hint, hint! There was that tiny mischievous smile
she'd occasionally given when making an obvious point,
and he'd missed it so much.

The ball was clearly in his court, and it was time for
him to say what he felt and mean what he said. Without a doubt he loved Carey. So, still being in caveman
mode, he bent down, swept her up into his arms and
carried her up the steps to his front door.

Once inside he planted another kiss on her, and got
the kind of reception he'd hoped for. But he knew he
couldn't get away with a mere display of affection. If
ever a person deserved, or a time called for, words, it
was now. So he gently released her legs to the ground,
snuck in one last quickie kiss, and stepped back.

"Please forgive me for pushing you away. I was hurt.
And afraid. Still am. And if you don't think that's a
huge thing for me to admit, you don't know me like
you think you do."

"I totally understand how huge that is." She groped
around his shoulders and chest. "Just like the rest of
you."

He went along with her making light of things, because the topic was difficult and heavy and loaded with

old habits that needed to be set free. They'd both been through so much lately, but he had one more thing to say and he needed to say it now. He cupped her face between his hands.

"I'll understand if you can't see a future with me, because I'm sterile and I can't make babies with you."

"Stop right there," she said. "You really don't get it, do you? Did you not hear me say I love you? You may not be the biological father of the little lady here, but you've acted nothing short of a true, loving, and beyond decent father. Actions really do speak louder than, well, other actions in this case, I guess." She screwed up her face in a perfectly adorable way, having briefly confused herself. Right now there wasn't a single thing she could do wrong. "I know, terrible analogy."

He laughed lightly, while understanding exactly what she'd meant, because that was part of what was so right about them, they always *got* what each other meant, spoken or not.

"But it's all the family we need," she added, and he loved her even more for her generous thought. But the truth was a small family could never be his style, that's why he'd decided to never be in the position to have a family at all. Until Carey had shown up and changed everything.

"You don't want her—what are we going to name her?—to have sisters and brothers? How about Peaches?"

"Name my daughter after a piece of fruit?" she playfully protested.

"Our daughter, you just said it, so that gives me equal naming privileges. Besides, I thought Peaches might be significant since I'm planning to make the famous Matthews ice cream just for you after dinner tonight."

"You're making me peach ice cream?"

"How else can I make sure you'll never leave me again?"

"Ah, your father's secret ingredient."

"Yes. That. Plus the fact you have no idea what a hellhole it's been here since you left, and I'll never let you go again."

"And...?" she encouraged him.

"Because I love you and can't imagine my life without you." He kissed her again, because there was no way he could say what he just had without needing to touch her, with the best expression of love he knew. Physical touch.

"Neither can I," she said. "And if we want to give, well, I'll agree to give her the nickname of Peaches, but honestly we'll have to come up with something better than that for real. Anyway, if we want to give her siblings in the future, first one step at a time and all, right? Let's see how this little one turns out. But, honestly, in this day and age, if we want more children, we can find a million ways to do it. Right?"

"Right, as usual. Sorry I've been so dense about that topic for so long. I've been too busy wallowing in my pain."

"And *that* should never come into play with us again. Okay?"

"You got it. Because I intend to spend the rest of my life showing both of you how much I love you."

She sighed her joy and nuzzled into his neck, which felt fantastic. "That works out perfectly because I intend to spend the rest of the afternoon showing you exactly how much I love you."

For a guy who'd been up all night and who earlier could hardly keep his eyes open, Joe suddenly felt full of life, love, and, right this instant, intense desire. He pressed his nose into her hair and inhaled the smell of fresh coconut shampoo, thinking how he could contentedly spend the rest of his life simply doing this. He smiled widely, knowing she had a far better idea. "I like your plan."

She gave him a long and leisurely kiss in case there was any mistaking what her intentions were. He loved how well they communicated.

"For the record," she whispered into the shell of his ear, "you had me at homemade peach ice cream."

* * * * *

TAMING HOLLYWOOD'S ULTIMATE PLAYBOY

AMALIE BERLIN

To the awesome and lovely writers who populate the #1k1hr hashtag on Twitter: Without you this book would've never been done by the deadline.

And to the other awesome and lovely writers at the Harlequin Writer's Circle forums: Without you guys I maybe wouldn't have needed Twitter to make the deadline. But I've never had so much fun or felt so helpful and productive while procrastinating.

CHAPTER ONE

"Now for the hard part…" Liam Carter muttered, hauling himself out of the deeply comfortable chair in James Rothsberg's office at The Hollywood Hills Clinic.

"The hard part?" James asked, politely rising in tandem with him.

Why had he said that? James didn't need to know how shaky his plan was.

"Walking," Liam said, offering an explanation he knew James would believe.

"I can get you a wheelchair and have you wheeled down to the treatment rooms…"

"No." He raised a hand, laughing a little. Limping and still upright, even with pain, trumped being wheeled around. "No, I can make it."

Liam hadn't seen Grace in six years, and he'd damned well make her re-acquaintance on his feet. No matter how much it hurt.

He tested his balance and found it before he found the appropriate expression to conceal the pain.

James rounded his desk, hand outstretched to shake. "Don't be surprised if Grace insists on crutches."

Even without his desire to save face with Grace, if anyone saw him in a wheelchair or on crutches, word would travel, and the people he spent ninety-five percent of his life making happy would begin to question his suitability for the project.

Liam mustered a smile and shook the offered hand, then turned toward the door. "I'm sure we'll work something out. Grace always was good at creative problem solving." In their amicable past, the one that had ended for them that one night. The one he'd never have James know about, the land where nothing ever suddenly exploded. One terrible…and amazing night.

There had been plenty of great years before hormones had become involved, but the punctuation on that sentence assured their first meeting in years would be anything but normal.

For someone who lied for a living, doing so off script always left a bad taste in his mouth, so he left it at that. It had to be Grace…

Minimizing his limp as much as possible, Liam exited the office and made his way to the elevator he'd been directed to. The Hollywood Hills Clinic lived up to its reputation of clean, modern elegance, not that he could really appreciate it right now.

Two days and the best splint money could buy hadn't even put a dent in the pain that radiated up his leg with every step. Liam would swear his ankle hurt more now than the day he'd sprained it. But despite the pain and the all-looming discomfort, the prospect of seeing Grace Watson again still had him moving a little faster.

How would the years have changed her? Would he find her still the slender, athletic girl she'd been, light on curves but with quiet, supple strength? Maybe he was nervous for no good reason, and time apart could've extinguished that youthful spark between them. It might not even come up.

Through Nick, he knew that Grace had worked in

professional sports, helping athletes keep fighting fit. She could help him. He just had to convince her. Pretend their last meeting had never happened. They were both fully adults now, and adults ignored unpleasant things all the time in order to keep things cordial.

A short ride down and he stepped off the elevator. The more he walked, the more the spark of anticipation grew in his gut, and the faster he hobbled.

He just had to pretend. Pretend the image of her in that flimsy black lingerie wasn't still etched crisply into his mind…six years later.

Hard to believe it had been that long.

By the time he'd reached the treatment rooms, the buzz on the back of his neck was enough to drown out the constant pain grinding through his ankle, or at least enough to distract him from it.

He stepped through the door of the treatment room, and before he'd even looked over the various equipment and exercise areas, he knew she wasn't there. It felt empty.

Back in the hallway, he could see double doors at the end marked for the therapy pool. If she was anywhere, she'd be there.

Pools were as common as palms in Southern California and, while growing up, anytime she'd had a few minutes to spare, she'd spent them in the Watson family's pool.

He approached the edge of the pool just in time to see her turn underwater and push off the side. He knew from the way she moved that it was Grace even through the shimmer of water. Sleek and fast, she powered through the water toward the far end.

Mermaid. He shook his head and felt himself smiling despite the nerves in the pit of his stomach. At least that hadn't changed.

Maybe their reunion would be exactly like those old times. Maybe she'd reach the edge of the water and pretend to want a hand out, only to jerk him in with her.

Another underwater turn and she swam far enough before surfacing to speak of impressive lung power, then cut a path through the water toward him, straight as an arrow despite an unmarked lane.

Taking advantage of the seconds it would take her to reach his end of the pool, Liam ambled back toward the doorway to give her some space to exit the water, and avoid the urge to play with her. This wasn't the old days, and he wasn't seventeen anymore.

He saw her hand reach for the edge of the pool and heard her rapid breathing. She'd seen him when her head had cleared the water while breathing, or she'd seen someone there with her.

Grace's head now popped over the edge and before he knew it she was emerging from the water, toned, tanned, and with the kind of curves that made the black bikini she wore look exactly like that lingerie...

No, not exactly. She hadn't really had much in the way of hips last time. Now even her curves had curves.

His breath caught as their eyes met, but as she swung a leg up onto the edge of the pool one arm buckled and she toppled back into the water with a splash.

"Grace?" Had she hit something when she'd fallen back in? The concrete edge could do some damage...

He hobbled forward again.

Through training and sheer effort, Grace managed not to suck down a lungful of chlorinated water as she went under.

Broad shoulders.

Dark hair.

Eyes crystal and blue, like the inside curl of a summer wave.

Liam Carter.

What the devil was Liam doing there?

She grasped the edge of the pool and kicked hard as she pulled herself up again, turning immediately to plop sideways on the tiles, as graceless as a walrus, and breathing about as hard as one in full flounder.

Through sheer luck, she managed not to smash her face into the floor.

A walrus in a bikini was bad enough, one with an injury would just make it so much worse. And the last time she'd seen him, she'd— *Oh, God.*

Suddenly, she was eighteen again, and full to bursting with humiliation. Not the years-old variety—the kind you felt and then discarded—it felt as fresh as newly picked daisies, and her inner walrus wanted nothing but to escape back to the water.

Before the blazing heat roasting her cheeks could spread to the rest of her visible flesh, Grace snatched up her towel and climbed to her feet, whisking it around her before she'd even truly found her balance.

This wasn't happening.

This was...*chlorine poisoning.* Had to be.

Or maybe oxygen deprivation.

She needed a mask.

Or just to get out of there. Before he figured out her transparent panic. Or saw the scars. Proof of yet more foolishness. And she'd really like him to think she'd come through that unmarked, or that they were basically invisible...since he'd never even deigned to visit her hospital room after it had happened. Not that she'd have wanted him to.

Liam had his hands up, a gesture of surrender, but his eyes reeked of concern—she'd assume it was fake except she'd seen that look before. Same frown. Same posture. Different setting...

But she was practically in the same freaking outfit. It was too much to hope this wasn't real. She never got that lucky.

"You're all right." He said the words more than asked. "I didn't mean to interrupt. I was just here... Thought I'd say hello."

As he spoke, he backpedaled from the room about as smoothly as her first attempt to get out of the pool, strongly favoring one leg.

She tucked the corner of the towel to form a tight band above her breasts and, once covered, looked down at his feet—not only to indulge her curiosity but to have something as far from his head as possible to examine kept accidental eye contact from recurring.

Which was when she noticed one ill-fitting shoe, the sides bulging out from a splint supporting his ankle.

She coughed to force words through her tight throat. "You're usually a better actor than that, aren't you?"

Thankfully she hadn't also honked when she'd spoken.

Grace shifted, arms crossing over her waist as if that would cover her better, or make sure he didn't start drawing the same parallels between this and the last time she'd set eyes on him.

Pretend this was normal. Pretend the thought of running away didn't make her feet tingle and her knees itch with anticipation. Say normal person words.

"Are you here to see me, Liam... Mr....Liam?" She

usually tried to be professional when addressing prospective patients, but "Mr. Carter" felt even weirder than "Liam." But all of this felt wrong. Bad-dream wrong. Naked-without-your-homework-on-the-day-of-the-big-exam wrong.

What did a woman call someone from her past she no longer had a relationship with but whom she'd once forced to see her in her underwear? What was the proper, professional comportment for that situation?

"Or someone else, maybe?" Please, God, a lightning bolt would be good right about now. She could use a little smiting. Maybe not enough to die. There were lessons to teach actors to cry on command, where could she get lessons to learn to faint on command? Shouldn't there be some holistic expert in pressure points who could teach her something for this kind of situation? Just in case it should come in handy again in the future.

"I was thinking…" He stopped the denial and shrugged his affirmation. "Yes. I'm here to see you." He stopped his limping backward cadence and his arms fell lifelessly at his sides. "I sprained it. And with my schedule right now…"

Treatment. This wasn't a coincidence. At least treatment meant she had something to do other than stand around and wonder if he could see her nipples through her bikini top as he'd been able to do through that ridiculous bra. Or the other stupid thoughts shouting in her mental echo chamber, none of which would make him go away any faster. But treatment might.

Examine him. Offer advice. Refer him to someone else. Call it a day!

Good plan.

But get dressed first.

Act normal. Like nothing is wrong.

"Can you make it back to the treatment room?" She glanced into his eyes long enough to see the furrow of irritation marring his too-handsome features and was almost proud she finally sounded normal and professional.

"Of course."

"Okay. I'll just dry off, change, and then come check on you. Have a seat in one of the reclining chairs and get your foot up. It'll help with the throbbing." More sane words.

He paused a moment and then nodded. Without another word, he pivoted on his good leg and hobbled back out into the hallway, leaving Grace to make a beeline for the locker room to change.

Had Nick sent him here? Her brother was still friends with Liam. They had a bond that never weakened, even through the months when Liam was too busy to hang out or whatever it was they did together. Grace didn't know. She always tried her best not to know what Liam was up to, as much as was humanly possible in LA when she couldn't even go to the store to buy toothpaste without seeing his pearly whites gracing the cover of some magazine.

WORLD'S SEXIEST MAN!
  How Does Sexy Megastar Liam Carter Keep Those Rock-Hard Abs?
  Hollywood's Most Wanted talks life, love, and his favorite blah-blah-blah...

Or the ones she'd seen that morning when buying fruit: racks of tabloid headlines about Liam destroying his ex-girlfriend, who could only find comfort in the pills she got hooked on.

With minimal toweling efforts, she dried just enough to get her clothes back on without sticking, roughly combed her hair back into a ponytail, and stuffed her feet into sandals.

She'd go and examine him. Figure out what he was doing and what he should be doing to get back on his feet as quickly as possible. Fetch some crutches, maybe a different splint, and find someone to go to his house and give physical therapy. Someone who wasn't her. Someone who'd never thrown her pride to the wind and herself at a man who had clearly never wanted her.

Or at least not thrown herself at this particular man. Someone who'd always known you can't rehabilitate the bad boy.

But if you were lucky, maybe you could rehabilitate his ankle.

There had to be at least one such physical therapist in LA.

Liam half fell into the first chair he saw inside the treatment room. Not a recliner. Foot still down. All the better should he need to make an escape, an idea that stubbornly refused to go away. And the idea of reclining made his stomach roll, much like the first summer together when they'd all gone to Six Flags. Fifteen, stupid, with something to prove…jumping on his first ever roller coaster right after gorging himself with junk food and a milk shake…

The world felt tilted enough, without a chair adding to it.

Grace clearly didn't want to see him. First time that had ever happened. After that night he'd stayed away, but before that night she'd always been happy to see him, full of smiles.

Maybe it was shock. He just had to give her a few minutes to compose herself.

Maybe this was a mistake.

Reaching as high as he had meant every new relationship came with a certain amount of danger—personal or professional, it didn't matter. Not necessarily physical danger—though that was an unfortunate reality too—but it seemed like everyone was looking to make a quick buck selling any celebrity gossip they could get their hands on. More than just trashy network shows looked out for celebrity gossip. Now private websites and every form of social media got in on the scoops. It astounded him how fast a celebrity could fall from grace.

Grace.

She might not want to see him, but he could trust her not to be one of those people. Even if they hadn't had a history, she worked for a facility that guaranteed patient privacy.

But with their history... *Damn.*

He shifted the messenger bag back onto his shoulder and himself out of the chair to make for the nearest recliner. Convincing her to help him would be tricky enough without disobeying her instructions right out the gate.

He barely got settled with the foot of the recliner kicked up before she came bustling in, once again avoiding eye contact. It didn't take an expert to read that body language. Avoiding eye contact was a sign of vulnerability or of trying to hide something—given the situation, what she wanted to hide was likely that vulnerability.

She ducked into an office off to the side, saying in

passing, "Let me just stash my stuff and I'll have a look at your ankle."

Half her words came after she'd left the room, projected to carry through the open door, and she hadn't so much as glanced at him on the way through. That never happened these days. Since he'd become someone to be seen, everyone wanted to see him.

Everyone but Grace.

The problem with having an elephant in the room... he couldn't decide if it was generally a bad idea to mention it, or if he just didn't know how to mention it right. All he knew for sure was that neither of them really wanted to mention it—the idea of even trying summoned another wave of nausea. If she couldn't even bring herself to look at him without the subject coming up, it really wasn't the time to talk it out.

"I appreciate you taking the time," he offered lamely. What would he say to any other medical professional in this situation? Just talk about the job. Pretend. He was an actor, for goodness' sake. Just talk. "I've got a movie opening, three premieres to attend, and all the promotion that goes along with that. This couldn't have happened at a worse time."

She stepped back out of the office, finally letting him actually look at her in something other than her bathing suit. The clothes she wore didn't flatter, but she still wore them well. Her black scrub bottoms sat low on those hips, occasionally giving him another glimpse of golden skin when she moved.

"What exactly happened?" She dragged a stool to the reclining foot end of his chair and sat down. Only then did she look at him.

Ignore the elephant. Focus on the ankle.

"I twisted it while running." He answered her question and then fished for the bag he'd stashed beside him. "There are X-rays in here."

She didn't take the bag, but she did take the hint. "Did the doctors say it wasn't broken?"

Her hands gently lifted his leg and she worked his shoe off, then began unstrapping the splint—the only thing that had been keeping him upright today. He tried not to wince but any jostle pinged like someone poking at a bruise. Annoying, but more capable of creating tension in his shoulders with the promise of bigger pain around the corner.

"They said it didn't appear broken."

"Okay, it could still be a minor fracture, but until it starts to heal it might not show up on film."

He'd heard the same thing yesterday. And though she was gentle, his hands locked into the arms of the recliner, braced and ready to pull his leg free, even if he had no intention of doing so. Being ready helped somehow, self-comforting actions he'd been reading on her since she'd focused on him in the pool room. She'd wrapped her arms around her waist like she could hug herself right out of the whole thing.

Liam had studied body language enough to read almost anyone if he spent enough time with them, but someone he had such history with…well, he'd been able to read Grace from the instant she'd recognized him.

The shock may have dulled now, but she was still a little afraid…of him or the situation. Either way, it couldn't be more wrong.

All the movement finally brought enough pain to rob him of anything else to say.

As she peeled away the layers of light brown elastic wrap, the extent of the swelling and bruising finally became apparent. She gave a low whistle and lowered his leg once more to the foot of the recliner so she could slide up the hem of his slacks. Her hands moved quickly and surely, but somehow she managed not to touch his skin the whole time she labored to fully unveil his foot and leg.

"You did a number on it. I'm not going to make you move your foot right now, but you really shouldn't be walking on this. It should be elevated with ice to help with the swelling." She reached for his calf, the first brush of her hand on his skin causing his gut to join in on the stiff tension knotting his arms and the rest of his torso.

Gently, she lifted his leg, craning her neck to look at the underside of his calf. There was soreness there, but there was something else in the feel of her cool, soft hands on his skin. It was nice, if you discounted the pain.

She felt it too. Her complexion had been leaning toward pale since the pool, but the first brush of her hands on his flesh brought color zinging back to her cheeks. She either felt it or suddenly just remembered her embarrassment—which was too probable for him to count on any silly theory about connections and strange touches.

His leg just hurt, and he was more aware of anything to do with it now. Even the fan in his bedroom ruffling his leg hair this morning had made him do a double take. The hair had felt like it had been six inches long.

"Does it hurt up here?" She lightly squeezed the top of his calf, up beneath his knee, looking him in the eye finally.

Liam shook his head, holding her gaze.

The pink blooming on her cheeks set off the rest of her coloring, and everything about her was golden—

from the light tan testifying to her active outdoor life, to the flecks of gold in her warm brown eyes. Her hair was darker than he remembered—she'd always spent so much time outside that her light brown hair had always looked sun-kissed, but now, wet and pulled back into a ponytail, it was hard to tell whether she remained the quintessential California girl or not.

"Slightly sore, but not actual pain," he murmured. The undercurrents and tension made things weird, just not weird enough for him to change his plans. Grace had to be the one.

"I can see you had it elevated right after the fall and blood pooled up the back of your calf. You're sore up there because you're black-and-blue to the back of your knee." She laid his leg down again, and then went on talking about the injury. Something about tearing or stretching tendons, and all he could think about was the contrast between black lace and golden skin...

She paused long enough that Liam looked back to her eyes. Was he supposed to say something?

"Did they say anything like that?"

"Like what?"

"Like surgery to repair it?"

"Surgery?" The word snapped his attention back to what she was doing rather than how she looked. "No. I really don't have time for surgery. I have a premiere tonight in town. Two more tomorrow—a big one in New York and a small, local one where the movie was filmed in Virginia. And then another day of interviews when I get back here..."

She sat back and looked at him over the tortured ankle, one brow lifted screaming *idiot* at him, even if she held off actually giving the word voice—he recognized that Watson family expression.

Get it together. This is business. He still saw one of the Watsons on a regular basis, which made this mental trip down memory lane ridiculous. He'd lost her six years ago, not six minutes ago.

"I know you can wrap it with tape to give it support enough to power through this," he said, lifting his foot away from her hands and putting the recliner arm back down. Getting upright would help. "That's why I came to you, Grace. You've worked with athletes injured mid-game, kept them playing and all that. Certainly you can work with me long enough to simply keep me walking for a couple of days. And then I will do whatever it is you tell me to do in order to recover. But right now...I need to play through this."

"Those athletes who get taped are only mildly sprained. They can bear weight, just need some extra support to keep up with their range of motion. This is not that kind of sprain. You need crutches."

God. Another person with the crutches. "No. No crutches. Athletes—"

"Don't use them on the court," she cut in, sounding irritated with him now. "I know, but I told you—this is different. And even if it weren't different, there's a big difference between taping an ankle before it starts to swell and after. And you're already terribly swollen. Tape won't do anything for you, it can't give you any support when there's an inch of gelatinous *squish* between the tape and the joint."

"There are medications that reduce swelling."

"Yes..." She sat back again and looked at him. The more they engaged about the injury, the more comfortable she looked. The blush had already faded to a hint of pink. Maybe the weirdness would abate if they just stayed focused on the work. "Diuretics are used for chronic conditions that cause water retention, and as preparation before a surgery that will cause massive swelling—mostly orthopedic surgeries. But not really for injuries like this."

"Can't we use them that way anyway? And ice? And elevation? Get the swelling down enough to tape it?"

"I don't know," she said, standing again, one hand rubbing her forehead. Another self-comforting technique—her embarrassment may have faded but she still felt the stress of the situation. "I don't prescribe medication. Let me talk to Dr. Rothsberg and see who I can find in New York to—"

She started to turn and Liam lunged to grab her hand. Instantly that feeling returned. Connection. Warmth. "Grace." He said her name. Maybe if he held her back with words he could let go of her hand. "Talk to Rothsberg about the medicine, please, but I came to you because I need you."

Her hand turned slightly in his, not so much pulling away, just giving the smallest slide of flesh on flesh. Every nerve in his hand fired and tingling heat spread up his arm.

Her hands were small but he felt the strength in them. So soft in his, and warmth he could spend a year studying… He found himself stroking her skin in return, his thumb making lazy exploration of the back of her hand.

Something else, he'd been saying something…but whatever it was left him.

They'd always had chemistry, but he'd never let himself explore it. He'd always kept touching to a minimum or carefully relegated to non-sexy situations for so many reasons, not the least of which had been loyalty. The senior Watsons and Nick meant a lot to Liam, but no matter how kind they were to him even Liam knew that would all end if he gave in to that lust that colored his vision every time he looked at her. Grace was off-limits, all he could have of her was his imaginings.

And this added a new element to the fantasy of the untouchable Grace Watson.

What would her hands feel like on the rest of his body?

CHAPTER TWO

GRACE STEPPED CLOSER to Liam's chair, her arm outstretched, hand captured.

How many times had this happened in her youth? How many times had hands clasped to do something mundane and helpful? How many times had her teenage self been sprawled on the grass near where Liam and Nick had hung out—doing whatever it was that teenage boys did—with her beside Liam just so she could beg for a hand up when it was time to go in for dinner? She'd used any excuse to make him hold her hand, even for just a couple seconds.

But it had always been at her instigation.

She'd been the one dying to feel her hand in his.

The only kind of flirting a dumb kid could come up with to try and make Liam see her as something other than Nick's kid sister.

And the least ridiculous, as it had turned out. When she'd hit eighteen and the time apart while he'd been at school had turned her desperate, her tactics had become the stuff that couldn't be lived down.

"I know you don't want to come with me," Liam said, his hand still in hers, even though he'd stopped stroking her skin now. It didn't really help clear her thinking, though.

She needed to make him let go. Get some space. Maybe her thinking would unfuzzy.

She took a slow deep breath and gestured back to the stool as she pulled her hand from his, indicating that she wasn't fleeing so he'd let go.

Please, don't mention it.

She might be able to force herself through this without having to face the embarrassment head-on, but if he wanted to talk about it…

He hadn't so far, but she could see it on his face every time she looked at him. Who could forget something like that?

"We haven't seen one another in a long time, I know," he said, nodding to his ankle. "Could you rewrap it? It feels better when it's got something around it."

"Yes. Of course." She grabbed the bandage, thankful for something to do, and began rolling it up to make the rewrapping easier. Focusing on a task was better than focusing on emotions that would make everything so much worse. Liam settled back again, his hands in his lap. She could still feel the weight of his eyes on her.

"I have no one else to turn to, Gracie. It seems that when everyone wants something from you, it gets harder to trust." The edge she'd heard in his voice drained away and he chuckled, sounding something like the old, charming Liam. The old Liam, the only one she'd ever let call her Gracie. "You probably hear some variation of that from entitled celebrities every day, whining about their success and how much it costs them."

He lifted his leg as she began wrapping, allowing her to pass the elastic wrap under and around his leg, snug enough to stop further swelling but not so tight that it would hamper circulation. Something she knew how to do, unlike the rest of this. And as painful as it looked, the physical pain was so much easier to deal with. And he really had hurt himself, but there were things that could be done to speed recovery. Things she could help him do after a few days of healing rest, but this insane plan to keep walking on it...

"I'm sure I could find someone skilled enough to help me through these next few weeks, but I'd have to keep my guard up, and that's really hard to do twenty-four hours a day. I know you're not going to secretly record me or take pictures to sell to the tabloids. I know you're not going to pay more attention to the limelight than to my recovery. And if I ever had any doubt, after seeing how badly you don't want to get involved... I'm certain of it now."

Her stomach bottomed out, hearing those words, almost as sure a hit as if he had mentioned the other. "It's not that I don't want to help you. I can see you need help and I'm sure you hate having to come ask for it." The words tasted of lies. She didn't want to help him, but none of that was his fault. It was her fault. He wasn't holding grudges and she wasn't either, but... "Maybe I could get you started and then after your premieres you could come back. That way I wouldn't have to let down my other patients either."

"James said you have a light enough schedule that the other therapists can cover it."

Of course he had. Because even if he'd known about their past, James would've still wanted to do what was best for the clinic, and that meant taking excellent care of the patients, not turning them away for wholly emotional reasons. Way more professional than her reaction had been.

She should just say yes, let him stop convincing her...

She opened her mouth to agree, but he was already saying something else.

"The Watson family has always been my safe place. There's no one I trust more than Nick and you. Even when the whole world felt barbed-wired and booby-trapped, I always knew I could come to your house and—"

"Okay, I'll come." She blurted the words out before he tried other guilt tactics. Guilt worked every time, especially since all of this awkwardness was her fault. He was the victim here. Heck, if the situation had been reversed and he'd come to her house in a trench coat and scanty underwear, it would've probably been considered a sex crime. And it definitely would've made all his other relationships with her family tense and awkward, maybe even worse than this.

It had been all on her and her childish fantasies that Liam Carter could've ever thought of her the way she thought of him. No. The way she *had* thought of him. The only thing she felt now was horrified at her own behavior. And desperate to never have to acknowledge or explain, to never experience that level of vulnerability again.

Holding the loose end of the bandage with her wrist, she fished fabric tape from her pocket and pulled off a strip to tack the bandage down before taping it more thoroughly.

"But, for the record, I was going to say yes before you added that little bit about trust and our childhood."

There'd been no way for him to win that situation, just like there was no way for her to win this one. No polite, professional, or *kind* way at least, and he deserved her kindness. She'd spent years trying to figure out what he could have said that would've made the rejection better at all.

Should he have just slept with her so she hadn't felt stupid about the hours of vigorous waxing and grooming to make herself irresistible? Wasted hours and needlessly tender post-waxing flesh…

"You mean I'm wasting my best lines?"

His question jerked her back from pondering the futility of her tender bits after that tragic home wax/shaving experiment. The smile she found when she looked at him softened the memories of bad razor burn and gut-churning humiliation.

"Was that a line in one of your movies?"

"Don't you watch my movies?" The words rang with obviously faked horror and he laid a hand over his heart as if the mere thought would do him in.

Silly.

Cute.

He was trying to make her feel better.

Before she could stop it, she smiled back. He certainly hadn't lost that natural charm.

But that kind of dangerous thinking had to stay as far from her scrambled gray matter as possible. The only way to get through this was to just focus on the injury, not the man. Not the way her insides expanded when he smiled at her, which they shouldn't even do anyway. Playful banter might as well be a sledgehammer, he could knock all sense out of her with one strategic swing.

She took a breath and eased the smile off her face.

Playful banter fit nowhere, it had to go for the next couple weeks.

Playful banter could make her forget.

Playful banter could make her stupid.

No playing with Liam Carter.

"When do we go?" Grace asked instead, bringing the conversation back on track.

"How fast can you pack?"

Grace strapped him into the splint, which at least was of excellent quality and slender enough that it could probably be hidden beneath his dress pants. "Driving home will take—"

"No. I mean whatever medical supplies you need. We'll pick up whatever personal items you need for tonight and the morning. When we get to New York, we'll get any restocking of supplies we need too."

"Your people will get whatever else we need, you mean?" She reached up to grasp the cuff of his pants leg and eased it back down over the splint.

"Yes." He smiled again, that lopsided, little-boy grin that always made her heart speed up.

She wouldn't smile. No smiling. Business didn't need so much smiling. Taking care of him didn't mean she had to have a sweet bedside manner, just a professional one.

"I'd rather deal with my own clothes, but for now I'm going to get some ice for your ankle, talk to James about whether a diuretic would be acceptable in this situation, and pack a quick bag of supplies. You sit here until I'm ready. The ice might do some good before you get back on your feet." Grace stood, heading to the freezer to get things started.

This day had certainly taken a turn for the bizarre and uncomfortable. And as stupid as it sounded to her to try and push through this, it wasn't her job to make celebrities behave rationally. It was her job to try and keep the damage to a minimum, and also the whole rehabilitation thing. She could keep him going for a couple of days if he could ride it out.

That was her job.

And swimming together, in or out of therapy, was right out. At least for the immediate future. The only way she was going to retain some semblance of her sanity around Liam was to keep The Trench Coat Incident as far from her thoughts as possible.

Grace settled into the forward-facing black leather backseat of the limo, dropping her bag onto the floor at her feet as she settled.

In the quiet interior of the car, the speed of her heart registered. She'd felt it before, hovering in the fringes of her awareness, but here she could hear the speed and analyze the force of the beast tangoing in her chest. It hadn't really ever come back down since the second she'd seen him standing beside the pool. He probably could hear it now, even sitting three feet away.

She fixed her gaze out the window.

It was still hard to look at Liam too long, even if she knew she was going to have to get used to it. The door shut behind him, and the darkened interior of the limo kept him from reflecting in the glass.

Finally, something going her way. Any brighter in there and the only place to keep from seeing him would've been the insides of her eyelids. And that never worked out, she was too good at seeing him there.

"So, about your clothes. You need to let me handle that."

If she had to look at him, it would be in bright, open places. And if she had to talk to him, it would be about strictly professional subjects, which clothing was not.

"I know I didn't have time to pack anything but medical supplies, but what I am wearing right now will serve for this afternoon. While you're at the premiere, I'll go home, grab some clothes and come back to the hotel."

"I have a personal shopper."

Out of the corner of her eye she saw him fish his phone from his pocket and flip it on. Two clicks later, he had it to his ear. Not listening to her at all.

"I don't need a personal shopper. I can get my own clothes." She tried again.

"They will be your own clothes afterward."

"Liam." She said his name, forcing herself to become reacquainted with the way it felt on her lips again.

Ten years ago, simply saying his name had made her happy. She would've sworn it even had a taste—a slick, plump fullness, luxurious and sensual, like her tongue sliding across her lips to suddenly find cinnamon chocolate fudge...

Now, instead of sweets, his name felt like rocks and sand in her mouth. Sharp. Awkward. Gritty.

"It's really not a big deal."

He listened well enough to carry on the conversation, but he clearly wasn't hearing her.

Ugh.

This kind of thing never happened to her. It probably never happened to anyone outside of *Cinderella* and *Pretty Woman*.

And that would make her the prostitute in this situation. Great.

Grace licked her sandpaper lips and took another purposeful breath through her mouth, because although the car might provide her with the ability to stop looking at him, it only amplified the heady cloud of good smells clinging to the man. His scent had been indelibly imprinted on her memories, earthy and rich, like salty air, old forests, and even older heartache. She found herself breathing slowly and deeply.

This was such a bad idea.

She was supposed to be acting professionally. Yelling at a client wasn't professional. And rolling in his scent was an extremely creepy reaction to being in his presence again.

Everything would be okay, she just needed to get ahold of herself. And maybe explain better, if she could come up with the words.

"I'm sure your personal shopper is lovely." Diplomatic. Good opening. "But that's not really the point. I already have clothes. I can take care of my own clothes. We're not going to be in another state until tomorrow so I have time."

He stopped participating in the conversation as someone had answered and now he was in full Hollywood mode, greeting and no doubt smiling.

Would he be doing this if she were anyone else?

"My other clients don't buy me clothing." She'd had some bring gifts, the kind that had made her feel awkward and—

"What sizes do you wear?"

The close confines of the darkened interior of the back of the limo felt entirely too intimate without him asking personal questions about her clothing.

She shifted to another seat to make room and redirected the conversation. "Turn sideways on the seat so you can stretch your leg out there. Any elevation will help with the swelling." Ice would have been more helpful, but she hadn't brought any.

A few seconds ticked by and she heard, "You're ignoring me?" Incredulity rang in his voice, making her want to turn and look at him.

Then again, everything made her want to look at him. He was singularly the most attractive person she'd ever seen in person—even years later and working at The Hollywood Hills Clinic, which was peopled daily with the beautiful and glamorous.

And her reaction to him was precisely the reason she needed to avoid looking at him excessively or, as it would probably be called, staring in a starstruck and creepy fashion. Though, admittedly, the more he banged this shopping drum, the less she felt like gazing at him like a lovesick cow, and more like smacking him in the back of the head.

Precisely why she needed to keep all talking strictly professional.

"I'm pretending you didn't just ask a c—" The word *creepy* nearly sprang out of her mouth, but she managed to stomp the sound down before she used unprofessional language. "It's really not workplace etiquette to ask those kinds of questions. So, just let me handle any clothing needs I may have on my own."

"We don't have time for this, Grace. I'd really rather you blend in, and the clinic logo and your name on your shirt do not help you blend in." A pause and he repeated into the phone, "I'd like her to blend in with the group."

His group—she was going to assume that meant his people, in the ol' I'll Have My People Call You scenario. So Liam called them his group.

"Right. Slacks. Blouses. Shoes. Accessories…"

Accessories. Of course, how could she forget accessories? She had accessories. She just hadn't thought to mention them.

"No. She's tall, but not six feet. Probably about a head shorter than me. Compact and slim, but not so much skinny as athletic. She's…"

He wasn't going to stop. Next thing he would be trying to describe her curves or ask her cup size, which would just bring that stupid trench-coat situation back to his mind. This was worse than just giving the fool her sizes. "Please, Liam." She tried his name again.

"I'll snap a photo of her and send it to you when we get to the hotel."

"For goodness' sake, stop!" Exasperated, she turned to look at him, holding out her hand for the phone. "Stop and I will text her my sizes."

"Him."

"Him! Whatever!" She held out her hand for his phone, her voice rising with her blood pressure. "I will text him my sizes if it will get you off this and get your foot up on that seat. Every minute it is down on the floor like that, it's swelling more. You know that, right, Superman?"

"Text coming," he said into the phone. "And the picture in a little bit. If you can have them at the hotel in the morning, we're leaving for New York at seven." He hung up before handing her the phone and turning to prop his foot up, as she'd all but shrieked at him.

Good thing she wasn't interested in seducing him. There was probably a reason that the low, velvety voice analogous with seduction was the opposite of a shriek.

A minute later, she double-checked the details she'd sent to Shopper Tom, as he was known to Liam's phone. If he picked clothing she hated, she'd wear it the one time and then find someone at work who wanted the clothes. They were temporary, just like this assignment.

The thought failed to comfort her, and she returned her attention to the window, thrusting the phone at him and settling back into her not-speaking routine. She couldn't display her freak-out voice if she wasn't talking.

* * *

In order to maintain security, and probably so Liam wouldn't be seen traveling with a woman whose shirt announced her position as physical therapist, the limo had gone around to the rear, private entrance of the hotel, where his group had met them.

Now, with him limping down the marble hallway in front of her—which no doubt led to the supremely classy yet neutral color-schemed heaven on the top floor—there was no room to doubt how bad an idea it was for him to be on the carpet tonight.

His three assistants bustled along with him, informing him how they'd set up the interviews. More walking, him making rounds to meet with reporters in different areas of the suite...

"That's not going to work," Grace cut in, and three sets of eyes turned to her. Liam's didn't, but his people had no idea she'd been complaining about him walking on it for at least ninety-seven percent of the time since she'd seen him. Mostly because it was a bad idea, and partly because she couldn't complain about what she really wanted to complain about...

"What would you like us to do?" Liam asked, stopping at a nondescript elevator and pressing the call button. Maybe he came this way all the time?

"One, you need to be off your feet as much as possible if you're going to have any hope of getting through the red carpet tonight. Two, you said you don't want this advertised. Which? You're limping like you've just suffered a back-alley amputation and are walking on a bloody stump."

He smiled at her description and then nodded to his people. "She's right. I don't want to walk any more than I absolutely have to."

Despite the smile he'd put on, there was a white ring around his mouth and his forehead glistened, though it was far from hot outside. Concealed pain. Ridiculous that he was so driven to conceal it.

But at least he wasn't arguing.

Their elevator stopped again at the very top of the hotel. "A suite, I'm guessing?"

"The whole floor." Liam nodded.

Naturally.

"Okay." The door opened to a tiny room with an ornate fancy door. One of the assistants handled the lock.

"Here." She thrust the rather large bag of medical supplies to the closest assistant, a pretty, petite thing who made Grace feel the antithesis of her name, and didn't pause to see if she could bear the weight.

"I'm helping you, Liam," Grace said, in what she hoped was a tone that brooked no argument. Even if she had to come back for the bag, she wouldn't have the thing smacking into him and upsetting his already precarious balance. A second later and she had his arm over her shoulders and her own around his waist, "If you have the whole floor, no one is going to see me helping."

A nod and he leaned, letting her take some of his weight, confirming how much his leg was hurting. As they made it into the suite, she began issuing instructions.

"We're going to need crushed ice, and find one of the rooms to set up and have the press people come here instead. We need a table, a chair, long tablecloth…and a footstool that can be hidden behind the fabric."

"Two chairs," the man at her left said, probably taking notes the way he rattled off her requests.

She turned Liam toward the closest comfortable-looking chair and kept arguing. "One chair. The reporter is going to stand. Or sit across the room. Or away from the table. Or levitate. I don't care. If they're at the table, they might bump his ankle or crash their feet into the stool. We don't want them getting curious for any reason and looking, right?"

"Right," Liam confirmed, nodding to a different chair to indicate his seat of choice.

A moment later, she had freed herself from the heat and natural cologne of his body to deposit him in the chair, his foot propped up on a table with a cushion padding the heel. "This will have to do until we get the other set up."

"Grace?"

She stopped and turned to look at him.

"Thank you. I suddenly feel like my brain isn't functioning at full power."

"When did you last take medication for pain?"

"I took something this morning."

"Any reason you can't take anti-inflammatories? Any kidney problems?"

He shook his head.

"Good. They'll help more, reduce swelling. I am also going to…" She paused and directed her attention back to the one remaining assistant. "Get some food up here. Also, the room you set up in should be close to a bathroom."

"Why?" Liam's question came from behind her.

"Because you're going to take a diuretic, remember?"

"Oh, right."

"And you don't want to have to walk a bunch to get to and from it." Having tasks to occupy herself with helped. Top of the list now: water. She detoured to the bar and came back with a fresh, cool bottle of water and, after she'd rifled through the work bag the woman had lugged in, fished out a few blister packs with the medicine Dr. Rothsberg had agreed to. "Take this. And this."

"What's that?"

"Potassium. If you take this diuretic, it will flush the potassium from your body. So you take it with potassium." At least he was still with it enough to ask the right questions and not just blindly take any medicine handed to him.

"The other? The pain medicine, it's not narcotic, right? Not the anti-inflammatory mixed with something you get with a prescription?"

There was a sound in his voice that made her stop and look at him, like a pinch or something else causing pain. It took her a second before she worked out why. His parents. How could she have forgotten about their addiction?

"No narcotic in it," she said softly. "It's a prescription-sized dose of ibuprofen, but we're faking it by taking extra over-the-counter versions of the same drug. Nothing addictive..." She regretted the word before it had even fully passed her lips. Some words had a chameleonlike ability to become hurtful depending on who heard them. With his history, and his recent addict ex-girlfriend... If she was going to be working with him, she'd have to be more mindful.

Before the statement could settle, or turn the room acid, she changed to what they needed to do. Work could always save them. "How long do we have to get you settled before the interviews have to start? And what time do you have to get ready for the premiere?"

One of the assistants, Tall, Blond, and Slight—or Miles, as the others called him—answered, "As soon as possible on the interviews. Most of the reporters are here already, and from there about four hours before he has to get dressed."

She stood a little straighter, knowing that her words were going to irritate them. "Okay, then make sure it's no more than two hours for the reporters. He needs a couple hours with his leg up higher than his head, and iced."

"Liam?" Miles looked around her to their boss.

"She's in charge this afternoon," Liam said, all but pulling the words from her mind. "And if we have to sacrifice a few angry reporters in order to put in a satisfying show on the carpet, then that's what we have to do. If you're worried, double them up. Bring in two at a time. Limit the number of questions they can ask. We can keep them moving. You gave them all the script, right?"

"Script?" Grace asked, zeroing in back on him.

"Miles puts together all the information that we want them to have, they hand out copies and that keeps me from having to repeat myself. Sometimes they want a direct quote in my own words and the copy we've handed out is wasted, but usually they are a good way of shortening interviews."

Miles added, "I'll limit them to three questions. Or maybe a time limit would be better. Three questions or...seven minutes."

"How many crews are there?" The math started sounding more than ridiculous.

"You don't want to know," Liam said. "They were planning to have four hours to do this, but I threw a wrench into things by going to The Hollywood Hills Clinic for you first."

And she needed to be there in order to intercede, but Liam didn't want people seeing her shirt. "Do you have clothes here? Other than the ones for the trip and the premieres?"

He nodded. "Why?"

"The crews are here and Shopper Tom hasn't had enough time to get something here for me to wear. Thought maybe I could snag one of your button-downs and wear it instead of the polo until he gets here."

He nodded toward his female assistant. "Show Miss Watson what's available in the wardrobe. The shirts I wore when I leaned out for that role eight months ago would probably work best."

Grace followed the woman.

He'd leaned out?

In general, looking at Liam's chest was a bad idea if Grace wanted to keep her wits about her, but she couldn't help herself now. His shoulders were broad, had always been broad. How much weight had he lost for a role? Everything looked normal to her with his clothes on… What other tortures was he putting his body through for this job?

What would she have put her own through to turn pro? More than was sane. She'd done plenty during rehab when she'd been hanging onto a shred of hope. She had just never managed to get back there.

CHAPTER THREE

SOMEHOW GRACE HAD made herself the boss of Liam and his assistants, and Liam didn't have any desire to dissuade her from that course of action.

She got the crews in and out, and guarded the door in between. And the shirt she'd selected from his clothing didn't fit. Hell, it might as well be the only thing she was wearing for the way it distracted him. The collar unbuttoned deeply enough to tease at her cleavage, and the material tied in a knot at her waist, granting glimpses of solid abs and golden skin. No way would she be mistaken for a medical professional in that. She looked like his girlfriend or his lover, bossing everyone around and protectively fetching him water while still nagging him about this and that.

He liked that idea way too much.

But only because it was the perfect cover. No other options there.

If she didn't watch it, the story the reporters took away would be that Liam had dumped Simone and caused her to turn addict…so that he could shack up with the golden vixen managing his suite and tending to his needs while his assistants stood by and looked at her balefully. Yep, it all but screamed The Other Woman.

She escorted the fourth crew back and came back

to him, alone as she did every time. "How are you? Do
you need a break before the next?"

"I do. I need to use the…facilities." He gestured.
"And I won't ask you to stick around there, but someone to lean on would be appreciated."

"Just a second. I have crutches with me."

"You brought them anyway? How?"

She dug into the big duffel and started pulling out
parts. Somehow, in that big bag of supplies, she'd managed to break down and stash a set of crutches. She
flipped metal bits this way and that, pressed buttons,
and adjusted the height. "Don't worry, when you're
seated again, I'll stash them under the sofa so no one
can see them. I just want you using them anytime you're
not in front of the public. I'm serious, Liam. You are
damaging that further every time you put your weight
on it, and there is a window where you can get away
with it, but past that it's going to heal wrong and you'll
sprain it again. You'd be surprised by how little pressure a weakened ankle can withstand before it rolls out
of the socket. Pain is a signal. It's supposed to dissuade
you from acting like a he-man."

Arguing was futile.

"Fine. Give them to me. It might shock you to hear
this, but I don't want to do more damage than I have to.
I've rated it as high as I can beneath the top priorities."

She helped him get the crutches positioned right, and
walked beside him toward the bathroom.

"What do you think you're going to have to give
up by bowing out of these premieres and interviews?"

"It wouldn't take much to wreck the momentum my
career has gained in the past two years. You know how
the gossip is. You don't have to make huge scandalous
mistakes for the climate to turn. People are already mad

at me about Simone, and that's all speculation. I could keep making a series of small mistakes or demonstrations of bad judgment and the tide would still turn, just not as sharp a turn as if I went around punching people and biting the heads off live kittens."

He felt it before he even looked down and saw the face she pulled while walking beside him. She turned her lips in and bit them, the way she'd liked to do to hide smiles, or keep from saying something she shouldn't. Simone. She wanted to ask about Simone, how could she not?

No way. He wasn't up for talking about his ex with the woman he'd spent years comparing all his former girlfriends to.

"I know that's a silly example. What I want you to know is that I need to make the most of it while I'm in the position I've managed to reach. Do the most work I can, bank it for the inevitable downturn. And in the meanwhile get the best parts and stretch myself—increase the work that people think I'm capable of." He swung into the bathroom and turned to try and drill the importance of his words into her. "The next project is a really good one. It's also the kind of work that will keep me from being stuck in either the rom-com hero or action hero typecasts when I get too old for those kinds of parts."

She opened the bathroom door and waited for him to enter. "I'll wait out here."

It closed with a click and Liam shook his head. No comment on what he'd said. She thought he was being unreasonable just out of stubbornness. Or, worse, she thought it was ego. That his pride would sacrifice his leg if it meant the chance to prowl the carpet and be told how awesome he was.

He caught his reflection in the mirror as he passed it, scowling so deeply that he had to pause. Even speculating that she held him in anything but high esteem made him feel fifty pounds heavier, and it showed on his face.

Afterward, while avoiding looking into the mirror, he washed his hands and grabbed the crutches again.

"Door." He'd let her wait on him if she wanted to take it this far. "You think I'm being ridiculous."

"I think that you think you're invincible. I remember feeling that way myself, but when it goes? It's a really rude awakening."

"Liam?" Miles called from the door. "The media are getting restless."

"Right. Let me get settled and then bring in the next person. Wait at least ninety seconds." The crutches were awkward at first, but he'd played parts where they were needed in the past. His body remembered the way of it soon enough. He picked up speed to his seat, sat, and thrust them at Grace. "I'll take care of settling my foot with the ice on it."

His group were competent and cautious people and he even fully trusted two of the three of them, but having Grace take care of things felt the most secure.

When this was over, he'd have to make sure she knew how much this meant to him. Maybe she'd stop looking at him that way then. Maybe he'd stop looking at himself that way.

He should probably also give his group bonuses. He'd seen Miles—his longest-employed assistant—giving Grace the stink-eye at least twice today.

With a quick bend and tuck, she stashed the crutches beneath the sofa and out of sight. Liam made a point of not watching her bend over.

Twenty minutes and another trip to the lavatory later,

she was helping him back to the chair and paused to have a look at his foot before putting the ice back on it. "It's working. At least we have that. If the swelling keeps going down, your insane plan might actually work. Providing you can stand the pain. How's it doing right now, on a scale of one to ten?"

He could lie—and the professional side of his personality almost demanded it. If he told her that it was a solid four even when he was sitting still, and that it shot up to seven or seventy-five when he walked...

"It's pretty sore," he said, shaking his head. "And it is worse when I walk on it. The crutches are helping, but I'm only using them here."

"We've been over that," Grace said, heading toward the couch with the crutches. "But you didn't say a number."

"Three when I'm sitting." It wasn't really a lie. All these numbers were subjective. It just felt like a lie.

"And when you're on it?"

"I don't know. Six."

She straightened with a grimace and a shake of her head. "Before you go, if you insist on going, I'll give you a staggered dose of painkillers to help a little more. But you remember this tomorrow when sitting is a six and walking is a ten."

With the new rules limiting the number of questions they could ask, and doubling up on crews, they managed to get them all through with only a little extra time shaved off the required rest period Grace had given him.

And the remainder of it, all one hour and forty-seven minutes he'd spent flat on his back on the floor, his leg propped up on the seat of the chair he'd spent the afternoon in, his foot above the level of his heart, seemed like the easiest way to accomplish that.

However hard he'd thought it'd been to avoid her, he now fully recognized how much he'd missed just seeing her. Even considering the tension in their first minutes and the frequent flashes he saw in her eyes when she looked his way, things were going much better than he would have hoped.

She still thought he was being completely foolish, but she was getting him through what he needed to. And what he really needed now was another trip to the damned bathroom. Note to self: great for reducing swelling but lousy if you're not glued to the en suite.

"Grace!" he yelled from the floor. "Is my time up?"

"You have one minute, but I guess we can get you up early. Why? Do you need something?" She asked the question so innocently, he almost missed the teasing light in her eyes—small as it was.

"Uh-huh."

"Can you wait until I've had a second to look at it and tape it if possible?"

"Do we really need to delay? It's a quick trip."

"Yes, but any time with your foot down it's going to start swelling again."

And she'd made enough of a deal about it earlier that he didn't want to test her patience with him. Funny, he usually had a harder time letting go of his way than that.

"All right. If you can do it fast. Like in five minutes."

"I've taped on the sidelines. I can tape an ankle in under two minutes, but I need a couple more minutes to see your ankle once we've got the wrap off."

A minute later, she'd moved her supplies over and offered him a hand from the floor. "I thought you didn't want me to put it down."

"I want you to stand up and sit in the chair so I can tape it easier. You know, so I can get the tape under it without you having to strain to keep it off my lap and I don't have to give myself backache bending and twisting to get in past the seat back."

Liam shrugged and bypassed her hand. He could still stand up.

He sat up and flipped to one hip to push up off the floor without assistance, keeping what was left of his macho intact—or as much as it could be while hopping on one foot.

Sitting back down, he held his leg up and waited for her to make with the unwrapping, though really it was loose enough that she could probably slide it off like a sock at this point. He could only consider that a win.

When the skin was exposed, he prompted, "So?"

"So, this is not an instant decision. I'm going to need to move your foot around. I'm sorry, it's going to hurt, but I will try to be gentle. I need to make sure that what I diagnosed earlier was correct. Inversion sprains usually involve certain ligaments, and the method of taping is slightly different depending on whether it's the top one or the bottom one. I won't bore you with the names."

"So it can be taped? When you know the right taping procedure…"

She didn't answer yet, just gently moved his foot in the joint—pointed up, pointed down, side to side. It was the side motion that had him hissing loudest.

"Anterior talofibular ligament. And possibly the calcaneofibular."

"I thought you weren't going to bore me with the names."

"I'm just showing off." The tiny smile she gave came with a wave of relief in its wake. Almost normal. Her twisting his foot around might hurt enough that his jaw ached from clenching it, but physical pain could be borne much easier than what they'd been sidestepping since the second she'd pulled herself out of that pool.

"There's so much bruising I'm still not sure that there isn't actually a tear and not just too much stretching."

"Grace." He said her name a little louder, forcing her to stop what she was doing and look at him. "Can it be taped?"

"We're going to find out. I'm going to tape it, you're going to have people help you shave or whatever here in this chair, and keep it elevated until you absolutely need to stand up to get dressed. It might also be a good idea for you to—at the last minute—gently walk around the suite to try and get the motion down. When you've got your ankle locked, it changes the method of locomotion. Hip and knee flexing becomes more important. And it will also probably make your back hurt before too long, so don't walk any more than you absolutely have to."

Once more she went into that bag, this time coming out with an electric razor and some other supplies.

"I'll use my own razor when you're done."

"This isn't for your face. I'm shaving your leg."

"You are?"

"You want me to tape it?"

"Yes." He sighed and leaned back, letting her have her way again. "Just don't shave anything else."

"I'm not here for manscaping. I'm here to save your skin from the tape."

"Couldn't you just put something under it?"

"I am. But I use a light adhesive spray too so it doesn't slide and cause blisters."

"Fine, fine."

A moment later she had his foot cradled between her knees and was shaving halfway up his calf, all around.

Seconds only, and while it wasn't exactly a close shave, it got the job done. Then she hit it with the spray and grabbed a thin, blue stretchy wrap. It went on next, covering his leg from just below the toes, around the heel, and just over halfway up to his knee.

Grace hadn't been lying when she'd said she could do one in under two minutes, a wrap that would be tight and functional but maybe a little bulkier than she wanted. She'd take her time and do it in three or four minutes this time. After a couple of strips to anchor it, she flexed his foot up at a good right angle and laid down the stirrup strips. And then heel locks and figure eights of tape around the foot and ankle.

"How much tape are you going to use?"

"I'm going to make sure that none of the pre-wrap is showing except where the ends poke out a bit. No holes. It needs to be closed up completely or it might start to come off. So maybe the whole roll of tape. And maybe some other tape on top of it. I want to see you walk on it first. Then if we need the stretchy tape, we'll slap another layer on, just to add that little bit extra support."

He made some noise of affirmation, but stopped asking questions. Which gave her an opening. "I know you don't want anyone to find me out, but if I just go to the theater and lurk in the crowds by the carpet, that should be all right. I don't want to be up here sitting, waiting, when you might need me on the ground. I'll stand out of the way somewhere."

"I guess that's okay. I mean, you'll try to stand out of the way somewhere, but there's a lot of jostling that happens along the carpet. Not just from the cameras but also the fans lining up to snap pictures and shake hands. It's a big deal for them. If that happens, just go back to the limo and sit. I really don't want to have you helping me in public either. If I fall over, I fall over. Better that it looks like a fresh accident than something that I had to bring health professionals with me to manage."

"You really want to fall on camera?" she asked, hand fumbling in the bag beside her for the wide athletic tape.

Liam made a noise and shook his head. "But we're not talking about what I'd like, we're talking about what might provide the best public reaction. If I fall and limp off to the limo, I can just claim the doctor said I need to stay off it a couple days and that it will be fine, but if I am there with a physical therapist…"

"This is ridiculous. A fall is a fall, everyone will react to it the same way. They might even be happy that you're bringing someone like me with you in order to try and minimize the damage. Though I dare say that they'd strangle you if they found out that you're planning on walking on it unassisted in this condition. That might make them think you're out of your mind and incapable of the part. I know that's what would push me over the edge."

"You're a medical professional. And this is your job. Regular people, and especially people in the industry, want me to be a superhero."

"Is that what the part is for? A superhero?"

"No." He denied it too quickly, and for a man used to acting—basically lying for a living—he didn't pull the denial off at all.

"Your left eye just twitched." She stopped what she

was doing, though she hadn't really gotten started wrapping the thing yet. "It's *so-o-o* for a superhero. Who?"

"It's not what you think. It's different. He's a kind of medieval superhero, I suppose."

Before she could stop it, Grace felt her eyes roll and she scooted back and went to fish the crutches out. "Just until you get on your feet and have taken a few practice steps. Ease into it. Let your arms carry you until you find the right stride. And don't be afraid to call it off if you come to your senses."

Another moment without arguing. He took the crutches and carefully began to crutch-walk, easing onto the poor tortured foot. While he did that she got him the next round of over-the-counter painkillers.

"I think I want the stretchy tape."

"I think you do too," she murmured.

As bad as it was, the stretchy tape would add a tiny bit more support but it was kind of like painting the door when the house was falling down. But maybe it would help or have a placebo effect.

"I'll get it. You take these, and I'll send the anti-inflammatories with you. You can take them when the movie is playing—take water with you if you don't have drinks or whatever. I don't know how premieres are. Do they run the refreshments counter during one?"

He gave her a strange look but swallowed the pills down without water.

"Don't do that with the medicine. It needs to be taken with food."

"I'll handle it. Whatever is necessary to make this work. Now get out, I need to get dressed."

She handed him a blister pack with the appropriate dose, then headed for the door to the foyer area and yet more exceptionally tasteful shades of beige. She snagged her tablet as she walked out to where they'd been staging the reporters, out of sight of Liam and his crutches.

"Manage and document his dosing schedule so they can't screw it up, and add it to his chart." Along with his inability to heed much of her advice, and her rigorous objections to him walking on it.

Not that it would matter to anyone, but it made her feel a little better. The tablet accepted her words without argument.

Liam braced himself as the door swung open and he stepped out.

The first official step of the night, and it would have to be on his bad ankle. One thing he couldn't control was the direction from which cars arrived to drop off passengers at the red carpet. But it figured that he'd have to get out of the car on his bad ankle.

With a deep breath, he stepped down and used his arms as much as possible to haul himself from the car. Smooth.

Luckily for him, he had actually managed to control when he arrived, delaying his arrival until there were already plenty of people there to look at. Maybe the effort it took to get up would be missed.

Maybe the effort it took to keep his face a calm mask would also be missed. If he was lucky. But since his fall Liam had felt anything but lucky.

The gait that Grace had returned to his suite to demonstrate and practice was unnatural, but nothing he hadn't had to do before.

He had to use the hip and knee, propel himself forward with the other leg as much as possible to disguise the fact that he wasn't really pulling off heel-to-toe locomotion anymore.

She had made it look easy. But she'd probably had to do that walk a thousand times for other patients.

In this whole mess, she was the one bit of luck on his side. Not just that she hadn't pushed him out of her office immediately, and not even that she had agreed to come with him—those were things he could actually put down to James Rothsberg's influence as everyone wanted to please their boss at least a little bit. But his luck was that she still smiled at him on occasion.

After that night had gone down, at first he'd stayed away, hoping to give her some time to get over it, but soon enough he had been so busy with all the menial gigs actors did to get by before their chosen career began to pay off that he'd put checking on her at the bottom of his list of things to do.

He'd been unable to ever ask Nick about how she was.

Neither could he have asked Mr. or Mrs. Watson— David and Lucy. Or gone directly to Grace either.

Eventually, giving her time had become just plain staying away. And he'd kept busy enough not to do anything but acknowledge that the situation had made him sad. There had always been another low-wage gig to go to, until those low-wage menial gigs had become low-wage acting gigs, and then higher-wage acting gigs as his skill had increased…

The long hours of daylight meant that he had to do the walk under the kind of light that mandated he use those skills and give an exceptional performance now.

If it weren't for the amount of radiation he'd sucked up being reassured that he hadn't broken it, and his desire not to have any more X-rays at present, he might go back to the hospital and demand another set of films. How anything could feel this bad and not be broken was beyond him.

He'd known he and Grace had been broken by that night, but only here, in his own time, when she was nowhere around since he'd forced his way back into her life, had he even realized that he was angry about it.

It had been there in his expression in the mirror, but he'd put it down to pain. But the truth was…as conflicted as he had felt in that moment, and as guilty as he'd felt since then, he'd also felt anger that he'd lost her over it.

Not angry at her, not even angry with himself, just angry and frustrated.

No more than ten steps in and he'd been noticed. Cheers started in a wave, from the first to spot him, the advance warning system for the crowd, until it was all heads and flashbulbs.

And he could feel his brows furrowing. It wasn't the time for that, it was time for smiles.

This would be easier if…he didn't have to do it.

Wave. Smile. Stop for pictures. Shake hands. Don't show the pain grinding up his leg or the conflict churning through his gut. It had all worked out for the best anyway, Grace deserved someone who could stay forever, and his relationships came with an already determined expiration date. Something he couldn't do to her, even if he could get past all the family conflicts.

When this was over, when he got back to the hotel, Grace would take care of him. She might lecture him, but she'd do it with her gentle hands and a level of exasperation that told him she still gave a damn. Even if the mortification of that night had stayed with her more strongly than he would have liked, she still gave a damn about him.

That was something to feel lucky about. Something to feel grateful for.

Even if it would make things harder.

CHAPTER FOUR

THE TIME BETWEEN Liam leaving and the time that Grace had managed to make it to the theater swelled to the point that now, despite the fact that she'd not arrived for forty-five minutes after Liam had, she wedged herself through the crowds enough to catch sight of him still working the carpet.

Granted, he wasn't running up and down the length of it, but he did move from one side to the other, shaking hands, taking pictures, signing anything that people thrust at him.

Shopper Tom, or as she called him now, Tom, had come barging into Liam's suite about three minutes after Liam and his crew had left, then had insisted on making Grace try on clothes to figure out what gave the best fit. Were these shoes the right size? Did these slacks ride too high at the hem to wear with the heels he'd picked up for her to pair them with?

Did she even know how to walk in heels?

What about this color?

How did she like blouses to hang—did she prefer a very close fit that showcased her figure or did she want to go for the old Hollywood style with flowing material?

Did she even know how to put her hair up in anything but a ponytail?

By the time she'd managed to usher him out of the suite she'd had a scalp-stretching bun forced on her, as well as more than half the clothes that he'd brought with him.

This nonsense was going to last two days. Two days. Not twenty. In two days, she'd be back home and in her own clothes, she wouldn't have to blend in with Liam's Group. She could wear what she wanted. She didn't need five pairs of slacks. She didn't need blazers and blouses, and why in God's name had Liam included accessories and shoes for every outfit?

Grace flexed her toes up and then gave them a wiggle in the strappy sandals she'd still managed to succumb to wearing with the suit—aka the last thing she'd agreed to try on. She didn't blend in. The crowd dressed casually. She looked like she'd come straight from closing down a tenement for the poor and disenfranchised. Or, actually, she probably looked like she was trying too hard to look important.

While Liam looked tired. And in pain.

And like he needed to be knocked out, since that apparently was the only way she was going to get him to behave and actually take some time to heal.

Anyone who watched him right now would likely come to the same conclusion. He tried, bless his little idiotic heart, but his limp was still there. Pain had a way of overriding willpower and concentration. It also distracted from a person's ability to judge anything accurately, like how well he was doing pretending it didn't hurt.

By the time he made it to the double doors and out of her vision, Grace's irritation had turned to worry and her head ached from the way her brows refused to un-pinch.

No matter where she stood in the crowd, she wouldn't be able to keep an eye on him now. The only thing she could pray for was that Miles, the assistant who hated her, would keep an eye on him and not let him overdo things.

As if that would happen. It'd mean going along with her demands, and if she'd picked up anything from him this afternoon it was that his last priority was pleasing her. Liam wanted to keep going, and Miles would facilitate that, regardless of whether or not it was best for Liam.

With a growing sense of dread she turned to push her way back through the crowds. They were sticking around to be there and see those shining people they'd come to see on their exit back out of the theater. One trip, two chances to catch sight of them, no matter if they had to stand waiting two or more hours in between.

Not Grace.

Let Miles help keep him on his feet. The trouble with having no control over a situation? No matter how much she told herself that he'd be fine, that he was an adult and could make his own decisions, she still worried about him all the way to the street to catch a taxi. And likely would continue to worry for the remainder of the night, while she sorted out only the clothes she'd wear in the next two days and lumped the rest together to be messengered back tomorrow.

But at least that would give her something to do besides fret.

Two hours later, Grace dragged the crutches out from beneath the cream-colored sofa. She'd intended on doing so when Liam hobbled in the door of the massive suite she'd been pacing since the ten minutes it had taken her to sort the clothes out.

But, amazingly, he'd called and asked her to bring them down to the back entrance.

She couldn't decide whether it was a good thing or a bad thing. Passing her bag of supplies, she grabbed it for the splint and implements stashed inside, just in case it was a bad thing.

A short ride down, and she hurried to the back entrance.

A small part of her wanted to believe this request for the crutches was a positive thing. That he had decided that he should do what she wanted, and had given up on whatever macho idiocy that had him feigning invincibility.

When she stepped out the back, the limo was waiting. He hadn't even hobbled inside without them.

Liam sat sideways at the opened back door, pale and slouching, his tie undone and his shirt half-unbuttoned.

"Good grief, you look horrible."

"Thanks," he muttered, glancing down.

His look led hers and that overwhelming urge to shake him reared up again. "Oh, God, Liam. Did you try to chew through this tape?"

"It's cutting off circulation, which I would have thought would make it hurt less. But it doesn't!"

She propped the crutches against the side of the limo and dropped to her knees, glad she'd brought the bag. It took only a moment to locate her gauze scissors and she slipped the safety end under the tape to cut through what he'd managed to make impossible to remove any other way.

"Did you tape it like a puzzle on purpose?"

"Yes, actually. I taped it like a puzzle on purpose because that's the way you get the best support without cutting off circulation. Unless you hobble around on a badly sprained ankle despite medical advice, make it swell up and cut off circulation anyway."

Pitting edema. It had swollen so much that the scissors left a groove down his leg as she cut and tugged the tape away. "If you just keep going around and around with tape, it gets far too constricting. I taped it specifically to support an inverse sprain."

He grunted in response, but that sound became a low, pained hiss as she got the last of the wrapping off and blood rushed back into the skin.

It hurt when the blood got back into the area too.

She tilted her head to try and see the damage, but the low lighting didn't make that possible. Examination would have to wait. "Let me get the splint on."

"No!" He couldn't snatch his foot back from it, but he did lift it. "I'll use the crutches and hold my foot up. I won't put any weight on it. Just don't touch it until we're back upstairs."

"You don't mind if anyone sees it?"

"We'll go fast."

Grace shrugged, grabbed the debris and stuffed it into the hands of one of his assistants, handed the bag to another, and rose to help him up on the crutches. "Don't go fast. Go slowly. I've never seen anyone else come out this way, have you? It'll be fine."

Once inside, the light let her see just how pale he was. He almost looked like he'd been dusted with white powder, like an extra at King Louis IX's court.

She wouldn't nag. Wouldn't yell at him. She'd just get him upstairs, tie him up and refuse to let him go to New York tomorrow. Yeah, that was a plan.

The look he gave her as he leaned against the inside

of the elevator let her know that her yelling wouldn't
do any good anyway. He had the look of a man who'd
been converted. In fact, the labored breathing and shaky
hands said he'd probably have asked her for a wheelchair if there had been one in the suite.

By the time they got him upstairs, whatever civil
facade he'd been putting up crumbled and no sooner
had the door closed than he was announcing, "Everyone out. I need space."

Miles and crew turned right around, Hailey dropping
the bag she'd carried by the door on the way back out.

What did that mean for her? Should she go?

Grace stepped back and gestured to the bar. "I've
got ice waiting. Do you want me to help you get situated before I go?"

"You stay," he muttered, and continued through to
the bedroom, which was elevated by a few deeply carpeted steps.

With the way he shook, Grace didn't trust him to
navigate the steps on his own and scrambled along with
him, hands at his back, ready to grab and lower him to
the floor if he started to go.

"Stop. I'm fine."

"You're not fine. You're shaking hard enough for it
to measure on the Richter scale. And you were using
your foot for balance when it was splinted or wrapped.
Now you're just a walking tripod. And I know how to
control falls. I do it all the time. So shut up and take
the steps. I'm not going anywhere. Be glad I don't have
you by the belt. Yet."

He stopped at the foot of the steps and looked over
his shoulder, "Your hovering is going to make me fall.
Step off. If I fall, I fall. I'll roll the other way and protect my foot."

"No." She turned his head to face forward. "Looking back compromises balance. Move it, or I am going to do a fireman's lift and carry you up there, if for no other reason than to prove to you I'm not a delicate flower who can't help you."

"I'm just doing this to save your fool back. We can't both be laid up." Liam shook his head but took the steps as directed. Despite the bone-deep shaking in his frame, he got up them with ease and went to flop on the end of the bed. "You want to help me? Take off my pants."

Grace stopped in her tracks, her hands going to her hips as she regarded him. However pained and cranky he felt right now paled to the irate tilt of her head as she looked down at him. "Your hands work fine. Take off your own pants."

He unfastened them and then looked up at her, giving his best pitiful but harmless look. "Come on, Gracie. Don't make me stand up again. All I want to do is kick back, take some flavor of painkiller, eat, and sleep. And maybe ice it once it stops throbbing…"

"Fine. If you're going to play imbecile, I'll help you with your pants."

"Don't you mean invalid?"

"Nope, I'm pretty sure I meant imbecile. I went to the theater. Even with your limp it shouldn't have taken more than five minutes to make it the length of that stupid carpet, but I didn't leave here for forty-five minutes because Tom came by with clothes and made me try them on."

She hooked her fingers in the belt and tugged as he lifted with his good leg. He fell back on his elbows and watched her toss the trousers over her shoulder as she knelt to get a look at his foot. God, that thing hurt. If she touched it, he might cry like a baby. Maybe then she'd give him a little sympathy rather than her anger.

"Liam Jefferson Carter! What did you do?"

Uh-oh. The middle name had come out. She wasn't even going to pretend not to be furious.

One cool hand cupped his calf and lifted, contrasting with the fire in her eyes. "You know, I was thinking we might switch you to heat—ice is usually only for the first forty-eight hours after the injury, but it's worse now. That's why it hurts more, that's why it swelled despite the tape. Might as well be a new injury."

"I know," he muttered. "I'd actually say it hurts more right now than it did when I fell. So, congratulations, you were right. But you know I wasn't doing this just to be a pain in your butt. I have to, Grace. That's what this life is, if you're lucky enough to get this high, then your whole life is schedules and obligations, and when I sign a contract to do a movie I also sign on for the promotional aspects at the time of opening. It's contractual."

"And is it also contractual that you go in there without any support? You could have done this a lot better with crutches, Liam. Then you would still have met your obligations."

"No, I couldn't."

"Tell me why. Tell me exactly why, because…"

He lay back fully on the bed, pinching the bridge of his nose as if that would dispel his headache. The whole night had taken him to the end of his tether, so if she didn't get off this, he might kick her out with the others. Then he could sleep and let tomorrow worry about itself.

"Liam."

"I don't need a lecture. If you're going to keep after

this, then you maybe should just go to the other room. Or your own room."

"We didn't get me my own room. I've been here all the time." She straightened and leaned over the bed, looking down at him.

He couldn't deal with this right now. "Then we'll get you a room."

Just when he was about to scoot up the bed to reach the phone, she touched his face and stopped him.

That warmth again. She slid her hand to cup his cheek and his frustration all but left. And with it his ability to care whether or not he should enjoy her touch. It comforted him. It meant she still cared, and this wasn't just a job. She cared about him. And it felt good, he felt better.

Closing his eyes, he tilted his head into her hand and held it there with his own hand.

"Liam?"

"Shh. Just wait…" he said, not opening his eyes, just letting the warm strength of her hand soak into him.

Her thumb stroked his cheekbone in a soothing arc. "Tell me why it's so important. I need to understand this if we're going to keep working together. Because right now I know you're frustrated and in pain, and it isn't just hard to see you hurting yourself like this, it makes me feel ill. If you want me to stay, tell me why you have to do this."

He wanted her to stay. Hell, he wanted her to stay right there. Or maybe put his head in her lap and stroke his weary brow. That would be nice.

But staying was actually important for more reasons than his hedonist tendencies.

It wouldn't matter if he gave her what she'd asked

for. This was Grace, not someone who'd use the information against him.

"I'm starting another project in a few weeks—a part I've been dying for—and I don't want the producers to think that I am going to slow down production. It was between me and one other, right down to the wire, and they went my way. If I show up limping around now, they're going to reverse course." He opened his eyes and looked into hers, and then slid her hand from his cheek to his chest but kept holding it there. "We haven't even signed the contracts yet. It's all verbal agreements until there's a signature on the dotted line. And even then sometimes contracts can be broken."

"What's so special about this part?"

"It's a book…" With her hand in his and her eyes fixed on him, he could tell her why. Maybe not everything, just give her an idea. "Sit here with me." He patted the bed and transferred her hand to his other one so she could sit.

When she had, and turned her hand over to wrap her fingers around the edge of his palm in return, he took a breath to steel himself.

"Don't laugh."

She shook her head, squeezed his hand.

"Do you remember, well, your parents would just come home with little gifts sometimes?"

She nodded, still not speaking.

"The book was the first time… I'd been hanging out at your house pretty much every day for about six weeks, and then one night they came home from work and had stopped at a bookstore. Lucy got you some book you'd wanted—I don't remember what it was—but then she reached into the bag and pulled out two copies of another book, handed one to me and one to Nick."

"Mom liked to do that—still does that, actually. Now they're making that book into a movie and you want to be in it?"

She didn't get it, but he could see in her eyes that she was trying to.

He might be able to explain, but he couldn't do it while looking at her. Letting his gaze fall to where their hands joined in his lap, he tried again.

"It was the first time anyone ever gave me a gift for no reason. Birthday and Christmas presents were real hit-and-miss with my folks, depending on what they'd done with their money that week. It wasn't really about the book. I was just included, like I was an extra son who'd sprung up and was automatically accepted. So… it was the first time I had any idea of what it was like to be in a family."

When he looked back at her, her eyes were damp and she was silent, clearly working through what he'd told her, and the implications of it all.

"Plus, it's outside my usual roles, so it's kind of a big deal career-wise that I have this part, Gracie."

Lifting her free hand, she swiped her eyes quickly and nodded. "Okay." Accepted. "I'll do whatever I can to help you, but understand something for me?"

He turned just a little to look at her better but kept her hand in his.

"It doesn't just anger me that you're causing yourself more pain, but I'll try to ignore that as much as I can. I'll help you do what you need, but please take pity on me, and make all these things you have to do as easy on yourself as you can. No unnecessary walking. Put your foot up anytime you can."

"Come with me to the premieres tomorrow." He said the words before he'd really thought about the urge.

But the desire was real. He hadn't been at his best on the carpet tonight, and not just because of the ankle. He'd also kept wondering what she was doing. Just how angry she was with him.

"I thought that my coming with you to the premieres was what this was all about?"

"No," he said, letting go of her hand so he could move around her and his foot was propped up on the bed beside her. "Come as my date."

She opened her mouth to say no, and he held up a hand, energy coming from some unknown source to give his words some urgency. "Every time I've gone solo to a premiere or event, I end up doing way more walking around. Come with me. Be my date. Keep me with you and I won't do as much walking."

"I don't know. I don't have a gown or anything."

"Tom can fix it."

"It's late, he'd have to do some night shopping or very early morning. We're leaving at seven, right?"

"Yes, but he can do a lot from the plane. He's got numbers for both coasts. We'll go to New York and then take a short flight down and back from Virginia. He can have prospective gowns waiting for you. And whatever you need to help get you ready."

She didn't look convinced. The furrow in her brows could be doubt or worry. What would make her come around?

"You can be my walking stick. So I can lean against you a little and not put weight on my bad leg when we're not walking."

Her frown deepened. "Will you use a cane?"

"If I have you, I don't need…" Her look stopped him. "I'll carry a cane if Tom can find me something that could look like an accessory. And then I can use it if I need to."

The frown stuck and he caught her hand again, looking for any way to make it sound plausible. "You know, the movie is a historical. Gentlemen used canes. Maybe I could play it as a nod to the movie and theme."

"You just thought of that now?" Shaking her head, she pulled her hand free. "Where's your phone? I need to call Tom if we're going to do this."

He pulled off his jacket and handed it to her. "Inside breast pocket."

She hung the jacket on the back of a chair and retrieved the trousers she'd thrown on the floor. "Scoot up to the head of the bed. I'm going to talk to Miles about the travel stuff and call Tom. You order dinner—the phone is on the table."

He could do those things. Scooting up hurt, but he could do it.

She walked to the door, dialing as she went.

When he'd asked her to help him out, it had never occurred to him that she'd have to do so much for him, but it was like a godsend, having her here.

He hadn't thought about telling her about the project earlier. He knew it was silly and sentimental—there could never be resolution with all the dark parts of his childhood, even if the role felt like giving a gift to the child he'd been. A kind of resolution. His parents were dead and gone, so there couldn't be any peace from that corner, but David and Lucy had been the only real parental figures in his life.

And Grace…he could make things right with her. He could make their tentative friendship a real friendship again. Talk it out. Maybe it was time to talk it out now that she'd grown comfortable enough to yell at him. That had to be some kind of sign.

He just had to think about what to say, make sure that he planned it out and didn't do anything to make things worse between them.

Tomorrow. He'd think about it tomorrow. Tonight he'd eat, do whatever she told him to do, and tomorrow, when some of the pain had abated…

CHAPTER FIVE

"WHAT TIME ARE we taking off?" Liam asked, leaning back in his seat with the foot rest raised.

The private jet loaned to him by the studio had all the bells and whistles, and none of the executives—both of which he was thankful for. The circle of people in the know was already large enough between his crew, Grace, and Tom—who'd been sworn to secrecy about the ankle situation and seemed happy to go along with the ruse.

"We're supposed to take off in fifteen minutes." Miles's voice came from the seats behind where he and Grace sat.

Grace had the ice back on his foot, and she'd managed to get another couple of diuretics from James. Liam looked up at her. "Shouldn't I take one of those swelling pills again?"

"Not when you're flying," she said, settling into the seat beside him.

Despite the understanding they'd reached last night, she still didn't look happy with him or being there.

"Why not?"

"Being dehydrated on a flight increases the chances of a blood clot forming. Really, you should be drinking more water right now, especially since your mobility is lessened—you can't get up and walk around much, and you can't put weight on that ankle to flex the muscles well enough to—"

"But I'm not dehydrated right now. I'm just overly hydrated at the ankle. And our window between when we arrive and when we have to get ready is small."

"I know. We're doing the best we can."

"I'll risk it."

"No."

"Grace, it took three hours last time to get the swelling to go down."

"I know, but we'll just have to try and make it work. Maybe keeping your leg elevated on the flight will help it."

"It's not that elevated."

"You can lie on the floor after takeoff and put it on the seat again if you want to."

"It takes an hour to kick in. You want me to compromise on things? You have to compromise too, Grace."

Shouldn't she be happier with him now? She knew this wasn't just about ego.

"I will, when it's not life-threatening levels of dangerous." Her mouth said yes, but the shake of her head made him doubt she meant it. "Just relax for now. You have a long flight, and I know you didn't sleep well last night. Maybe you can sleep now that the worst of the pain has passed."

"I doubt it."

"Well, I have a way to pass the time if you're all done fighting," Tom, the middle-aged stylist, snapped at Grace, and pointed to the front of the plane. "I need a few pictures of you."

Grace made a face. "Liam sent you a picture yesterday and I'm here in person today. Have you deleted the picture already?"

"No, but that was one angle, and it was from behind. I was flying blind on what your chest was like until I met you last night."

"And now you've seen it."

"He saw your chest?" Liam asked, frowning dramatically, wanting to cajole her out of her glowering a little. "That hardly seems fair. I'm the one footing this shopping expedition."

"He didn't see-it see it." Grace made an annoyed sound, unbuckled her seat belt and went to stand where Tom had directed. She suffered through a series of photographs as he had her stand full front facing, then three-quarter profiles both left and right, and then again from the back, and three-quarters profile back…

By the time they got to the last couple of photos, her hands were on her hips and she repeatedly took deep, disgruntled breaths.

"You're very pretty to be so camera-averse," Tom mumbled, letting her off the hook with a gesture for her to go back to her seat.

"I don't even want to know why I did that," she muttered, buckling back in beside Liam.

"You're probably lucky he didn't have you strip down to…" The statement died in Liam's throat.

Since last night he'd been mentally working through ways to bring up that trench coat, but that was not the right way to do it. Especially here in front of everyone.

The hint of color creeping back into her cheeks confirmed that her thoughts had gone to the same place. He had to say something else to drag her out of it, so he went with the real explanation. "He's probably looking at gowns on his tablet and some books. He wants to see you in the right profile so he can easily picture how a dress would work for you."

"I guess." She reached for a magazine stashed on the wall beside her seat, shutting the conversation down.

But if that look she'd given him was anything to go by, he had an inkling how she was going to react. Not great, but maybe if he did this right, it wouldn't be so bad.

"Body frame is very important when it comes to the style of a gown," Tom confirmed.

Just another reason he didn't want to talk about this all here. The small cabin made it possible for everyone to hear every word. They didn't need all their issues on display, this uneasy alliance was already juicy enough.

But he didn't want to dance around the subject anymore. She didn't need to know all the gritty details but he could apologize. Tell her it wasn't a reflection on her that he had sent her away. Remind her about the loyalty and kinship he felt to her family that kept him from considering her as anything other than a friend. She didn't need to know the other reasons, the ones that made up the bulk of his present resistance.

So he'd tell a lie. But a white lie. A lie he wished was true. The loyalty part was there, but it still didn't help him not consider her as anything other than a friend. He considered, he considered so much that sometimes he even got confused about who they actually were. It just wasn't a situation he could pursue.

He'd spent years thinking of the incident in the only way he could minimize it: she'd been embarrassed but had then probably put it from her mind and moved on. Thinking about it any other way left him angry with nothing to fight against.

Twenty-four hours in her presence had brought a few

other revelations he might never have come to on his own without seeing her again.

This mess wasn't about her feeling humiliated because they'd both wanted each other but couldn't go there.

She thought she'd been alone in that desire, and that's what hurt her. If that were the case, it meant she hadn't been smart enough to read him right. It labeled her dumb, clueless, or cocky that she knew but didn't care how he felt about the matter. Mostly, in every incarnation of the situation where she felt alone in the desire, there was no making it better.

He'd have to tell her that he'd wanted to drag her to bed and that even now, years later, it had been the sexiest night of his life.

Then tell her that nothing could happen because of his loyalty to her family. If they were both shutting down the attraction with good reasons that had nothing to do with desirability, that might take the edge off the situation for her. It would help him were the situations reversed.

Last night's conversation about the book had been way too revealing for his peace of mind, but maybe that reason was something she'd accept now. He just had to come up with some way to make this all right.

There were very few good things about never pursuing real, lasting relationships—but the one thing he would change right now was not having the tools to instantly know how to fix this. All he really knew was that he had to try.

When they were alone.

The pilot's voice broke into his thoughts, announcing their clearance for takeoff. He had five hours to come up with the right words. And three hours to start hounding her for that other swelling pill.

"The wrap is getting looser," Liam said, gesturing to the foot he still had propped up on pillows piled atop the footrest.

The jet had just landed, and they were currently taxiing away from the runway.

She stashed the last magazine back in the rack and leaned over to look at his foot. "The pill is working already."

"Oh, it's working..." he murmured, doing his best not to give her anything else to be angry about. All this nonsense, as she referred to it, didn't make him happy either. He was getting his way, kind of, but it was hitting home that his way was stupid.

"I hope it means that some of the bruising is dissipating. Seems like that might make sense, there's blood pooled there, and fluid is being whisked away by a medicine. Maybe it will take some blood with it. I really don't know if it works that way, but it would be nice if it did. Might take some of the soreness," she said, then turned in her seat to look at Tom. "Did you find a good cane for him to use and pretend is just for show?"

"I did. I have a friend in antiques, he called around and found something nice and the right length. It has a sword hidden in it."

"So, if we're set upon by bandits, I can defend you." Liam smiled at her. She might not be trying to talk him out of his plan at every turn now, or telling him that it was stupid, but their conversation definitely hadn't diminished her surliness over the situation.

"I think it's more likely that if we're set upon by

bandits, they'll be aiming to kidnap you. Ransom you for shiny baubles."

And she was grumpier the closer it got to the premiere.

"Is there any way you can do the carpet prowl thing and then come back here and skip the actual movie?"

"We'll skip the early movie in Virginia, go strictly red carpet, then fly back to New York," he answered quickly, then redirected her attention back to his ankle and away from worrying about tonight. "The bandage is loose enough to feel irrelevant. Think you could wrap it again before we disembark?"

She leaned over to look out the window. "I guess there's no flight attendant to tell me to stay buckled in until we get to the gate. So, sure."

She unbuckled to head for the other side of his seat. He watched her flick the tape off and then unwrap the loose dressing. "How does it look? Think you can still tape it like before?"

"It doesn't matter if I should or not, but if the swelling continues to abate, we'll tape it. I'd be happier if it were also in the splint."

"I think my ankle feels a little better." He changed the subject to something that he hoped would ease her. She hadn't smiled the whole trip. Even when he'd assured her that it certainly felt better than last night.

It made him feel better at least. Reviews had come out that morning before the flight, and those had made him feel good too. Good enough that even if his ankle was hurting, he'd make the premieres.

The cane would help.

Having her there would help.

Two separate walks would not help, but it had started

to look possible that his foot wouldn't actually fall off and leave him with that bloody stump.

Now, if he could get any clarity on the trench-coat situation...

Liam's ringing phone echoed inside the back of the car sent to fetch them on the tarmac. Miles sat in the front with the driver, leaving Hailey and Dexter behind to get the luggage from the jet and catch up, and Grace all alone with the Sexiest Man Alive.

"You just turned it on. Does it send a homing signal for people to call you when you turn it on?" she asked. As soon as the words were out of her mouth she regretted them. Her mood had to improve. How many women would kill to be Liam Carter's red-carpet date? But every time he looked at her she felt like he was going to bring up that night. He hadn't, thank goodness, and he'd given her no real indication that he wanted to. Every instance when something had been said that might lead into that conversation, he'd changed the subject too.

She should relax.

"I think so."

He answered the phone and began talking. Reviews. Good reviews. Or what she'd call great, at least the ones she'd seen before they'd got into the air. And she had seen no mentions of his limp. So maybe he was right. Maybe she only noticed because it was her job to notice.

Tonight was the last night that he'd have to be on that ankle, and then tomorrow she'd get to go home, only see him at the clinic for treatment, and soon enough that would be over too. She'd get her quiet life back.

Today it was easier to look at him. Something had

transpired between them last night when he'd held her hand to his cheek and made his soft confessions.

The king-sized bed in his hotel suite would have comfortably slept them both, without either of them ever touching one another or even realizing that they'd been sharing a bed probably, but it was a move that Grace hadn't been able to accept.

Even though he'd offered.

Even though she'd slept on the couch and had got up every two hours for twenty minutes to wake him and ice his ankle.

Staring was bad. She forced herself to look back out the window. It was safer.

Even though she'd undressed him. Actually, the undressing was probably a big part of why she said no. Yes, he had been in his underwear in front of her, and that was similar to the outfit she'd worn at the scene of the Big Rejection. But things had been different. He was confident in his body, because... Damn. They had him shirtless in every movie for a reason, and it wasn't to display the dramatic black tattoo wrapping around one shoulder and crawling down the arm.

She became aware that the pitch of his voice had changed, and then began actually listening to the conversation. "Yes. I have an injury, but it's really not that big a deal. I twisted my ankle the other day on a run. It's..."

He paused and listened. When she made eye contact, his scowl communicated enough: she was wrong. They cared. They cared a lot.

"Is that your agent?" she whispered.

He nodded, mouthed, "Conference call."

So it was more than his agent. He squirmed in the seat, trying to find a more comfortable position. This car was much smaller than the one they'd used in LA. He could put his leg up, but he'd have to drape it across her lap.

Which might be uncomfortable for her, but it was better than him having it down, undoing all the good work the diuretic was trying to do. She waited to catch his eye and patted her lap, and whispered, "Put it up."

"I have my physical therapist with me. Actually, she's making me put my foot up right now, and she has been icing it and giving me the necessary medications since yesterday." As he spoke, he swiveled and put his leg across her lap. "You don't need to speak with her. I can answer your questions."

Why wouldn't he want her to talk to them?

A small argument ensued and he held the phone out, his expression grave. "Craig wants to talk to you."

"Is that your agent?"

"Yes."

"Who else is it?"

He listed several names and their importance, producer, director, blah-blah-blah.

She took the phone and answered questions. Who was she? Where did she work? What were her qualifications? It was like going to an interview for a job you already had, but once they got through the litany of questions they topped it with, "What's the diagnosis and prognosis for Carter's recovery?"

"He's got an inversion sprain. It's not the worst or the best one I've ever seen. It will heal and it's unlikely that he'll have much trouble with it in the future. We'll be starting actual therapy in a couple of days, once we're back in LA. Right now, I'm taping him and keeping him mobile."

* * *

Liam didn't watch her speaking. She sounded confident but, then, she was a pretty together person. She was also the only person, besides him, as bothered by the amount of stress he was putting the injured joint through.

Would it be better if he could hear their questions or worse?

"Yes. We'll return to The Hollywood Hills Clinic and start his physical therapy in a couple of days in the pool so he can start working on motion and strengthening without the need to bear weight.

"In three months? I doubt there will be lingering effects, but in three months, if he's having trouble, it would be as simple as taping the ankle before he does anything that might make it roll out. There are some pre-sized tape kits that come with two to three wide, sticky strips, and, when they are placed appropriately, entirely concealable.

"Yes. Colored and those that are a medium tan color, which would blend in with his skin tone. But I expect if you really wanted to conceal them, your effects people could do a light airbrush to… Yes. Yes. He'll be on the carpet tonight. I'm going with him and he's using some support in the form of a camouflage cane." She sighed. "No, it's not got a camouflage pattern. It's there to look useless but be useful."

"A prop," he whispered.

"A prop," she dutifully repeated.

There was another break in her answering questions directly related to him, where she listed several athletes she'd worked with and fished her phone out of her bag to thumb through it. "If it will make you feel better, I can provide references. Aside from Dr. Rothsberg, I can put in a call to former clients and have them call you if you need it."

Another moment and she hung the phone up and handed it to him. "You owe me. They know, they are convinced it's no big deal, and you can use your crutch at the premiere."

"Cane." He took the phone back, correcting her lest she get more ideas. She'd just told them cane, and if he showed up on crutches now, they'd need more reassurance. "Why didn't you tell them I'm the worst patient you've ever had?"

"Because you're not. You're just the worst one that I cared enough about to yell at."

Two minutes, that's what she'd said five minutes ago.

Liam leaned against the wall beside the elevator, all his weight shifted to his good leg.

This was the other thing that happened whenever he took a date to a premiere: waiting.

Just when he was about to send Miles after her, the door to the room adjoining his opened and Grace stepped out.

Or backed out.

There was some jostling of material and some muttering, which dispelled any doubts about who was in the gown, if he'd had any.

Pink? Flesh? Sparkly…silvery beige? What color was that thing?

When the gowns had shown up two hours ago, Liam hadn't even looked at them, just sent Tom to Grace with the garment bags and boxes of shoes.

"Are you going to come with me, Gracie?" he called. "Or are you going to stand there muttering at your skirt for the evening?"

She moved, shifting from the low light of her doorway into a halo of golden light from above, looking over her shoulder toward him as she did. The back was modest by most standards, bare shoulders and supple golden skin to the mid-back. Sexy. Understated.

Her eyes found his, deep and full of contradictions. Worry. Sweetness. Promises he had no business even considering.

Liam's heart stopped in his chest and then launched into a fast, skittering beat.

Gathering the front of her dress, she turned fully and let it fall, hitting him with the full effect.

Beautiful women in glamorous gowns were like Tuesdays in Liam's life. But he'd never seen anything like this.

"We have to go, Miss Watson," Miles called. Herding Liam toward his obligations was part of his job but even with his ankle aching he didn't want to hurry her. He wanted to look at her. Far away. Close-up. All the steps in between.

She still hadn't smiled at him, and he wanted it. The grumpiness plaguing her had been replaced by nervousness. She'd turned her lips in and chewed at the inside. He could act the fool, say something cute and meaningless, but…that wasn't the right kind of smile. Not amusement. Happiness. He wanted her to smile at him because being there with him made her happy, everything else aside.

"Of course. Sorry." She reached toward Tom, and a small flat handbag of some kind was passed to her, but as she began moving toward Liam it was a conscious effort to square the knowledge that this was Grace with the Gracie he knew.

She'd always been the girl next door. Pretty. Wholesome. Quietly unattainable. And he'd always wished he could attain her. Even during the time that he'd done his best to put her from his mind and had got on with living, anytime he'd seen that shade of sun-kissed light brown hair he'd thought of her. Every time he'd spoken to his best friend he'd thought of her, even if just to remind himself not to ask about her. He'd told himself she'd never fit into his world...but the truth was something else entirely. He was the misshapen one here.

But in that dress she was the best of Old Hollywood—flowing lines and glittering, silken elegance.

Her light brown wavy tresses had been braided somehow around her head, so the blonde highlights stood out. A style she could wear to the beach or on a picnic... He could imagine her poking daisies into the woven crown. More sweetness, and at odds with the gown and the glittering jewelry, but somehow on Grace it worked. This was how Grace would fit into his world, taking the best parts from both.

As she got closer, he felt an overwhelming desire to straighten. Stand taller. Say something to let her know, make sure she knew... If this were a movie, a writer would have given him a great line, something that would let her know just how gorgeous she was.

"You look..." He paused, completely at a loss. Oh, was he in so much trouble...

"Do my scars show?"

"Scars?" The word fit nowhere in his mind right now. "What scars?"

She held up one of her arms and turned it so that he could see the inside.

The pain in his ankle faded as he stepped forward, tucking the cane under his arm, and reached for her elbow so he could angle her toward the light better.

A blast of cold shot into his chest as his eyes found what she referred to. A thin puckered line led from the inside of her arm back, around her triceps.

Suddenly, his hands were the ones shaking. It had come from a large injury of some kind, or had it been a surgery? Something big enough he should've damned well known. "What the hell is that from?"

"You're going to get makeup on your hands. I don't want you to have tan handprints on your tux. Believe me, makeup stands out on black material about as badly as it does on white."

"It won't smudge," Tom said from behind her, interrupting Liam's questioning.

And she'd said scars. Not scar. "There are more?"

"Other arm too, but the rest are covered. Dress…"

More? He peeled his hands off her before he lost control, and took a step backward, still not using the cane but putting her outside of the reach of his hands so he didn't shake her until she answered him.

"What happened? What happened to give you scars?"

"They're from my accident."

"What accident?"

The elevator doors opened with a ding and Miles interrupted them. "The car is here, Liam. If we don't go down now, it's going to cut into your carpet time."

Confusion flashed in her eyes, and behind it regret. He didn't know about her accident. She might as well have said the words for how clearly he could read it in her expression. Another reminder of their time apart. Or was it memories of this accident when he hadn't come to visit her as she'd recovered?

Stepping toward him, she pulled his cane from under his arm and put it into the appropriate hand. "We'll talk about it later. Don't want to be late, right? We'd better go before you have to do something sensible like spend less time walking on your injured ankle."

A moment later the elevator whisked them downward, leaving him with too many questions to think about. But she was right. If they didn't go now, he'd have to move faster than his ankle would appreciate. Something else to talk about at dinner.

"Do I match you?"

"Match?"

He shuffled a little back so he could see her again.

"Like complement? Does my dress complement your tux? It's got kind of an old-fashioned cut…"

"It's made to look like something from the era." He confirmed the cut of his tux, but the nervous light that had replaced the regret in her eyes made him add, "I think it does, but really anything complements a black tie." Her nervousness redirected his teeth-gritting focus. "Besides, I'm pretty sure I'm the one complementing you tonight."

"No," she said, reaching up to smooth his jacket at the shoulders and down the sleeves. "That's silly. You're the star of the movie, which I'm looking forward to seeing." She stopped smoothing, her hand resting on his chest where she'd fluffed the silk kerchief in his pocket. "Are you sure you're up to this?"

Fretting. Fussing. Focusing attention away from herself. Away from the scars…which he hadn't even assured her barely showed. Later. He couldn't bring them up again right now.

"I'm up to it." He'd keep her hand resting on his chest all evening, keep her there in that small space in front of him, looking up in that way that made him feel…something he didn't want to feel. Possessive. And destructive.

But he recognized his chance to start evening things

out between them. "Even if I wasn't up to it, I'd be up to it...just to have you on my arm tonight."

For a moment the worry disappeared from her eyes, a kind of wonder replacing it.

Those were good words. Maybe not the perfect thing to say but it was close.

He shifted her hand from his chest to his elbow as the elevator stopped and opened on the ground floor, then planted the cane and used it to lead her out.

As they walked, she was still looking up at him, the wonder turning to shock. They passed through the lobby of red marble and dark walnut, and when they made it to the car she still looked shocked. He lifted a finger to her chin. "You're beautiful, Grace."

The urge to kiss her nearly overwhelmed him. If she were his, he would've.

Instead, he closed her mouth and let his hand fall to the small of her back to steer her into the car.

Did no one ever tell this golden angel how magnificent she was?

God help him, he was in so much trouble.

CHAPTER SIX

ON THE FLIGHT down to Virginia, Grace once more had Liam with his foot propped up, shoe off and a cold pack placed over those injured ligaments.

It seemed she'd no sooner settled herself in her dress than they were out of the plane and in a limo.

It all happened so fast. They stopped at the curbside where the carpet started, and when Liam had his cane in position and her on his other arm, he moved her forward.

People, screaming and cheering, lined both sides. Flashes came from all directions. A quaint refurbished theater with gilded fixtures on tall, heavy doors awaited them after a blessedly short carpet walk. Liam shook hands as they went, posed for pictures, took a couple selfies with a fan, then a number of group selfies with cameras Grace funneled toward him and then back to the crowd.

And then they were inside the theater, a manager leading them through to a back exit where the limo waited.

Grace couldn't swear she'd even taken a single breath before it was all over and they were back at the airport, with her once more settling a cold pack on his ankle.

"You all right?" Liam asked.

When she looked at him, he nodded to the seat beside him. "They want us buckled in so we can get back into the air."

"Right. Right..." She gathered her dress as best she could to prevent wrinkling, and sat down.

"You look shell-shocked, Gracie. Want something to drink?"

"No. I'm fine. I just... That was... A lot."

"Not to scare you but that was small. The next one will be much bigger. But it was overwhelming to you because it was your first. That's over. You've done it now, and we won't be in such a rush to get through the next one. Just lean back and breathe."

Breathe. She didn't really have anything to do but make sure Liam didn't walk all over the place. And she was very good at walking.

"Do you always go from one right to another one?" Grace asked Liam, sitting by the door in the back of the limo as it spirited them through crowded evening streets toward the New York theater.

"It's not unheard of, but not usually. We were on location in Virginia for three months, and the film was based on a book written by a local author, who's like a hometown hero to them. So that's why it was scheduled."

"I get that," she said, "But why have two on one day?"

"Sometimes they hold the theater launch back until after the premiere. Though it's pretty common to have more than one, and they don't want to hold the film any longer than necessary. It's all decided by the marketing people for best impact. I just go where they tell me."

He scooted a little closer and wrapped his arm around her shoulders, pulling her against him. "You thought it was all fancy parties where everyone stood around telling each other how amazing they looked, and drinking too much."

"Actually, I thought you all got dressed up, but then behaved like it was a frat party, with gobs of public nudity and body shots," she filled in, grinning at him. His heat felt good at her side. It was still summer, and the Virginia carpet had been hot, but the air-conditioning on both the jet and in the cars had been high enough to chill her.

Liam looked at her, the fondness in his eyes cutting through some of the chill too. Enough that she didn't know how to respond again. He'd done that to her earlier too, when he'd said she was beautiful.

"Why are you looking like that?" she asked, needing him to stop before he confused her again.

Not that he stopped, he just smiled too. "Because you finally smiled."

"Didn't I smile enough in Virginia?"

"You did. But you weren't smiling at me until now."

She felt her cheeks going pink and forced herself to look down. He'd said she was beautiful earlier, and now he'd looked at her like she was sunshine. In one day. What her earlier self would've given to hear those sweet words from him.

Even so, she couldn't keep the smile from her face right now, though she tried to edge back to the earlier subject. "My real mental image was that it was all about the after-party with champagne and wild behavior. If it is, I'd like you to keep that from me. I much prefer this, even if I'm really tired of posing for pictures."

He let her get back to it without doing anything else that might make her emotions go haywire. "We're skipping the after-party."

"Oh, thank God." That would be less time in the dress and less time with him on that foot.

"This time it will start the second we step out of the car. Hope your cheeks aren't too sore from the last round."

Half a block in front of them crowds had gathered, and police stood in front of barricades, directing traffic—regular traffic in one direction, and them another.

They'd just done this a couple hours ago, but he'd been sitting still since then. And when you did that with an injury... "Remember to use the cane more when you first put your weight on the leg. It's been resting for a while, so that pain is going to scream through your leg when you first—"

"I know. I've figured that part out." His hand moved to cup her bare shoulder, the pad of his thumb stroking the front curve.

The car stopped and her stomach lurched with it.

"You've already done this once," he said, obviously picking up on her discomfort. "You're the belle of the ball, Grace. Just remember to smile."

The door opened and she had to make herself move. "I'm the belle of the ball," she whispered to herself as she accepted a hand out from the man who'd opened the door. "Thank you." She stepped to the side, reminding herself to smile as she made room for Liam.

As soon as his handsome head appeared above the door, so many flashes went off that as she turned to look at him and check his balance, all she could see were spots in her vision.

"I'm okay, Grace," he said, before she could ask, then slipped his hand into hers and steered her around the door so they could make the walk. "Just follow my lead. Stop when I stop. Pose and smile. Just like before.

Only with more stops this time. We'll also make a wide zig-zag path down the carpet."

"How many zigs?" She stopped when he did and turned slightly toward him, her heel butting against the center of the other foot, just like Tom had told her to stand.

Pause. Smile. Walk.

"I don't know. Ten."

"Two," she countered. "The more you zig, the more you walk. You said I was here to keep you from having to walk too much. Otherwise why am I wearing this dress?"

"Because you're my date, and you have to wear clothes to a premiere, no matter what your freewheeling California inclinations say. Hippy."

She laughed despite herself. "Idiot." But his joking made her relax. "I'm willing to up to four zigs. Any more than that and I'm going to take your cane and start clubbing your fans so that they stay back."

"Five."

They were moving again slowly, with him waving, as they headed for the first point of the zig.

"Fine, but only because an odd number would flow better toward the door with you going in this direction first." She quieted down as he approached the edge.

Once again, pieces of paper, magazines, pictures… things were thrust at Liam, and he dutifully signed and shook hands.

Every time he was ready to walk again she joined him and they made their way back to the other side, pausing for photos along the way, and once to speak with a camera crew who called to him for an interview.

Why was he using a cane?
Who was his date?

Was she the reason he'd broken up with Simone Andre?

Though she saw a tic in his jaw with the last question, Liam answered everything politely. Sprained ankle. Grace Watson. No. He'd begged Grace to come with him last night, and she'd miraculously been available.

At the last leg of the carpet, a very little boy at the front asked about the cane. Even though Liam had given this answer at least thirty times since that first crew had asked, he stopped in front of the boy and shifted his weight to the good leg so he could pinch the pants leg and lift it, showing the expanse of white tape poking up above his sock. "I fell down when I was running."

"Does it hurt?"

"Oh, it hurts, but I wanted to come and have fun here tonight with everyone. Plus, they gave me a cane to use and it's got a sword in it." He pulled the handle up to give the boy a peek of the blade. "I couldn't pass up a chance to use a sword cane."

And he actually had been using the cane, and not just as a cool prop. Why he'd ever been upset to begin with still didn't compute with her.

There was some gasping over the awesome sword cane, the boy lifting his own pants leg to show Liam his bandaged knee.

As much as she wanted to usher him right off into the theater and make him sit, make him take the weight off it, there was no way she'd interrupt wound comparisons and "I fell too" stories.

By the time she thought her face would split from smiling, the little guy's mother opened her bag and after some digging produced and unwrapped a colorful bandage.

She watched as Liam lifted his cuff and the little boy crawled beneath the velvet rope to pull Liam's sock down and place the bandage right over the bump of his taped ankle, a cartoon character bandage in an expanse of white tape.

Her heart squeezed as she watched. He might complain about how crowds drained him, but he loved it too. He was so sweet to the boy she had to look away briefly to banish sappy tears.

He fought to be at all these events, and it wasn't just because he wanted his career to continue being wildly successful—although, of course, that had to factor in. It was something more.

He posed for pictures with the boy this time, and their matching bandages, then made it the last few steps into the theater.

"Let's find where we're sitting. I need to sit."

"Of course you do. It still took forty-five minutes to make it into the building."

"And that was fast, Grace. I've spent two hours out there before." He leaned on the cane heavily and gestured for an usher. Soon they were being led to a small balcony to sit down. "Will we have people here with us?"

He nodded and then proceeded to name names—all of which she'd heard before, and none of whom she'd met.

Before they got there, she leaned forward in her seat to look at his leg. The tape looked tight but not tight enough to cut off circulation. She pulled the sock up for him, and set it all to rights. "Will there be any empty seats?"

He did a quick seat count and then shook his head. "Probably not."

"Can we get a footstool brought up?"

"Oh, that we might be able to do," he said, and then looked at her long enough to demand her attention. "You're always concerned about my leg and pain level."

"Of course I am."

"Because you know how it is to have an injury?"

There was an edge to his voice, prompting her to make eye contact again in the low light of the theater.

"I'd like to think that I'd still care without that painful time in my past."

"How did you get hurt?" He didn't sound angry, as he had in the hotel, but there was more emotion in his voice than she'd expect from someone who'd stayed away so effectively. And who hadn't felt the same way about her as she'd felt about him.

Even if she'd avoided asking about Liam, she'd always thought he'd probably still kept up with her through Nick. Nick was a talker, and he had spent a lot of time in the hospital with her while she'd recovered. "Nick really didn't tell you about my accident? I thought you two told one another everything."

"No. He never did. Which is pretty weird…"

Yes. Weird. Unless Nick knew about them. "I had a motorcycle accident when I was nineteen."

"I never heard about you having a motorcycle either."

"I didn't. My boyfriend at the time… It was his motorcycle. After that, I had a lot of rehab. But it pretty much scratched professional swimmer off my career list. So I'm doing the next best thing."

He made some sound of affirmation, but it didn't sound settled.

Liam leaving had made her reckless, always seeking out the bad boy. That particular bad boy had made her go to the other extreme. Which made this premiere business so out of character for her that it could've been a joke. If someone had said to her last week that she'd be glittering from head to toe at a New York City premiere she'd have definitely thought it was some kind of joke where her dullness was the punch line. Because her life had been dull, probably. Other people would find the clientele exciting, and sometimes she did, but it was hard to be impressed by celebrities when she'd known Liam as long as she had. He was a real person, and that made them all too real and flawed as well.

Maybe they were all wounded too. Maybe it took that kind of hurt to get someone from talented to artist.

"I'm going to go find the usher," she said, mostly because she didn't know what else to say. "See if we can get that footstool."

Before her musings moved onto lamentations of what she couldn't have.

"The movie was good," Grace said, shifting in the back seat of the limo, not sure of where or even how to sit now that their charade of a date was over. "You were good. Not that I expected anything different. But all those period costumes, I loved it. It felt like a real story. Not just all the flash-bang stuff that goes on in your action movies."

For the entire evening she'd been pretty much plastered to Liam's side, and now, sitting with space around her, she felt cold. And lonely. Making useless small talk also felt awkward.

"Grace Watson, are you saying you don't like my action movies?" Unlike earlier, Liam had taken a spot up by the door, his legs stretched out in front of him.

"Still playful, that's good. I guess your ankle isn't hurting as much as last night?"

"You did not answer the question but you're correct, it's not hurting as badly as last night."

She crossed her arms and lifted her brows, giving him her best told-you-so expression.

Liam crossed his arms in response. "You want me to say it?"

"I do. It's a personal failing, I know, but yes. Yes, I want you to say it." She knew she looked smug, that was the whole point of the told-you-so expression.

"You were right. I should have listened to you all along, but then I would never have gotten to have the prettiest date tonight."

She snorted. The first couple of times he'd said it she'd been too dazed to really process the words.

"You know, the more you say it, the less I believe it." They passed a building she hadn't seen on the way to the theater and she stopped to get a good look at the direction in which they were traveling. "This isn't the way to the hotel. Are we going to the airport or something?"

"No, we're going to dinner."

"You want me to be right some more? You need that thing up and iced—it's been hours."

"I need to eat too if I'm going to take one of those blessed pain-reducers, don't I?"

"Yes, and it's called room service."

"I don't want room service. I want to eat at my favorite restaurant in New York, with my date."

She didn't say anything. Arguing with the man had done no good in anything they'd butted heads over so far. He'd only agreed to the cane after he'd proved her case for her. "How about we get it to go?"

"No. We're going to go in, sit at the quiet booth I've reserved, and if you want me to I will sling my leg up in the bench beside me to have it elevated. We can eat good food and relax with no responsibilities hanging over our heads. No one asking for interviews, or pictures. Have a little wine. Can I have wine with those pills?"

"No. I know I say that a lot, but you always want a little bit more, don't you? I want to go to dinner. I want to eat where I want to eat. I want to have pain pills and wine." She shook her head, but the tension she'd been feeling had already started to drain away. Probably had started the moment that he'd agreed to use the cane. It made it easier to tease him back. "How did you stay alive this long? Luck? Your looks?"

"Yep." He reached over, wiggled an arm behind her around her waist, and slid her over to him. "Fate lets me get by with stuff because I'm too pretty to smite."

She laughed even though she knew it just egged the fool on. "So that's why Fate sent me. I'm immune to your prettiness."

The car rolled to a stop and the doorman came to open their door. "You just adore me for my winning personality? Or is it my body? I feel so cheap."

And yet he grabbed his cane and got out of the car, stepped to the side and offered her a hand.

"This is not a date," she said, taking the offered hand if for no other reason than civility—even if she was currently ignoring the fact that navigating car doors in this dress wasn't really in her usual skill set. "And no wine. Or I'm going to whine."

"Fine, fine. No wine. But I'm eating red meat and you can't stop me." He passed her hand through the crook of his elbow and led the way inside. "I come here whenever I'm in New York, they have a couple of great private booths. And if you want, I'm sure they'll even bring out a bag of crushed ice. Which I will use, in the interests of making my date happy."

"This is not a date." Grace repeated herself, this time more quietly as they wandered through the restaurant to the promised private back corner booth.

"Okay," he whispered back. "In the interests of making happy the lovely creature who went to the movies with me, and who is now going to eat with me, I will ask for ice."

They stopped at the booth and Liam sat on the side that would allow him to kick his leg up on the seat like the heathen he'd better well be if he wanted her to eat dinner with him.

Grace took the other side, and resisted the urge to ask for the ice. He'd said he would do it.

Knowing better than to test her on this—or at least she liked to think that was the reason—he dragged his foot up onto the seat and winked at her.

Menus were place before them and a bottle of the vintage Liam preferred presented to him. "No wine tonight. Water. Iced tea maybe?" He looked at Grace.

"Just water for me." She looked at the menu, but the prospect of reading words seemed too much for her. "My feminist core is shrieking, but I don't want to order. Can I just have whatever you're having? I don't think I have any room in my head to make any decisions right now."

"It's harder than it seems, eh?" he asked.

"The stop and pose, stop and smile, stop and shake hands, stop and sign things, stop and chitchat route to the movie?"

"It was better tonight. It's always better with someone there but, you know, as much as we've avoided one another for the past several years, it's been really great to have you here, Grace. I hope that's all right for me to say."

She smiled, looking down as she did so, and nod-ded. "You too. When you're not being infuriating. I forgot how much of a playful charmer you can be. All I've really seen is Actor Man, he of the thousand faces, since... You know."

She cut that thought off sharply, and scrambled for something else to say. She wouldn't bring that subject up now. Their forty-eight hours together were almost done. From tomorrow on they could see one another once a day, she'd go back to her less glittery existence, and he'd stay out in the limelight, adored by millions.

"The little boy..."

"Brody." He said the name she'd missed.

"You asked his name?"

"He offered it. Brody, the budding physical thera-pist." He lifted his pants leg and showed off the color-ful bandage still plastered to his taped ankle.

"You were really great with him. As much as you say that this stuff drains you, it doesn't show. It didn't show. It only showed last night because of the limping, I think, otherwise no one would've known."

"I like kids. I don't really remember ever being that age. I mean, I remember being in kindergarten and, you know, young grades, but my life was..."

Bad. She knew his childhood had been really hard. She had always known that his mother had died from an overdose, but she just didn't know any real details. Before he'd told her about the book. That had cleared up all her confusion in a way that gave absolutely no other details. It had hurt him to even tell her that much, and it had hurt to hear it. She didn't want him to have to go through anything else like that tonight.

"Complicated," she offered quickly, giving him an

out in case he, too, wanted to avoid dissecting painful memories.

If she had her way, she'd know every single part of him, from his past, to the way he thought, to all his future plans... But it really wasn't her right to ask any probing personal questions. No matter how nice they both agreed it had been to be around each other again, he wasn't going to be around that long. Once he was back on his feet, her usefulness would be at an end.

"Complicated." Liam echoed the word. His childhood wasn't high on his list of things to talk about tonight. The waiter arrived and he tried to think of the least drippy foods to order, and shifted conversation on.

His list of things to talk about really only had two items: that night and that trench coat.

But that felt like an after-dinner conversation. So he steered them back toward small talk, safe and focused on subjects that would make her feel comfortable.

Memories they'd shared after Liam had been placed in foster care near the Watsons' home, and how he'd befriended Nick.

How she'd ended up at The Hollywood Hills Clinic.

Why she'd left professional sports.

Things he'd never let himself know about her, even when he'd wanted to know.

"I saw you once at a game," he said, as their dinner plates were taken away. "You were working on one of the players' knees. You want dessert? I want dessert."

The dessert he wanted definitely wasn't on the menu, but in the interest of sublimating his carnal desires...

"I don't think I need one."

"Split one. They have this chocolate cake thing with fruit that's really good." He ordered one and then took the ice off his ankle, sat up straighter, and slid toward her in the booth.

"If you don't want to eat it, just take one bite and I'll pretend we split it equally."

"I could move over there to you so you could keep your foot elevated."

"It's okay. We're not going to be here much longer anyway. And I think that those pain tablets are kicking in."

With a nod, Grace went about clearing a spot between them, shifting water bottles and cutlery as needed. Keeping busy.

"Grace, I need to talk about—"

Before he even got the words out her perennially straight posture went rigid, and beneath that California glow he could see her cheeks pinking up.

She still didn't want to talk about it.

"It's not what you think." He caught her hand before she could tidy any more and dragged it to his lap in the hopes that her attention followed.

"Oh, I'm sure it is."

"The thing is—and this is pretty selfish of me—I need things to be good between us. And be honest. You don't really owe it to me to listen to my explanations…"

"You really have nothing to explain." This time, catching her hand didn't settle her down and her voice rose a little as she looked everywhere but at him. "I don't blame you. I'm not mad. It was all my fault. You didn't do anything wrong. I put you into an unwinnable situation because I was young and stupid. Inexperienced in reading people's intentions…"

"Grace?"

"You've become really good at it, not that I blame you. How else are you going to keep out of those kinds

of situations, especially now that you're on the Freebie
List of at least seventy percent of the married women
in North America, and probably a significant number
of women abroad?"

"Stop."

"Barring sexual preferences, of course. Oh, then
probably men too. I just couldn't even ballpark a figure on that one."

"Grace, I wanted you," he blurted out, his heart suddenly thundering in his ears, and his confession probably carried halfway across the restaurant. The waiter
arrived right then and wordlessly placed the plate between them, then placed the silverware and left.

Grace rolled the hand that he held, not pulling away
but as if she couldn't dispel the tension in her body unless she moved something.

"Take a bite of this thing. Strawberry. Chocolate
brownie thing. Cream. Get all of it. One big bite." He
kept her hand, and she still didn't pull away, but she
also didn't look at him, focusing heavily on the dessert instead.

"I'm eating more than one bite of that," she finally
said, and when he let go of her hand, she reached for
her spoon.

"You don't have anything to say about my declara-
tion?"

She glanced up, an uneasy smile on her face now.
One of her hands slipped up to cover her collarbone protectively, then gave it a little rub. "You mean besides *I
don't believe you*?"

"You think I'd yell that in a crowded restaurant if
it was a lie?"

"I think…you're trying to make things right." She
chose her words slowly and carefully, he could see, but

the self-comforting actions had already started. "And I appreciate that, but you don't have to."

He reached over and pulled her hand from her chest, once more holding it in his own as the other fiddled listlessly with her spoon.

"What are you doing?"

"Comforting you," he murmured. "You covered your jugular notch, it's a self-comforting technique. Women often do that when they're feeling unsettled or emotionally unsafe, while men usually rub the back of the neck... There are other things that could be called tells. Like when you got out of the pool and you saw me there, your feet were pointed toward the closest door, and I knew you wanted to run."

"I wanted to go to the locker room and get dressed. And please don't do that," she muttered, bouncing the spoon in her fingers, having yet to use it for anything useful.

"Don't hold your hand?"

"Don't tell me what I'm feeling based on what my extremities are doing!"

"Fine. How about I tell you this instead: I wanted to drag you into that apartment, tear off every scrap of black lace, and make sure that you could *never* forget me. That's the truth." It was still the truth, but not one he was going to admit. He still wanted her in a way that defied logic, in a way he still had to fight his way through even when she was quarreling with him. "But because I couldn't have what I wanted—which was you, in case you're not paying good enough attention—I tried to forget it. To forget you. But I never didn't want you, Grace. You didn't read me wrong."

The spoon she bounced on her finger slipped and clattered off the table and onto the floor. She didn't reach for it; instead, she finally looked him in the eyes again, the kind of measuring look that at least said he had her complete attention. She was trying to decide what she thought.

"You were off-limits. I wasn't kidding when I said that your home and family were my safe place." She *had* to believe him. These confessions weren't easy, and if they were for nothing? "Or how much you all meant to me. Nick is my best friend, I love your family like my own. More than my own. They never measured up when they were around. It wasn't a rejection, I just didn't know how to do it right. You weren't the only one who was young and stupid. I may be older, but I'm definitely not the smarter of the two of us."

His heart beat so hard his lungs felt battered.

"There was a girl at the apartment with you. I only realized it as I was running off and I heard her call out to you."

"That girl?" He stopped, trying to recall who it was. Yes, there had been a girl... "You're going to call me a pig, but I actually can't remember her name. I sent her home right after you left." He let go of her hand and retrieved his own spoon. Once he'd got some dessert on it, he held the spoon to her lips to distract her.

Her lips parted and she leaned forward, taking his spoon into her mouth, her warm brown eyes never leaving his. He could feel the slow seductive movement of her tongue across the bowl of the spoon before he slid it back through her closed lips. Good God, he was getting too wrapped up in the idea that this was a date. His heart sped up for an entirely different reason.

"She wasn't the girl I wanted that night." His voice went hoarse and he had to clear his throat to add, "So I sent her away, and spent a long, miserable night, staring at the ceiling and waiting for Nick to get back from his date."

Here beside her, the goose bumps racing down her arms were impossible to miss. He ran the back of one knuckle down her arm, then shrugged out of his jacket and wrapped it around her, as much to warm her as to help his own willpower—hide that soft golden skin beckoning him. And maybe break the sudden heavy, sensual atmosphere that had descended on them. It had to go if he wanted to hold on to any scrap of his sanity.

No more feeding her or touching her. He needed to get the atmosphere back to a more playful, jovial mood. He took a bite for himself, an excuse to make himself stop gazing into her eyes. "Him getting back? Made things worse because your brother always seems to pick up screamers."

"Oh, God, I don't need those details," she said, laughing a little as she pulled the jacket around her and snuggled in, then focused back on him, latching onto what he'd said. "I didn't misread you. You wanted me?"

"I'm an idiot, but I'm not that big an idiot. Of course I did. You're…" He stopped again. "You're great." Great. Not perfect, he wouldn't say perfect. His heart felt too big for him in that moment. Enlarged. Sluggish. Sore. It all felt too big for him.

If he'd taken her up on it that night, maybe he'd be able to ignore that want now, but that wasn't Grace's style. Maybe she didn't even want him anymore the way he wanted her.

She shifted in her seat, turning more toward him. Open, inviting. Those walls were coming down. That had to be good. It was almost too much to hope that they could return to being friends.

"I spent the whole night thinking of what I wished

I could have done differently." She whispered her own confession.

"Just one night?" he asked, thankful for the opening to try and get things back on less shaky ground. "I spent considerably more time than that."

"No. Not just one night. But, well, my rewind fantasies of that night were not very, you know, good. In a sexy way. They were mostly about me dragging that girl out by the hair and keying your car."

That was easier to smile at. Like she'd ever do either of those things. "If you'd keyed that car I would've never noticed," he said, taking another bite of the dessert. "I still have it, though."

"You do not." The waiter replaced her dropped spoon, and Grace reached for it and helped herself to a bite this time.

"Yes, I do. It's at a shop that restores old cars now. They're gutting and rebuilding it. So, if you decide to key it in the future, I will notice and be very sad. So let's keep talking about how sad it is that we're both so hot and can't have one another."

"I never said I was hot."

"No, that was me. I implied it. I thought you'd be better at reading between the lines than that. Or we could talk about why your—what did you call them, rewind fantasies? Why weren't they satisfying? I'm told that fantasy me is a stallion."

She laughed then, so brightly that he instantly felt better. Like the whole of their history was being wiped clean. They could be friends, continue on in one another's lives, hang out with Nick and do whatever it was that people did when they hung out in groups. Go the movies without formal wear. Something.

"Well, that was the other thing." She sobered, shaking her head as her cheeks began to turn pink. "I wasn't… See, I had this idea that you would've been… my first time. So I didn't just make a stupid and unaccountably brave move for me, but for my experience level."

His head snapped back as her words settled and coldness washed over him.

"You were…?" He must have heard that wrong. "You were a virgin? You were coming to me because you were a virgin?"

CHAPTER SEVEN

"I HAD THIS HAZY, insubstantial fantasy heavily lacking satisfying details…about you being the first." Grace shrugged as she said it, like it meant nothing. Like that didn't make it worse.

Liam sat back, at a loss for words.

"I'm not still a virgin," she hastened to add. "I'm not still holding out for you or anything pathetic like that."

Once again, she had misinterpreted his behavior.

"No, I imagine if you were still holding out for me, you'd have been a damned sight happier to see me than you were," he muttered, his hand lifting to rub the back of his neck. "The guy you ended up with."

"Brad."

"Brad." He repeated the name, as if it weren't giving him those rewind fantasies about beating the hell out of *Brad*. "I don't want details! Just… Was he good to you?"

"I guess so. I haven't had very serious relationships. I always pick badly," she said, shrugging again.

"Stop shrugging. Was he the one with the motorcycle?" If her rebound guy had…

She nodded, mouth twisting to the side. No doubt she could tell by the tone in his voice, which he had no hope of disguising, exactly what he wanted to do to Brad.

"Did he survive?" Earlier, Liam hadn't thought to ask

about the ex-boyfriend, but now that he knew his name and that he'd hurt her after being her first…

"Yes. He had all the leathers and such. I was just in jeans and—"

"Okay! Stop. I can't know more right now. And to think I was hoping that this talk would make things better between us."

"It has," she said, putting her hand on his, so small and fragile to his eyes now. So breakable. He should've been there to protect her. He should've been there to make sure that Brad damned well knew he should give his date the damned leathers anytime he took them out on his motorcycle.

"Liam, I put you into a no-win situation. There was nothing you could've done right in that situation. Even if you'd done what I wanted, it's unlikely that things would've been good between us now. My rewind fantasies also included how later, after you'd come to your senses, you came after me. Sometimes with gifts."

He wanted to put his arm around her again and know that as long as she stayed by him he could keep her safe.

He pulled his hand free instead. "Those are normal girl fantasies."

"No, I mean quintessential boyfriend gifts. Like flowers, candy, and a kitten in one hand and a puppy in the other. Do you see what I'm getting at?"

"That you had relationship feelings." It had never just been about sex. She'd had relationship feelings, she'd wanted him to be the first. And now? It was worse, because his mind was exactly in the same place.

Hell.

"Right."

"Again, how does that make things better?"

"Because they're another example of my being irrational and sentimental. You were living away at that time. I was about to go to college at the other end of the state." She dropped her hand into her lap and once again the oversized shoulders of his jacket rose. "It's okay. I got over it. I met someone else."

"Brad."

"Brad," she repeated. "And then we broke up, and I met Austin. And then—"

"Stop. Please. I don't need your dating CV."

"Because this is not a date?" she prompted, grinning at him finally. "I feel better. I do. You shouldn't feel badly about events you had nothing to do with."

He felt badly about the event he *had* had something to do with. "If I had taken you aside and said *I want you but we can't do this*, it would have been better. Because then I could've been there to make sure Brad knew what I'd do to him if he hurt you."

"You assume that one change would have changed everything. Maybe it wouldn't have. Maybe it would've made everything worse. I know for sure what you telling me that would've done. It would have led to me upping my game."

"Grace, your game started with you at my front door in your underwear."

"No. My game started long before that, but then you went away and I got desperate. That was my big plan when you came back to visit. It was my grand gesture." She pushed the plate away and then flattened her hands against the tabletop. "I thought if I stopped beating around the bush, once you knew I wanted you, you'd be all for it. Everyone says teenage boys will have sex with any girl they find remotely attractive if offered the chance. I thought once the chance was offered, that the underwear would make you want me, and then everything would fall into place and they all lived happily ever after..."

"No reflection on your attractiveness, but that's not how it works. At least not for me."

"I figured that out later. But my point is that if then you had already wanted me and were just being rational? What eighteen-year-old girl do you know who cares about being rational when feelings are in the way? Heck, I barely care about rational now and I've supposedly had six years to grow up since then."

The waiter came, the dessert between them was only half-eaten, and he'd lost his appetite for the chocolate-strawberry confection. "Check, please." He nodded toward the jacket and said, "My wallet is in the pocket with the phone."

"No," Grace interjected before the waiter could get away. "Two checks."

Because this wasn't a date.

There had been moments when it had felt date-like, and then everything had gone pear-shaped.

The waiter looked at Liam for confirmation before he went to split the order.

She frowned, but didn't keep on with the subject. Instead, she slid the jacket off and handed it to him. "Thank you for the loan of the jacket. Mind if I visit the ladies while he sorts the checks out?"

"It's that way." He gestured and scooted back around to his side of the booth as she departed the table.

Before he moved to LA proper to start chasing the dream, he'd known about the boys who'd called Grace, and the few that she had tried—and quietly succeeded—in making him jealous of. He probably owed her for teaching him to hide that emotion, even though the ability had abandoned him tonight.

He called his driver and had him ready the car and pull around to get them. The waiter brought the checks before Grace returned, and Liam paid both of them.

When Grace came back he stood with his cane and offered her his elbow again. "Checks?"

"Paid," he muttered, and added, "I don't want to fight about the check. The restaurant was my decision, and you're here as my employee, right? It's not a date. It's not two friends having dinner together. It was my responsibility. And I tipped him well for his trouble. Clear?"

She didn't take his elbow, but walked ahead of him through the restaurant for the door.

He'd known she'd had a crush on him when they'd still been in high school. Idiot though he may have been, he had been love-deprived enough that he'd developed a keen way of detecting it in every incarnation. And if he was honest with himself, that was probably a big part of the draw of his occupation. He'd gone from having very few he could claim who loved him to having thousands, to having millions. He'd gone from the unwanted son of dead junkies to the man on top of every producer's wish list.

He could identify a lot of emotions on sight—studying body language to improve his acting had come with other benefits. He could tell the difference between fondness of friends, adoration of fans, and when past girlfriends were getting Too Close to Love—aka Time to Break Up. He knew the difference between the way his parents had looked at him the times they hadn't been looking through him, and the way the Watsons had always looked at him—loving and always a little worried about him.

He could identify love in its many flavors.

But apparently he sucked at spotting a virgin.

Liam had claimed he'd wanted honesty and to clear the air. Obviously he hadn't thought that through.

Grace was just trying to be completely honest, because all her instincts said to lie about the whole ordeal. Protect herself. But when her instincts were the most selfish, that's when she did her best to ignore them. Do the opposite. Do the hard thing if it could help someone else.

Protect Liam. Absolve him of his guilt. Don't leave him wondering why she'd been the one to hold on to it for so long, make sure he knew this had never been his fault.

But this was apparently also wrong. Now that she'd told him, they sat in the back of the limo in silence and tension even worse than when she'd been wondering when he was going to bring up how much he hadn't wanted her.

"You're gritting your teeth," she said softly, trying to fix this before it got worse. "I'm fine, Liam. You should be fine too. You were right."

"I don't want to hear again that it was the only course of action. I know that. I still know that, but that doesn't make this better."

"Why? Are you such a caveman that you're angry that I've had boyfriends?"

"No. God, no. I'm not angry."

"Have you told your face that? I don't think your eyebrows got the memo. Did you ever notice that the angry characters in children's shows either have a unibrow or they have just really heavy, straight brows that come together in an angry way?"

"I never played a Muppet," he joked, if that tone could be called a joke.

She scooted up against him, mirroring the way he'd dragged her to him earlier, and lifted his arm so she could get under it. "See? I'm completely at ease with you now. I understand limits. I understand why you felt that way. I really do. At least now. You felt like you should be more like a brother to me, only I didn't feel that way. You—"

"Couldn't have won. Let's stop talking about it."

"You were the one who wanted to talk."

"And now I want to stop talking," he said, sharply enough that she leaned forward, out from beneath the arm she'd just wrapped around herself, and slid away from him on the seat again.

He was going to be the end of her sanity. Should she have trusted that instinct to keep hiding things? She'd not trusted them because when she had, all those years she'd been wrong.

Mr. I-Know-What-You're-Thinking-Because-of-Your-Feet would never have that problem. He studied body language, she studied bodily injuries. Not the kind of emotional injuries that might help her understand him.

And maybe that was why he was good at reading people. Maybe it wasn't just study but something he'd developed during a rough childhood.

She sank back into her spot on the seat and looked toward her window as he uttered an expletive and dragged her back to him.

This time, rather than wrap an arm around her, he twisted and grabbed her by the hips. One second she was on the seat, the next she was in his lap. "You're going to hurt your ankle!"

"Shut up, Grace." He caught her by the back of the neck and pulled her against him, his mouth immediately on hers.

His lips, soft and sweetened with the lingering taste of berries, stroked and nibbled, coaxing her mouth open within seconds.

Her arms rested against his chest, but as his tongue sought hers and the kiss deepened, the fighting from the past long minutes fled her mind. Instinctively, her arms slid around his shoulders as his went around her. Wide, hot hands pressed against the cool skin of her bare back and on down to her hip to keep her close to him.

She'd seen him kiss countless women, and had always wondered what it was like even while envying them. Even when her coping mechanism was to pretend that she didn't think anything about him at all.

It felt like a drug. Like it heightened her senses and tuned her into him so acutely that her heart changed rhythm to match his beat. She breathed his air and plowed her fingers into his hair to kiss him better, get him closer. Every kiss dragged her deeper into him.

A kiss like no other. If it was because of all his practice, she didn't care.

If it was because she'd been starved for it for so long, had imagined it so many times, she didn't care what that said about her either.

Their time together was almost at an end. Soon they'd be back at the clinic, and frequent visits would dwindle to only a few and then back to none. None, because that was normal for them. They'd done all they could to unweave all their ties six years ago, and she had no illusions that he'd start unweaving them again once he no longer had to have her with him. He might still want her, but there were so many women who could be whatever he wanted. A girlfriend without their baggage, without their obstacles, without jeopardizing the friendship he held dear.

This bubble that New York cast around them, it felt like a different planet. A place where they could talk about that stupid trench coat, and a place where inexplicable anger and hungry kisses could confirm that old desire still clung to them both. The only place it could exist.

The door they sat beside opened, a blast of humid air hitting them both. Liam jerked his head back, eyes glazed and panting.

"Sir?" the doorman said. "Want me to close the door back up?"

Tonight they were at the front entrance. She'd forgotten that they weren't sneaking in and out through the back since he'd deigned to use the cane. A flash went off. Then another. Stupid cameras.

She felt him retreat before he'd moved an inch.

The wall came up, and he put her down gently. The next instant he had his cane and had climbed from the car.

This time he didn't wait for her to get his elbow but started forward with the cane and a stronger hobble.

She got her bag and accepted a hand out from the doorman, thanking him before she went to catch up with Liam.

Something had just happened, she just wasn't sure what.

Two days later, decked out in her classy, cotton, roomy, embroidered polo and slacks, Grace walked beside her morning patient at the clinic, holding on to the small woman's support belt as she used the double bars to take shaky but supported steps toward the end.

Finally, a patient who didn't confuse her.

A patient who liked her and listened to her advice.

"You're doing great. Don't rush."

"I want to sit down and the sooner I get to the end, the sooner I get to sit down," Mrs. Peters said.

"And every step gets you closer to needing to sit less. You're doing so well. I can honestly say you're the best patient I have had in days."

The woman stopped midway and Grace kept holding on to the support belt, as she always did.

"I need just a little breather."

"Take your time. You standing here without walking is still making you do work."

"Yes, it is. I don't know how I got so weak."

Grace knew. Stroke. It had been caught fairly quickly, but it had still had time to do some damage.

"Muscle weakens really fast. Many of the people who come visit me here don't actually even have direct accidents or illnesses to blame for the atrophy. It happens if you just spend too much time sitting. My gran needed a bit of rehab after she had particularly nasty flu, just because she wasn't active in that time. It sneaks up on you."

Mrs. Peters nodded and inched her hands along the bars, supporting herself that way before they took another step. "A good reason to keep going."

"You can wait a bit more if you want to. It's probably only...six more steps to the end. That was one. Five more."

Other physical therapists on staff came and went with their patients during the day, but the facilities came with the kinds of equipment that made it possible to do this kind of work with only one therapist. She had safety harnesses and leads that hooked to the ceiling if the client was too heavy for the belt, but Grace preferred the belt. She'd liked it best when she'd been rebuilding her own muscle after her accident. It was smoother than the cables. Felt more secure, even if that was the opposite of true. Being connected to a person rather than some apparatus brought trust into the equation, and she'd swear that patients who could use the belt with her help got better faster.

Together they counted the steps, and once Mrs. Peters got to the end, Grace helped her turn and sit in the chair that she'd already placed there. "Let me get you some water. Don't go walking around while I'm gone, now."

She stepped into the storage room and snagged a cold bottle of water from the cooler. Her phone rang when she was in there. She glanced at the screen and rolled it to voice mail.

She didn't want to talk to Nick. She was having a hard enough time finding ways to not think about Liam, without Nick talking about anything. He invariably talked about his best friend.

And she was a terrible liar, and what was she supposed to say if he asked about her weekend? *Great. I went to New York and made out with your best friend who I'd currently like to strangle because he's being a big taciturn jerk?*

After the steamy kiss in the back of the limo he'd gone to his room and she to hers, and she hadn't seen him again until the morning when Miles came to knock and give her the ten-minute warning before they went to the airport and she'd gone to Liam's suite to wrap his ankle.

Yes, he'd accepted the ice.

He'd been polite but had slept most of the flight.

He'd taken the anti-inflammatories when she'd foisted them on him.

But what he'd refused to do was talk. He didn't actually say, *I don't want to talk to you.* There had been no yelling. He'd just failed to engage about anything.

"I'd like to watch television for a bit, Grace," Mrs. Peters said. "I didn't sleep well last night and feel tired today, but my son isn't coming to pick me up for another half an hour."

Grace flipped the brakes off on the chair and wheeled the small, frail woman around to a wall-mounted television above where the treadmills faced. She confirmed that Mrs. Peters wanted her to phone her son to come and pick her up.

She didn't have any other clients this afternoon as her clients had been shifted to other therapists—she'd only had Mrs. Peters because of a scheduling misunderstanding.

What she should do was call Liam and check on him. Even if he didn't want to talk to her about anything else, he was the one who had dragged her into this patient-therapist relationship, so she'd do the job she was supposed to do.

She dialed.

Liam answered on the second ring. "Afternoon, Grace."

"Hi. Just checking on the ankle. Doing all right? Keeping it elevated? Heat instead of ice?"

"Doing all prescribed actions."

She opened her mouth but heard Liam's name on the television and turned to look at it.

"You're on TV. Mrs. Peters is watching something. Interview."

"I had a couple of interviews this morning."

"Did you use your cane?"

"I did. And they came to the house so I didn't have to go to them. Foot elevated and all that. I told you I'd do what you told me as soon as I was able to."

A picture of Grace flashed up on the television, all decked out in her beautiful deep taupe, sparkly halter gown. "They asked about me?"

Watching the interview and talking to Liam at the same time was...weird.

"Is that you, Grace?" Mrs. Peters asked. "You know that Liam Carter?"

"Yes. And it's... Yes." She answered Mrs. Peters first and then added into the phone, "Why were they asking?"

She stopped when Liam's eighteen-inch head began laughing off the idea of dating her. Just his physical therapist. Just a friend from childhood. Just there to make sure he didn't do anything silly with his ankle in wraps.

"Wow," she said into the phone, not even sure what she felt about the denial. The way bighead TV Liam phrased it, the notion was laughable. Like there had been no kissing. No history worth mentioning aside from having been childhood friends. Nothing romantic at all.

"It's just the way you handle the press, right?" he said, trying to lead her to the same conclusion.

But all she could say was, "Wow."

Mrs. Peters's son arrived, having just wandered back inside from the grounds. She needed to go.

"I'll call you tomorrow to set up your first appointment in two days." Before he could say anything, she hung up and stashed her phone.

The chair her patient was currently using belonged to the facility, so she needed to transfer her back to her own chair and remove the belt once she was securely seated. She could think about Big Laughing Head Liam later.

Right now she didn't have room inside her own small head for all...that.

"What the hairy hell, Liam?"

Liam winced into his phone at his best friend's voice crackling down the line, loud and sharp enough to peel the eardrum from his ear. He'd been expecting Nick to call all afternoon, but he'd expected to get a greeting out before the expletives came into play.

It took a little effort, but he kept his voice steady and calm. He deserved his friend's wrath, but knowing that still didn't make it easier. "Hi, Nick. I guess you've been watching the gossip blogs."

"No, television, actually. And there you were with my sister in New York. Together. Holding hands, and then more... So let me ask again, what the hairy hell, Liam?"

"I sprained my ankle." Liam had expected a call, but for some reason he hadn't expected anger. Even in the rare instances that he and Nick had disagreed, it had only ever gotten physical once. And that time? His temper had started it, over nothing of consequence, and it had ended after they'd exchanged punches.

He'd always skipped this part during his Interlude with Grace fantasies. Consequences were rarely fantasy material, so he'd cut off anytime his imaginings had strayed in that direction.

"And?" Nick said.

"And I went to Grace to get help to finish my press tour and go to the premieres, she went with me to the East Coast premieres because having a date helps keep me from doing as much walking as I do when I'm alone. Right now, I'm sitting with my foot elevated and a heating thing on it. I have physical therapy at the clinic starting in a couple days. After I've had a mandatory rest on it."

"That doesn't explain the shots of her on your lap in the back of a limo, man."

No, it didn't.

That he couldn't explain. He'd done precisely what he'd sworn he'd never do—he'd crossed lines with Grace. "That was bad judgment. A mistake."

"You could have found another date. You could have found twenty dates to take with you and keep you from walking around too much."

He gripped the phone and switched to the other ear, this one starting to hurt from how hard he'd been smashing it with the earpiece.

One mistake in fifteen years wasn't so much.

Especially considering that he had turned her down in that trench coat, not that he had ever told Nick that. And he wouldn't tell him now. Nick didn't know about it and Grace deserved more. "It's complicated, but it's fine. Everything's fine now. It was a kiss, we didn't do anything else."

"Then why isn't she responding to my texts or answering my calls?"

"I don't know. Because you're acting like a possessive older brother?" The words came out before he could stop them and Liam suppressed a sigh, trying again. "She's seen the interviews I did this morning, so she's probably not answering because she didn't want to talk about it."

"Why not? What else did you do?"

"Dude! Do you really think I'd ever set out to hurt her?"

He heard Nick sigh and after a moment he said in a quieter tone, "You're my best friend so don't take this the wrong way, but Grace is not a player. She's a good girl. She went through a bad-boy phase and she couldn't handle it. I'm not sure how she grew up around us and remained an innocent little angel, but she did. She can't handle you."

Nick saw what he wanted to see, but there was a naughty side to Grace that Liam would never expose. A side that family should never see. But other than that, she pretty much fit the word Nick had selected. "I didn't molest her."

"You don't have to. All you have to do is be yourself. She's been more than half in love with you since she was twelve years old."

"She had a crush."

"No. She had…she had feelings for you. That's why when she stopped talking about you I stopped inviting her out with us. You still come up in conversations, but she shut down after you left. For a long time. I don't know what she feels now, I just know that you're a weak spot for her. You might not mean to make women fall at your feet, but it could be messy with Grace. Even if you don't mean to hurt her…"

This understanding and caring older brother thing chafed his already raw conscience, and he couldn't keep the irritation out of his voice. "Are you telling me to stay away from her?"

"Do I have to?"

"No. I'm seeing her for my physical therapy, but we're not traveling together anymore. They've got me scheduled for, like…ten visits. Five days a week for two weeks, weekends off. And it will be in a clinical setting. She's good at what she does, and she understands what's going on. She's the one who was taping my ankle and keeping me upright this weekend." He could probably find all that with a different physical therapist, and that's where his conscience was catching. The secret was out, so any decent physical therapist could see him in the clinic for the next two weeks. There were probably even other PTs at the clinic he could see instead.

But he didn't want to go to them. And that he couldn't defend, so when Nick started cautioning him again, Liam cut in. "I know you're protective, but you don't have to protect her from me. I love your family, Nick. I've got to go, but give her some space. She'll call you back when she wants to talk."

He hung up before he started shouting.

Because, yes, he'd screwed up, and he kept screwing up when it came to Grace.

When she'd called earlier with that interview playing in the background, he'd been hoping she'd walk out of the room, or that someone would change the channel. It had been an example of what not to do: go to an interview without knowing what you were going to say about everything. He hadn't known what to say about Grace, so he'd stuck with the physical therapist story they'd sold to his producers. It was easy. It flowed off the tongue. He'd had to force the levity there at the end, and the laugh had rung false to his ears. But, then, he knew his fake laughs from his real ones. He'd gotten good enough at faking them that most other people didn't. Grace hadn't spent enough time with him in the past few years to even have a chance of recognizing them.

To her ears, that all probably sounded legit.

Everything with her had somehow spiraled out of control. That dress had made him stupid. Dinner. The conversation he should have never started. A smarter man would have just left that subject alone rather than pick at it, thinking he could fix it.

He dropped the phone onto the table beside him before he gave in to the urge to throw it.

He was supposed to sit still for three whole days. All he wanted to do was run. Run from all this, find a peaceful beach and let his feet pound wet sand.

And it was the first time he'd ever wanted to run from any of the Watsons.

When he'd first known them and he'd run, it had been toward their house. The safe place. The place with parents who'd made sure he'd done his homework, given him a standing invite to dinner, and had always picked up a third one of anything they'd bought for their own two kids.

Even when she'd shown up at his door in her black underwear, he hadn't wanted to run from her. Every step away had been sluggish and hard.

He didn't want to feel that again. He just didn't know how to fix things with her. It could be that they could never be friends. That there was too much there for them to resist. Too much pull. Too much need—to laugh, to kiss, to talk.

They might never be able to be friends, and if he kept trying, the one friendship he could hold on to would sour.

Because Nick was right. Even if he didn't mean to, he would hurt Grace in the long run. She was innocent.

She was good and loyal. She had a shining example of a long, happy marriage to aspire to.

And the look in her eyes when she'd talked about the bandage exchange with little Brody. Grace was mother material. Grace was built for marriage and the fairy tale. While he was doomed to be surrounded by addicts and to watch them fall off, one by one, she had white picket fences and playdates in her future. He was the product of something twisted and ugly. He knew enough about the way people passed their sickness on to their families, their children…and he couldn't risk it.

Nick was right. He needed to stay away. He just needed to keep things cool between them until then.

Professional. Being friends would never work. Not now.

Not after that kiss.

CHAPTER EIGHT

THREE DAYS SINCE Liam had last seen Grace, he walked with the aid of his crutches into The Hollywood Hills Clinic. After signing in, he headed downstairs, praying for a good reception.

Their first day back she'd called to check on him, but he hadn't heard her voice since that call. Oh, she'd still checked in on him twice each day, which was probably more than any other physical therapist did with unruly patients, but it had been via text. Short texts. Terse texts. One-word texts: Update?

And he'd taken the hint. Don't call her. Because what could he say?

I can't kiss you anymore because your brother will be mad at me?

I can't kiss you anymore because all I want to do is rip your clothes off and find new, creative, and wildly satisfying ways to hurt my ankle?

Without direction from her, he decided to go to the big room with the equipment rather than the pool this morning.

"Morning." Her greeting came from the office area and he forced himself fully into the room.

Liam tilted an ear, rolling her words and tone around

in his mind as he called back, "Morning. Am I the first patient?"

Come out of there, Gracie. I need to see you, to see how you are...

"You're my first patient," she confirmed, stepping out of the office. "Everyone's got their first appointment of the day. You're not late, I just scheduled you about fifteen minutes after theirs." Busily tapping on the tablet she carried to make notes, she didn't even look at him.

Which told him enough. She was still very unhappy with him.

"Where are the others?"

"I don't know. There are three of us here, and a few different therapy rooms that can be used. We're going to one of the private rooms since we're starting light this morning." She gestured for him to follow her and stepped back out. A short distance away a bright corridor turned off and he followed her to the last room.

Inside there was a work table along with some chairs and counters. All very modern, clean, and comfortable looking as far as examination tables went.

What he should be aiming for was to handle this in a wholly professional capacity. It would be wonderful if they could be friends without all the rest of it, but it just didn't look likely. So feeling let down that she didn't want to look at him made him an idiot.

"Where do you want me?"

"Hop up on the table if you can," she said, putting the tablet down and grabbing a rolling stool for herself.

"Of course I can. I've been navigating stairs with these suckers for days. I'm just about to go pro in the Stair Climbing with Crutches event." He maneuvered himself up onto the table and scooted back, finally letting himself look at her more closely when he settled.

All that professional nonsense aside, part of him still wanted her to smile at him. He had to do better than this.

Back in normal clothes, back in their own corners, she looked at him much like she had that first day: like she wanted nothing to do with him.

"I'm just going to unwrap and have a look at it. Have you been having any trouble wrapping it?"

"Yes. I am not nearly as good at it." He leaned back and held his leg out for her to do whatever she was going to.

Still not looking at him, which was probably for the best. Eye contact led to words, and he had no words to offer her. Every time he tried to think about what to say, his mind invariably turned to replaying the limo ride, the way every time his tongue had slipped into her mouth she had rewarded him with moans and sighs, with pressing closer, with her hand tangling in his hair.

God. Stop it.

All he'd managed to riddle out was the fact that they'd have to go back to operating in strictly separate worlds after this ankle business was finished. If he were a stronger man—a better man—he could control himself. But apparently he couldn't do that.

His foot bare, she stashed the support implements to the side and gently turned his leg this way and that to examine it.

And there would be no wincing. He might not be strong in mind but he would be…strong in pain control.

"How does it look?"

"A little better. The bruising where the blood pooled isn't much different, but it's almost gone from the higher areas, away from where the actual damage occurred. But we really can't push it today. We're going to measure range of motion, what you can do on your own without my help, and what you can do with a little help from me. Did you take any pain medicine this morning?"

"I took the one you have to eat with. It helps more than the other."

She nodded and got some kind of protractor and a chair and began walking him through basic movements.

Businesslike, but still gentle with touches.

His range of motion was really bad. She had him moving until it hurt, and she would gently press until he cried uncle.

The up-and-down motion, the usual walking foot motion, was better than he'd thought it would be but any rotation in the socket made him want to jerk his leg out of her hands.

She got him down from the table and into one of the recliners.

"Want my foot up?"

"Not yet. We're going to do a paraffin bath first."

"Wax?"

"Yep, hot wax. It's not as hot as drippy candle wax because it melts at a lower temperature, but it is like no heat you can apply at home. It'll feel…" She stopped when her phone rang and she fished it from her thigh pocket. A quick scan and she gave the barest shake of her head and swiped it out. "What was I saying?"

"I think you were saying the hot wax was going to feel good."

"Better than good, really. We'll dip, I'll wrap your leg in hot towels and let you sit in it for about twenty minutes, and then we'll measure again."

The phone buzzed.

She grabbed it again and glanced at the screen. Then

turned the thing off completely and dropped it on the counter. The expression on her face…well, it was exactly the expression he'd imagined on her face every time she'd sent her one-word texts the past couple of days.

"Something wrong?"

"My brother is hounding me." She knelt and rolled up his pants leg. "We'll do this every day before we get going so you might want to wear shorts in here. Just an idea. No one to impress. No danger of it getting on your slacks."

"Okay." He looked at the phone and then at her stiff shoulders. He shouldn't ask, but it wasn't about kissing. Not exactly. Only kind of. And about the fact that his best friend thought he was a louse. Think about that. Focus on the consequences. "He's been upset with me."

"Yeah, I worked that out our first day back."

She didn't ask. Did that mean she didn't want to know how that had been going? With the way she was ignoring texts, he had to wonder what Nick had said to her.

"Both of those were him?"

"Yes. I'm not speaking to him right now."

"Why not?"

She settled the cuff above his knee and wheeled the paraffin thing over to him, but stood and retrieved towels he could only guess were hot before she guided his foot up and into the bath.

"Is he telling you to stay away from me?"

"Is that what he's telling you?"

"Pretty much," he muttered. "I told him you were helping me."

"Yep. That's what the physical therapist is supposed to do."

Zing.

She submerged his leg to mid-calf in the deep bath, and though it was plenty hot she didn't leave him soaking, just shook out one towel and as soon as his leg was out she wrapped the towel around it. And then another, and another.

Soon she had it completely encased, and nodded at the lever on the side of the chair. "Put the foot up now. I'm going to put you on a twenty-minute timer, and then we'll get you out of it."

"Is it going to turn hard?"

"Somewhat."

"So how do we…get out of it without causing pain after it gets hard?"

Grace stood up and went to wheel the bath away from him. Something she'd been asking herself for days. *How do we get out of this without causing pain?*

He had been referring to the wax, presumably, but it didn't feel that way. They'd now resorted to talking in code, because no one could say what they really meant. Which was just…great.

"It'll feel good for a while." The whole while, without a doubt. "You probably won't want to come out of it by the time it's done." That she was less certain of, at least if they were talking in code. If he was just talking about the wax, her problems were actually far less significant than she figured them to be. He got much less sexy if she also made him an idiot in her mind.

"I don't doubt that at all," he said, his words so quiet she might have missed them if she weren't so primed and tuned in to him.

Definitely talking in code.

She rolled her stool back, needing to make the room

a little bigger…because all she really wanted to do was stand up and beg him to kiss her again. "I suppose it's about risks. What you're afraid of and what you're willing to risk."

Risks. She shouldn't be the one who had to take all the risks. Was that what this would require? It hadn't seemed that way in the limo because that had been Liam's doing. For once. He'd been the one reaching for her. And then he'd laughed off the very idea of them being together. She couldn't even wish he wasn't so close to her family, because she knew now exactly how much his time with them had meant to him, and how it had probably saved his life.

"Well, you shaved my leg before, so that should help."

Was he still talking in code?

"Right. Not going to rip hair out." She twisted to snatch her phone off the counter and turned it on, checked texts and messages, then stashed it in her pocket. "I'll be careful, Liam. I have no desire to hurt you."

"Me either," he said, both hands lifting to rub over his face.

"You want me to leave you alone to soak in it?"

He dropped his hands heavily in his lap, finally looking her in the eye.

She saw regret there, matching what his voice told her. But Grace knew how terrible her instincts were with regard to this man. "All right."

A quick detour and she retrieved a remote control to give to him, pointing out a sticker on the back with the Wi-Fi password on it. "For your amusement in the meanwhile. I'll be back in twenty, and we'll roll the wax off and check your range of motion, then go through the exercises you're to do today and tomorrow. I don't need to see you tomorrow, but I will check in. And you can call if you have trouble. It's only a few gentle exercises today and tomorrow, mostly just about keeping the joint working without interfering with the healing. I'll go over the instructions when I get back. And bring in a package prepared for you to take with you with a moist heat pack and sheet with exercises in little pictures."

Liam took what she handed him and let it drop to his lap. "Thanks, Grace. I...I owe you."

"No, you don't. You pay me to do this, just like all the double time you're being billed for travel and round-the-clock care."

She wanted more, she knew that now, but she had absolutely no idea how to go about turning this mess into something more. Or even if she should try. The only thing she knew she had to do was try to keep things going, get through this, and see what happened.

That's what she always did.

Since her accident the only risks she'd taken had been with regard to Liam. All the rest of her life was Safety First. But in his presence? She kept throwing caution to the wind. Which should probably tell her something.

She stepped out of the room, set the timer on her phone, and headed back to the office. If he was going to be in therapy for the next two weeks, she should probably invest in some kind of wall padding or helmet for all the beating her head against the wall she'd no doubt be doing.

Once in the office, she closed the door and called her brother back.

She loved Nick. She really did. She knew he wanted

the best for her, and he probably felt compelled to protect her.

But she was a big girl, and it was past time he figured that out.

Grace had RSVP'd Freya Rothsberg and Zack Carlton's wedding weeks ago. She even had a dress and new strappy sandals picked out. What she didn't have was a date.

Today she'd begun to feel the pressure of that. She'd blame Liam. How in the world was she supposed to find a date for a wedding when she had movie stars in her eyes?

The problem with having stupid squishy feelings for a celebrity patient was not just knowing that she shouldn't—ethics got involved because he was her patient. She could hold out and feign something professional for the few hours a week that they spent on his rehab, which should have made things easier, but it hadn't.

But the ethics mattered to the clinic, even in their case where their history was so deep and complicated that it made the ethics question reach new depths of murkiness.

This morning's early visit would involve time in the water to get him walking in a near-weightless environment.

Which meant it was time for her to change into her bathing suit.

Normally, she'd use the one-piece that came with shorts and really concealed her assets. But due to a series of phone meetings today Liam was coming in a good two hours before they usually started seeing patients.

And she was going to make the most out of that situation because, murky ethics or not, she did want more from him. She just had to start laying the groundwork now even if she couldn't act on it while he was her patient, and also because her grand gestures to seduce the man had never seemed to work out the way she'd envisioned.

She was going to wear her black bikini, the one she kept for swimming when no one else was in the pool. The one she'd been wearing that first day when he'd stumbled over her.

Because in the four days since she'd seen him, Grace had come to some realizations.

She could deal with humiliation, but she couldn't handle not knowing what it would be like to be with him.

Liam got under her skin more than anyone ever had, and if that never happened again, she'd regret not experiencing it.

Yes, anything to do with him made her completely unable to predict how it was going to go—she couldn't make a safe play because she didn't know what was safe when it came to Liam. Not trying and going another five, or fifteen, or fifty years wondering what if? Or living with the humiliation she'd become so accustomed to if he turned her down?

Knowing he wanted her made that at least easier to stomach.

It wasn't a great plan, but she'd lived a safe life too long. She needed some risk. Liam wouldn't be the death of her, and if she was lucky, it would give her the kind of symmetry that her heart needed. Finish something that had started back then.

She went to change.

And if this bikini didn't work, that was okay: it was stage one. She had something much flimsier to try if she had to break out bigger ammunition for stage two.

Maybe she should convince him to go for a house call. His pool or the one at her place. There were pools to be had in LA where she could lure him with privacy and tempt him with tiny bikinis.

Not a great plan, but it was better than the trench coat. At least in theory.

"This exercise is not as advertised," Liam said, sliding into the hotel's rooftop pool he'd rented for the evening and had closed an hour early for his therapy with Grace, watching her across the pool where she stood in a black bikini so small only microkini enthusiasts would say it wasn't revealing enough.

The woman's bathing suits just kept getting smaller.

She dropped the towels she'd been carrying at the edge and slid into the water.

"It's water. We're going to be walking and swimming tonight, working the joint in three different ways."

"And we could have done this at the clinic. I know what you're up to, Watson."

Driving me crazy.

The use of her last name got her attention and Grace swam to his side of the pool, no doubt because it was faster than walking, even though the water wasn't more than waist deep on him. She stopped and stood in front of him, the water sluicing down her body, rippling over that soft, golden skin. He sighed and leaned back against the side.

True to her guarantees, his ankle improved a little every day. But his willpower? That was now limping along.

What came next? Topless pool therapy day?

Having a private pool suddenly seemed like a really legit reason for investing in real estate.

If he were into one-night stands, he'd find some woman to get naked with just to relieve the stress that spending every day with Grace in progressively smaller bathing suits was putting on his libido control.

"Not going to deny it?"

"Deny that I'm up to something?" The smile she gave him flashed so wickedly that he had to look anywhere but at her.

She maneuvered until she was beside him, facing in the same direction, and murmured, "You need to go a little deeper."

Deeper. Yes. Really…deep.

"Quit that," he bit out. "Just tell me what to do."

"Quit what?"

Like she didn't know what she was doing. "Don't play innocent with me. I'm onto you. Don't do that… provocative…well, it wasn't exactly dirty talk but you know we do that. Sexy double talk."

She pointed across his chest to the deeper end of the pool. "So you knew what I meant. Good. Move a little that way. The water should come up to your ribs. We're going to do some walking in the water. Back and forth here for a warm-up and then each time we'll move a little farther up the pool to progressively shallower water, so you'll be taking more weight on it each time. See how far you can go up. Then the same thing tomorrow."

"Is this the new measurement system?"

"Yes. Your range of motion is greatly improved so now we're working on slowly increasing strength."

"And are you going to admit what you're up to?" He asked the question but started walking in that slow, mostly submerged, bouncy fashion across the short length of the pool, staying in the same water depth.

She stayed beside him as he did as instructed, like he needed help or a safety net. Would it be better or worse if she were out of the pool and he got a view of her skimpy bikini every time he came toward her?

"You want a confession?"

"Yes." He stopped at the other side of the pool and turned around to start the return trip.

"I thought you didn't want to know all the details of what's going on in my head."

Frustration reaching snapping point, Liam paused long enough to brace his good leg against the bottom of the pool for support.

Grace stopped and looked at him, concern in her eyes.

Before she could say anything, he grabbed her by the waist, jumped as high as he could, and chucked her a few feet away from him in the water. He'd thrown that woman in the pool more times than he could count as teenagers. Usually in more shallow water, or from the side of the pool, where he could really get a good fling on her and send her flying. The ribs-deep water made that harder, but she still went under with a satisfying splash.

When she came up sputtering and laughing, he nodded and continued walking. "I don't. But apparently it's the only way through this. So out with it."

"I'm done playing it safe," Grace said, still smiling from the reminder of their old, more innocent games, as she approached him again to resume walking.

"That means what?"

"That means that I've realized that just because I'm afraid of losing again it doesn't mean that I can live with myself if I don't try."

"You should be able to." God help him, he wasn't going to make this easy on her. She had to get the idea to stop. "It isn't going to work. No matter how nice it might be. It can't."

Grace took a deep breath and as they reached the edge of the pool, ushered him about a foot higher, into somewhat more shallow water. "Again," she said, dealing with the therapy first while working out what she wanted to say. Considering the way they'd been circling one another for days, she hadn't expected him to approach this head-on. He wanted it all out in the open again, or so he claimed. No matter how badly that had gone last time. And she was completely out of instincts on it. It had all boiled down to simple facts: he enjoyed kissing her. He'd wanted her then, he still did now. That wasn't going to change because she found her spine again and tried to convince him.

"I've spent years wanting that night to have gone differently and I want to know. I want my night. With you."

"Grace—"

"Just wait. I know what you're going to say. We can't because of Nick, who I'm sure is putting just as much—if not more—pressure on you than he has been on me to stay apart. He said you're a player and I will just get hurt. Just like your last girlfriend was."

"He's right. About us. You're built for forever, and I won't ever marry. It's not for me. So you would get hurt."

"You're not a player. You're a serial dater, but you're not a player. You have relationships, otherwise they couldn't end up badly and in the news. The only reason I was news was because of how recently you broke up with Simone Andre, and because now she's in rehab."

One thing to be thankful for. At least Grace didn't

sound like she blamed him for Simone's drug problem, but he didn't want her thinking that. It didn't have anything to do with them, but he didn't want her to see him as recent gossip had been painting him.

"The stuff about Simone isn't true. I didn't just get done with her and move on. I didn't break her heart and turn her into an addict. I broke up with her because she *was* an addict. And I wanted her to get help. And she has. She's in rehab and I'm really glad, but, like I told you before, rumors and gossip spring up about everything, even stuff that isn't true. I don't need to make her life worse, and she's not the one telling people all this, so I don't correct the idiotic stories I see that paint me as the bad guy. Right now, I'm the stronger one. I can carry this for her. I can handle lies, it's the true stuff that hurts."

"You're making assumptions about what is best for me. You and Nick both are, and I'm a big girl. I can make my own decisions. I made some admittedly stupid choices in the past, but I was a bit younger then, you know. And we've already talked about being young and stupid. So that argument doesn't hold water, and you're doing me a disservice when you act like I need to be protected from you or that it's your job or Nick's job to do it."

"Got it. You don't need to be protected from me. But, to be clear, I would try and protect Nick from making a bad decision too if I knew in advance he was trying to make one. So I can't get mad at him for doing the same thing with me."

"Because you're about to make a bad decision with me?"

"That's what it looks like to Nick. I did make a bad decision in the limo."

"My point is, I would regret it more if I didn't try

to finish this than if we go to bed once and you never speak to me again. I'm pretty sure that you're never going to speak to me again anyway when this is all said and done. So what would you regret more?"

He stopped once more at the edge and gestured toward the shallow end again.

She nodded. "One more and then maybe we'll stay there for a couple of passes. This one worked your ankle a bit."

"This isn't too bad."

"It sounds like you're in pain, though." In pain and angry. Maybe she should just let this alone. She'd made her point. She'd put herself out there, and at least she'd done it with who she was this time.

"A little." At least he admitted to the physical feelings, and moved another foot down and shaved another few inches off the water depth. "And all that stuff I told you about my limits because of your family and our history?"

"I'm not going to announce it to Nick or Mom and Dad, Liam." She kept pace with him, letting him set the speed now. "I'm not going to go whining when it ends. I know I don't fit into your world. It's going to be over between us when you're recovered, one way or another. You're going off to some film location and, sure, you might send greetings through Nick in the future or ask how I'm doing, but we're not friends." She touched his arm, stopping him in the middle, forcing him to look at her.

"We're not friends anymore, Liam. Right now, we're pretending to be friends because if this attraction wasn't between us, we would be friends. I genuinely like you, and I know you like me. I know you care about me, and you care about my family, and our history... But

it's never going to be what it was when we were kids.
If it ever was that anyway. I can't be friends with you
without all this between us."

Liam watched her in a way that said her words
had been in his mind before she'd said them, and she
watched as he reached up to rub the back of his neck.
The man shouldn't have told her that body language
tell. He felt emotionally in danger, that's what he'd said
men did when they felt that.

"So it's going to end because of all the reasons we've
talked about. Why is that going to be easier than if
we've made one amazing memory together first?" She
stepped back, one step, then another, her courage abandoning her at the end of her forward, angry confession.
Now she had no choice but to flee if she wanted to keep
breathing or keep from protecting her jugular notch.

Every time he said he wanted her honesty, it went
like this, with his words drying up and her left trying
to fill the gap.

"I want you to do another three passes here, back
and forth. And then swim. Gently, not like you're being
chased by sharks. Kick and flex your feet separately
or together like a fish, but don't frog-kick your legs.
Use your feet better, and don't overdo it. Do the same
thing three times tomorrow. Morning, afternoon, and
evening."

"Are you leaving?" he said finally, stopping in the
center of the pool where she'd left him, the water lapping at his hips.

"Yes." If there was any fairness in the universe, he
wouldn't hear her voice wobbling. "I'll see you in two
days at the clinic. Text me what time you want to come.
Morning, I'm guessing. Which would be fine. Or night.
I can come back or stay late from work. If you want

to meet at night, then do the exercises that day before you come, and we'll switch things when you get there."

He nodded, apparently not disagreeing with any of it.

She turned and headed for the side of the pool where her towel was, and kicked out of it.

The bikini business had to stop.

If anything were going to happen between them now, it had to be his move. Her cards were on the table. So many cards. God, what was she thinking?

Shaking the towel out, she wrapped it under her arms and clutched it there to head for the changing area.

Dry off. Get out. Go home.

Find some way to stop her words from playing on repeat all night. No rewind fantasies this time.

She couldn't take it if he once more failed to live up to them.

CHAPTER NINE

TIME TICKED ON. Grace met with Liam daily to check on him, changed his exercise regimen and measured his progress every other day. The days that she didn't see him he still came in to use the pool. Exercise in only his hotel's pool limited his ability to exercise several times a day so lately he'd spent more time there than the twenty minutes she prescribed three times a day.

And not once in all that time had Liam's poker face slipped an inch. She had no idea whether or not her words to him had made a difference, all she knew was that she was out of gumption to chase things.

Three days ago she'd added dry-ground exercises to his program, in addition to the pool strengthening techniques. They'd see him through to the start of his first project, and he'd reached the point that he didn't need monitoring. That meant today he was being discharged from supervised rehabilitation.

Grace stepped out of her office, clipboard in hand with the discharge paperwork snapped in, and headed to the pool therapy room, hoping to catch him before he got into the water.

"Liam?" She called him out of the locker room.

Hearing a splash, she turned back to the pool in time to see him rising above the closest edge, every muscle in the man's arms and chest flexed, the tattoos he bore on his shoulder rippling in some breath-catching combination of strength and water running off tanned skin.

The clipboard in her hand felt as heavy as her tongue.

This was it. This moment was the end of whatever insanity they'd been cycling through for the past three weeks. She'd talked to him before about the papers, now she just had to find some way to remind him. Some words to say.

She had nothing.

He was going to let it go without a backward glance. She was probably already in his rearview mirror.

Spinning the clipboard paper side out, she gave it a little shake and then laid it on a nearby bench with the pen.

There. Message delivered.

She showed him her keys too as farewell, then turned and hurried out.

Someone else would lock up. They stayed late. She needed to go.

At least this time it wasn't humiliation eating a hole in her, even if he clearly didn't want her as badly as she wanted him.

Whatever it was could just remain undefined. She didn't have any energy left to roll it around in her mind. Not when there was wine chilling in her fridge and yoga pants waiting for her.

A knock on the door interrupted Grace's night of sulking and drinking.

She flopped back against the plush pillows on her couch and stared at the ceiling.

It was probably Nick. Yesterday, when she'd called him to catch up, she'd refused to talk about Liam and had hoped that would be the end of it, but that's never how things went with her protective older brother.

At least since her accident. Before that mess he'd pretty much left her to her own devices when it came to the guys she dated. Which probably informed his protectiveness now because no matter if she chose hot bad boys to date, they were never good for her. And they were never a good enough stand-in for Liam for her to keep playing that game when it became clear to her how fragile her hold on this life could be.

Another knock came, but no yelling. Not Nick.

She took another drink of her wine to fortify herself, and to empty her third glass, set it down and peel herself up off the couch.

Emboldened by booze, she flipped off one security device after another, locks and stoppers designed to allow her to peek without subjecting herself to the danger of a full door opening.

But the security in her building was too good for that to be a real issue.

She flung the door open and there Liam stood.

Or leaned, one shoulder resting against her door-jamb, hair wet and disheveled, his black T-shirt clinging to him like he'd not taken the time to even dry himself properly before throwing his clothes on and coming to find her.

The heat and hunger in his eyes sent sparks licking all over her body and burned away any doubts she'd been nursing through her second glass of wine.

Once again she was struck by her inability to predict this man.

"I don't have a trench coat," he said finally when she'd failed to come up with even a single word of greeting. "Can I come in anyway?"

Instead of answering, Grace reached directly for his belt and dipped her fingers into the front of his jeans. Soft hair brushed the backs of her fingers and she closed her hand around the buckle to tug him insistently through her apartment door.

One step inside and she launched herself against him, arms flying around his shoulders as she pressed as close as she could get, hungry mouth glued to his.

He managed to close the door and flip some locks, then she was against the wall, the tank top she'd donned to laze around the house inched up. Soon her belly burned with the heat of his firm, muscled torso against her.

More. She wanted more skin, the only thought strong enough to barrel through years of need coiling in her belly.

When her shirt reached her arms she let go of Liam long enough for him to whisk the material over her head.

He tossed the flimsy tank top and then stepped away from her, his eyes rolling down her body, which heated her skin too, just not as well as his skin against hers.

She once more closed the distance between them, needing his flesh against her. Before she could slide her arms around his shoulders once more, his hands landed on her hips and he pressed her back against the wall, falling to one knee as he did so.

He was going to hurt himself. A trickle of rationality made it through her fuzzy brain. "Your ankle." The getup he had on might be meant to tantalize, but he'd still known better than to take off the boot cast he'd been in since they'd returned from New York.

"It's fine," he said, pressing his face against the flat plane of her belly, then trailing wet kisses from one hip to the other, the stubble he wore so well rasping along her skin.

When he dug his fingers into the waist of the pants and dragged them down, along with the flimsy panties, she realized his intention.

No sooner had they wrestled her legs from the cotton tangle than he had one of her legs over his shoulder and his hot mouth pressed into her.

His tongue stroked and his lips plucked as if he were starved for her, as if he'd spent every night for the past six years dreaming of exactly this. She couldn't tell whose moans were louder.

All she could do was grab the frame of her front door for support as pleasure blazed through her, arching her back so hard she would've fallen without his hands clamped to her hips.

The fervor with which he loved told her he wasn't stopping until he'd wrung her out for their first course.

All the bad boys she'd dated...there could be no comparison. It might not be her first time but deep inside, for that girl who'd yearned for him for so long, it was her first time.

But she needed to touch him so, sparing one hand, she plowed her fingers through his hair, down that tattooed shoulder and the muscled arm...until she found the hand that held her hip. Instinctively, her fingers wrapped around the first digit she could get hold of.

Connection completed, the orgasm given by his greedy mouth almost split her in two.

The name that had secretly echoed in her heart for every lover finally passed her lips. She cried his name, and then again. And again.

When the last spasm burst, her supporting leg buckled, unwilling to hold her anymore.

Quickly, he turned the fall into a controlled slide, and once she touched the floor he crawled up her body, still hungry.

"Here?" He panted the question more than asked, eyeing the open window not ten feet away before he looked back down at her. "Not here."

"We're going to do this right. If it's the only time… and it is, right? You…you agree that it's the only time?" He pulled her up against him but stayed where he blocked the window.

When she nodded, he pulled his T-shirt off, baring that sculpted perfection that was his chest and belly. He wrapped the black cotton around her hips and tied the corners. "Then we need a bed. I want…everything to be perfect. Cool cotton sheets and pillows…"

"Bed. That way." Her words still slurred just a little, drunk with pleasure.

But she scrambled to her feet and offered him both her hands to tug him back up, her faculties slowly returning. "Use the booted foot to stand. The other one can bend…"

"Don't worry about my ankle," he said, but he still took her hand and did as she instructed. "It's fine."

She backed toward her room. Looking at him was too good. He didn't try to hide his want at all, and the front of his jeans strained over a heady ridge of flesh.

Oh, God, this was real. He was really there. Not just here in her mind, not a fantasy.

She didn't even want to know what had changed his mind. Later. She could ask later, or not. Maybe it would be better if they didn't talk about anything else, didn't get more attached. Just one time, and then…let it stay perfect in memories.

Don't think about after.

"My turn," she said, as they passed through the door into her room and she felt the edge of the bed against the backs of her legs and released his hands to let hers roam up and down over his chest, alternating gentle touches with little scratches anywhere she found hair. Down, over his belly, and she fell to her knees beside the bed.

"No. I can't wait. Next time." The words strangled in his throat, and it only took one look into his eyes for her to know the reason for it.

There would be no next time.

This was supposed to be a farewell.

The thought almost put her off the whole thing.

Almost.

Grace was a big girl. She was the master, not her emotions. And this had been her idea. Her only chance.

She unfastened his belt, unbuttoned his jeans and eased the zipper down, her eyes still locked on his.

"Please? Just for a moment?"

He read people, he knew what was on her mind. He could call the whole thing off; now would be the time...

The moment lengthened, with him clearly struggling with all this as much as she was. When he didn't say anything, she took his silence as consent and brought the head to her mouth, letting her lower lip rest against the crown, letting him stop her.

No stopping. He nodded, jerkily, and reached down to touch her face as the impressive manhood she held in her hands bobbed against her mouth.

"One night," he managed, as the heat of her mouth enfolded him. "I want the whole night."

She nodded, and she worked him deeper into her mouth, letting her tongue luxuriate in the slick skin and the salty evidence of his need. He slid his fingers into her hair, his eyes on hers, letting her see what every flick of her tongue did to him.

Right now he was hers, without barriers, and that was enough. It'd have to be enough.

It wasn't long before he gasped and gestured urgently, trying to pull himself free of her mouth. But she didn't want that, she wanted everything she could get from him tonight—her one and only night—and grabbed his hip and drank him down.

When she finally moved back, he collapsed onto the bed, hands closing on her arms to pull her up to him so that her cheek rested on his chest and he tangled one hand in her hair.

"No holding back. One night, no holding back," she whispered against his skin, kissing her way back down to his boot.

"Okay."

A couple of strategic Velcro rips and she had his foot free. "Thank God, you've got the bandage too. I don't think I could control my fingers enough to wrap it."

He laughed. "I'm already on the bed and I'm not sure if I can get up to the head of it."

She crawled up onto the bed, fetched condoms from the nightstand to have them within easy reach. "For when you're able."

He nodded, and just pulled her back to him, still struggling to catch his breath.

"Aren't you able yet? It's been at least fifteen seconds. I thought you had stamina." She couldn't stop herself from teasing. She wanted that too—no holding back meant giving everything, pleasure and passion and the playful side of both. That's who they were. That's what she wanted, the real Liam, not the polished celebrity adored by the masses.

He dragged himself more fully on the bed and reached for her. Soon they lay face-to-face, him on his good side—and she let him as it'd minimize the pressure on his ankle. "Can't have you doubting my stamina. But in my defense that was a cripplingly good orgasm. I might need a minute to get my mojo back."

His humor had returned to match her own. She couldn't stop herself smiling. "So long as you're not done."

"I'm far from done," he assured her, running his hand over her hip as if he couldn't quite believe that he had his hands on her. "I'm going to need at least two more rounds before I'm done. Maybe three. If you don't fall asleep."

"Me?" She laughed and scooted closer so that their noses all but touched. "Let me remind you that I'm the one who worked for this. Seducing you is exhausting, Mr. Carter."

He took her tease in the spirit it was offered, and slid his arms around her as she hooked a leg over his hip to keep him close, little adjustments to get closer and closer. She could already feel him growing hard again against her inner thigh.

His expression sobered a little. "I'm sorry. But you know it's not because I didn't want you. You wouldn't believe how I've imagined this. So long. You got me through some dark days, Gracie. Actually, this is probably going to sound pretty creepy, but when I was penniless in LA, doing all those awful jobs that got me from audition to audition, my favorite pastime was thinking of you. Off at school. Standing in front of that apartment door with the trench coat open and sheer black bra and panties...I could still draw a picture with every detail preserved. If I could draw."

"You pictured me a lot?"

"Every day."

"Just dark times?"

"No, of course not. Good times too. When I had some time alone. Going to sleep. Running."

"Was I the carrot?" she asked, leaning down to kiss him again, her fingers combing through his hair in a way that was both soothing and arousing at the same time. Increased pressure encouraged him to roll over, and she went with him.

"Sometimes," he murmured.

"Sometimes it was some other woman in her underwear?"

"No," he said, pushing her hair back from his face, the tenderness in his eyes making her inexplicably teary. "I don't think I've ever daydreamed about another woman like I do about you. But I don't always run happy. Sometimes…"

"Sometimes you run mad? Sad?"

"Yes. Though that doesn't always work out well. Running if you're too distracted can result in a sprained ankle."

Sprained ankle? She probably shouldn't ask, but it was right after he and his girlfriend had split. "Because of Simone?"

"No. No, not Simone." He slid a hand around the knee she had hooked over his hip and rolled to his back so that she was on top of him.

She sat up then, settling herself against him at the wrong end for penetration, but still in a place where she knew he'd enjoy a little friction.

"What were you upset about? The part?"

"No. Less talk. More… Where's the condom?"

"Not until you tell me what made you fall," she said,

flattening her hands against his chest and grinding her hips down just enough to slicken him.

His eyes got that unfocused look of pleasure and he grabbed her hips to keep her right there, even as he groaned his complaint. "Not fair."

"I don't play fair." She usually played fair, actually, but if it wasn't important, he wouldn't be trying to hide it. "No holding back. You agreed."

He sighed then and stopped her hips. "It was the anniversary of my father's death. It's always a bad day."

A bad day, he'd said. Like those words were powerful enough to carry all the meaning that went with them.

When she'd first met Liam she remembered thinking he was different, and the discussion she'd had with her parents about foster care, and why Liam was in foster care. Her parents had told her enough that she'd have been nice to him even if he hadn't been the most handsome boy she'd ever seen. But Liam wasn't much for sharing. He minimized things. And she was beginning to understand that the things he minimized most were the things that hurt the most.

"Did I kill the mood?"

Grace realized she'd been staring at him a long time and that she had tears in her eyes.

That no-holding-back rule... "Does that happen on your mother's anniversary too? Or were you too little when she died to really—?"

"I don't remember much about that." He lifted that tattooed shoulder, minimizing further.

"But you do remember your father's death. Were you there?"

"No. I found him later." His words were delivered so flatly and emotionlessly...

Her heart ached, her eyes burned, and she leaned forward to kiss him, unable to say anything.

Warmth slid up her body as his hands crept to her cheeks, and as he accepted and returned every wet kiss, his thumbs brushed away her tears.

When she'd kissed him enough to give him a glimpse of all the sorrow she felt on his behalf, she leaned up to look at him again. The tears still came, but his eyes were dry.

"Don't cry. I'm okay now. You got me better."

"It's not that. It's not that you got distracted and fell. Can't I just be heartbroken for you? Because I am."

"I'm not."

Lies. Lies he might have even believed.

He reached to the side, grabbing one of the foil packets she'd put out and tearing it open as he sat up, pushing her up as he did so, freeing the erection once captured between them for the condom.

"Liam…"

"Do you still have those panties and that bra?"

"No."

She knew what he was doing. He'd done what he'd promised, he hadn't held back, but now he was getting this fantasy-fulfilling evening back on course.

"I went home and burned them. They were all tainted with unrequited longing and…"

A little shifting and she felt herself stretching to accommodate the hardness pushing insistently into her.

"Do you have some other ones? I think… I deserve some black underwear to complete this memory."

She wanted another night. Another ten thousand nights wouldn't be enough.

CHAPTER TEN

ANYTHING SHE WANTED. After their night, when they'd both been drunk on pleasure and each other, when the idea that everything would be okay somehow had dominated his mind, Liam had announced he'd give her whatever she wanted. Ask him anything, he'd say yes.

And he had. Even when she'd asked him to be her date to a wedding.

So dumb. All of that was going to make this harder. Consequences.

Liam tossed his keys to the valet and went to offer Grace his elbow. The boot that made it easy to walk without support didn't go with his formal wear, so he was back to tape and a cane. Only today it didn't hurt much at all with the tape. Unlike before. A sign of progress: that he'd healed enough for tape to work. At least physically, though his heart and conscience were starting to feel battered from the effort.

He looked down at her smiling face and the pit of acid eating a hole through him widened, and he had to work to swallow it down. Whatever was between them was usually flirty and playful. Even when she'd been grumpy with him over his ankle, they'd still found their way back to that playful relationship.

And there was the problem word. They no longer had one fantastic night, they had a relationship.

This was a date.

A date to a wedding, of all things. Because Grace was made for the fairy tale.

He should have figured out some way out of that promise. But he'd considered it, and the fact that they'd be staying alone together in a hotel had overridden his sensibilities. One night had turned into one more night.

But he hated broken promises, with all the promises made and broken in his childhood, so making promises lightly should be the last thing he'd ever do.

And the Liam from Grace's bed—the one satisfied down to every last atom—would've kept that promise. So today, even though he'd had two days to come to the conclusion that this was a bad idea, he had to keep his promise to Grace. He just couldn't keep it well. The spirit of the promise was different from the tangible semantics of it.

Tonight had to end differently than she wanted. It had to end differently than even he wanted. Because what he wanted was the opposite from what was right. Tonight had to be a bad night. To help her see things clearly. To knock the stars from her eyes.

She gasped softly as they walked through the lit estate. Cool night breezes rolled off the ocean below and all the trees glittered with white lights.

"I guess this is what the wedding of the children of Hollywood royalty looks like," Grace murmured, squeezing his arm. "Your ankle okay?"

"It's fine."

"Are you sure? You look like you're in pain."

"I'm okay."

"You're scowling," she said, waving with her free hand to different people they passed.

Security took their names, and an usher came to escort them off to more white and gold, to rows of chairs in two blocks facing an astonishingly lit gazebo and a sea of puffy white flower balls that Liam couldn't identify.

"I'm…" He started to deny it, but then lowered his voice and his head to her so no one else would hear. "I'm not a fan of weddings."

"But it looks like a fairy tale."

Fairy tale.

Seated, Liam shifted around, trying to get comfortable. "Yes. It does."

"You're not happy for Freya and Zack?"

"Don't know Zack, but sure. Freya's a good person." Liam didn't know her well, but they'd spoken a few times at some event or another. It was impossible to move in the same circles for years and not interact on some level. He had gone to The Hollywood Hills Clinic because it was attached to the Rothsbergs, after all. "She's smart and she's worked for what she has. So, sure. This is what they want? I'm happy for them."

Grace leaned back a touch, studying him. Since they'd been around one another for this second chance…or whatever it was…she'd watched him study people. Been told a few too many times what she was thinking because he studied her. And she'd picked up a thing or two.

He'd carefully positioned himself on the chair beside her so that they weren't touching. His arms were crossed as he waited and other guests were shown to seats around them, and he didn't even look at her when he spoke.

Liam didn't just not want to be there, he didn't want to be there with her.

Or was it a case of him not wanting to be there with her in front of people who moved in his circles? She only moved in adjacent circles that had some people who moved in his circles…

Her blue dress was nice but not designer. It fit her well, but wasn't couture. She hadn't gone to a stylist to have her hair and makeup done. She hadn't paid a week's salary for her shoes or her handbag. And the simple diamond teardrop necklace she wore for special occasions wasn't big enough to be specially insured. She looked nice, but far from glamorous.

Liam, on the other hand, wore a handmade suit. His shoes were probably also made just for his feet. And he smelled like sin, but who even knew if that was a cologne or just the way he smelled? Not her.

So was it the family thing again? Somehow, after their night together, she'd thought he was coming around to that. Nick wouldn't be at the wedding. There were so many people there that even if camera crews gatecrashed, it wouldn't be to see if Liam had brought his physical therapist again. No one in her family had to know yet, so it couldn't be the circumstances tonight. It was about Liam not feeling it between them, even though she knew this path had to be leading somewhere if he'd just walk it with her.

Off to one side of the gazebo, musicians lifted their instruments and began to play. As the groom and groomsmen stepped up into the twinkling gazebo, beautiful string music began to fill the air.

She reached up and touched Liam's elbow, causing him to turn and look at her finally. "It's starting. You might not want to keep your arms crossed. It sends the wrong impression."

Everyone rose, so they did as well. Liam's arms unfolded to hang at his sides, but tension still screamed from his frame. She should have stood at the end, at least then she wouldn't be looking over his broad-shouldered surliness to see Freya in her dress.

Well, his surliness wasn't going to ruin the wedding for her. She wouldn't let it.

Unlike Liam, Grace loved weddings. She loved them even more when they seemed built to last rather than just being another notch in the bedpost of some star.

As Freya passed their row, it was impossible to miss her glow. She belonged there under the twinkling lights. Radiant in her pregnancy, the twins she carried only added to her blessings.

When they sat again, Liam kept his eyes forward, but at least he didn't cross his arms again.

She had to stop looking at him.

No matter what she felt, no matter what she believed could be theirs, it didn't matter if he didn't see it too.

She really had to stop trying to be with him. Leaving a door open to him was just as bad, she'd be the only one aware of it and waiting for him to come back through if she did.

They'd said one night, but it had been such a wonderful night, when he'd said yes to anything, she'd wanted to believe he felt it too.

He'd probably just felt the need to shut her up so he could sleep.

Six years hadn't made her any smarter about relationships.

The ceremony was crafted of beautiful words, and

all around her Grace saw handkerchiefs out and plenty of eye dabbing.

Did Zack take Freya? Yes. He did.

Did Freya take Zack? Yes.

They kissed.

Loving, honoring, cherishing. Forever. Not just one night. Not just one night that got dragged into two by one pushy person. But the beauty she could identify she didn't feel. By the time it was over, all she could do was force a smile.

That's what her situation with Liam lacked: they weren't both in it. She was the only one there, waiting for him to make up his mind.

The wedding party walked back down the aisle, and Grace stood, clapped with the rest of them.

Eventually they moved from the site of the wedding up the stairs built into the hillside to another plateau, this time at the top. The large cliff-top oceanside overlook had been set up to host the reception. Dinner. Marble checkerboard slabs defining a dance floor. Candles twinkling on every table, and an open wood framework above supported thousands more of the twinkling white lights. More stars in the sky than ever for Zack and Freya.

Perfection.

"Bar," Liam said, drawing her attention back to him with one word and gesturing hand. He pulled his elbow from her limp grasp and started away, saying as he left, "Find our seats?"

Find our seats? That implied he'd come and find her when he'd dulled his senses with bourbon or something higher proof if he could find that instead.

This evening couldn't end fast enough.

Grace turned to survey the tables to decide where

to start looking. She wasn't really one of the elite, she just worked with them. She wouldn't be seated at the kiddie table, but it would no doubt be farther from the action than Liam would've been had his name been the one on the list and she'd been his plus one.

Like that would've ever happened.

The cheerful sound of people laughing and chattering hurt her head, and the whole situation hurt her heart.

She checked a few of the peripheral tables, found her name, and pulled out the chair.

Time to fake a smile and sit with him through the dinner. Time to pretend for the benefit of everyone else, so she didn't come off as one of those women who became depressed at weddings. If he hadn't driven them there, maybe she could just go and give her love and her congratulations to the couple and tell Liam they could go. Another reason why it would've been better to have stayed dateless for the occasion.

Was he still taking the pain medication?

Was it her place to ask if he was mixing alcohol and his anti-inflammatories?

No. He wasn't her patient anymore. And he clearly didn't want to be more.

This was what came from her making bold moves in Relationshipville. She should have just been happy to have gotten him into bed. She'd had her night. And it had been so good it had made her stupid. Her IQ always seemed to drop a few points where Liam Carter was concerned.

She forced a smile as people joined her, introduced herself, made the expected small talk. Eventually, Liam came over, placed a drink on the table for her and took his seat beside her, much to the delight of everyone at the table except Grace.

Drinking the fruity concoction gave her a cover for not being chatty and personable. Liam was the one everyone wanted to talk to anyway, and it suited her.

She'd muddled through difficult situations before. She'd survived being rejected in her underwear, she could handle this rejection too. But it would've been nice if it had come before the wedding. Then she could pretend easier.

By the time the dancing rolled around she was so ready to go but had to wait until the bride and groom were off the dance floor.

"Pardon me," she murmured to the table at large, scooted her chair back and wound her way through the tables to the clearing and into a copse of trees on the far side.

Just a moment alone. That's all she needed. Somewhere quieter to breathe.

She wandered through the trees until she got to the edge of the cliff, out of sight, somewhere she could see the water, and leaned over.

Now what?

It wasn't long until she made out the sound of movement in the trees behind her. And voices. At first quiet, but then loud enough for her to recognize one.

James Rothsberg.

And he was talking to a woman.

Grace leaned around the tree just enough to see who was there, and considered her escape route.

This was what came from her going to the edge, there was nowhere to go besides over the cliff into the water and rocks far below, or past James and...

"Mila, you look good."

Moonlight filtered through the treetops, a shaft illuminating the woman's face. Romantic.

Oh, hell.

Grace leaned back again, looking at the ledge between the trees and the cliff face.

Was that wide enough for her to skirt the trees without plummeting to her death in her high heels?

The last thing she wanted was to see her boss having A Moment. Especially tonight. Could she not get away from the magic in the air anywhere?

"Do I? I looked better at our wedding."

Their wedding? Okay, maybe it wasn't going to be that kind of a moment.

Grace couldn't stop herself. She had to look again.

Should she clear her throat? Climb the trees and see if she could get in touch with her inner primate and balance-beam her way across the limbs without breaking her neck?

There was some talk of another woman, which Grace didn't entirely catch.

But then Mila raised her voice. "I don't care who you're dating. Or who you're not dating. Or who you're maybe thinking of one day dating. It's not my business anymore. My business is Bright Hope and my patients, that's what's most important to me now. Let's leave it at that."

"A truce, then?"

"I haven't been picking fights with you, James."

"I'm not picking a fight either, but that's how things keep going. So…truce. Let's just try to keep things professional."

"Yes. That's what I've been trying to get across to you."

"And once the photo shoot for the South LA Clinic is done, we'll just keep to our separate corners. No need for further interaction."

"Sounds good."

Grace could feel the emotion tingling in the woman's voice, but considering this wedding business and another woman...well, who could blame her for being roused to a quiet fight with her ex?

James and Mila had once been married, or something...and now they were stuck working together? Maybe not smoothly working together but they were trying. She knew she'd heard the word "truce" in there. Because that was the adult way to handle these kinds of relationship issues.

Which made her hiding in the trees until it was time to leave clearly not the adult way to handle this mess with Liam.

Freya wouldn't notice if she slipped out before face-to-face congratulations, she had so much else going on this evening.

Grace peeked around her hiding tree again, but no longer saw James or Mila so she darted through the trees and back to the reception.

Get Liam.

Get out of there.

And just get it over with.

She should've stuck with just the one night.

Liam hadn't expected her to want to leave before the first dance but, then, she probably wouldn't have let him dance on his ankle. And she'd spent so much time away after dinner it seemed like his plan to make her dump him was working.

His stomach soured at the thought.

But if she did the leaving this time, she wouldn't feel rejected. It would be her turn. And he could take it.

With her silent and tense at his side, Liam opened the door to their hotel room and held it for her.

Grace stepped past him and went straight to the mini-bar. Ten seconds later she'd poured herself a straight vodka and in less time than it took for her to lift the glass to her mouth the clear liquid was gone.

The drink must've burned as she breathed hard, coughed a little, and put the glass down. Pulling her shoulders back first, she turned around to face him.

"I don't know how to do this. Never thought it would come to this, but it's just one more way I'm delusional when it comes to you." She stopped, rubbed her head and paced away from him, then back.

Self-comforting. Dispelling tension.

It was happening. He could smell it in the air like salt by the ocean. His stomach rolled and he stuffed his hands into his pockets, lest she see him shaking.

Unlike the dinner where he'd brought up the trench coat, she wasn't hiding her gaze from him tonight. It was all right there, spelled out for him.

"Whatever stupid idea made me invite you tonight, consider me over it. I thought that things changed between us that night. I thought that you had finally stopped running from this. I thought you felt..." The words dried in her throat, and she looked back at the empty glass. "Something."

"It was supposed to be one night," he said, avoiding all that talk of feelings, because even now, even though this was what had to happen, he wanted to comfort her.

"I know!" Grace blurted out. "I know that's what we'd said. But that was before we were together, and one time became one night, became one whole night, became yes to whatever I wanted. That was the perfect example of a situation changing, right? It seemed that way. It seemed like…"

She stopped facing him and went to the balcony doors and opened them, pulling the drapes back so that the cool night air could blow in, and breathed deeply.

He didn't know what to say, aside from the apology clawing at the back of his throat. He shut his mouth so she'd keep going, make it go just as he'd rehearsed in his mind all day.

"I didn't ask you to come with me because I was trying to collar you. I haven't been writing 'Mrs. Grace Carter' on my notebooks. I just wanted to be with you and see how things went. I didn't invite you here as some grand gesture to hint for you to start making commitments. I know that there are extenuating circumstances to be careful of with my family. And I know you're just out of a relationship."

"That relationship has nothing to do with this one."

"No? Because you don't care what people say about you and Simone?"

"No. I care about what your family could say about us. That would be true. Unless this leads to marriage, then it's a betrayal of the trust that David and Lucy put in me when they welcomed me into your home."

"Why?"

Damn. She was going off script. This wasn't how it was supposed to go. She was supposed to yell and leave. Demanding explanations meant she saw through his tactics, and there was a danger of this turning into him rejecting her again.

"Because you're built for marriage, Grace. You are a cry-through-the-ceremony woman. But I don't want to be married. Not ever. I don't want kids. Any of it. I am not your white-picket-fence future. But that's what you want, or what you'd come to want, because that's who you are. And you would get hurt."

"I'm hurt now! Because you're lying to yourself and to me. I love you, and I know you love me."

Rolling stomach turned to nausea at her words. Ignore it. Ignore them. He drew a deep breath, looked her in the eye, and said, "I don't love you. Not like that."

The words felt like mud in his mouth. Mud and blood. Acidic and wrong.

She shook her head, tears in her eyes. "Yes, you do. You might not want marriage and children, but you feel more for me than lust. I'm not nothing to you."

"I never said you were nothing to me. But even if I did love you, love doesn't make things magically work out. My parents loved one another. They did. They probably loved me too in some twisted way—why else would my father refuse to grant permission for me to be adopted for so long but to keep from losing me? They were full of love, for each other, for me, and for their heroin. They still spiraled into death and destruction together."

How had this gone so far off course? There was no easy way out of it. No one else had forced him to say words he'd never wanted to give voice to, there was no one else he felt compelled to bare his soul to. Another reason to get out now.

She poured herself another drink.

"I loved my father, Grace. I loved him and I still couldn't save him. When Nick went to school and I moved into my own place in LA? Before my acting took off, I sought him out, moved him in with me. I thought maybe if he was there and we had a relationship, if he had someone to count on, someone to talk with about Mom, I thought he could heal. But he didn't.

He died, Grace. He died alone on the living room floor of my run-down little hovel. Love didn't help him. Not once. Not ever. Love doesn't fix things, it just makes losing harder."

The tears in her eyes spilled over her cheeks and she stepped toward him, her instinct to comfort him. Always to comfort. Even when they were fighting.

"I'm sorry," she whispered, stopping before she got to him, lowering the hands that had half reached for his face. "Your love couldn't fix him. Are you telling me this now because you want me to come around to the notion that my love can't fix you?"

"Yes." He felt his heart hammering against his chest. "I'd ruin you. That's what I'm built for. That's the example I have to draw from."

"You're wrong."

"I'm not."

"Yes, you are, because you don't need fixing. You didn't kill your father or your mother. Fate handed you a terrible situation, and you survived it. And you learned to thrive. You didn't ruin Simone. You didn't use me and throw me away, even when we were stupid kids and I offered you everything. You tried to do what was honorable at that time, you tried it later. I know you're trying now, but it just so happens that you're wrong." Her voice stayed confident and certain until she got to the end, and then it broke. One aborted sob followed by a short, bitter laugh—a sound nothing like the full-throated laughter he loved to hear from her. "Don't feel bad about it. I keep screwing up with you too."

"You give me too much credit. I agreed to one night with you because I crave you like an addict craves heroin. And you have the same addiction. I didn't care. Even now, I don't care. I want to stay because I want to be with you, but for the need to do better by you than what I learned from them. And if we keep on the way we want to there would eventually be a child. Or you'd want one. And people learn from their parents' example. My parents were abusive, neglectful junkies. Is that what you want for your children?"

"That's not what would happen. I saw you with Brody. But if you want to blame someone for this situation, then blame me. I'm the one who couldn't let go. And if you're guilty of anything, it's being too afraid to take a risk on me. I'm not afraid to take a risk on you. I know a sure thing when I see it. You might not see it, and I don't think you even want to see it, but you're an honorable man, Liam. Or else you'd still be with Simone."

Grace swiped her cheeks, picked up her handbag and then went to grab the handle of her suitcase.

"Where are you going?" His palms started to sweat and the air felt thick, soupy, hard to breathe.

"We're broken up, right? I can't stay here with you in this hotel room." She unlocked and opened the door. "Take care of yourself, Liam. You couldn't save your father, what happened to him was due to his own decisions. And I can't save you from this, because it's your decision. Only you can save yourself. Don't just do it in your rewind fantasies of this evening, and don't take too long... I'm not going to wait for you forever, even though I know that's how long I'll love you."

She pulled the door open, her head up and her shoulders back. And she was gone.

CHAPTER ELEVEN

SWIMMING IN THE pool at work had rules, and one of those rules was the hours of operation. But at two thirty in the morning, after tossing and turning her sheets into a sweaty tangle, those rules meant very little even to the perennially law-abiding.

The last place Grace wanted to be was somewhere she'd spent so much time with Liam, but work was the only place she could find a pool where she knew it would be safe to swim alone at that hour.

It took a little explaining to get her past the guard, but as she flipped on the lights to the pool room she could already feel the stress starting to abate.

A swim was what she needed. Exercise to burn off excess energy. The comfort of the familiar. Maybe the water could give her even the metaphorical weightlessness she wanted, some way to return to her usual mental and emotional buoyancy.

She dove in and prayed the water would work its usual magic on her.

How long had it taken her to get over Liam the first time? Really get over him, not just take out her frustrations by kissing every cute boy who hadn't immediately bored her?

Well, that was a depressing thought.

Because she'd never got over Liam. Not really.

She had eventually got to a place where it had hurt less and she hadn't cringed when she'd heard his name. By the time his face had been plastered everywhere, it hadn't even really hurt anymore. She'd built up a callus, which she'd vigorously exfoliated when she'd gotten tangled up with him again.

Kicking harder, she turned under the water, completing her first lap.

Three days and she hadn't heard anything from Liam. Tonight she'd come to the conclusion that she wouldn't. The paparazzi who'd found out where she worked had mostly given up following her—all except for a couple intermittent stragglers. Why bother watching her when Liam was clearly nowhere around? She went to work. She went home. She swam. It wasn't terribly interesting.

Even if they saw what she did when she was home, it would probably only inspire pity in them.

She was considering getting some cats.

And learning a craft of some kind.

And moving in with people who shunned cell phones. Anything to keep herself from asking Nick about Liam. He'd stopped talking about his friend anymore when they spoke, and she didn't know if Nick and Liam were even speaking to each other.

If they weren't on speaking terms any longer, that would mean that her desires had interfered with her brother's relationships. And if they were, it would be just as awkward between her and Nick, even if it was a different kind of awkward.

Cats, crafts, and shunning technology seemed like the safest outlets to turn her attention to.

Or maybe it was time for a change of scenery. Take

another job with a sports team, somewhere other than California, New York, or Virginia. Maybe if she went far enough away, she could figure out how to put it all behind her.

Liam sat sideways on the sofa in his hotel suite, trying to wrap his ankle before his guest arrived. It had probably gotten to the point that he could stop wearing all the wraps and splints if he was careful, but he'd be cautious a little longer. He just couldn't call Grace up and ask her.

He couldn't call Grace up for any reason.

But Nick he had called, and Liam was now waiting for his oldest friend to arrive. With all that had gone on with Grace, and then with Nick's reaction, he needed to figure out where they stood.

By the time he worked the little metal thing into the bandage to keep it in place, the door opened and Nick strolled in. "Hey, Miles let me in. He said you were working on your ankle."

Nick stopped by the sofa and looked down at the bandaged limb. "That looks like the same technique you use to wrap gifts."

"I don't wrap gifts anymore. Hailey does it now," Liam said, dragging a smile on his face even if it was just for show right now. He used to also have someone who would wrap his ankle for him, but that was over. And the reason why seeing Nick for the first time in more than a month felt like walking to an execution he'd volunteered for. "Thanks for coming. Want a drink? Bar's stocked, as always."

Liam got his sword cane and used it to meander over to the bar. Talking at the bar felt better than talking on the sofa. Less intimate, and Nick wasn't the Watson who Liam had a history of getting intimate with.

Nick followed and reached for the Scotch and two short tumblers. A minute later they had ice and whiskey in them. Liam had given up the pain relievers last week, just in time for this conversation that required alcohol.

"So, do you want to talk about my sister?" Nick slid a glass to him.

Right to the point.

Liam nodded, took a drink of the Scotch and looked for the words. Unlike with the Trench Coat talk, he hadn't planned any of this beforehand. He was by turns apologetic with Nick and angry with him, but before he got to his apologies, there were things he needed to know.

"Yes. And I asked you here because you're my best friend so if there isn't honesty with us, then this friendship isn't worth saving."

"Is there some reason it's going to be in jeopardy?"

"You might think so after I tell you what happened with your sister." Liam downed the Scotch and slid the glass back to Nick with a nod to refill it. "But first I need to know something."

Nick didn't sit. He stayed standing on the other side of the bar where the booze could be easily reached. "I think I know what happened with my sister. You dated her. You kissed her. You said you weren't going to do anything else, and then you ended up at a wedding with her. So I'm guessing that something else happened in there somewhere."

"Something else happened."

Another two fingers of booze slid back to him and Liam took another good pull at it—they always stocked the good stuff at this hotel, but this bottle could be smashed over his head just as successfully as rotgut.

"More happened. A lot happened. But, speaking of things that happened... You've known about her feelings for me for a long time. So I have to ask—when she had her accident and was in the hospital, why did you never tell me? She's got scars, she said that a motorcycle wreck derailed her from her career goals, and I would swear on a stack of bibles that you never said one word to me about her getting hurt."

"That's because I didn't." Nick rubbed the back of his neck and then leaned on the bar. "Your dad died that day, Liam."

It was a week and two days since the wedding, Grace spent most of her evenings alone with wine and movies. Tonight she'd added her cell phone, and now sat replaying a voice mail over and over, with her thumb hovering over the delete button, unable to bring it down.

Liam's bosses—the producers and whoever she'd spoken to on the phone about him—had called to offer her a job on their set.

High action, medieval, dragon-chasing fantasies could injure the actors and stunt crew just as effectively as thrillers and movies where the good guys fought the bad guys with high-speed chases and pyrotechnics.

Even though the phone call had felt like a job interview at the time, she really hadn't expected anything to come from it. And she still didn't know how to respond.

She wanted to say yes, and she wanted to scream at them to lose her number.

It was just a reminder of that door she'd left open for him. A door that any sane person would've closed by now.

She took another drink of her favorite sweet red wine and set the glass down, then pressed the button.

Delete.

The doorbell rang, and she continued to sit. Dealing with people didn't sound like something she could do right now.

She got up and turned to her bedroom to get as far as she could from the door. After she got another glass of wine.

"Grace?" Her name shouted through the door reached her just as she was about to shut herself in her bedroom.

Her hand started to shake.

That was Liam's voice. Liam was at her door.

The bottle felt heavy and awkward as she headed for the door, gripping the bottle with both hands lest she drop it.

Opening locks and latches with her hands full of wine bottle didn't work. She bent and set the bottle on the floor. When she finally got the door open, the first thing she saw was his eyes.

Still dark blue. But hopeful. He'd shaved and the man's trademark stubble was gone, leaving that broad, manly jaw completely bare.

She looked down at his feet next. Wrapped, but not in the splint.

And wearing nice dark gray slacks and a button-down shirt. No tie, and also no sexy lean or smoldering looks. This wasn't Hollywood's Beautiful Bad Boy. This was…not a booty call.

This was him trying to make a good impression.

Without saying a word, she focused on the various things in his hands.

A bouquet of daisies and roses in the crook of one arm.

A heart-shaped box of candy in the crook of the other.

And in each hand a ceramic figurine. A kitten in one hand and a puppy in the other.

Her words came back to her.

Her old rewind fantasies.

Quintessential boyfriend gifts because…he had relationship feelings.

One hand flew to cover the base of her throat and she held back a cry that wanted to collapse her chest.

Worry in his eyes, Liam stayed standing there in front of her, waiting in silence.

It took her a minute, but when she managed a full breath without whimpering Grace lowered her hand again and folded her arms across her ribs. She wouldn't touch him. She wouldn't throw herself at him. He'd shown up, and that was a lot, but he had to say some stuff too.

Her stomach had just tied itself in a knot, and she probably couldn't even have moved from in front of the door if the apartment had been on fire.

Don't say the wrong thing.

She nodded to his hands. "What's all this?"

"It's candy, flowers, a kitten and a puppy," Liam said, not a hint of their usual flirtation in his tone. He looked nervous. And he sounded insane.

"The kitten and puppy were supposed to be real. And alive. Not ceramic."

"I'm new to commitment, Gracie. I didn't think I could handle taking on two animals if you told me to get lost so I went with figurines." He nodded to the apartment, and then to his arms. "Can I come in? Or can you take the breakables?"

"Are you here to ask me to go steady?" Even as she said the joking words, her heart leaped at the idea. It was a beginning. And they'd come this far. If he took this first step, he wouldn't turn back. Liam didn't know how to quit.

"Yes. And anything else you're willing to risk on me."

She unfolded her arms and opened the door wide enough to reach for the flowers and candy, relieving him of the items perched most precariously on his arms.

"Did I have four arms in your rewind fantasies? Or a pet carrier with the animals in it?"

"It's a lot to carry. I did say those fantasies were insane at the time." She stepped back from the door and nodded to him and the floor. "Don't kick the wine."

Turning to the hall table, she set down what she'd taken from him and then looked back, waiting. Afraid to let her hopes get too high. Terrified because they were already soaring.

"I had a long talk with your brother," Liam started. He stepped in and set the knickknacks down then closed the door.

"About me?"

Vulnerability, she saw it in his eyes. It was there in hers if he was looking closely enough, and he always looked closely. "And me."

His hands rubbed together roughly. He seemed to realize what he was doing and stuffed them into his pockets instead. "And also why he didn't tell me about your accident."

It was something she'd wondered too, but hadn't been able to bring herself to ask Nick yet. And right now it seemed very important for her to hear anything Liam wanted to bring up. Let him talk. At least as long as he had something to say he wouldn't go. She could hear his voice. Watch his mouth forming words—any words.

She could see that he'd nicked himself shaving before coming over.

"Why didn't he tell you? Was it because he knew about…my trench-coat antics?"

He shook his head.

"He didn't tell me when I called him, because it was the day my dad died." The words came softly, but he made no move to hide the rawness in his voice. "And he knew I'd still drop everything and run to your family at Cedars. He said it was the last thing I needed to deal with."

Grace nodded as she absorbed this. Nick had done what he'd thought was the kindest thing to do for Liam, and she might've made that same decision. He'd had no way of knowing what had been going on with them—she'd certainly never told anyone about the night she'd gone to his apartment. He'd probably only known they'd stopped talking about one another, if he was even perceptive enough to pick up on that at twenty. "That was probably the right thing to do."

"No, it wasn't," Liam said, taking a step closer to her, close enough to touch her if he wanted to. Or for her to touch him if she was brave enough. "It was an attempt at kindness, he did it because he cared. But the truth is… Cedars would've been the best place for me. I tried to make a family with my father when I got old enough, but we were both too damaged to know how. And when that ended, the best thing I could've done would've been to go to my real family. The best thing for me, I mean. You all had a lot to deal with at the time. So I could've understood if he'd not told me because you all couldn't deal with one more broken thing that day."

She still didn't know if she should touch him, but she needed to, and he needed it too. He'd come as close as he could and had left that final step to her, so close her head craned back and she could feel his breath fanning her skin. Accelerated, scared. She lifted a hand and rested her palm against the solid heat of his chest, and then used the other to brush away a trace of blood beside that razor nick. "That would never have happened."

"I know," he whispered, catching the hand at his jaw and holding it there while he looked down at her, his worry fading as fast as hers started to fall away.

"But I realized something after my talk with Nick. Something I'd been missing. Family takes care of each other, I got that part right. But the part I messed up is… real family never give up on one another. They never…" His eyes closed and he bowed his head forward until his forehead lightly touched hers. Slowly, his arms crept around her waist, the slightest tremble evident in his broad frame.

This was real. He was really doing this. It may not have come easily, but it did come. And she was going to say yes to whatever he offered because she'd learned those lessons early about how to treat the people you love, and he was still getting there.

"They never give up on someone they love," he said, as if touching strengthened him enough to go on. "My parents gave up. On life. On me. On everything. They worried about their desires first. When you were hurt, Nick didn't keep the information from me to keep me away from you or your family, he did it because he was trying to protect me. And maybe he was trying to protect you too, because you have terrible taste in men, Gracie."

She laughed, her hands moving up to cup his cheeks. "No, I don't. I had good taste when I picked you. But when it didn't work, all my efforts to find a stand-in

Liam failed. Turned out bad boys are easy to find but it was impossible to find one with your heart. With your charm. Your kindness and honor."

Tears rolled fat and wet from her eyes.

He tilted his head, kissed her eyes and nosed away the tears on her cheeks. "Don't cry. I don't ever want to make you cry again. If you'll still have me."

"What am I having you for?" She leaned back to look up at him once again, and slid her arms around his neck.

"Whatever you want. I'll take whatever I can get."

He held her gaze, those deep blue eyes open and full of love. He hadn't said it directly, but she'd known beyond doubt that he loved her since their only night together. She just hadn't believed she could wait for him to come around to the same knowledge.

"Do you want marriage?"

"I want you."

"Do you want children?"

He said again, "I want you."

"But you were worried about those things before, them being…contraindicated in a relationship with you."

"Contraindicated?"

"It's medical talk. It means don't mix this and that. Like ibuprofen and wine, and I suppose that in this case I'd be the ibuprofen…"

"You would certainly be the ibuprofen, you dull the pain and keep me upright. It's not sexy, but it's not wrong," he said, and then answered her question. "My objections have all been about the ways that I would screw it up and knowing I couldn't live with myself if I did. I told myself I didn't want marriage and children because I don't trust myself. I still don't trust that I'll have the right instincts. I've been terrified that I'd fail them and you. But after I talked to Nick, after I pieced together his motivation, my motivation, and your motivation, I realized what's been missing in me."

She shook her head, not understanding.

"When you Watsons screw up in relationships, when you make the wrong calls for the people you love? It's because you're trying to do what is best for them. When I've been making the wrong calls, it's been because I was afraid and trying to do what was best for me. But I know it now. I see the difference. I finally get it. And I know I can do better."

He stopped, tears standing in his vision. So open. If he said another word she'd break. They both needed a moment to touch before even one more word came. She tugged his head down, the barest urging needed.

His mouth closed on hers and he pressed her back, two steps and he had her once again against the entry wall. Only this time the need that drove him was toward closeness, to starved kisses, until they were both left gasping for air.

"Please take another chance on me." His forehead went back to hers, the rest of his body melding to hers. His words came slowly, with pauses for breath, but he didn't stop long enough to catch his breath properly. "I can promise, right now, that I'll want you. Forever. I'll love you forever."

He'd said it! Again a breathless laugh bubbled up, and she could only nod.

"Be patient when I screw up, because I'm going to screw up, I know I will, but I'll do it for the right reasons. Teach me how to make a life together—a real life, not some surface-deep Hollywood sham of a relationship. I want you, Gracie. I love you. And I understand now."

One tear fell onto her cheek, and then another. It took her a moment to realize they were his.

"One life, nothing held back. Deal?" Her voice, still not strong, wobbled over the words, and she smiled even as they both cried.

He nodded. "Deal."

"Now take me to bed."

He laughed, nodding and swooping her into his arms to head for the bedroom. And she let him. His ankle was wrapped, and it felt too good to be cradled against his chest.

She leaned up and kissed his ear, then nuzzled in close and whispered, "I got some new lacy black underwear…for next time…"

Because there would be a next time. A lifetime of next times.

* * * * *

WINNING BACK HIS DOCTOR BRIDE

TINA BECKETT

To my husband and children…always!

PROLOGUE

Six years ago

THERE WERE CERTAIN benefits to returning to civilization, texting being one of them.

Without it, she doubted she would survive this party.

No. Not party. "Charity event," as these A-listers liked to call their swanky affairs.

Whatever.

Mila Brightman's thumbs glided over the keys with remembered ease.

will let u know.

C'mon, Mila. He's gorgeous and newly single.

Perfect. Just what she needed. A *charity* date to go with the charity event. She grinned at her own witticism. Okay, so her mental play on words hadn't been all that funny. But, then again, neither was this party.

He's ur bro. You have to say that. Does he even know u r trying to set him up on a date?

Not yet. But it'll be fine. And he is cute. Promise.

She hadn't even told him yet. Mila rolled her eyes, thumbs already responding.

That's what u said about the last guy.

She'd let her new friend Freya Rothsberg talk her into going on a different blind date a week ago. That particular man had been good-looking all right, but their date had stalled when he'd road-raged his way down Hollywood Boulevard. She'd ended up hopping out of the car at a stop-light and hailing a cab to take her home.

This is different. PROMISE.

Uh-oh. Her friend had used the word *promise* twice in a row. This time in caps. Never a good sign. Freya was on the other side of the room, waiting for her supposedly gorgeous brother to arrive. Time to head her off at the pass. Maybe she could use humor to soften the blow.

With my luck ur bro is probably short and squatty. A real toad.

The screen stayed blank for almost a minute, and Mila wondered if she'd offended her friend. Then it lit up.

A toad? Really?

A smiley face followed the words. Whew! Not offended.

Yep. T.O.A.D. Warts and all.

Another long pause. Maybe the Wi-Fi reception in the hotel ballroom was glitching or something.

Why don't you look up and see?

Something about those words caused a shiver to ripple across her midsection. Swallowing, she glanced over the top of her screen.

Freya stood right in front of her. Eyes wide. Mouthing something. "I'm sorry."

In that instant, Mila realized her friend was no longer holding a cell phone. Neither was she alone. And the person standing beside her was neither short nor squatty.

Oh. My. God. Her thumbs pretend-typed the words as they sprinted through her head.

The man in the tuxedo was tall. Very tall. And gorgeous?

Yes. Oh, yes. He was also holding something up, turning the object to face her.

A phone—with all Mila's text messages surrounded by a bold blue bubble. The air left her lungs, and she struggled to breathe.

He'd read what she'd written. And suddenly the banter didn't seem quite so innocent. Or funny.

Before she could apologize, one side of the man's mouth tilted up, the movement carving out several craggy lines in his face. If she were a swooner she'd have keeled over by now.

"You know what they say about kissing toads. One of them might just turn out to be a prince."

Her brain fought to process anything other than that low sexy tone. Although she could have sworn the word "kiss" had been in there somewhere. At least, she hoped it had.

She gulped, her eyes straying back to his mouth just as the other side tipped to form a smile that scorched across her senses. If she moved she feared she'd crumple into a pile of ash.

As if reading her thoughts, he passed the phone back to

Freya, his gaze never leaving Mila's face. "Shall we test that theory?"

"Th-theory?"

Before she knew what was happening, he'd swept her out onto the dance floor and off her feet. And when his kiss came a few hours later, just as the party was winding down, it was indeed magical. Only there was no need for any kind of transformation. Because James Evan Rothsberg already looked like a prince. A prince whose kiss was every bit as deadly as his smile.

Right then and there Mila knew, without a doubt, her world would never be the same.

CHAPTER ONE

Present day

Bzzzzzz...

No matter how many different ringtones James tried—and it seemed like he'd tried them all—he still hated receiving text messages. The flat sound of his current tone was no different. His pulse sped up and his throat went dry, even though he knew it wasn't from Mila.

Losing the fun, sexy messages they'd used to exchange had been one of the hardest adjustments he'd had to make after calling off the wedding, and his no-texting rule was his way of trying to deal with that.

He shook himself from his stupor. Six years had changed nothing. No matter how right he'd been to break off their engagement, he couldn't blot out the image of the horror in his ex-fiancée's gorgeous hazel eyes when she'd realized it was over.

So were the intimate texts. All texts, in fact, since everyone around him was aware that he preferred actual phone calls to typed messages.

Besides, Mila had taken off to parts unknown soon after he'd skipped out on her, going back to Brazil, where she'd been doing relief work among indigenous people.

Until now.

He'd had a damned good reason for leaving her at the

altar: a panicked phone call from a former girlfriend telling him she was pregnant. And an unexpected betrayal by his father.

It didn't matter now that the whole thing had been a setup. That deception had turned out to be a blessing in disguise. Mila had been saved from being dragged into the reality that was his family, with its arguments and its never-ending scandals. His famous parents had been the darlings of the paparazzi for that very reason—even after their divorce years ago.

Mila might not have seen it at the time, but surely in the years since then she'd come to realize the narrow escape she'd had.

He'd never tried to contact her, even after he'd discovered what Cindy had done.

The phone sent him a reminder buzz.

He forced himself to look down at the screen as he exited his car along with the damned photographer the clinic had made him bring along to this meeting. The text was from Freya. The no-text rule had become a running joke with her. She would text him just because she knew how much he hated it. To try to provoke him to answer. It never worked. He always responded with a phone call. Or not at all.

It would seem she was still at it. And under the circumstances it was in extremely poor taste.

We saw you pull up. Waiting just inside.

We. That could only mean one thing. Freya wasn't alone inside that tiny building. Although he'd known she wouldn't be.

Hell. He'd hoped to have a moment or two to get his thoughts together, although he'd had plenty of time to prepare for this photo shoot. Over two months to plan his words down to the final punctuation mark.

Had he done that? No. He had not. Even during the twenty-minute drive out of the more secluded Hollywood Hills and into the city of Los Angeles itself he'd done no advance planning.

Morgan, the photographer the PR department had contracted, had been more than happy to keep up a steady stream of conversation. She might have been fishing, but James didn't care. He was no longer biting. He was fresh out of yet another superficial relationship, which the paparazzi had followed with glee. He was definitely not ready to test the waters again. Especially not with this meeting with Mila hanging over his head.

He'd avoided thinking about that particular woman. He'd decided that if he kept his head in the sand long enough, this whole damned situation could have just dissolved into nothing.

It hadn't.

And he knew exactly who'd be on the other side of the door once he walked through it.

Mila Brightman.

The woman who'd almost become his wife.

The woman who'd barely escaped that particular fate.

Thank God she had.

He didn't bother to respond to his sister's text. They both knew he was here, so there was no point. How, exactly, his sister had talked him into this arrangement he had no idea. The Hollywood Hills Clinic had been gliding along just fine without another addition to their efficient little family.

Except this was Freya. And Mila. Two women he'd always had trouble saying no to.

Sucking down a resigned breath and dragging a hand through his hair, he waited for Morgan and then he headed up the walk, stopping short when he spied a ragged square of cardboard taped to the outside of one of the clinic's windows. He was so used to the pristine opulence of his own medical center that the squat building huddled on the corner of a busy street seemed as foreign as the relief work Mila had once done. But the sign painted at the top of the clinic was bright and cheery, a bevy of colorful handprints forming an imaginary sidewalk that led to an artist's rendition of the building—only whoever'd painted it had had quite an imagination because although the edifice was the same shape, the painted version was a welcoming place. And there were no cardboard patches in sight.

The photographer raised her camera, aiming it right at the broken window. James wrapped his fingers around the woman's, stopping her short. "No. Not that."

Morgan frowned at him but lowered the camera. "So you only want the positive stuff?"

His eyes were still on the brown square in the window as they reached the front entrance. "That's what we're here for."

Bright Hope Clinic. The painted lettering on the glass door matched the colors of the handprints on the sign. And the glass doors were spotlessly clean. His glance went back to the cardboard patch.

A sliver of unease worked its way through his gut. Not about Mila's safety. Of course not. About the soundness of his decision to allow a branch of this clinic to open inside his own. Freya's doing. Not his. But his damned board of directors had put him in charge of overseeing the opening of the facility. Which was why he was here, pricey photographer in tow.

The woman took a few shots of the sign and the door, dutifully avoiding the window. "We can go inside anytime you want."

Before he could even reach for the door, however, it was flung open and Freya stood there. "Come on, James, what's taking you so long?"

"What happened to the window?" He nodded toward

the offending cardboard, not sure he even wanted to know the answer.

Although he couldn't see Mila, she was just inside the dark entrance of the clinic. The growing pressure in his chest told him that. Schooling the rest of his body to mimic the bland mask he wore on his face, he made no move to go inside.

"Oh…um…" Freya glanced behind her. "It's nothing. Probably just a stray baseball."

James turned his attention to the busy street behind him. Cars clogged the asphalt as they waited for the light to change and allow them to head on their way. Baseball? He didn't think so. Not on this road. He lowered his voice, to avoid Morgan hearing him. "Tell me you weren't here when it happened." His sister was seven months pregnant and did not need any stress at this point.

"No, it was sometime last week." She waved off his concern, a frown appearing between her brows.

Biting back his next words, knowing his sister wouldn't welcome any brotherly advice, he sighed, hoping she'd catch his drift.

"It's perfectly safe, James."

Safe? With Mila somewhere inside? He didn't think so.

But he was here. And the sooner he got this over with, the sooner he could be on his way. The space they'd set aside in The Hollywood Hills Clinic was on the other side of the building from where his office was, so it wasn't like he'd see her every day. And he was pretty sure she would split her time between this facility and the new one.

With that bracing thought, he motioned the photographer and Freya inside and then followed them.

The interior of the clinic was as cheerful as the sign. Bright colors were splashed on every available surface, as if a painter had opened his cans and tossed the contents onto the walls and countertops.

"Wow," Morgan said, already snapping shots of the interior.

Wow was right. The place was so very...Mila that it made him smile.

His gaze came back, zeroing in on her at last with a swallow.

Her hair was much longer than it had been when they'd been together. Back then, it had been cropped into short waves above her ears, allowing the delicate bones of her face to shine forth. Not that they didn't still. But unlike the easy-care locks of days past, the new Mila appeared cool and polished, the curls tamed into long sleek strands that ended just below her shoulder blades.

He swallowed again and extended his hand in a fake formality that would make the PR department proud. "Mila, nice to see you again. Thank you for letting the clinic do some publicity shots."

Right on cue, the camera clicked multiple times, reminding him of how often he'd been caught unaware on the streets of LA. During his parents' ugly divorce, he'd barely been able to go anywhere without some member of the paparazzi lying in wait, hoping to get him at the worst possible moment. He tensed, before forcing himself to relax his muscles.

He didn't ask how Mila was doing, and for a split second he thought she'd refuse his greeting. Maybe it would have been better if he'd kept his hands in his pockets, but then she reached forward and curled her fingers around his.

Big mistake. The contact scattered images through his head that were every bit as vivid as the paint on the walls. Memories of Mila's head nestled deep in his pillow as she'd slept, of making love into the early hours. Laughter. Late-night texts. And finally the tears.

Damn it.

As if plagued by the same thoughts, Mila snatched her

hand free and turned away. "Nice to see you as well. And it's fine about the publicity. You're used to it by now. Besides, I'm sure your clinic wants to show off its newest investment. So how about a quick tour? I didn't schedule any patients this morning, but you should be able to see—"

He touched her arm to slow the torrent of words. It worked. She swung around, but he noticed she took a step back, the distance just enough that he couldn't touch her again.

"The window. What happened?"

Freya broke in. "James, it's fine. Don't go all protective big brother on us."

Not very likely. The last thing he felt toward Mila was brotherly affection. But he did feel a niggle of worry.

He narrowed his eyes on his sister. "I think we have a right to know the risks involved in taking on this little venture."

He glanced toward Morgan, but she was ignoring them, still exploring the waiting room, where brightly colored plastic chairs perched on top of acid-stained concrete that had been polished until it gleamed.

"*Little* venture?" If Mila's voice had been cool before, it had now dropped to well below freezing. "Afraid you might lose some of your high-dollar clients if they spot a pair of humble flip-flops cruising down the fancy halls of your clinic?"

His jaw tightened. Not at her words but at the disdain in her tone. And the fact that she had hit a nerve. The board had discussed at length how to handle their newest addition.

The voting members had made a motion to add a separate entrance so that Bright Hope could be accessed directly from the parking lot, instead of its patients coming in through the huge double doors at the front of the clinic. The decision stuck in his craw because putting in another door made it seem a little too much like a service entrance for comfort.

He'd gone along with it only because if he hadn't, the vote to allow the opening of the clinic might not have gone through—and Freya had her heart set on it. It had only passed by a slim margin as it was. And the financially challenged kids of LA did need access to what The Hollywood Hills Clinic could offer.

Telling Mila any of that, however, would not make her feel any better. If he knew her, she had only agreed to Freya's idea because his sister had insisted.

Which meant Bright Hope was not doing as well financially as she had made it seem.

"Let's just say we'd rather not have a gang war break out in one of our hallways."

Mila's eyes flitted sideways away from his.

Damn. He'd been joking about the gang war. Had that broken window been caused by a hail of bullets? "Do you have security?"

"Yes. There are cameras, and a security guard is here during business hours."

But only during those hours. Did Mila come here when there was no one else around? The question tickled the back of his throat, but he ignored it. He didn't want Morgan going back to the board with any tales that weren't true. He took another tack instead.

"Did the police catch whoever broke your window?"

"Not yet, but I've turned the surveillance video over to them. Hopefully they'll find the culprits."

Culprits, plural. "Do you keep drugs on the premises?"

She threw him a stormy glare that he recognized all too well. "Of course not. Nothing stronger than over-the-counter pain medication. There's a pharmacy around the corner, if we need something stronger."

That was smart. "Was anything taken?"

"They didn't try to gain entry."

Strange. Maybe she was right. Maybe it had just been a stray ball from a kid.

And from her curt answer, that was all he was going to get out of her. "Well, then, let's take that tour, so Morgan can shoot some pictures, and I'll let you get back to whatever you were doing."

"So she *does* have a name." His ex-fiancée leaned closer with an amused smile, one brow raised.

What was that supposed to mean?

Oh, hell. He'd seen the women shake hands but he'd forgotten to introduce them. Bad manners on his part, but he didn't exactly think straight when Mila was around.

Well, even if she thought there was something going on between him and the photographer, who cared? She'd been dating Tyler, that brawny firefighter, until recently, hadn't she?

With the same fixed smile, Mila indicated for them to follow her down a small hallway to an exam room.

This space was decorated in tropical island hues. Ocean-blue walls and sand-colored linoleum were a smart choice. As was the artist's rendition of a palm tree painted in the corner. The same beige from the flooring flowed up onto the bottom half of the wall, meandering across it, giving the lone tree a place to root and thrive. Individual grains glimmered under the overhead lights, much as they would beneath the sun. A few painted conches dotted the surface of this imaginary beach.

All in all, it was a tropical paradise any child would love and not a cold, sterile exam room. This was a place of adventure, not of fear and pain. And as skillful as Morgan might be, there was no way she was going to capture the feel of this room.

He wandered over and ran a finger across the textured

paint that made up one of the palm fronds. "This is pretty amazing, Mila."

Maybe they should incorporate some of these designs in the new clinic to tie the two centers together. It would be a little different from the posh chrome and Italian marble in the rest of The Hollywood Hills Clinic, but maybe that would be a good thing. It might even give the board a reason to rethink having a separate entrance for Bright Hope. And it would make Mila feel more comfortable with her surroundings.

He knew firsthand she didn't like over-the-top extravagance. She'd practically cringed every time she'd had to get into his car six years ago.

It highlighted one of the biggest differences between them. Orphaned as a child, when her parents had been killed during a home invasion, Mila had been left a huge inheritance by her famous Hollywood parents. But she didn't live like it. In fact, she gave her money away whenever she got the chance. James, on the other hand, enjoyed the security that money could buy. Security he hadn't felt during his childhood years, even though his parents had been just as wealthy as Mila's, if not more so.

He gritted his teeth until his thoughts were back under control.

Surely by now even Mila could see that he'd done her a favor by breaking off their engagement. They'd been doomed, even without Cindy's deceit.

"Can we get some pictures of the three of you in front of that mural?" Morgan asked.

Freya gave a horrified snort. "Oh, no. Not me, thank you very much. I'm about to pop, and I'd rather not do it in front of a camera." She threw her brother a look. "You and Mila should be in it, since you represent what this partnership is all about. It would be good to have some publicity shots of you two, anyway."

Why the hell hadn't he thought of the possibility of having to cozy up to his ex in some of the pictures? Because he'd figured Freya would be in them as well.

Nothing to do but get it over with. He gestured for Mila to go ahead of him. She hesitated for several long seconds, then her shoulders dropped in resignation and she trudged over to the mural. James moved in as well, standing a good five feet away from her.

"Can you move closer?" Morgan waved her hand. "You're blocking part of the tree."

Was it his imagination, or did the photographer have a slightly "gotcha" smirk to her expression? Maybe he should have been a little less standoffish when she'd been flirting with him in the car because right now it looked like she was enjoying having him at her mercy.

He took a couple of steps to the left, trying to talk his way through his discomfort. "Who did your paint job? It might not be a bad idea to match this look in the new clinic."

She didn't get a chance to answer, because Freya grinned. "Mila did it. She painted the clinic signs as well. Aren't they great?"

His sister's pride was evident. As was the warning gleam in her eyes that told him not to say anything that would hurt Mila's feelings. As if he would.

The photographer snapped a couple of pictures right as that news was relayed. Even he could feel the shock on his face. He hated to think what it would come across as on film.

He glanced back to get a closer look at the tree. It was good. Very good. Right down to the smooth green of the coconuts hanging from it. He could have sworn she'd had it done by a professional. But then again she had lived in the tropics of Brazil so it made sense that she would have had learned to improvise and do more than practice medicine. And she had always loved children.

A trait that seemed to be missing from his family tree.

Another area of incompatibility. If only he'd been looking at their relationship with a clinical eye six years ago, he would have seen it. It had taken a shock from an ex-girlfriend and an offer of payment from his dad to make him see the reality of what Mila would be subjected to if he married her.

Another flash of Morgan's camera, but he was too busy with his thoughts to take much notice.

Mila had survived. Improvised.

Had she improvised with some Brazilian man after he'd broken things off with her?

A thought he had no business dwelling on.

"Can you both turn toward the front? I'd like a couple more in this room before we move on."

They both swiveled on their heels and faced the photographer.

"So do you think you can replicate this over at my clinic?" he asked.

She threw him a glance, the brow from earlier edging back up. "Beaches and palm trees won't exactly match the theme you have going on over there, would it? What do you call it, by the way? Moneyed Green? Or are you just hoping artwork like this will highlight the differences between your clinic and mine—your patients and mine?"

The camera went off again.

Damn the woman. A muscle in his jaw clenched. "I was trying to pay Bright Hope a compliment. Forget I asked."

Fingers landed on his forearm, and her eyes closed for a second before reopening. "I'm sorry, James, that was inexcusable of me. Can we start over?"

It was far too late for that. But if cold indifference was the way she wanted to play this game, then she would find he could match her, ice chip for ice chip. Except she'd never been an ice queen. Far from it. In fact, he'd always liked

Mila's hot temperament. It had matched the places she'd been. Stoked his own internal fires.

But he'd better figure out how to extinguish that particular flamethrower. And soon. First, though, he had to get rid of that damned camera, which seemed to be recording their every expression.

She'd almost blown things. As Mila gave James and his photographer the grand tour, and it wasn't much, with the tiny size of her clinic and the money crunch they'd been under for the last few months, she tried her best not to let her animosity toward him show any more than it already had. Six years after the fact, she should be over their breakup. But his comment about her decorating choices had made it fizz up like the head on a beer. And he hadn't even meant it as a cut.

She drew in a deep breath. It was up to her to calm the waters.

Only how was she supposed to do that when the waters churning inside her were gray and choppy? And with that photographer giving him the eye for most of the visit?

She pushed open the door at the far end of the hall. "And this is our business office."

The head of her young assistant, Avery Phelps, popped up from behind her rickety desk, her brown eyes widening. She backed out of the narrow space on her hands and knees and climbed to her feet, tugging the hem of her blouse down over her tanned midriff. "Hey, Mi. Sorry. I was just trying to get this stupid cord to stay in place for once."

"The computer again?"

"Yes. And I lost an hour's worth of work this time."

Mila groaned as she glanced at the empty screen of the computer monitor. "I'm so sorry. I keep meaning to have someone come out and take a look." It was still weird to her to have to rely on technology to keep up with things when she was used to taking patient notes on actual paper, with an actual writing instrument. She preferred jotting things down, it seemed more personal.

But she couldn't ask Avery to do that when things in the US were all done via computer. The young woman had been with Mila from the very beginning, when she'd rushed into Bright Hope as the frantic single mom of a very ill three-year-old girl. It had turned out Sarah had type one diabetes. Once they'd gotten her blood-sugar level under control, Avery had wanted to give something back and had insisted on donating several hours a week to the clinic—after working her own full-time job. She'd been at Bright Hope ever since, eventually becoming an employee rather than just a volunteer, and Mila had no idea what she'd do without the woman.

"Do you want me to take a look at it?" James's voice rumbled over their heads.

Yeah, it would have been pretty tempting to ask him to crawl around underneath that desk, but she was afraid her body would go haywire and send out pheromonal signals that could be detected for miles. "It's just a loose power cord but every time the desk jiggles, the power blinks in and out, and Avery loses data."

He gave the old machine a dubious look. "Not good for your system. Do you have any tape?"

"Tried that a couple of times." She was proud of herself for being one step ahead of him. Although it was really Avery who had thought of that. And how embarrassing was it to have this exchange in front of a camera?

"How about surgical tape? Or even phlebotomy tubing?"

How was that supposed to work any better than what they'd already tried?

Before she could ask, Avery said, "I'll get you some. Anything to keep the darned thing going."

Mila made a mental note to get someone techy out to

look at the machine. The last thing she wanted was for James to have to come out to fix things.

Like her practice itself? If Freya hadn't gotten him to agree to pump some funds into Bright Hope and allow her to open a branch inside The Hollywood Hills Clinic, people like Avery would have very few options. Mila had gone through most of her inheritance in the years since her aunt had passed away. Not that she missed the money. She didn't. But she missed what it could do.

Within a minute her assistant had come back with a roll of latex tube tourniquet and wide surgical tape. "Pick your poison." Avery said it with a smile, but a shiver went over Mila. Maybe because her poison had been James once upon a time. And like a slow-acting toxin, he'd killed the part of her heart that she'd handed over to his care.

"Let's try the tubing first."

Freya, who'd been silently watching the exchange, smiled. "My brother the handyman. Always trying to fix what's broken."

Was her friend talking about the eating disorder she'd overcome years ago? Mila remembered James's sometimes heavy-handed tactics when it came to his sister, but Freya said that things had mellowed between them over the last year or so. Especially now that she and Zack had fallen in love and gotten married. Their twins were weeks away from being born, and the pair was ecstatic. Mila had done her best to be happy for her friend, but it struck too close to home. That could have been her and James had he not decided that a wife whose passion was working with various relief organizations would cramp his Hollywood style.

That might not be exactly true, but something had given him cold feet. He knew she wasn't interested in being a big earner, so she'd always assumed that had had something to do with it. Only James had never seen fit to tell her why he hadn't wanted to marry her. Just that she was better off without him.

And she was.

Definitely.

And he could keep his reasons for breaking their engagement to himself. After all, she was used to being kept in the dark. Her aunt had loved her, but in trying to protect her she'd left Mila unprepared for the shocking reality of her parents' deaths. They hadn't died in a car accident, like her aunt had told her. In fact, her mother had lingered for days in a hospital after being shot. Ten-year-old Mila had never even had the chance say goodbye. It had taken her a long time to forgive her aunt for that once she'd discovered the truth.

The Mila of today did not believe in holding back information no matter how unpalatable or difficult it might be. To do so was to destroy her trust. So James's refusal to level with her had made it easy for her to walk away and never look back.

His voice came from nowhere, jerking her back to the present.

"I'll need some scissors." He tested the flexibility of the tubing he'd been handed.

What was he going to do with it?

Avery grabbed a pair of sharp scissors from the desk and handed them over.

Somehow wedging his large body between the leg of the desk and the wall, he grunted a quick oath at something and then remained silent for several minutes.

And the view from where she was standing was exquisite.

A length of tubing appeared on one side of the computer. "Can you grab that, Mila?"

Conscious of the pencil skirt she'd donned for the photo shoot, and praying the photographer didn't catch a wardrobe malfunction, she knelt down and took hold of the tubing that he'd pushed beside the computer. Only it now had a dark stain on it. Red. Wet.

"Are you bleeding?"

She glanced up at Avery, who read her wordless request. Within a second or two she handed Mila a bottle of hand sanitizer and some gauze. She quickly wiped down the tubing and lobbed another question toward James. "What's going on back there?"

"Tie it at the front of the computer."

She frowned. How was this supposed to fix anything? "How tight do you want it?"

"Pull it taut and then start the computer up."

Mila tied the two ends together and made a quick knot in the rubber. "Okay, let's see if that did it."

Pushing the start button, the screen leapt to life, along with a warning that the computer hadn't shut down correctly.

"No kidding," her assistant muttered, staring at the monitor.

"It's going, James. Thank you."

A few seconds later the man edged backward and climbed to his feet. The fingers of his right hand were pressed tightly against the sleeve of his dress shirt, where another stain had formed. "Oh, my God, what did you do?"

A series of clicks went off behind them. Mila ignored the sound.

"It's nothing. Just found some old tack strip along the wall."

Oh, no. The building had been carpeted when they'd first moved in. Mila had immediately gone to work removing it and then prying up the tack strip. By the end of the process she'd been dog tired, and since the office desk had always been there, she'd left the lone strip where it was. She'd forgotten all about it until now. It was a wonder Avery hadn't cut herself on it. She threw the woman a look. "I'm sorry, I totally forgot about it."

Her assistant gave her arm a gentle squeeze. "It's fine. I've never had any problems avoiding it."

Avery was a lot smaller than James, so that was probably true. Still, it didn't make her feel any better.

"Let me see." She held her hand toward him. He eyed her for a second and then shook his head.

"It's nothing. Just a scratch."

"Then you won't mind if I look at it."

His jaw tightened, but he didn't argue with her again. He let her take his hand. The second his skin touched hers, a frisson of awareness trickled up her arm and circled her chest. She did her best to beat it back, turning his hand over to get a better look at it.

The flash of a camera went off in the background, making her suddenly aware that Morgan had been snapping away as nobody had told her not to. The last thing Mila wanted was a shot with her and James holding hands. But if she said something, he would know, so instead she found the spot where he'd cut himself. Long jagged lines ran parallel to his little finger, going up the side of his hand. Nasty looking but not deep enough to need stitches. "Have you had a tetanus shot recently?"

James's brows went up. "Yes."

Of course he had. He was a doctor. Her face burned, but she forced her voice to remain steady. "Avery, would you mind getting me some more gauze, please? And some alcohol from the cabinet in the exam room?"

The photographer slid sideways, her camera still up to her eye as she snapped shot after shot.

Evidently James had had enough. "I think you've taken enough pictures, Morgan, don't you?"

Whether he didn't want their picture to pop up in the society pages with speculation about them rekindling their past romance or something else, his low words had their desired effect. The woman murmured something that might have been either thanks or an apology and put her camera back around her neck. She then glanced at her watch. "Oops. I'm late for my next appointment. I'll just grab a taxi, if you don't mind. Thank you, though, for letting me hitch a ride to the clinic."

James nodded, but said nothing. Freya offered to see her out.

The pair left, leaving Mila alone with her ex.

"Nice touch," he said, indicating the hand she still held.

"Excuse me?"

"The clinic has been trying to improve my image. Evidently my bedside manner isn't always as soft and cuddly as the board would like it to be."

A thought came to her. "Did you cut yourself on purpose?"

"No." He nodded at their joined hands. "Did you do *that* on purpose?"

She released him. "Of course not. I was just trying to help."

His gaze came up to spear hers. "And so was I."

There was something about the way he said that that made her... No. It had nothing to do with their past.

She squared her shoulders. "And you are. Thank you." She gestured toward the computer. "For that, and for convincing The Hollywood Hills Clinic to take on Bright Hope."

"It'll be good for our image."

All of the warm feelings that had bubbled up a few moments earlier popped, leaving her feeling oddly flat. "I'm sure it will."

"Hey." He slid the fingers of his uninjured hand beneath her chin. "I didn't mean it like that. I meant it would be good for my clinic's image…and for yours. Your patients will know they're going to get quality care."

He cut off the words before she could say them. "Not that they wouldn't be getting that at this location, but we will lend you instant credibility. You might not like what that brings with it, though. Prepare to be inundated."

If he was trying to scare her, it wasn't working. She'd been swamped with patients plenty of times. In fact, the more she worked, the less she thought of her sad lack of a personal life, and how poor Tyler had pressed and pressed for a decision about taking their relationship to the next level, to the point she'd finally had to break things off with him. She couldn't do to him what had been done to her. And she'd at least had the guts to hand him the truth rather than dish up a halfhearted fabrication.

Like her aunt had about her parents' deaths? Or was she thinking of James and the way he'd ended things?

"Don't worry about me," she said. "I can handle just about anything."

Avery came back into the room with the items she'd asked for, and Mila hurriedly cleaned up James's hand with the alcohol, although he waved aside the need for any kind of bandage. "It would just get in my way."

"Are you sure?"

"Yes." He glanced at her face. "I'll let you know when the photos come back so you can look through them."

Good. That way she could weed out the ones that made her and James look a little too friendly toward each other.

Because things between them were anything but friendly.

And if she was smart, she would keep it that way. Despite the fact that they were going to be seeing a lot more of each other in the future, she would have to protect her heart. Because James had already hurt her once. She had to make sure he never got the chance to do so again.

CHAPTER TWO

DINNER PROBABLY WASN'T the best place to do this.

But it wasn't like he wanted these photos flashed around the corridors of The Hollywood Hills Clinic. At least, not all of them. Which begged the question of why he hadn't just tossed the more questionable pictures.

Why? Because he didn't trust his own judgment, that's why. He could be seeing things that weren't there. Things that were remnants of days gone by. Maybe Mila would glance through them and not bat an eye. It wasn't like there was anything suggestive about them.

They just looked…cozy. Not a word he would use to describe their current relationship.

Strained. Awkward. Difficult. Those were much more accurate terms. And if Mila didn't desperately need the funding that his medical center could provide, he had no doubt she would have refused to work with him in the first place.

All of this was because of Freya.

He eyed the entry plaque of the Très Magnifique with its gold-plated edging for the fifth time. Still no sign of his dinner date. He had always been punctual to the point of an obsession, while Mila had taken on the characteristics of the Brazilian people she'd worked with over the years. With them it was about relationships and not about the hands on a clock.

And exactly which relationship was she cultivating this time? The one with that firefighter she used to date? Was she seeing him again? If so, what did the man think of his girlfriend going out to dinner with a former lover?

It wasn't dinner. It was a business date.

And yet it made his skin chill to think of Mila as anyone's girlfriend. But he'd given up the right to that title—or the title of fiancé—a long time ago. One stupid lie had changed everything. And it hadn't even been his lie. But that, combined with his father's dark suggestion, had made him rethink the direction his life had been taking.

Everything with Mila had happened so fast, a flare-up of emotions he'd never realized he'd had.

But Mila was all about family and helping those in need. Maybe because her parents had died, and she'd been left alone.

Family, unfortunately, was the exact thing James hoped to avoid. His own family had been a disaster. Between the tabloids, the violent arguments and his father's very real infidelities James had always been leery of steady relationships. Then Mila had come along, and he hadn't been able to resist anything about her. For the first time he'd started thinking about forever.

Until Cindy and his father had destroyed the fairy tale. And that's all it had been. Mila had never tried to contact him once he'd ended things. Never really tried to ask why he'd backed out of their wedding at the last minute.

If she'd truly loved him, wouldn't she have wanted to probe a little deeper? Instead, she'd accepted his "it just won't work between us…we want different things out of life" explanation at face value.

"Sorry to keep you waiting." The breathless voice rushing toward him brought the gavel down on his thoughts.

Tightening his hold on the attaché case he carried, he turned to look at her. The fact that the first place his gaze parked was her lips, looking for any signs that she'd been kissed recently, irritated him. He focused on what time it was instead. "I see some things never change."

That soft mouth he'd been staring at tightened in warning. "I had a patient."

Damn. She was a doctor. Why had the possibility she'd gotten delayed due to a case never crossed his mind?

Maybe for the same reason that he saw coy glances passing between them in those pictures.

And she was only six minutes late. It only felt like he'd been waiting for her forever.

Hell, he remembered thinking almost those exact same words at their first meeting. The one where she'd called him a toad.

Unfortunately for Mila, he'd never really perfected the transformation into a prince. And she'd discovered far too late that she should have bypassed kissing him altogether.

Except he hadn't given her much of a choice, insisting that she dance with him.

Forcing himself to come back to the present, he motioned toward the door. "They're holding our table for us. Shall we?"

Mila glanced at the sign, and then the hand-carved door, her teeth catching her lower lip.

Had she been here before?

Not likely. This wasn't the kind of place the Mila he'd known would have frequented. So why had he brought her here?

The hostess guided them through the front part of the fancy establishment, and James tensed as his glance trailed over Mila's formfitting dress and the staccato twitch of her hips as she followed the woman. She didn't generally like dressing up, and when she'd heard the name of the restaurant there'd been a long pause over the phone before she'd finally accepted the invitation.

Now that they were here, he realized he should have made sure the restaurant knew this was a business dinner and nothing more—because the employee was taking them back to the table he was normally seated at when he dined here: a secluded spot in the very corner, away from prying eyes…and cameras.

He probably should have chosen a different place to eat. But they knew him here and it was generally easier to get a last-minute reservation than at the places where celebrities normally hung out. There were some of those at Très Magnifique as well, but the dim lighting, specially coated glass and tight security made it hard for the paparazzi to gain access to its patrons. Another reason why this was one of his go-to restaurants.

The distaste of having his face splashed across the tabloids was a holdover from his childhood, when his parents' every move had made the front pages. James had seen his own mistakes—including his broken engagement—paraded for all the world to see. Because of that, he'd become adept at avoiding the places those kinds of photographers frequented.

Mila slid into her seat, setting her small clutch purse on a corner of the table. "I assume you have them with you."

He had to smile at the way she lowered her voice, since it mirrored some of his own thoughts. Leaning forward, he mimicked her hushed tones.

"Yes. I have them. They're in my briefcase. But I think you went into the wrong line of work, Mi."

"Come again?"

"You should have been a spy."

Her lips went up as well. "Am I being too paranoid about this whole thing?"

A possible reason for her behavior slid up from somewhere inside him. He didn't know if she'd started seeing someone else since breaking up with Tyler, but it was a possibility. Or maybe they'd even gotten back together. "Will this be a problem for your boyfriend? I'd be happy to call him and explain, if you'd like." Although the last thing he wanted to do was call Mila's boyfriend and tell him this meeting was purely platonic.

Not when the last thing he wanted it to be was platonic.

Not with her sitting across from him in a dark green dress that hugged her form and showed just a touch of creamy curves at the neckline. Curves he'd once explored at his leisure. He forced his eyes back to her face, noting she was biting her lip again.

What the hell? Had she gone and gotten engaged or something? His stomach sank like a rock.

"No. You don't need to explain anything."

Because this guy, unlike him, would need no explanation as to why Mila was dining with her ex-fiancé? If she were still *his*, he sure as hell would have wanted to know why she was having dinner with another man. Especially since she was a physician and not a CEO, which meant there was no need to dine with clients.

"He must trust you." He forced the words to sound impartial.

"It's not that." She toyed with the clasp of her purse for a second or two. "I'm not seeing anyone. I told you I'd broken up with Tyler."

She had told him. But people changed their minds.

James stared at her for some clue as to what might have gone wrong between them.

"It was me," she continued. "This time."

Said as if she needed him to know that James wasn't the only one capable of backing out of an unwanted relationship.

"I'm sorry."

Sorry for the way he'd treated her? Or that his past actions might be affecting the way she navigated current-day relationships?

"Don't be. I don't believe in stringing someone along when I know how the story is going to end."

The barb sank deep. Because that's exactly what he had done to Mila. Strung her along, even when he'd known that he was eventually going to break things off. Both because of Cindy and the bombshell she'd dropped, and because of his own father's response to it. He couldn't follow in the award-winning actor and egotistical bastard's footsteps. He would not father a child that he would be no good at nurturing. Or throw money at the mother of that child to make the whole thing go away. So James had done neither, deciding to break it off with Mila and do the right thing by Cindy. Only it had all been a lie.

Mila's dreamy words the last time they'd slept together about starting a family had hit him at the worst possible moment. Their courtship had been such a whirlwind affair that children had never been discussed. And then Cindy had dropped her bombshell and almost immediately afterward Mila had wistfully expressed her own desire for children.

His reaction had confirmed what he'd believed about himself all along: that he truly was like his celebrity parents, who had left him and Freya to the mercy of a string of nannies. He was no nurturer.

Even his attempts at standing in for his parents when it came to his sister had ended in disaster. He'd been overbearing and overprotective. In some ways he blamed himself for the eating disorder Freya had developed, wondering if it was because he'd been too controlling about what she did…who she went out with. He sure hadn't practiced what he'd preached back then, because he'd gone out with scads of women who'd meant nothing to him. Including Cindy.

Hell, he'd been the worst possible role model for her.

His regrets over his mistakes with Freya and the scare

of that unplanned pregnancy with Cindy had given him a fear of having children of his own. It had gotten so bad that he had stopped treating children in his medical practice, referring them instead to colleagues. Which had left him treating insipid socialites and celebrities. People very much like his parents—a peck on each cheek, a little nip, a little tuck, and they were good to go.

Only he'd grown tired of it all. Weary in a way that he didn't understand.

"Drinks, sir?"

He blinked back to the present as the server handed them each a menu.

Maybe Mila had been lost in her own thoughts as well because she wasn't staring at him like he had two heads. He waited as she asked for a glass of wine, and then he did the same, adding an order of stuffed mushrooms—something he remembered her loving. Although why he felt the need to do anything other than toss the pictures across the table and eat a quick bite was beyond him. Except he probably wasn't going to get to sit across a table from Mila Brightman ever again. And maybe a part of him wanted to relive the days he'd left behind. Now that he knew she didn't have someone waiting at home for her, that urge had grown stronger.

The server left to get their drinks, and Mila propped her elbows on the table, staring at him. "So how does this work, exactly?"

He frowned. Had she read his thoughts? The idea of taking up where they'd left off flashed through his head. Somehow he doubted that's what she meant.

"How does what work?"

"The pictures. Do you want me to look through them before we eat? Or after we're done? Just how bad are they that we're even sitting here?"

Ah…so she had realized something was up when he'd asked her out to dinner. "They're not bad. I just…"

He hadn't expected to have to explain his reasoning. He tried again. "I just thought we should go through them without an audience. That might be hard at the clinic or even at Bright Hope."

Especially with a few of the more intimate shots. And Morgan had seemed to be quite adept at catching them at just the wrong moment. A woman scorned who was doing her best to embarrass him? Or was it inevitable that he would see the pictures through a different filter than other people?

Mila's lips curved. "Did she catch you crawling under that desk or something? I can see how you might want to hide that particular shot."

He laughed. "I take it the view wasn't all that flattering from where you were standing."

"Let's just say it was interesting."

Interesting.

He couldn't be sure with the low lighting in the restaurant, but he thought maybe a bit of color had seeped into her cheeks, and he couldn't help but follow this trail just a little further. Especially since he could picture several office desk scenarios he wouldn't have minded exploring once upon a time. "Interesting good? Or interesting bad?"

"I think the photographer thought it was good, that's for sure."

Had Mila noticed the other woman's interest? He thought he'd made it pretty clear that she was there on a professional basis only. He hadn't been interested.

"And you. What did you think?" Okay, so this was pursuing it a little too far.

"I think maybe we should stick to the subject at hand."

Not exactly a denial. More like an evasion. Which meant

maybe he wasn't the only one who was struggling to keep their old relationship where it belonged: firmly in the past. But he'd better make more of an effort, or he was going to find himself in a very uncomfortable place.

"Fair enough. Why don't we sort through them now, then?"

Mila swallowed as she shuffled through the sheaf of glossy photos that James had brought out of his leather attaché case. Now she saw why he'd wanted to bring her to a place where the tables were private and the lights were low.

Even with the dim lighting in the restaurant these shots made something in her belly come to life. These were not the kind of publicity pictures one wanted for the grand opening of a charity clinic. At least, not some of them.

One of the photos in front of the mural did more than light a fire in her gut. It made her face heat. Because she and James were gazing at each other, and while she couldn't exactly read his expression, hers was filled with dread—with a side order of longing. A longing that had made one of her hands stretch toward him a bit? Coaxing him to move closer to her like Morgan had asked? Lord, she hoped not.

Maybe she was simply gesturing toward something in the mural. But she didn't think so.

She flipped through a couple more, and then paused once again. James was watching her as she said something to Avery, a slight smile on his face, hands stuffed in the pockets of his dress slacks. He looked so endearingly at ease that it made her chest ache. It was as if she'd been sucked through a time warp and was looking through a window to the past.

Their past.

She could remember glancing toward him and catching

him with this exact same expression. As if he loved watching her go about life.

Swallowing, she looked up at him. "Is there anything in here that can be salvaged?"

She had no idea if there was a software program invented that could change these pictures into something they weren't. And it made her feel a little queasy that the emotions she felt on the inside were so very visible on the outside. At least in these shots.

But then again, hadn't Morgan caught James off guard in them as well?

"Some of them aren't as bad. But I wanted us to decide that together."

"I can see why."

Their server returned with their appetizers and wine. Mila handed the photos back to James for safekeeping. Or was it simply so she didn't have to look at them anymore this evening? She had a thought. "Maybe you can come to Bright Hope once we finish up here and we can spread them out on the reception desk."

"That sounds like a plan. Speaking of Bright Hope, did you get the glass in that window replaced?"

"Yes, someone came the day after your visit. It's as good as new."

"No other attempted break-ins?"

She paused in cutting one of her mushrooms. "It was just an accident. The police seem to think so as well."

Was it her imagination, or had James just relaxed in his seat? Maybe. She knew how relieved she'd been when the officers had said it looked like a rock kicked up by a car or something. There had been construction on that street not so very long ago.

Popping the morsel into her mouth and chewing, she studied the changes in James over the past six years. His hair seemed even more golden than it had before. From spending time in the California sun?

He'd once been an avid sailor, his sleek schooner making the trek back and forth to Catalina Island every chance he'd had. Hours on his boat would explain his deep tan. And she loved the way the crinkles at the corners of his eyes were lighter than the surrounding skin, as if he smiled more while out on the water than he did at other times. He had when they'd been together, anyway.

She swallowed, trying to nip her speculations in the bud. It was none of her business what he did or didn't do. Not anymore.

"What are you thinking about?"

Time to scramble. She didn't dare stray too far from the truth, because he'd read it in her face if she told him a complete lie. "Do you still go out on the water?"

One side of his mouth twisted into a half smile. "Every chance I get."

"On the *Mystic Waters*?"

His smile slid away this time. "Yes, I still have her. I can't imagine giving her up for anything."

Unlike Mila, who he'd been able to give up with a snap of his fingers. It stung to know that his boat had been with him longer than she had. Since they'd actually spent quite a bit of time on the schooner during their romance, the images it brought up were unbearably intimate. For all her discomfort about displays of wealth, the boat was one place she'd felt at home. Maybe because James had gone to great lengths to put her at ease.

It normally took four hours to sail from Los Angeles to the port of Avalon on the island of Catalina, but it had often taken them even longer, because James would stop every time she'd squealed in delight over some new sight, whether it had been porpoises trying to catch a ride on the boat's wake, or something else. And when he'd taken her below...

Her eyes shut for a second or two before reopening and finding him watching her.

He knew. Knew exactly what she was picturing. Damn him!

"The boats I spent my time on were a little different from your schooner."

"Rubbing my nose in the fact that you've given back more to humanity than I have?"

No. She wasn't. And she had no idea why she'd spouted off like some self-righteous prig. Maybe because it still hurt to know how easily he could toss her aside.

It seemed like every time she'd trusted someone, they'd broken her heart. Her aunt. The men she'd dated in the past. James.

His betrayal had been the worst of all of them.

But he'd gone to bat for her with the board of directors at The Hollywood Hills Clinic. That meant something. He might have founded the medical center, but that didn't mean he made all its decisions. Still, his support was probably the main reason they'd deigned to back a joint venture with Bright Hope.

Freya, as part-owner of the clinic, had helped push it through, she had no doubt. But James was the driving force, the one who'd made sure it happened. Who'd helped make sure disadvantaged children and their parents got the help they needed.

And the fact that she'd just wiped any trace of a smile off his face made her feel sick. When had she turned into such a shrew?

Bracing herself for the impact, she set her fork down and reached across to touch his hand.

"You've given back plenty, James. I remember you working on that little boy whose face had been damaged in that car—"

"I don't do that kind of work anymore." If anything, his

jaw tightened even more. "I've gone back to traditional practice, leaving post-traumatic facial reconstruction to… other doctors."

She sat back in her seat, shock washing over her. He was a gifted plastic surgeon so traditional practice had to mean that he…

She truly was a fool. A fool who'd once hoped James would join her on her treks to other countries, helping those who'd been disfigured, either through birth or through some kind of violent act. So had he only pretended to be interested in those things?

Evidently. Until he'd lost interest in her. Those long intimate conversations about the future and the good they could do together had meant nothing.

Nothing.

So why had he even tried to help Bright Hope get a foothold in the Los Angeles community and beyond?

It had to be because of Freya.

Mila had allowed herself to hope that maybe…just maybe James remembered their time together fondly and had used the funding from his clinic to show her that.

The waiter had set their dinner plates in front of them at some point, without Mila really paying attention to anything except James. The thought of eating now made her gut churn.

Maybe he read something in her face. Maybe he'd just realized how his words had sounded, because he leaned forward a bit, snagging her gaze with his.

"I'm happy about what you do, Mila. Glad there are still people like you in the world." A muscle in his throat worked. "I'm just not one of them. Those cases, they…"

He shook his head, not finishing his sentence.

"They bother you?"

Was that it? He couldn't bear to look at what humans could do to each other?

"Yes. They bother me." And this time Mila swore she saw a glimmer of something in his face. Compassion. Or maybe anger. She really couldn't tell. But it beat that blank mask he tended to wear.

Except for in those pictures. Then it had slipped when she wasn't looking. The camera had been watching, though, and it had caught him in the act.

Only Mila had no idea what any of it meant.

"They bother me too, James, but someone has to help them."

"I know." He lifted a shoulder. "It just can't be me. Not anymore."

"Why?"

The muscle in his jaw went back to its rhythmic pulse. "I'm just not cut out for it. I do better with the celebrities and socialites, like my parents. We come from the same world. We understand each other."

She shook her head. "I don't believe that."

"Believe it. It's true." He picked up his fork and cut into his thick slab of steak. "Don't let your food get cold. Très Magnifique does a wonderful job."

Mila had ordered beef tips with mushrooms over pasta. Spearing a bite-sized piece of meat, she tried to figure out what was going on with him. Only she was no good at reading this man. Not anymore. Maybe not even when they'd been together, since she'd been so sure he'd been as happy as she had.

Except he hadn't been. Not toward the end. He'd been pulling away, and she'd found herself becoming something she hadn't liked. A grasping, frightened girl, trying to do her best to hold a fading romance together all by herself.

Never again.

She would never throw her heart back into the ring like she had during her time with James. Tyler had known the score and had been willing to wait for her to trust him fully.

When she'd realized she'd never be able to give him what he needed, she'd broken it off.

And she missed his friendship. Especially now. Especially when confronted with a man who still had the power to wound her with the tiniest of barbs.

Like his unwillingness to work on those who so desperately needed his skills?

Yes.

But there'd been something behind his words. His relationship with his parents had always been rocky at best. And at the very end, when he'd broken off their engagement, he'd said something about his father. The loathing in his voice would have shocked her under normal circumstances but the agony she'd felt in realizing their relationship was over had drowned any other thoughts for a very long time.

Had the man threatened to cut James from his will for marrying a shy do-gooder who shunned the celebrity scene?

Somehow she couldn't picture James caring one way or the other. He'd made his own way in the world, his wealthy clientele willing to pay exorbitant prices to be ensconced in the luxury and prestige of his clinic and be catered to by some of the best physicians in the world. From cardiac surgery to face-lifts, from cradle to geriatrics, the medical center gave the finest care available.

She'd never understood what had happened between them, other than she hadn't been enough to make him happy. And she'd been too angry to ask if his surface explanation—that they weren't right for each other—was the truth. After discovering what her aunt had done, she'd decided she was never going to try to pry the truth out of anyone ever again. They could either tell her or not, but if they chose the latter, she was done with them.

Forcing herself to swallow, she pasted a smile on her face. "Thank you. You were right, the meal was delicious."

Not that she'd actually tasted much of it beyond the first few bites. "I'm ready whenever you are."

"Would you like coffee?"

She hesitated. James had always liked to finish his meal with a nice strong java, no matter what the time. Caffeine had never seemed to affect him. Neither had anything else. But she suddenly wanted out of the intimate confines of the restaurant and to finish this back on her own turf, where she knew what to do to protect her mind from stray thoughts... and her heart from stray emotions. She decided to go with escape.

"I have a small apartment above the clinic. I can make us a pot of coffee if you want, and we can go over those pictures."

He frowned. "You live in the clinic?"

"Not *in* the clinic, no. Like I said, I have a small studio apartment above it. It saves on transportation costs since I don't have to drive to work."

And it also made it easy to take those middle-of-the-night emergency calls, since all she had to do was throw on some scrubs and walk down a flight of stairs to get to her clinic.

"Were you there when that window was broken?"

No, she'd been in the process of breaking things off with Tyler that night. It had taken her almost three weeks to get the window repaired. Something she wasn't going to tell James, because she had the strange sensation he wouldn't be happy about that. Why he would even care, though, was beyond her.

"I was out that night. But it turned out to be nothing. No big drama. No one was hiding inside the clinic."

His frown deepened. "You went in by yourself?"

No. Tyler had gone in and checked the place out, even though she could tell he'd been crushed by their breakup.

She'd tried to take a taxi home, but he'd insisted on driving her.

He was a good man, a simple man with simple tastes, and Mila wished with all her heart that she could have fallen in love with him. But you couldn't control who you loved. She'd found that out the hard way—had mooned after James, even as she'd flown off to the jungles of Brazil to get away from her pain.

And it had worked. She'd come back a changed person. At least she'd thought she had. Now she wasn't so sure.

"No, I had someone with me."

James swallowed, if that jerky movement of his throat could be called a swallow.

"I'm glad." He called for the check and slipped a credit card into the padded folder. "I'll take you up on that coffee, if the offer is still open. It'll give us a chance to pick a couple of pictures and get them to the marketing department in time for the opening in a few weeks."

As soon as the waiter returned with his receipt, James pocketed it and his card and stood. Mila followed, now wondering if it wouldn't have been better to have their coffee here. She'd wanted to get back to her own territory, but was it really wise to invite the tiger into your sanctuary?

Melodramatic, Mila.

But as she slid into the leather seat of his luxury car, she wondered if she really was being ridiculous. The closer they got to the clinic, the more her nerve endings twitched in dismay. This was a mistake. She knew it was but it was also far too late to change her mind, not without him knowing she was afraid to be alone with him.

They turned onto the road where her clinic was located just as her cell phone sounded with a weird chirp, the one she'd preprogrammed to sound if the silent alarm on her clinic was tripped.

"Oh, no."

Just as James glanced her way, a question in his eyes, she saw her worst fears were realized. The glass door to her clinic had been smashed wide open.

James saw it too, and screeched to a halt just outside the entry. Before either of them could say a word a figure in dark clothing dashed out through the opening and sprinted down the street.

CHAPTER THREE

"STAY HERE!"

James gritted out the command as he threw open the door to his vehicle and dashed after the intruder. He turned the same corner as the man, only to be confronted by a spiderweb of alleys and apartment fronts. There was no sign of anyone. No witnesses. No perpetrator.

If Mila hadn't still been in the car, he would have ventured farther to make sure the jerk wasn't hiding in one of the dumpsters or behind one of the parked cars, but what if he had an accomplice? What if, even now, Mila had decided to go inside her clinic on her own?

"Hell." He should have just called the police and stayed with her, but the instinct to chase down whoever it was had been too strong. And now he was at least five minutes away from the clinic.

Pivoting toward the opening of the alley, he took off the way he'd come, his gaze seeking out his car as soon as he turned the corner. And found the passenger door open, the seat empty.

"Damn it, Mila!"

The muttered words were swallowed by the flow of traffic on the busy street. Why had no one stopped to help when they'd seen someone breaking in? Maybe because this wasn't the safest area of town.

And Mila lived here…had just gone into that dark clinic all alone.

Reaching the door, he found it still locked, so he stepped through the opening, glass crunching beneath his shoes. His instinct was to call out to her, but if someone else was lurking in the shadows, he was afraid he'd tip him off. Instead, he stopped for a second and listened.

He heard someone talking. Was it just Mila on her phone, reporting the break-in to the police? Or was someone else in there?

Picking his footsteps a little more carefully to avoid snapping more glass, he made his way through the inky interior. She hadn't turned the lights on. Why?

He reached the narrow hallway and drew up an internal map of the clinic from his visit a week ago. The voices were coming from the right, from the direction of the exam room he remembered seeing. Pausing outside the open door, he again heard Mila's voice, the low sound coming across as calm and soothing…as if worried about spooking a frightened animal.

It was then that it dawned on him. She wasn't speaking English. It was Spanish. She'd trekked through the Amazon basin, so she knew both Spanish and Portuguese.

He took a deep breath and spun around the corner, a streetlamp shining outside the window making it a little easier to see.

Mila, who was crouching in the gloom, grappling with someone or something, squeaked out a warning. He braced himself for attack.

Only the fear on her face was aimed squarely at him, not whatever was next to her.

"God, James, you almost gave us a heart attack."

He'd almost given *them*…? The thing next to her was evidently a who…not a what.

"What the hell is going on?"

Reaching to the right, where he remembered the light switch being, he flipped it on. Two pairs of eyes blinked up at him. His attention swiveled to the small figure huddled close to Mila.

It was a child—a young boy around three years old—not an armed intruder, like he'd feared. Which meant the man who'd run away from the building was what? A father? Boyfriend? Some kind of sexual predator...? His brows drew together in anger. Who broke into a medical clinic and dropped off a kid?

In one hand, the boy clutched a gray blanket, the satin edge frayed and missing in spots. The child's other hand was balled into a fist that he held against his mouth.

No. Not a fist. The child was sucking his thumb, fingers curled tightly into the palm of his hand. And those hollow, tearstained eyes...

The child stared at him for a second or two longer and then whimpered, cringing closer to Mila. James forced his frown away, realizing he probably made a scary figure standing over them, the emotions churning within him clearly visible.

"Está bien. No tengas miedo." Mila's voice was soft and comforting, even as she sent James another scathing glare.

She was telling the *child* not to be afraid?

What about him? She'd almost set him flat on his ass when he'd seen her kneeling there, envisioning all kinds of terrible things.

But this child was thin. Very thin and... His gaze stopped, chest squeezing tight enough to stop him from breathing for several seconds.

His feet. The boy's feet. They were turned inward at an unnatural angle as if they were pairing up for a duel.

Clubbed. Both of them.

His inward curse rattled his ribs and shunted the pressure that had been gathering around his midsection to his throat. The deformity should have been corrected when the child was an infant.

He knelt next to the pair, his glance meeting Mila's. "Is this one of your patients?"

"No." She placed a hand on the boy's head as if protecting him. From what? James's fury?

He wasn't angry. Not at the child, anyway. "I thought I told you to wait in the car."

"I was going to, but I heard crying coming from inside the clinic." She glanced toward the door just as the sound of a siren swept through the interior of the space. "And I knew the police would arrive at any second."

Not soon enough to stop a bullet, though, if Mila had come upon something other than a frightened child. His anger came back in a rush. "You should have waited for them, then. For your own protection."

Her face quieted, becoming an icy cold mask that stopped him in his tracks. "I don't need you to protect me, and you're not the one who makes my decisions. Not in the past. And certainly not now."

She was right. She was a grown woman, and this was her clinic. Not his. "I was worried. I lost sight of the man I was chasing, and when I came back and saw the car empty…"

Mila's mask cracked, then fell away. "I'm fine." Her head shifted toward the boy. "He said his uncle left him here. I think he was hoping to get the boy some help."

"Medical help, I assume." He nodded toward the boy's feet.

"Yes."

"And then just ran off? What kind of a—?" He bit off the word, not sure how much English the boy understood. "What kind of person does something like that?"

"Fear can make people do things they wouldn't normally do."

"Like abandon someone they're supposed to love?"

As he said the words he was gripped by a huge sense of irony. Fear had caused him to do that very thing. Abandon Mila on the cusp of their wedding, leaving her hurt and alone. No matter that he'd thought it a necessity at the time. And then when he'd discovered it hadn't been necessary, when it had been too late to take it all back, the tabloids had exploded with the news of their broken engagement, comparing it to his parents' ugly divorce years earlier. It had reminded him of all the reasons he should just leave things as they were. Mila deserved better than him and his dysfunctional family.

Freya had been there to pick up the pieces for her friend, and to rake him over the coals. He didn't think his sister had ever quite forgiven him for what he'd done to her dear friend.

The sound of voices shouting from the entrance to the clinic cut off anything she might have been getting ready to say, and they were soon caught up in chaos as the police rushed in, followed by the emergency technicians once the all clear was given.

Worse was the fact that a lone firefighter showed up, right on the heels of everyone else. Concerned eyes took in the scene, and Mila stood to hug him, leaning in to whisper something in his ear.

The man shrugged with a crooked smile. "I know. I was worried. Sorry. The address that came over the com was for Bright Hope. I had to check it out."

Tyler Richardson, Mila's ex. He evidently wasn't out of the picture as completely as Mila had said. And he was evidently allowed to worry about her safety, whereas he himself didn't have that privilege.

Taking in the lean muscle and short cropped hair of the other man, James stiffened. Emotions he'd thought long dead surfaced as he watched her describe what had happened, including the police officers in her explanation.

Mila never once lost her cool during the events that followed, and she didn't allow James—or even her ex—to speak for her, not that the man tried. He knew enough not to, which made James's chest tighten further. Tyler knew the woman Mila was today.

He forced himself to stand a few feet back and watched her, a strange sense of admiration rolling through him. She was confident and matter-of-fact. So different from the shy but passionate woman who had taken his senses by storm six years ago.

She'd traveled the world. Alone. Had probably faced hundreds of situations far more dangerous than the one they'd found at the clinic.

Would she have gotten the chance to grow and change if they'd stayed together? Or would the overprotective nature his sister accused him of having press her into a box she was afraid to leave? Or worse?

He had no idea whether he was trying to assuage his guilt in leaving her, or if it was a genuine question for which there was no answer. But, whatever it was, Mila had been changed in some undefinable way.

The firefighter who still stood by her side seemed to respect her as well. In fact, the three of them—woman, child and man—looked like the kind of family you saw on greeting cards.

And James didn't like it. At all.

He moved in closer to diffuse the picture. "I know Bright Hope hasn't officially opened its branch at The Hills, but I'd like to transport him there to do a workup and make sure there are no medical issues other than his feet. We have state-of-the-art equipment."

It was true. Not just that. His medical center was also equipped with suites to house patients who were having surgery so that their privacy could be guaranteed. A nod to battles he, his sister, and his parents had fought with the paparazzi. The center could also accommodate those patients who needed physical therapy after a procedure. And they always kept a few of the small apartments open for emergencies.

"That would be great. Thank you, James."

Tyler's head abruptly cranked around to look at him, narrowed eyes meeting his.

Was it his imagination or was there a veiled threat in the firefighter's gaze? He met the look and matched it with one of his own. Neither looked away, until Mila cleared her throat and glanced from one to the other.

James took a step back. "I'll call Adam Walker and see if he has any openings in his schedule. He's one of the best orthopedic surgeons around."

Mila's eyes closed for a second. When they opened, they were a warm shade of hazel that he hadn't seen in forever. "Thank you. I owe you."

"Nope. You don't."

If there was a debt owed by anyone, it was him. And it was more than he could ever begin to repay. For helping him discover something that had set his life path in stone. Or maybe he had Freya, his dad and Cindy to thank for that. Cindy's lie had saved two incompatible people a lot of grief and heartache. Mila might not have appreciated that back when he'd broken things off, but she probably did now.

It took almost an hour to sort through the red tape of having Leonardo—the name the boy had given them—declared a temporary ward of the state so that they could transport him to The Hollywood Hills Clinic. Mila had gone outside to say goodbye to Tyler and then had headed up to her apartment to pack a small overnight bag, insisting that she was going to stay with Leo at the medical center.

What if he got scared? Or had a nightmare? He shouldn't be alone.

"Are you sure you want to stay?"

The department of children's services wouldn't be there until morning. Maybe it was just as well, because James was suddenly bone tired in a way he hadn't been for a long time. Whether it was physical exhaustion or exhaustion that came from the emotional upheaval of the break-in and seeing Mila's ex, he had no idea.

"I'm sure," she said, walking with the EMT workers to the ambulance and then climbing in beside the boy. "Would you mind running by the store and picking up a few things for him, like clothes and a toothbrush?"

"Excuse me?"

"Oh, sorry." She peered out of the vehicle before opening her purse.

He stopped her with an upraised hand, realizing she'd misunderstood him. And he was glad that she'd chosen him to run her errands, rather than Tyler. If he refused, he had no doubt she would call the other man and ask him to get the items. Not going to happen. "I don't need your money. I just have no idea what size he wears."

Up went Mila's brows. "Um. He's around three years old. So a size three should do it. Get some underwear and socks too, okay?"

Kids' clothes sizes ran by age? Who knew?

"I'll meet you back at the clinic in an hour or so."

"Thanks. I'll see you soon."

The doors to the ambulance slammed shut and the vehicle sped away from the building, lights flashing, leaving him standing there alone.

Just as well.

He needed time to untangle exactly what had happened here tonight. And why the fishing hook he'd been toying with a few hours ago at the restaurant had just been suddenly and expertly set by some distant fisherman, leaving him little or no chance of escape. Not without inflicting some major damage to some of his internal organs. Although, if things got too bad, he might have to just rip free of the line and hope for the best.

Adam Walker met her at the door.

Mila tried to calm her still shaking legs. She'd been shocked that Tyler had rushed over to Bright Hope to try to help. Especially with James there. She'd felt guilty enough for breaking things off with him. She certainly hadn't expected him to show up right after she'd been wined and dined by her other ex.

Lord.

It was over. With both of them. She had nothing to feel guilty about.

And yet she did. That line of guilt ran from her to each man, and she wasn't sure which side made her feel worse.

Neither. And her mind should be on Leo right now, who needed her help.

"Let's get him to an exam room." Adam stretched his palm toward the boy, who, seated in a wheelchair, hesitated for a split second and then placed his small hand in the other man's. With kind eyes and tightly curled brown hair, the orthopedic surgeon had worked with children before. It was there in the easy grip of his fingers, in the way his right shoulder stooped low so Leo's arm wouldn't be stretched too high by the difference in their heights as Mila pushed the wheelchair.

Mila smiled, despite herself. Whereas James had seemed vastly uncomfortable in the boy's presence, Adam was a natural. Judging from the gleaming gold band on the man's left hand, he might even have children of his own at home.

They got Leo up on the exam table, and while a nurse worked on getting the boy's vitals, Adam rolled the bottoms of the child's threadbare jeans up a few inches to get a better look at his feet and ankles.

His jaw tightened as he examined the twisted appendages and slid his gloved hand along the outside edges of Leo's feet. "They're both fixed in the varus position."

Mila knew that there were two main forms of club foot, equinus—when the toes were pointed toward the ground—and varus, when the bone malformation caused the outer portion of the foot to swivel downward, forcing the toes toward the center. "I haven't seen him walk yet. I'm not sure if he can."

"You may not have seen it, but he does." Adam gestured her closer. "See this callusing over the tarsal and metatarsal? He walks on the edges of his feet."

"Wow. It should have been corrected when he was a baby."

Adam shrugged. "I've seen more of these cases in developing countries than here in the States, where corrective surgery is the norm. Maybe his folks couldn't afford it. Or maybe they immigrated here from somewhere else."

"He only speaks Spanish, from what I've seen. And he said his uncle left him at my clinic. The authorities are still trying to locate him."

The surgeon rubbed a hand behind his neck. "I can fix his feet. But we'll need permission from someone before I can do anything."

"I'm scheduled to speak with a social worker tomorrow. Surely they'll make a way, even if we can't find the uncle. He can't stay like this."

"I've done a few pro bono cases that have come through the courts when the system's doctors were inundated and couldn't get to them." He gave the boy's shoulder a squeeze. "I'll be happy to help in any way I can. Just get me the release forms."

"I'll get to work on it."

James pushed through the door, his arms loaded with packages. Not from the local store but from one of the upper-end clothing chains in the area. The orthopedist's brows went up, bland amusement sliding through his eyes. "Doing a little late-night shopping, James?"

"Sure. That's what I normally do with my free time."

His voice was a little sharper than she'd expected it to be, and she blinked up at him. Maybe he really had minded going to the store. She could have asked Tyler to go, but since they were no longer an item, she hadn't felt right doing so. She didn't want to give him any false hope.

So why had she been okay with asking James? Maybe because she hadn't been worried about him getting the wrong idea. He'd been the one to break off their engagement, not her, so he wasn't likely to want to rekindle anything at this late date.

And neither was she.

Oh, maybe she'd taken one look at that rugged face and piercing blue eyes and had seen stars for a second or two. But that had been pure fantasy. The real-life version of that relationship had gone up in smoke. And if she were stupid enough to harbor any ideas, she'd better snuff them out now because the man hadn't wanted her back then, and he undoubtedly didn't want her now.

Adam filled James in on what surgery to Leo's feet would entail and how long it and the ensuing recovery would take, while Mila peered into the bags of clothes.

Hmm. Superheroes. She never would have pegged James for a superhero kind of guy, although he was aloof and secretive. And he never snatched at publicity. In fact, he'd always shunned it while they'd been together, even though reporters had dogged his every step back then.

Was it because he hadn't wanted to be seen with her?

He'd asked her to marry him, for heaven's sake.

And yet he hadn't been able to go through with it in the end. How humiliating it had been to see cringe-worthy pictures of herself beneath headlines that had screamed things like "scorned" and "dumped." She'd fled to Brazil to get away from the onslaught…and the pain.

Pulling her mind from the past, she ripped open the packages, instead. "I wish we could run these through the washer before putting them on him, but I guess it's better than staying in the filthy things he has on now. I'd like to get him to a room and get him cleaned up, if we can."

James pulled his cell phone from his pocket and made a quick call. "Okay, mark the suite as occupied. Oh, and, Stella, make sure you have an extra trundle bed set up."

Good, he was taking her at her word that she wanted to stay in the room with Leo.

"Yes, I'm aware that the room already has one. I need an extra, in case there are any problems."

"Problems?" The panicked word slid from her mouth before she could stop it.

Adam, as if sensing a storm was brewing, gave a quick wave. "Let me know what happens with the social worker, or if there's a problem during the night. I'm on call."

She mouthed, "Thank you," to him, still trying to wrap her head around the bombshell James had just dropped. Why on earth did he need an extra bed? Did he think she couldn't handle one small child on her own?

As soon as the specialist was out of the room, she turned toward him. "I don't understand."

"You don't know this child or what he's like. It's just for one night, to make sure things run smoothly."

Smoothly? He was making Leo sound like he was just another chart to be dealt with.

As if realizing he needed to clarify matters, he said, "If it's true that his uncle dropped him off, the boy is bound to be frightened. He might even try to run away or the uncle could show up, which could cause legal problems for the clinic if the Department of Children and Family Services comes by tomorrow and the child has disappeared. I thought we could take shifts and watch him. See how he does."

Okay, so that made sense. Although she wasn't sure how he expected a three-year-old to sneak down the hallways unnoticed and make a daring escape. But he could get lost. Or hurt. Or someone could appear, claiming to be one of his parents.

At least James's reasons for staying with them were now perfectly clear. It had everything to do with protecting the reputation of his precious medical center.

And nothing to do with her.

She heard something.

Cracking her eyelids, Mila found a dark, silent room.

Not her bedroom.

Lying there for a moment, she waited for her vision to adjust.

Another murmur of sound.

Leo! She was in a hospital suite. Rolling to the side, she almost tumbled off the narrow cot until the events of the previous evening came flooding back to her. The boy. His damaged feet. James's insistence on spending the night with them.

She somehow managed to get her legs beneath her and staggered upright as a quiet sniffle and whisper slid past her.

Yanking down the T-shirt she'd retrieved from her apartment, she tiptoed toward the sounds, hoping she could get there before Leo woke up James. If she could do that and leave the lights off, she would.

More snuffling, and then a deep sigh.

She could finally see enough to make out the cot where James had been.

It was empty.

She relaxed. Maybe he'd decided not to stay after all. If he'd had as difficult a time getting to sleep as she had…

Well, *her* stupid insomnia was due to having James sleeping in the same room.

She made her way toward the hospital bed, almost reaching it before she realized there were two figures there.

Her heart squeezed so tight she almost couldn't breathe. There in the bed was James, eyes closed, one arm loosely draped around Leo, keeping him from falling off the edge. The boy, dressed in the new set of superhero pajamas, was half-sprawled across her ex's chest. Tears pricked her eyes.

Their future could have looked exactly like this, only she would have been in the bed beside James, and Leo would have been their son.

She had to blink several times to get the chaos swirling within her to settle down enough to move closer. Leo must have woken sometime during the night. James had evidently heard him and she hadn't and he had gone to him.

Since it looked like one of Leo's hands was clutching James's shirt, rather than his ratty blanket, he probably couldn't ease away from him.

How long had they been here like this?

From James's posture, it had been a while. His right arm was curled beneath his head, as if using it for a pillow, since the actual pillow was on the boy's side of the bed. Except Leo wasn't using it. He was using James's chest instead.

She crept closer, fascinated, just as she'd always been, by how her ex's face looked as he slept. His lashes made slight shadows beneath his eyes. The furrow of concentration he normally had between his brows was softened in sleep, and just the slightest hint of a depression remained.

She should go back to bed and leave them alone, but

she couldn't. It wasn't fair to let him shoulder the burden when she had been the one to insist on staying with him in the room.

So she leaned down, close to his ear. "James," she whispered.

His lids flicked open in an instant, all traces of sleep gone. Blue eyes sought out hers and the arm holding Leo to him tightened slightly.

The frown was back. "You okay?"

"Yes." She nodded to the sleeping boy. "Did he wake up?"

"He had a nightmare."

There was something about whispering with James in the dark that made her swallow. How easy things had once been between them, and how simple they'd seemed.

In reality, nothing had been simple. They'd known each other for too short a period of time to commit to staying with each other forever. She'd known almost nothing about him and yet she'd planned on spending the rest of her life with him.

An ocean of hurt welled up inside her, making its way to her eyes once again.

James didn't miss it. Then again, he didn't miss much of anything. His arm came from beneath his head and he snagged her wrist. "Hey. Are you sure you're okay?"

"Yes." Her voice betrayed her, though, even at a whisper.

"Mi." He eased out of the bed, leaving Leo asleep, and his hand moved from her wrist to the hair falling over the left side of her face, coaxing it behind her ear. The soft touch made her shudder. Before she could move away, though, his fingers continued from her ear, curling around until they reached her nape. He paused.

Then his head came down, lips brushing against hers in a soft kiss that broke her heart.

"I'm sorry," he murmured. "For everything."

Sorry.

An admission of guilt but nothing else.

A word rolled through her, bouncing around like a giant ball that had been trapped in a small room for far too long. There was no exit unless she made one. But, try as she might, her pride wouldn't allow her to ask the one question that had haunted her for six long years: why?

CHAPTER FOUR

JAMES FELT AS if he'd been kicked in the skull by a donkey.

Exhausted, and with a pounding head to boot, he'd been forced to take a couple of painkillers. Something that went against the grain, after dealing with his mother's addiction problems. Problems that had probably contributed to Freya's own addiction to controlling her food. Thankfully, his sister had overcome those issues and was now leading a happy, healthy life.

He paused outside the door to the exam room, bracing himself for his "emergency" patient, Peggy Smith, better known as Patricia Stillwell, award-winning actress. It was always an emergency, it seemed, whenever she stepped into his office. With raven hair and thick dark lashes, she'd been compared to Elizabeth Taylor on several occasions.

She also won the award for being his most difficult patient, obsessed with maintaining an ageless appearance that was not realistic. He'd talked her out of many a procedure, using a computer manipulation program that showed her what the results would be. And when putting up before and after images didn't work, he then resorted to showing her what she would look like ten years down the road. So far it had worked, but he knew the day was coming when she would no longer be willing to listen and would start demanding he comply. When that day came, he would refer her to another doctor.

He was pretty sure she wouldn't go quietly but would trumpet some ugly rumor about him to the tabloids to make him pay. She'd done it with her primary care physician when he'd refused to prescribe her a heftier dose of sleep aids. That doctor had wound up in the divorce courts by the time Patricia had finished with him.

It was just as well that he had nothing to destroy as far as romantic ties went.

He pushed open the door without bothering to look at the chart. The sight that greeted him, however, was not Patricia Stillwell, petulant actress. It was the tearful, scrubbed-clean face of a terrified woman.

Holding a bloody towel up to her cheek, she looked devastated. And slightly out of it.

James did flip open the chart at this unexpected turn of events. "What happened?"

"I…slipped…in the shower." Patricia's voice was uneven. Not slurred, exactly, but there was an odd tremor to it. "Cut my cheek a little."

He punched the button for the nurse. Unlike what he would have expected from the actress, she didn't once mention her appearance or ask about scarring. That made him even more uneasy.

"Who brought you in?" He'd seen no one waiting in the hallway, not even her current love interest who was also an A-list actor.

"Allen." Patricia wouldn't quite meet his gaze. "But he had a casting call and had to drop me off at the back entrance to the clinic."

Another warning flag began fluttering in his head. Allen Claremont had a reputation for losing his temper both on the set and with his fans and paparazzi. He'd been arrested on assault charges on a couple of occasions, but the charges had always been dropped. "Let's take a look."

When the towel came down, James caught his breath.

This was no "little cut." Neither was it the jagged split he would have expected from a hard fall, but a clean, straight, slice that ran from the corner of her mouth up the side of her cheek. Blood immediately gathered along the wound. He swore under his breath and grabbed a sterile gauze dressing, ripping it open and pressing it to the injury to slow the bleeding.

He didn't hold back the question, didn't even consider doing so. "Did Allen do this?"

"No! Of course not! If the press even suspects, it'll ruin him."

The answer had come much too quickly. As if she'd been rehearsing the words. The nurse came in before he could ask anything else, and Patricia's shoulders slumped.

"I'll need to flush it and test your nerve function." He hesitated to go any further, but she needed to know that this wasn't something that he could wave a magic wand over. "This is a serious injury. The placement makes hiding it more difficult. And if there are nerves involved, we'll need to call in Damien Moore, our head of reconstructive surgery."

"I'll be able to go back to work, though."

That strange slur was still there. The arm holding the cloth to her cheek had obscured some of her mouth movements, but James was worried. There was an abundance of nerves and vessels in the cheek. If the cut was deep enough, it could affect muscle function.

"Of course you will."

But at forty-five, she'd already complained that the quality of the roles she was being offered had declined. This injury could be life-altering for her.

Allen, in his thirties, was almost a decade younger than Patricia. He was a sought-after actor in romantic comedies, for sure, but he was still climbing the ladder. There was talk that he was using Patricia's success as a way to boost his own, using her contacts and prestige to cement his position. If what he suspected was true, though, Patricia needed to report him.

But would she?

"I need to leave without the paparazzi wondering why I came here."

The clinic valued the privacy of its patients because James insisted on it. With that in mind, one of the first things to go in had been an enclosed entrance where drivers could pull up and drop off occupants and then slide back out without anyone being able to see, thanks to a stone wall that faced the street. The result was a blind spot where it was virtually impossible for photographers—or anyone else—to spy on the comings and goings of patients.

That reminded him. He'd won a small victory this past week with the board of directors. He'd convinced them that Bright Hope should have an entrance inside the main part of the clinic. The argument that those patients had as much right to privacy as The Hollywood Hills Clinic's own patients did had evidently held water. They'd scrapped the plans to permanently close the door that connected the two wings. The clinics would now be linked in every sense of the word.

"That won't happen for a while. We need to clean out the wound and check for damage to the structure of your face."

"Can't you put some of your famous tiny stitches in and make it go away?"

This wasn't going away. Not completely. It would leave a scar. Maybe it wouldn't be noticeable to the cameras of the paparazzi but it would be there nonetheless.

Kind of like the scar he carried around? It wasn't an external scar but he still felt the pull inside him when his heart got too involved with a patient. That warning tug that told him to take a few steps back.

"Stitches, yes. But we're going to have to do it under

anesthesia. It'll take a couple of hours, and I'd feel better if you stayed overnight."

Her eyes widened. "But Allen—"

"Will be fine. And if you're lying to me about his part in this, then you need to wise up and put some distance between you. Do you want him doing this to someone else?"

"He won't. I know he won't."

That was the closest to an admission he was going to get. "How do you know?"

She shrugged an overly thin shoulder. "I just do."

Because he'd told her he was sorry? That he'd never do it again? He could remember his father promising the same thing to his mother after each infidelity.

Maybe Allen—unlike Michael Rothsberg—meant it. After all James meant it when he said he wasn't having children. And so far he'd kept that promise. But life was full of unknowns. He hadn't expected Cindy to claim she was pregnant and force him into a decision he'd never expected to make.

He sighed and shook his head. "I want you to think about something while I set up for surgery. If that cut had been three inches lower, we might not be talking about restorative surgery. We'd be fighting to save your life. Next time you might not be so lucky."

James took that "next time" philosophy to heart in his own life. He always, always used protection, no matter how insistent his current partner was that she was clean and on birth control. You never knew what someone was capable of.

Like Cindy.

Or his father.

The bastard.

Evidently Patricia was opting to learn about personal failings the hard way. As difficult as she was as a patient, he didn't like knowing someone had purposely tried to destroy her life. And for an actress, a maiming slash to the face was to strike at the heart of how she made a living.

But who knew what went on in the heads of some of these celebrities? He certainly didn't claim to know his famous parents, whose public meltdowns had probably kept half the tabloids in America in business. His mom's repeated stints in rehab had probably done the same for the other half. He barely had contact with them anymore.

"Think about it," he urged.

Patricia's chin wobbled, and her hand went up to the gauze pad covering her damaged cheek. "I will."

A muscle contracted in James's jaw. "What do you want us to do if he comes to visit?"

"I don't know." Her eyes closed for a second. "Can I decide that after I wake up from surgery?"

"Yes." It was the best he was going to get for the moment. "I'll put a no-visitors order on your chart." Which he did even as he spoke, pushing a button on his tablet and checking the appropriate box on Patricia's chart, quickly typing what he wanted done and when. The tablets were connected to a central system that would flag the next available surgical suite and reserve it, along with his team. Then he called Damien and asked if he could come in and give him a second opinion.

The other surgeon promised he could be there in twenty minutes.

While he waited, he gave Patricia a local injection of lidocaine with epinephrine to numb the wound and slow bleeding and flushed the area with saline, examining the edges of the laceration with his magnifying headset. Thank God, she wasn't dealing with full tissue laceration as the wound didn't penetrate the mucosal or muscle tissue, but it was deep enough that he would have to do the repairs in layers. He mentally calculated fifty stitches on the surface and absorbable suture material inside the wound.

He noticed that as she'd talked, that slight defect in her speech had cleared up. Maybe it had been caused by stress, rather than nerve damage.

A knock on the door pulled him from his work and he sat up, tipping the loupes to the top of his head. He glanced at his tablet. Maybe one of the surgical suites had come available sooner than they'd expected.

Nope. The projections still put them at an hour out. Luckily the face had an overabundance of blood vessels, so there was a longer window for repairs than for some other areas of the body, where the lack of blood supply created a need for quick intervention.

He glanced at the nurse. "Can you stay with her for a minute?"

Patricia grabbed his hand. "You're not leaving me, are you?"

His heart went icy. Those were almost exactly the same words Mila had used on the last night they had been intimate. He'd gotten out of bed almost immediately, guilt eating him alive. She'd known something had been wrong and had tried to get him to talk.

You're not leaving me, are you?

He'd denied it at the time, even as he'd known he was indeed going to leave her. He'd fallen into bed with her in despair, days after Cindy had told him he was going to be a father. He'd meant to talk, not have sex, but once the deed had been done, it had been easier to play the denial game than to have it out with her. Then it had been too late. He'd broken things off just as he'd learned that the tabloids were going to break a story about how he and Cindy had been seen together at a hotel days earlier—when she'd told him she was pregnant.

And then his father had…

Not the time, James.

This wasn't about him. It was about Patricia. "I'm not leaving. I'll be right back."

When he opened the door he swallowed hard.

The woman he'd just been thinking about was standing there, worry in her hazel eyes. "What is it? Leo?"

He stepped into the hall and closed the door behind him.

She nodded. "They think his uncle has fled to Mexico. All they found at his apartment was a note saying the boy's parents had been killed by one of the drug cartels and that he wanted a better life for Leo than what he could get in his home country."

Her face was as white as a sheet. Mila had told him her parents had been murdered when she'd been a child and that her aunt had lied to her for years about how they'd died. Was she remembering that?

Gripping her hand in his, he lowered his voice. "I'm so sorry, Mi. Are you okay?"

"What am I going to tell him?"

"Nothing, for now. He's only three years old." He took a step closer. "If you're thinking about your parents, this isn't the same thing. You were older and your aunt *never* told you the truth, and she should have. Just not when you were Leo's age."

"Maybe. But after a while it becomes easier to let the lie stand than to have the courage to do what needs to be done. I don't want his trust destroyed like mine was."

A shot of hot bile stormed James's throat. He'd done exactly that with Mila. Destroyed her trust. And, yes, it had been far too easy to let the lie stand. Even now.

"Was his uncle abandoning him a better choice? I don't think so."

Hell. Why did every word out of his mouth seethe with accusation? But not at the wayward uncle. At James. At what he'd done six years ago.

He'd wanted Mila to have a better life than what he could

give her. To do that, he'd done much the same thing as Leo's uncle had. And Mila's aunt. He'd lied to protect her.

From the angry flash of her eyes he wondered if she knew what he'd done six years ago. If so, there was no plastic surgery known to man that could repair that particular scar. It was far too old and covered too great an area. He'd thought cutting things off with her would leave a clean line…an easy fix.

How wrong he'd been.

He opted to change the subject. "What did DCFS say?"

"That as long as he's in the hospital they can hold off on putting him into foster care, but the second we release him…"

"Will he be deported?"

"If they can find the uncle? Almost certainly." She licked her lips. "I'm thinking about applying to be a foster parent."

"What?" Of all the impulsive, ridiculous things… But that was Mila. Putting others ahead of herself. Always. That had included him once upon a time. "You need to think this through. You're just getting ready to open a clinic here. How are you going to have time to take on something like a child?"

She blinked up at him. "Some*thing*? I don't know. It just feels like the right thing to do."

"You don't even know this child."

"No. But I've known children like him. And maybe this is my chance to change a life. To really, truly—radically—change the future for this boy." Her chest rose. "His parents were killed. Murdered. And he doesn't have an aunt to see that he gets the care he needs, like I did. She loved me, James. No matter how much I disagree with what she did in the end, I know she was trying to keep me from being hurt."

A host of emotions crawled along his nerve endings, none of them good. "Why are you telling me this?"

"Because…" she licked her lips "…I want to use you as a personal reference on the paperwork, if that's okay."

Mila's head swirled as she waited for his answer. She wasn't sure why it was important for James's name to be on that form. Avery would certainly agree to be a reference. But she wanted James. Did she still need his approval somehow?

No. It was strictly a tactic to show she surrounded herself with respected professionals. People with money, although that went against everything she believed in. But since she was asking DCFS to expedite the process, she would use any tactic she could think of.

What she'd told James was the truth. Now that she was back in the States, she still wanted to make a difference. Bright Hope was one thing, but bringing hope to a child who was an orphan like herself, who had nothing… no one…suddenly seemed vital. Maybe she was trying to make sure Leo didn't feel the way she had when her parents had died, leaving her with no living relative other than her aunt. Or the way she'd felt when James had walked away from their relationship, making her feel just as alone as she'd felt after the death of her parents.

"Why me?" His low voice rumbled past her ear and she couldn't tell if he was angry or just puzzled by her request.

Mila wasn't sure she even knew why herself.

"Because you started The Hollywood Hills Clinic. You've worked with DCFS cases before."

"Only a few times. And that was years ago." He frowned. "How did you even know about those?"

"Adam Walker said the clinic has helped DCFS out in the past. And Freya said *you* used to take some of the harder reconstruction cases that no one else wanted."

"Ah, yes. My sister. I should have known."

This was a mistake. A stupid, impulsive mistake. The

prospect of working so closely with someone who'd once broken her heart must have addled her thinking somehow. Time to undo it, if she could. Starting with...

"Never mind. I needed a professional reference, but there are plenty of other people I've worked with that I can ask."

He leaned back against the wall and regarded her through hooded eyes. "Like Tyler Richardson?"

She'd actually been thinking of Avery, but what if she did ask Tyler? What was it to James? Something made her pursue that line of thinking. "I'm sure Tyler would be happy to provide me with a reference."

"I'm sure he would." He sighed. "I didn't say I wouldn't give you the reference. I was just surprised you would want it."

"Whatever gives me an edge." Even as she repeated those words inside her head she knew they weren't strictly true.

"I guess I should be flattered, then." He gave her a slow smile. "Yes. You can use my name. I'm sure you've used it before, although not in quite as positive a way."

She smiled back. "No. Probably not." She remembered biting out his name in anger on more than one occasion, usually accompanied by a black period of name-calling and plastic-plate throwing—something her therapist had suggested after she'd found out the truth about her parents' deaths. She still threw around nonbreakable dishware from time to time. Not over James, but just when various frustrations crossed her path. Although if she got Leo, she would have to stop that.

It would be a small price to pay.

She drew a relieved breath. "Well, thank you. I'll get you the paperwork—"

"You haven't heard my conditions yet."

The air in her lungs stuck for a second before whistling back out. "Conditions?"

"I have a cottage on my property. I want you and Leo to live there until you find something else."

"What?" Shock held her immobile for several horrifying seconds. Stay on his property? There was no way.

"Do you really think DCFS is going to let you keep a child on a property that has been broken into on two separate occasions?" His words said one thing, but his eyes said something else, dark shadows preventing her from seeing below the surface.

"But the broken door was Leo's uncle. The window was probably his handiwork as well."

"You don't know that. And unless you can convince them there is no risk to Leo…"

She couldn't. In fact, both incidents had left her shaken. But what else could she do?

It wasn't like she could just up and move to Hollywood Hills. There was no way she could afford to live in this part of the city, even with the increase in her salary. Besides, her tendency was to keep just enough to live on and sock the rest of it away with the small remainder of her inheritance, ready to sink into whatever needy cause caught her attention.

And taking Leo in? Didn't that top the list of good causes?

What about finding James with the boy sprawled across his chest last night? Oh, that had touched her deeply. So deeply that she wanted him to approve of what she was choosing to do? Possibly.

But live within a few yards of his house? As icy and detached as James liked to appear to those around him, he cared. Why else would he agree to be a reference…or insist that she move him onto his property? Did she want to dig any deeper than that? No. She needed to be grateful and leave the explanations for another time.

"Thank you. I accept your condition."

"Good. The place is furnished, but I'll send someone for anything you want to put in there this afternoon."

"It's not permanent. As long as you have the basics, I'll just bring a couple of suitcases of clothes. And once I find a better solution I'll be moving out."

His brows came together but he didn't argue.

She rushed ahead to finish. "I know you have a patient waiting, so I'll let you get back to it. I'm sure DCFS will be calling you with some routine questions. I would appreciate it, though, if you didn't mention our past."

His mouth quirked, and he took a step closer, edging dangerously close to her personal space.

"Do you think they won't find out about us, Mila?" His voice, low and silky, brushed across nerve endings she hadn't even known existed. "All they have to do is type your name into a search engine and mine comes up as well. I've done it, and there are still plenty of pictures of us out there, courtesy of the paparazzi."

Her tummy went wobbly, as did her legs. Only there was nowhere for her to retreat, except to turn and run back down the hall.

How did he know there were pictures of them? He said he'd typed her name in? Why? And what exactly had come up when he had? Six years was a long time for stuff to hang around. But when you had famous parents, as they both did, it stood to reason that people would be interested.

"I'm sure they can find anything, if they look hard enough. I have nothing to hide. But if you could avoid giving them a reason to dig any deeper, I would appreciate it."

He reached out and touched her cheek, and the wobbling became a full-fledged tremor. "Afraid of your skeletons, Mila?"

The correct response came to her in a flash of self-preservation. "No, I'm afraid of yours."

There were probably pictures of him with every starlet or

model he'd ever dated. She didn't know if that would hurt her chances or not, but she didn't want to risk it.

His hand fell back to his side, and his eyes cooled back to their normal color. "Don't worry, those particular skeletons will remain safely out of sight."

"Thank you." She hesitated. "For everything."

Just as she started to turn away James touched her arm. "For what it's worth, Mi, you'll make a great mother."

Another doctor came striding down the hallway headed straight for them. James greeted him with a wave and together they went into the exam room, leaving Mila standing there to digest the shocking developments, not only about his cottage but his statement about her being a good mother. Did he really believe that?

She had no idea, but if she was smart she'd forget he'd ever mentioned that.

The question was, was she smart? Where James was concerned? Absolutely not. Sighing, she decided to head down the hallway and look to see how the newest branch of Bright Hope was coming along.

She made several turns down the corridors, catching sight of a couple of people she thought she recognized from the celebrity magazines, but she knew enough not to stare or stop to get a closer look. Then she found a glass door inscribed with the same logo she had on the LA clinic.

Bright Hope.

She'd looked at the plans, and James had told her about the board's decision to allow access through the main part of the medical center, but the reality of seeing it made her heart swell. Soon there would be patients here and a bustling staff. They could reach so many people.

Moving closer, she ran her fingers over the paint. It reminded her that James wanted her to paint a mural on the wall in the reception area similar to the one at her other location.

It was official. In a few short weeks they would open their doors. Which meant she needed to get busy and hire some staff besides Avery. Unless James planned on pulling them from his current pool. Except she wanted to do the hiring herself, to make sure that the clinic personnel wouldn't act put off if someone came in looking a little less than perfect. Surely James would understand that.

She went to push open the door, only to find it locked, which made sense.

Peering through the glass, she smiled when she spotted comfortable-looking furniture in pale, muted colors, rather than the modern black and chrome found in most areas of The Hollywood Hills Clinic.

Maybe she could do the mural over…

A huge framed picture on the wall opposite where she stood caught her eye. She stared, her breath getting stuck in her throat for several long seconds.

Damn. It was a framed enlargement of one of the photos taken at the LA location that James had shown her over dinner. With everything that had happened with Leo, they'd never had a chance to go through them again.

In this particular shot, James had hold of her hand and they were gazing into each other's eyes.

To someone who hadn't been there, it appeared the normal handshake of two businesspeople. But she had been there, and that touch had been no ordinary clasp and release. No, it had been as intimate as his touch in the hallway a few moments earlier. She quickly averted her eyes to glance at the words that appeared under the picture frame.

In beautiful script appeared the words:

The Hollywood Hills Clinic and Bright Hope
Two powerful beacons serving our patients and our community.

That was when she knew the picture was there to stay. No matter what she said, the board of directors or whoever had chosen that particular photo had made the decision.

For as long as the two clinics collaborated, there would be handshakes and meetings and unexpected sightings. But there would be no more kisses. Not like the one in Leo's hospital suite.

Moving onto his property where she would see him almost every day would make that a challenge. For her, at least.

But somehow she either needed to become immune to his presence or risk facing some devastating consequences. If she couldn't, then she needed to find someplace else to live as soon as she could. And then have as little as possible to do with this clinic. And with him.

CHAPTER FIVE

THE SOCIAL WORKER was due at his house at any moment, and
James still had no idea how things had gotten so screwed
up. One second he'd been telling Mila he would be her reference and the next he'd been demanding she use the guest
cottage behind his own home.

The thought of her staying above that shabby clinic
downtown made his gut churn. It wasn't safe. Not only for
Leo but for Mila as well. And since she only had a security
guard during the day…

It was a wonder she hadn't been hurt or killed.

Besides, no one stayed in the cottage. He'd purchased
the property right after he and Mila had gotten engaged,
with the intention that he would use the extra residence for
either of his parents, should they choose to visit. Only he
and Mila had never made it down the aisle, and he'd never
invited his folks to come and visit. In reality, his father
wasn't welcome in his home. And his mom, probably unaware of what Michael Rothsberg had tried to do all those
years ago, hadn't even asked.

But that didn't mean he should immediately offer the
place to Mila to help her become a foster parent. In fact, the
thought of having a child on the premises twenty-four-seven
made him shudder. And yet he'd done it anyway. And Mila
had accepted his offer, which had been another surprise.

It had been a little over a week since she'd turned in the

paperwork—a little over a week since he'd been foolish enough to press his lips to hers in Leo's room, although he could still remember every second of it. It seemed the DCFS had indeed expedited things.

The problem had been that Leo couldn't stay at the clinic indefinitely, and once he left, he would be dumped into the foster-care system, which brought up a whole new series of complications. One of them being that The Hollywood Hills Clinic wasn't included on the list of medical facilities that DCFS normally used. So if any of their normal doctors were available, the agency would use them, leaving Adam Walker—and Leo—out in the cold.

And Mila wanted to make sure the boy received the best care. She was willing to become a foster mom and live right under James's nose, if need be, to make that happen.

Mila was at the cottage right now, setting up things in the spare bedroom. She'd stuck with her decision about bringing nothing more than a couple of suitcases. And she'd tried to pay him rent.

Rent!

There was no way in hell he was accepting a dime from Mila. It wasn't a permanent arrangement, and Mila was already looking for a place that allowed children. Which was ridiculous. The child wasn't a puppy. Or a pet. He was a human being.

Something he'd been far too conscious of as he'd held the boy that first night at the clinic. It was the only night James had stayed with them because having a small trusting body curled against him had done a number on his gut. Worse, he'd fallen asleep, and when he'd woken up, Mila had been standing over them with a softness to her eyes that he hadn't seen in a very long time.

He didn't want her getting any strange ideas. Not that she would. There was no way she would ever take him back after what he'd done to her all those years ago. And he wouldn't dream of trying to persuade her otherwise.

And yet he'd been willing to persuade her to live—and sleep—within a hundred yards of his house.

As if sensing he was thinking about her, Mila peered around his open back door. "She just texted me. She's running about a half hour late."

There was something telling about the fact that Mila had come over in person to let him know, rather than simply shooting him a text like the social worker had done with her. It just confirmed the days of sending lighthearted messages back and forth were long gone.

Mila evidently texted some people, though, whereas James chose not to send messages at all. Everyone around him knew about his weird predilection, including his sister, although she just chose to ignore it.

"I'm making coffee," he said. "Would you like a cup?"

"Love one. I have to tell you, I'm nervous. What if she doesn't like me?"

Since James had never met anyone who didn't like Mila, he couldn't imagine that happening. "She will."

"You don't know that." She perched on one of the tall leather chairs that flanked the round bar table and propped an elbow on the black marble surface.

He hesitated. "Are you sure you want to do this, Mila? It could be a long-term commitment."

"Maybe that's what I need. A long-term commitment." She studied her nails, not meeting his eyes.

His gut twisted. It was the one thing she'd needed from him, and the one thing he hadn't been able to give her. "Are you thinking of adopting him?"

"I'll cross that bridge when I come to it. It depends on what happens with his uncle and whether they can locate him."

He poured a mug of coffee, adding flavored creamer and

a squirt of whipped cream he had in his fridge. He topped it off with a sprinkle of cinnamon.

When he carried it back to her, she was staring at him strangely.

"What?" he asked.

"You remembered."

He glanced down at the cup, realizing he'd automatically fixed the brew the way he had in the past. The exact way that Mila had drunk it back then.

Setting it in front of her, he swallowed. "I remember a lot of things."

"Like the way I drink my coffee." Her words came out in a husky rush, her tongue tipping forward to moisten her upper lip.

He remembered that gesture too. It had normally ended with him kissing her—with them falling into bed.

"Among other things." Like the way she tasted. Felt beneath his hands. His mouth. A sense of hot anticipation began to roll through him.

The chair was tall enough that it wouldn't take much to lean down and...

She picked up her cup and took a quick sip, then set it down again. He should move away and fix his own cup before he did something stupid.

Really stupid.

Too late.

He slid his fingers into the thick hair at her nape, the delicate bones of her skull also something he remembered far too well.

"James?" The inflection at the end of his name said it was technically a question, but the soft sigh put it in a different category altogether.

Cupping her face, he met her halfway, his lips brushing over hers, his eyes closing as bittersweet memories—

more sweet than bitter—swept him away on a cloud of forgetfulness.

Forgetting the pain he'd caused her.

Forgetting the horror of Cindy's fake pregnancy.

Forgetting the fury caused by his father's attempt to buy her off.

All that remained was the woman sitting at *his* table in *his* kitchen in *his* house. And he'd forgotten nothing about her. Especially not the needy press of her mouth on his or how it made him want things he'd never dreamed he could have.

One of her hands came up and wound around his neck, her fingers warm from where she'd held the cup of coffee. A feeling so familiar it sent a ripple through the muscles of his abdomen, the sensation pooling in his groin.

This was right where he wanted to be.

He slid his thumbs beneath her chin and tipped her head just a touch, taking a step closer, until his thighs pressed against the outside of her leg.

How easy it would be just to swing her up in his arms and head toward his bedroom. The room where they'd made love time and time again.

Bzzz... Bzzz... Bzzz...

Something vibrated on the table and a flash of movement caught his eye.

Damn! Mila's phone.

She jerked away and grabbed the instrument just before it slid off the table.

The past came rushing back to greet him. All the regrets. All the mistakes.

Mistakes he'd vowed never to repeat.

She pulled her phone toward her, glancing at the screen. She didn't say anything for a second or two, then murmured, "The social worker. She'll be here in five."

Even he could hear the tremor to her voice. And her lips

were pink and lush and full. From his kiss. Another thing he hadn't seen in ages. All he wanted to do was lean down and take them again.

But the last thing either of them needed was for someone to jump to the wrong conclusions.

Ha! What kind of conclusions would they be? That they'd been on their way to devouring each other?

"Why don't you run to the restroom, and I'll wait for her."

"Thank you."

With that, Mila slid off the chair and headed down the hallway to where she already knew the restroom was. Which was good. Because it also gave him a chance to try to collect his thoughts. Not that there were many of them floating around his head at the moment. Just a jumble of emotions that he needed to shove to the back of his mind.

Mila was back in two minutes. Much sooner than he'd expected. Her hair gleamed around her face, and those pink, natural lips had a coating of artificial color slicked on, hiding any trace of what had happened. Even her hazel eyes seemed cooler. Much different than the warm ocean green they'd been just before he'd kissed her.

He smiled, half in relief and half in regret. "You look poised and ready."

How easy it had been for her to wipe away any trace of what had happened. Had it been just as easy for her to erase what they'd once meant to each other? He had spent many sleepless nights thinking about her.

If only there'd been a lip balm back then that could have erased the memories of her mouth opening beneath his. Of sinking deep into her and losing his heart, his soul… his mind.

This was not helping.

"Do you want to meet her here or at the cottage?"

"The cottage, since that's where we'll be staying. At

least in the beginning. Thank you again for suggesting it. And you were right. My apartment wouldn't have worked. I would have worried constantly about Leo. Especially after what happened."

Thinking back, James was pretty sure the first broken window was related to the boy and his uncle as well. But she had a point. There'd been a police report filed about the first incident. And the second. That wouldn't have played in Mila's favor during the home visit.

"Speaking of which, I had a lease agreement drawn up. I should have mentioned it earlier, but it's just a technicality. Just in case the social worker wants something official."

And to make it look less like a friends with benefits arrangement. Because they weren't friends. Not anymore. And there were definitely no benefits attached.

"I never even thought of that. Thank you. I'll pay rent, of course."

"I already told you that isn't necessary. It was just sitting empty, anyway. My housekeeper did her best to keep the place clean but—"

"It was spotless. And I won't need her to clean for me. I'm a big girl, I can take care of myself."

"And I'm a grown man, but we both have very demanding schedules, and yours is about to get a whole lot busier with the opening of the new clinic."

In fact, it had been James's mother who had hired his housekeeper years ago. He'd protested at first, but when he'd seen how Rosa's face had fallen when he had tried to let her down as easily as he could, he'd had second thoughts. He'd justified it the same way he'd justified it to Mila, telling himself he was busy and it wouldn't hurt to have a little help on the side.

But a big part of it was that he couldn't bear to let one more woman down, as if by keeping Rosa employed he was paying just a little bit of penance for letting Mila down. For letting his mom down by not telling her what his father had done. So Rosa was there to stay.

"Still—"

"You'll hurt her feelings if you try to refuse her help. Besides, she loves children. I think it would be a plus in your favor if the social worker knew you'd have someone to watch Leo when you weren't home."

"I don't expect Rosa to do that without asking her first."

His housekeeper was off on Fridays so that she could spend weekends with her nephews who lived in Fresno. Since she stayed on the premises the rest of the week, it also gave James a few days of privacy when he could unwind. Or pass the time in female company.

Come to think of it, it had been a while since he'd spent time with a woman. Maybe that's what was behind his sudden urge to kiss Mila. He needed to have sex.

With anyone *but* Mila.

The doorbell rang just as he was trying to convince himself of that. That any woman would do.

Except there was a little voice deep inside that rumbled that that was a lie. There was only one woman who would do, and she was the very one he couldn't have. The very one he shouldn't touch.

Not anymore.

James could charm the pants off a giraffe.

The social worker had been hooked from the moment she'd laid eyes on him, flipping her fake blond hair over her shoulder every other second.

Good thing the woman had arrived when she had, though, because James had almost charmed the pants off her as well.

The last thing she needed was to fall back under his spell. Hadn't she learned her lesson the first time?

Evidently not because she was practically living under

his roof. In fact, that damned lease—the one she'd scribbled her name on just before they'd opened the door to the social worker—said she had free rein, not only of the cottage but also the main house. She could come and go as she pleased. Use the pool, or anything else that she wanted.

Including him?

No. Not including him. And she would not set foot in the main house any more than absolutely necessary. She would take him up on his offer of the pool, though, because she imagined that swimming would be a great low-impact therapy for Leo as he recovered from surgery.

Depending on how long the little boy was with her.

It bothered her that in two weeks she was already starting to think of him as a part of her. She'd spent every night at the clinic with him. And as he was going to be released to wait for his surgery date, they would naturally come back to the cottage.

"Do you have any children of your own?"

The social worker's question brought her back to reality. Only it wasn't aimed at her, it was aimed at James. Why the hell did the woman need to know if he had children?

Maybe because she wanted to know if other kids would be on the premises. Yeah, it could be that. In fact, the woman probably rationalized the intrusive question with just that intent. But in reality Mila got the feeling she was fishing to see if he had an ex…and children with that ex.

Because there was no ring on Evelyn Scott's left hand, was there?

She squinted a little closer. No, there was not.

A popular song came to mind, the dancing figures in a music video telling some unlucky guy that he should have given her a ring before it was too late.

Ha! James had given her a ring. For all the good that had done her. She'd mailed it back to him from Brazil, where it was better not to wear expensive jewelry.

Even if it had been completely safe, she still wouldn't have kept it. In fact, James had never acknowledged receiving it. Had the engagement ring even made it back to the States?

It didn't matter.

"No, I don't have children." If Evelyn sounded curious, James sounded peeved. Had he too felt the question was inappropriate?

"Well, it looks like everything is in order. And the cottage is adorable." Evelyn stuffed her papers back into her briefcase and snapped it shut. "I'll give my recommendation to the court that they make an emergency motion for placement with you. It'll just be temporary until we can file the rest of the paperwork. You'll have to let me know of any plans to move. And you can't take him out of state without permission."

"How about on a boat? Within local waters?" James asked.

A boat? What…? Surely not. Was he thinking of taking Leo sailing?

She blinked, trying to find some reason to be outraged, but she wasn't. She was happy. Happy for a little boy who'd probably never had the luxury of seeing—much less visiting—a boat like *Mystic Waters*.

Evelyn looked from one to the other, clearly a little dumbfounded. "I'll have to check, but I don't see why not. As long as you stay within California waters."

"Absolutely."

Mila had completely lost the use of her tongue, at least as far as forming words went. But she was grateful. Grateful for his willingness to take on a boy who was not his responsibility and provide him with a referral to one of the best orthopedists in the business. Not only that but he'd given the boy permission to live almost under his nose.

She stood beside James as he said his goodbyes to the

social worker, assuring her she could stop by anytime she wanted. Evelyn nodded, flipping her hair once more and telling him she was sure she'd be seeing him soon.

As soon as the door shut, he leaned against it, blowing out a breath. "Looks like you're getting your boy. I hope you know what you're doing, Mila."

"I do. And thank you for everything." She hesitated. "Did you mean it about the boat?"

He nodded. "I thought it might be a good way to get his mind off things. Especially since he won't have surgery for another couple of weeks. We could even take him on an overnight trip to Catalina. It's still considered part of California."

Wow. He'd taken her to Catalina. And she'd been in awe of the beautiful island. It was everything the tourist pamphlets promised it would be. But maybe that was because of the man she'd had at her side when she'd visited it.

Well, this would be a little different. And Mila had to make sure that she didn't lose her head. Not this time. Besides, he hadn't offered his boat because of her. It had been because of Leo. She had to remember that, and she would.

And she was definitely going to make sure she kept James at arm's length, because anything else was dangerous.

Dangerous to her. And dangerous to a little boy who would be looking for a father figure after the disappearance of his uncle.

Unless she wanted to risk Leo being as emotionally damaged as he was physically, that father figure could, under no circumstances, be James.

Now came the test.

"Are you ready?"

Patricia Stillwell slid a hand up to touch the stitches on

her cheek. "I think so. Are you sure the scarring will be minimal?"

Examining the tiny stitches he'd painstakingly made, he said, "If someone knows it's there, they'll be able to spot it but, other than that, it should be barely noticeable. And a good makeup artist can erase all traces of it."

"What about the sinking you mentioned?"

Whenever there was trauma to an area, there was the risk of fat cells dying off, creating depressions on the surface.

"It's too soon to know. If it happens, we can transplant fat from another area of your body into your cheek to even it out. We should know within a month."

"What about scar reduction surgery?"

There was that need for perfection again. If he had been Patricia, he would be more worried about what else her boyfriend was capable of. But every time James had tried to bring the subject up, Patricia had stopped him by either changing the topic or by defending him.

How she could defend a person like that was beyond him. Did she ever even ask herself why she stayed with him?

Then again, Mila hadn't asked him why he'd walked out on her. Even in Leo's room when he'd apologized for what he'd done. Wasn't she the least bit curious? Or had she just not understood what he was saying sorry for?

It's been six years, James. Give it a rest. She doesn't care anymore.

And he shouldn't either. But he did. Maybe he felt the need for absolution. To get it all off his chest and have her say she forgave him.

Kind of hard when he hadn't forgiven himself.

"Are you ready to have the stitches out?"

"I am."

"Remember the redness won't completely fade until it finishes healing." Patricia had never had the problem of decreased melanin production in surgical areas that could sometimes cause the skin to become paler than the surrounding tissue.

"I've been through this before, Doc. I know what to expect."

She'd been through *surgeries* before. When he operated, he took the utmost care with what his scalpel touched and what it didn't. This was the indiscriminate slash of a blade without any concern for what it might damage. Patricia hadn't been through anything like this before.

And he hoped she never went through it again. The warning signs were there, though. If she didn't heed them, she could wind up back on his exam table. Or worse.

He gave a mental shrug. Not his decision to make.

Just like Mila's decision to apply to be Leo's foster parent hadn't been his to make.

Asking for the scissors, he prepared to cut the first of the line of sutures. He could have let his nurse handle this part. A lot of surgeons did. But he wanted to make sure everything was okay and that the scar didn't do anything unusual once the tension was released.

He snipped the first line, next to the knot. James was in the habit of tying off between each stitch so that he could control the tightness along the whole incision. It prevented stretching or buckling during day-to-day muscle movements or sleeping. It also meant that when he went to remove the stitches he had to cut behind each knot and pull the suture out section by section. But a good outcome was worth the extra effort.

And the outcome with Mila. Would it have been different if he'd put a little more effort into the courtship process, instead of rushing through it to get to the prize?

He had no idea, but he was getting pretty tired of having everything in his life bring something to mind about his failed engagement. And about Mila, who was now back in his life. To stay, evidently. For as long as the partnership between The Hollywood Hills Clinic and Bright Hope continued.

By the time he got to the last stitch, he'd put his thoughts firmly on his patient and what he needed to do. Cutting the suture, he used his tweezers to pluck the tiny piece of filament from her skin, dropping it into a plastic dish that held the rest of the stitches.

He examined the skin, checking for any areas of weakness that might open up at some point. Everything appeared solid, the healing process well under way.

"It looks good." He reached for the mirror the nurse was already holding out. "Have a look."

Patricia peered into the reflective surface. "What about the holes where the sutures were? Will they show?"

"Some of that depends on your skin. But we've never had a problem with that in your case. I'll want to see you back here in a week to see how you're doing and check everything. If anything feels warm or starts to hurt, call me right away."

He looked up at her. "You know I'm not one to give advice."

Patricia raised her brow. Okay, so he'd advised her against having additional surgery from time to time, but this was different. This was her life.

He smiled. "Okay, but it's only because I care."

It was true. He did care for all of his patients. It was how he'd gotten through his broken engagement and how he got through life.

"I know you do," Patricia said. "And I think I know what you're going to say, but I'm not ready to walk out on Allen. Not yet. I promise, though, if he loses his temper again, I won't stick around."

That was the best he was going to get. "I'm holding you

to that promise. He has a reputation, and evidently there was more than a hint of truth behind it."

"Exaggerations. He's a great guy."

A great guy who cut open someone he cared about?

Yeah, well, hadn't some of his own patients raved about what a good guy *he* was? How good he was at his job? How compassionate he was with his patients?

And yet he'd been able to walk into a room where the woman he loved stood and slice her with words that would cut her to the core.

Some great guy he'd turned out to be.

Angry with Allen Claremont, with Patricia Stillwell, and with himself, he gave her some last-minute instructions about scar care that would help keep the area as smooth and supple as possible. And then he walked out of the room and headed off for his next appointment. As he knocked on the door, he put Mila out of his mind once and for all.

CHAPTER SIX

"It's called a sailboat, Leo. *Un velero*."

Mila smiled as the boy looked around in obvious awe at the pristine white surfaces of the *Mystic Waters*. She remembered feeling the same awe. But not about the sailboat. About James, when he'd stood across from her the night they'd met. The night she'd joked about toads and princes.

Her eyes had probably held the same wide-eyed wonder that night. She'd certainly let him hustle her off to bed fast enough.

Glancing at James, she saw he was watching Leo as well. Only he wasn't smiling. In fact, there was a solemnity in his gaze that took her aback.

They were supposed to be celebrating her getting temporary custody of Leo. Well, if the man's expression was celebratory, she'd hate to see funereal.

They weren't going sailing today but had made plans to head out to Catalina in a few days. But for now there was a picnic lunch Rosa had packed for them to enjoy. It was a rare day off for her, and for James, evidently, who'd managed to clear a large block of time to come out on this outing with them.

Why had he, though? Especially if he was so glum about being here.

Was he regretting letting them use the cottage? He'd been the one to offer it. And it had worked. The social worker had given them her seal of approval. And so had the judge who they'd met yesterday. He agreed it was in Leo's best interests to keep things as stable as possible for the moment. Especially when the child had the opportunity to have his surgery done at The Hollywood Hills Clinic.

She went over and nudged James with her elbow, keeping Leo in her sight. "Hey, is everything okay? We can skip lunch, you know, so you can go back to work."

It took a moment or two to get a response from him, but then the right side of his mouth tilted up. "That bad, huh?"

"You certainly don't look overjoyed to be here."

"Just thinking about how lucky Leo is to be placed with someone who genuinely cares about him. Not everyone gets that kind of childhood."

Was he talking about children in general? Or about his own unhappy childhood? She knew that James and his father had never seen eye to eye. And there had been talk of his father's philandering in the tabloids. But in the days leading to their breakup he'd spoken of the man with a contempt that had floored her. And knowing about Freya's struggle with an eating disorder, she wondered exactly what had gone on in that family. She had her friend's account of fighting and angry words between the famous parents, but Freya had never talked much about her brother's interactions with them, only that he'd been left to practically raise her at times. Maybe Freya figured it was James's story to tell and not hers.

"No. They don't." This time, instead of nudging him, she let her elbow maintain contact with his arm, feeling the need to touch him. While the truth about the deaths of her parents had devastated her, her mom and dad had been loving and kind people. At least from everything she'd read and from her own memories of them. In that her aunt had told the truth. They'd also made sure she'd been well provided for. She hoped they'd be happy with the way she'd used their fortune, to better the lives of those less fortunate. "My keeping him might not have been possible without the use of your cottage. Thank you again for that."

"It's a small price to pay."

And yet he didn't act like it was a small price at all. In fact, Mila had noticed that aside from that first night in the clinic he hadn't touched Leo any more than necessary. He had lifted him onto the boat. But it had been a quick heave-ho, setting him on his feet. It had lasted all of five seconds.

"But it was a price you were *willing* to pay."

Unlike marrying her.

James's frown deepened. Because he'd guessed her thoughts? Time to change tack.

"Why don't we break into that basket Rosa packed for us?"

The furrows softened. As badly as he'd hurt her six years ago, she couldn't find it in her to lash out. Not now. Back when it had happened? Oh, yeah. She'd raged, written terrible destructive things in her journal for months afterward. It had been cathartic somehow. And now all she was left with was regret that things had ended the way they had. That he hadn't loved her the way she'd loved him. In reality, she should have guessed by the way he'd been acting in those last weeks that they weren't going to make it.

Except when she'd pressed him for reassurance he'd always given it to her. And once, while in a panic over the growing emotional distance between them, when she'd mentioned starting a family, he had murmured all the right things...told her he loved her.

Only those reassurances had been every bit as much of a lie as her aunt telling her that her parents had died in a car accident. Neat. Clean. Easy on the ears. But still lies.

Pushing back the tide of the past, she lifted the large picnic basket onto the folding table James had set up on deck, saying it would be nicer to sit out in the cool autumn sun than be stuck below deck. Besides, Leo was kitted out in a life jacket, which James had produced before she'd even had a chance to suggest it herself.

"Tienes hambre?" she asked him, as she spread the tablecloth, tucking it beneath the wicker basket.

"Si. Mucho."

James had introduced Leo to a pair of crutches, but since the boy was used to walking on his twisted feet, he'd quickly discarded them.

But watching him slowly shuffle his way toward them, his face contorting a time or two as he struggled to force his limbs to obey, Mila's heart squeezed into a hard little ball.

His surgery couldn't come soon enough.

James helped her get things set up. As soon as she pulled the last of the containers from the basket, though, her fingers brushed across something shiny and smooth. Peering inside, she saw a folded pamphlet. "What's this?"

"Something I wanted to discuss with you over lunch. Away from the clinic."

Was this why he'd suggested coming out to the boat? Her heart sank. She'd thought he'd been trying to give Leo a nice outing. Instead...

She lifted the leaflet, and started to open it, only to have James place his hand on it. "Let's get Leo's plate set up first."

A stray cloud caused a shadow to drift across the deck, matching the one that was sliding through her heart. Whatever it was, it was bad enough that he expected her to protest. Why else would he have wanted to get her away from the clinic?

"We could have discussed this at the house."

"I wanted to show it to you in a neutral setting."

Neutral? Was he kidding? This huge boat was anything

but neutral. They'd made love in the cabin below—one of the reasons she thought James had wanted to eat up on deck. How wrong she'd been. He didn't see this boat as anything but a sailing vessel. As his property.

Fine. He wanted to talk about whatever was inside that pamphlet? She would surprise him by not reacting at all.

She was going to remain cool, calm and collected. No matter what James said or did.

"They want us to what?"

The horror on her face would have been comical if it hadn't mirrored his own feelings. This was exactly why he'd wanted to get her away. And knowing she wouldn't go anywhere without Leo in tow, he'd been forced to pretend it was an outing planned just for the boy.

Only that had backfired. Leo's obvious joy at being on his boat had made his chest burn in a way that it hadn't since he'd brought the ax down on his and Mila's relationship.

"You knew the clinic would want to plan some special events surrounding the fund-raiser for Bright Hope."

"Yes, of course. I knew there was some kind of ritzy ball coming up. But a regatta? Is that why you wanted to show me this while we were on your boat?"

He'd been just as surprised by the request. The parade of boats by clinic patrons was nothing new. They'd done that several times in the past. Except this time they wanted James and Mila to glide into the docking pier first and start the festivities off with a bang, since they were each the head of their respective medical facility.

"I thought this was a good place to discuss it, yes, since we'll be sailing in on the *Mystic Waters*."

James didn't like this any more than she did, but it was his responsibility to make sure this venture was a success.

He'd put his reputation on the line for Freya's pet project and he had no choice but to see it through to the bitter end. Especially with Freya so close to giving birth to her twins. He would let nothing hurt her, either physically or emotionally.

So there it was. And since it was actually his sister who'd suggested they arrive together—even mentioning James's prized boat to one of the board members when he hadn't been around to shoot the idea out of the water—he was stuck.

"Freya didn't mention anything about this to you?"

"Does it look like she did?" Mila cast a quick glance at Leo as if trying to make sure he didn't understand. But so far the youngster was busy making roads in his mashed potatoes with his spoon, making engine noises as the utensil sped through the white surface.

"If it makes you feel better, I didn't know about this either until just the other day. I knew the clinic was putting on a gala to celebrate our partnership, and we've held regattas in the past. But us arriving together was new."

"So you knew they wanted us to, but you're only now telling me about it." She flicked the pamphlet toward him. The same picture graced the cover that was on the wall at her new clinic. Promising an event that was "not to be missed." "You couldn't have warned me before these were printed? What if I said no?"

"Part of your clinic's agreement with us states—"

"I know what it says. I signed it, remember? But I didn't know that it would entail playing dress-up and parading around in front of a lot of rich…" She cut off her sharp words and set down her fork. "I just want to help people, James. Maybe I should just go back to my little clinic in LA and do what I set out to do."

"You could do that, yes. But you would be letting down

a whole lot of people. People like Freya." He steeled himself and went for the jugular. "Children like Leo."

Mila's breath hissed in, eyes widening in shock and dismay. "Is that a threat?"

"What? Hell, no. What do you take me for?" He dragged a hand through his hair, leaning back in his chair. "Forget I asked that. I know exactly what you think of me."

"Then give me a reason not to." There was an element of pleading in her voice—maybe about the past, maybe not. But the time for confession was over. Not that there'd ever really been an opportunity once he'd broken things off. Truthfully, he hadn't wanted to. The shame of the lifestyle he'd once led and the consequences of it—real or made up—and his own screwed-up family had made him choose to remain silent about Cindy.

He'd loved Mila too much back then to subject her to the ugliness that had gone on behind the scenes to avoid a scandal for his famous parents. When he had refused to go to Cindy and offer to pay her to have an abortion, his father had done so instead. Only Cindy hadn't been pregnant. But she had threatened to sue his parents and had even secretly taped the conversation between her and Michael, saying she was going to sell it to the highest bidder unless James agreed to marry her.

In order to spare Mila the humiliation of being dragged through the mud right along with him, he'd ended their engagement. And somehow the whole mess had just gone away. He had no doubt his father had shelled out some ungodly sum of cash to make that happen. By the time he'd found out Cindy had never been pregnant at all, Mila had been long gone, and James had never heard another word from her.

He realized she was still looking at him, waiting for his response. "All I can tell you is that the way this regatta was laid out wasn't my idea. But I think it could benefit both of our clinics. It's one night, Mi. Surely you can stand to sail with me one more time. Once we dock and go on shore, we can do the obligatory dance to kick off the gala, head to our own separate corners of the ballroom and go home unscathed."

She seemed to consider that for a moment. "It's not that..." She gave a rueful grin. "Okay, so it is partially that. But the worst thing is that you kept this to yourself until you couldn't hide it any longer. You could have trusted me with the truth."

"I had some idea of how you might respond."

This time she laughed. "Okay, so you got me there. So much for not reacting."

"Excuse me?"

She waved away his question. "Never mind. So we get on your boat in our black-tie best, eat a few hors d'oeuvres for the benefit of some wealthy donors, and then when the gala is under way..."

"Then when the gala is under way...we dance."

She shook her head. "We dance badly. So badly they let us off the hook almost immediately."

"The worst anyone has ever seen."

Mila picked up her fork and cut into her fried chicken. "All I can say is that you'd better make it look believable. And the bad dancer isn't going to be me, mister. It's going to be all you."

He laughed. A spark of the old Mila had just emerged from the ashes of the past, an energetic playfulness that he'd missed more than he'd realized. For the most part he'd seen only the professional self-assured Mila of the here and now. Except during those kisses.

Oh, she'd been knocked for a loop all right. He'd sensed it. And he'd been knocked just as hard.

That was one of the reasons he agreed their dance should

be short and sweet. A quick, awkward shuffle that would get them off the floor as fast as possible.

If he played his cards right, not even the intuitive Freya would realize his and Mila's dance fail was anything other than the real deal.

She shouldn't dwell on how right James looked carrying a sleeping child. Because if things had been different, Leo could have been theirs. An ache settled in her chest that made it hard to breathe.

Not a smart place to let herself land. Especially not after the meal they'd eaten together on the *Mystic Waters*. Or after learning that they would share the opening dance at a fancy ball.

Just like the dance they might have shared at their wedding.

Leading the way across the dark rustic path that wound around to the back of James's property, she didn't dare close her eyes, even though the dull ache had turned into a jabbing spear that reached the core of her being.

"There's a light switch on the post to your right." His low voice slid through night air. Leo had fallen fast asleep during the car ride back from the boat, but when Mila had gone to wake the child, James had given a slight shake of his head. "The boy's walked enough today," he'd said.

As reluctant as James had seemed about getting involved, his words had said something different. He did care. So did Mila. Maybe a little too much.

But what was to stop her from eventually adopting Leo if his uncle was never found or if he didn't want his nephew? Even James had hinted at that possibility.

Too soon to think of that, Mila.

She pressed the glowing button on the wooden fence post and the area came alive with twinkle lights. Beautiful and romantic, the tiny overhead beacons glinted off the water of the L-shaped pool and made the small courtyard between the two buildings seem unbearably intimate. Her brows went up. Before she could voice the question, or even wonder if James had designed this place for seduction, he answered her question.

"Rosa likes to sit out here at night and drink her coffee. I didn't think she should sit in the dark." A flash of teeth from beside her. "*I* wanted to put in floodlights. She wanted something that wouldn't 'blind' her, as she so tactfully put it."

Mila smiled back. "I don't think the word 'tact' is in Rosa's vocabulary."

The housekeeper was warm and kind, but opinionated. She'd told Mila in no uncertain terms that she would do the cleaning in the cottage—and had offered her services to babysit without hesitation.

"No. It's not." He shifted Leo in his arms, and the working of his biceps made her swallow again. His free days had always been spent on his boat, and he must still do that whenever he could. She could remember how heavy those booms were to move, and hoisting the sails made her own muscles scream with fatigue. But she'd learned to love it, even though she hated to think what its price tag must have been. When they were out there, it was like they were in their own private world. A land of promises and make-believe.

Make-believe was all it had been in the end, though.

Kind of like this beautiful night.

They reached the front door of the cottage and she hesitated, not wanting the magic to end just yet but afraid to say anything, afraid she'd come across as needy and pathetic. They'd had such a wonderful afternoon. And those lights looked so peaceful…so inviting.

She forced herself to give him an out, though, as she

turned the key in the lock. "Do you want me to take him from here?"

"I'll carry him to his room."

His room.

And that sounded just as right as the sight of James holding him.

"Would you like some coffee? I have decaf, if you're worried about it keeping you awake."

He glanced at her as he entered the cottage. "Do you have an early day ahead of you?"

So was that a yes or a no?

"I don't have to be at the clinic until nine."

"In that case, I would love some. Let me tuck him in and I'll come and help you."

Relief swamped her veins, although why she should care one way or the other was beyond her. She just had a feeling that tomorrow would bring something different, and she wanted the ease she'd had with him right now to last just a little longer.

"There's a video monitor in his room. If you could switch it on and make sure it's aimed at the bed, that would be great. The receiver is in my room." She hurried to add, "Sometimes I think I hear him crying and then realize it's just my imagination."

"I know what you mean."

He did? Since Leo didn't live in the main part of the house, she had no idea why he'd be thinking he heard him. "If he cried loudly enough for you to hear him all the way to your house, I wouldn't need a baby monitor."

He turned down the hallway, his next words barely audible. "I wasn't talking about Leo."

He wasn't? Then who?

Oh, Lord, maybe asking him for coffee hadn't been such a smart idea after all. There was a minefield stretching between them that made navigating safe topics almost impossible. Because sooner or later… *Boom!* Something from the past would explode, sending both of them running for cover.

Or her, anyway. James seemed pretty impenetrable.

Except for that last inscrutable comment.

She'd just switched on the coffeemaker and was stretching up to reach for the extra coffee cups when an arm brushed hers, easily retrieving the mugs. A shiver went over her.

"Thank you."

"You're welcome." He glanced at the counter. "Rosa must have outfitted this after getting the news that you'd be staying here. If I recall, the cottage had furniture but not much else."

"You don't have people stay here? What about your parents?"

He stiffened for a second, before placing the mugs on the counter. "They're busy. I'm busy. But to answer your question, I think you're the first person who has actually stayed in the place."

Mila blinked. She'd halfway expected this to be his own private love nest but maybe his women stayed in the main house. In James's bedroom.

Of course they would.

Her stomach clenched. She pushed aside that thought and went back to the previous one. His relationship with his dad had always been rocky, but surely his mom had visited him in the time since James had broken their engagement.

The coffee pot gurgled as it finished churning out the last of the fragrant brew.

"Do you want to take it in here or out in the courtyard?"

He picked up the video monitor, glancing at the image of Leo peacefully sleeping. "How far does this reach?"

"The package lists the range as up to eight hundred feet, so that should give us plenty of room. If we start getting a lot of static, we'll come back into the house."

"I closed the baby gate you had in front of the door. Hope that was okay."

She'd installed the gate to keep Leo from wandering off in the middle of the night. She had no idea what his uncle had used to do at his old house, and closing the bedroom door didn't feel right to her. But James had a pool, and the last thing she wanted was for Leo to decide to go for a swim when she wasn't looking. Then again, she didn't want him waking up and feeling trapped. The gate had seemed like a good compromise. "That's perfect."

They each fixed their coffee, then James loaded their cups and some cookies that Mila had pulled from another cupboard onto a tray and headed to the deck that stretched between the cottage and the pool. A round café table perched on the stone patio and looked out over the water. James set the tray on the table and moved the chairs so they faced the pool. Mila peered at the receiver of the video monitor. There was Leo, as clear as day. When she thumbed the roller button on the side of the device she could raise the sound enough to hear Leo's soft snoring. No static at all. She turned it back down so that they would hear him cry but not every little shift of the sheets.

She dropped into a seat, while James went over to another set of posts, which had a hammock strung between them, and turned a dial. The overhead lights dimmed even more.

Sighing, she closed her eyes for a second, allowing the still-warm autumn air to brush over the skin on her calves, where the skirt on her sundress had slid up. She fiddled with one of the thin straps of her top. "This is nice. I would be out here every night, if I were you."

"I don't have much time for anything but work and sleep."

She nodded at the tanned skin of his forearms. "You have time for your boat."

"I sometimes sleep out there so it serves a dual purpose."

He slept there? When he had this beautiful home? Then again, she could remember spending some enjoyable nights on that boat.

Picking up her cup, she took a sip of her coffee. The warmth trailed down her throat and hit her belly with a splash of heat. "I think I'd be in the pool, floating my cares away."

He smiled. "Would you? I seem to remember you being afraid of water."

"Not any water. Just the ocean. You can't see what's down there. I've seen enough shark movies to know what happens when you venture in. As soon as the music starts, you're a goner."

"You do realize movie sharks aren't real."

"Of course I do. But sharks exist. And they do have teeth."

His grin widened. "You have more of a chance of—"

She put up a hand. "Save it. I already know the statistics. I've also read the stories. Seen the surfboards. It happens and I'd rather not be one of the few unlucky ones. Besides, if I felt anything against my leg, I'd be dead of a heart attack."

"Not everything that brushes against your leg in the water is dangerous."

She went still, very aware of that minefield she'd thought about a half hour ago. Did she dare take another step through that grassy field? Or did she retreat?

"No. Not everything."

"Did you bring a suit with you?"

She ventured forward another step, not sure where all of this was leading. "No. I didn't think about it."

She should have, though. Leo would want to go in the pool eventually. But she didn't think that's what James was talking about at the moment.

"It's still fairly early. And it's a warm night. Do you want to take a quick dip?"

Hadn't he heard her?

"No. Swim. Suit. Remember?"

Surely he didn't mean to...

"You can leave your dress on." He gestured at his board shorts. "And these are almost like swim trunks."

She was tempted. Oh, so tempted. He'd said they would keep their clothes on, so what was the harm?"

"What about Leo?"

He picked up the monitor. "Let me see if this reaches a little farther." He walked the few yards to the pool and nodded. He set it down on one of the lounge chairs. "Crystal clear," he said.

Her mind scrambled around for a reason to say no, although somehow she would be crushed if she actually found one. "Won't Rosa think it's odd to see us swimming around in our clothes?"

"Her bedroom is on the other side of the house. And the pool is screened from view, anyway."

Had he planned that to hide his late-night swims with bimbos?

Stop it, Mila. Just enjoy the night.

"If Leo wakes up—"

"I'll be out of the pool so fast you'll swear I was never there in the first place." He frowned. "Is he a light sleeper?"

Except for that first night in the hospital, he wasn't. In fact, he'd slept straight through to dawn ever since. "He doesn't seem to be, no."

"What's the problem, then?"

There was one. She was sure of it. She just couldn't find it at the moment, so she shrugged. "I guess there's not one."

James downed the rest of his coffee. "Shall we, then?"

Thinking this was probably one of the stupidest decisions she'd ever made, she set her mug down and stood to her feet, kicking off her sandals. Before she could put one foot in front of the other, though, James suddenly scooped her up in his arms and headed straight for the pool. In the daytime she would have shrieked with a mixture of laughter and alarm, but afraid she'd wake someone up she settled for hissing, "What are you doing?"

James didn't stop moving until he reached the very edge of the pool. "What am I doing? Something I haven't done in a very long time." He gave her a smile full of intent. "You know the drill. Hold your breath."

And with that he stepped off the side of the pool and sank, feetfirst, into the chilly water.

Taking Mila with him.

CHAPTER SEVEN

WHY HAD HE done that?

He had no idea. As Mila spluttered to the surface and then gripped the side of the pool, he only knew that walking into the house with that child in his arms had made his chest tighten. A sensation he didn't like. And then watching his ex-fiancée's hips twitch from side to side had made something else tighten. Something a little lower. Presented with a choice of which one to focus on, he'd gone for the easier choice: lust.

Something that jumping into a cold pool should have remedied. Only it hadn't. Because Mila's white sundress now seemed to have become almost invisible, every spot where it was plastered to her skin becoming pink and inviting. And there was a whole lot of plastering going on. In some very strategic places.

"Are you crazy?" She finally looked his way, eyes wide.

It would appear he was. Because instead of the water chilling any uncomfortable urges, it simply reminded him of another time in the distant past when they'd done this very thing.

Only there hadn't been any sundresses involved. Or any other clothing, for that matter.

He slicked his hair back from his forehead. "I was afraid you'd chicken out. And it *is* a warm evening."

Getting warmer by the second.

"So your solution is dunking me?"

"You were going to get in anyway."

One of the straps on her dress slid down her arm, carrying a wide swath of fabric with it. She hurriedly yanked it back up. "I was going to get in slowly. One toe at a time. But you didn't give me a chance to do anything but…" She glanced down, her words stopping. "Oh, my God."

She ducked down until only her head was showing above the water line. "Why didn't you tell me?"

The muscles on one side of his mouth pulled up. "I was going to once you stopped talking."

"You…you…"

One of her feet connected with his thigh, but the water kept the kick from feeling like anything except a sensual slide of flesh against flesh. He reached down and grabbed the offending limb. "Now, now, Mila. I think we've been down this road before."

And they had. That kick had probably been pure muscle memory from the past. And every time it had ended the same way, with him gripping her calf and hauling her closer until the lower half of her was snugged to the lower half of him.

And like the crazy leap into the pool, he couldn't resist the impulses that were beginning to pulse through him.

He tugged.

And she didn't pull away. Or screech at him to let her go.

Instead, she hooked her heel around the back of his thigh, just beneath his ass. Like she'd done so many times in the past.

Pure need ricocheted through his system the second she connected with his flesh. He wrapped an arm under her butt, lifting and holding her in place as he pivoted, trapping her between the side of the pool and his body.

"Hell." He couldn't stop the word from exiting any more

than he could force a certain part of his anatomy to soften and recede.

Wasn't happening.

He could just touch the bottom of the pool so he concentrated on more pressing concerns. Like the fact that all he had to do was slide a hand beneath her dress, ease her panties to the side and…

"James…" Soft eyes met his, and he could have sworn he saw the same urgency in them that was thrumming through his body. "What are we doing?"

Leaning forward, he allowed his lips to trail along the moist skin of her cheek until he reached her ear. "What are we doing? Anything you want."

"But, Leo…"

His eyes skipped to the monitor that was less than five feet away. The boy hadn't moved an inch. "Leo is sound asleep. Parents everywhere are envious."

Parents? Bad choice of words, James.

Mila blinked a time or two, seeming to be torn between a couple of options. Then her heel pressed firmly against him, and all the waiting pressure points tightened even further.

He had his answer.

Their lips tangled in a fury of need that had probably been building over the last six years. The contrast between the icy coolness of Mila's skin and the molten desire he sensed in her kiss turned him inside out.

He hitched his fingers beneath her other leg and hauled her up so she could hold on. Which she did, wrapping her legs around his waist and looping her arms around his neck.

Leaning back just a bit, he smiled when her lips followed his, her wordless protest nearly making him forget what he'd been about to do. But the sheer fabric of her dress had been calling to him for the past several minutes and he couldn't ignore the siren song a moment longer.

He palmed her breasts, the heady feel of her nipples

against his skin cutting through him like a knife. Whether her body's reaction was from the chill of the water or from need, he had no idea. It didn't matter. Because the whimper that erupted from her throat as his thumbs skimmed over the hard peaks said she wanted every bit of what he was doing. Of what he was going to do.

Her neckline was rounded and stretchy. Elastic. He used it to his advantage, allowing one hand to creep beneath the edge and tug until he'd exposed an expanse of creamy skin. His mouth watered.

Gorgeous.

Everything about this woman.

And what she did to him…

Hell.

She'd also been fairly vocal during their lovemaking in the past. And with that monitor just a few feet away…

"I'm going to need you to be very, very quiet, Mi, for what I'm about to do. Can you do that?"

She licked her lips. "It depends."

Instead of answering her, he leaned down and covered her nipple with his mouth, letting his tongue scrape over the tip.

She moaned. Quietly.

It ramped the simmering tension into a vortex that drove him to the edge of ecstasy. And despair. He forced it back.

Not yet.

But it had to be soon, or he wasn't going to make it.

Pulling back, he wrapped his hands around her hips and with a single quick movement lifted her up and out of the pool, parking that fine ass of hers on the concrete deck, her legs splayed on either side of his shoulders.

Very nice.

He scooted her bottom closer to the edge, then eased her dress slowly up her thighs, gulping when blue satin winked at him from beneath it. He followed the strings on the sides, expecting to find bikini underwear. Instead it was…a thong. How had he missed that when he'd been manhandling her behind?

He had no idea. But he liked it.

Liked that she'd worn it while out on the boat. Had she put it on with him in mind? She'd used to wear a much more chaste version of panties when they'd been together. Slightly sexy, but not outrageously so. Nothing like what she had on now.

But the thong matched the new air of self-assurance she carried with her. All the more reason why leaving her at the altar had been the right choice.

He frowned at the thought.

Mila had evidently "found" herself while they'd been apart. She'd probably done a lot of soul-searching about what she really wanted out of life and what was important. Maybe he should have done a little more of that himself. Yes, he'd loved the person she'd been back then.

But now?

Not something he was going to let himself dwell on. Especially now.

To distract himself, he concentrated on what was right in front of him. Not that it was all that hard to do. His fingers tightened on the string of her thong. "Lift up."

There was a second of hesitation when he wondered if she was going to change her mind. But maybe the past beckoned her like it did to him. She put her hands on the pool deck just behind her and pushed up. Just enough for him to tug the panties down.

And off.

He shoved them in the pocket of his board shorts. She wasn't going to be needing those anytime soon.

Mila's head swiveled to the side, glancing toward the monitor.

"Still sleeping. I checked."

And he had. Despite the raging need that coursed through his veins, he was very aware of their responsibility to that child.

Their...

Now, there was a funny word.

"This feels naughty." Her words were soft.

"It is naughty. Very, very naughty." His hands went to her thighs, thumbs tracing slow circles across the pale inner surfaces.

"When you do that, it feels very, very good."

"And so do you." He leaned forward and placed a kiss just below one of his thumbs. "Mmm...and you taste just as good."

A shiver went through her, and her hands went to his head, fingers threading through his hair. "God, I need you, James."

He cupped her behind as he propped his chin on the very edge of the pool, just inches away from where he wanted to be. "Then come and get me, honey."

Would she? Or would she chicken out and make him haul her forward? Where he could kiss her until those shivers became moans of desperation?

And hell if she didn't take the initiative and edge closer inch by inch until she was right there in front of him, fingers still deep in his hair. Tightening.

"Perfect. So perfect." He lifted his chin and ran it along the place where the satiny skin of her leg gave way to a much more erotic zone. A place where everything was smooth and bare.

Another surprise.

In slow passes, he brushed against the silken flesh with his cheek...his chin...his nose. And finally his lips. Right at the heart of her.

When he glanced up her body, he found her head back, eyes closed as he continued to explore.

He couldn't get enough. Wanted to touch her with every single part of his body. He nibbled. Licked. Breathed. Everything he could think of.

Mila squirmed against him, using her grip on his hair to pull him even closer. And he was happy to oblige.

Her breath came in desperate-sounding puffs of air, the whispers curling past his ear and messing with his head. He'd told her to be quiet, but maybe he should have let her scream and yell and moan because this quiet, writhing woman beneath his mouth was doing something to him that demanded he pull her back in the water and finish it.

But not until he finished her.

Bringing one of his hands back around, he entered her with two fingers, pressing deep, while his mouth kept doing exactly what it had been. She was warm and wet and deliciously sexy. And he needed her. Desperately. Loved the pumping of her hips as she tried to find release.

Release he was more than willing to give her.

Suddenly, Mila's grip on his hair became frantic and she pressed herself hard against him.

There!

It came suddenly, in sharp waves that tightened and contracted and rippled against his fingers. He gritted his teeth and held on to his own need with everything that was inside him.

Because he wanted to be inside her.

"Now, James. Please!"

Wrapping his arms around her hips he carried her down into the water, shoving his shorts down in a rush and in one sudden move entered her.

A growled curse came out as he went deep, pressing her hard against the side of the pool as her body continued to convulse around him.

He couldn't hold on. Didn't want to. Needed her.

Letting go, he pumped like a wild man craving everything she could give him.

And give she did, her fingernails digging into his shoulders, her mouth finding his and using her tongue to mimic what he was doing to her.

He gave one final thrust and wrapped a hand around the back of her head as he exploded, trying to absorb every sensation, drawing it deep into his mind…his body, his soul. His kiss slowed…softened until he finally got up the nerve to ease away. Even then, he let his mouth trail along her eyelids, her cheek and then back to her lips. Nibbling. Still tasting. Still connected to her.

"Wow. That was…wow." The soft words breathed against his neck made him smile.

Yes, it had been. For him too.

Something rattled at the back of his mind as his senses gradually returned. He caught sight of his wallet on the table next to the baby monitor. He glanced at the image of Leo, who was still sleeping peacefully, and then his eyes tracked back to the wallet.

His wallet.

Crap! The one containing his token "just in case" condom.

He pulled free of her in a rush, swearing in a voice that was the antithesis of quiet.

"What's wrong?" Her hazel eyes blinked in surprise, an uncertain frown contracting his brows.

"I didn't use protection." His brain sought an explanation and came up empty. "Damn it, I'm sorry, Mila."

How could he have done that? He'd broken his cardinal rule. But somehow the memories from the past—when Mila had been on the Pill and condoms had been an unnecessary evil—had clouded his thinking.

Maybe…maybe she was still protected.

She must have read the question in his eyes. "No. I'm

not. Not anymore. Some of the places I travel…it's hard to get the prescriptions filled. So I just gave it up. B-but I just had my period a few days ago, so surely it'll be okay."

Surely. The word disasters were made of.

"You might need to make sure." The sentence came out before he could stop it, and his soul froze inside him. That was something his father would have said. Exactly like it, in fact. He'd said those very words when he'd told James to bribe Cindy. *You might need to make sure. It doesn't pay to take chances.*

Mila's reaction wasn't much better than his own had been. Her words were small and cold. "You mean like the morning-after pill? Don't worry, James. I'm not going to saddle you with child support payments."

Hell, that wasn't what he'd meant at all. In fact the thought of her downing that pill made him sick to his stomach. But he was also worried about his stupidity costing her in a huge way. A life-changer. Wasn't that the phrase that was so popular nowadays to describe a catastrophic illness…or unplanned pregnancy? "I don't care about that."

But was that really true? He didn't care about the money. At all. But he didn't want to be a father. It wasn't in his plans. Not now. Not ever.

And yet…

No. Do not go there, James.

Too late. His mind had dredged up the image of Mila holding Leo in the back of the car as they'd made their way to the clinic. His eyes strayed to the baby monitor.

Mila shrugged, bringing his attention back to her. "Like I said, it's okay. Let's not make it into a national tragedy before there's a reason to."

It sure looked like there was a reason to from where he was standing. What kind of birth control had she used with her firefighter?

Not a question he was going to ask. Neither did he want to picture Mila with anyone else, doing what they'd just done. Or wonder if she'd ever gotten so carried away that she'd forgotten all about birth control.

Like he had?

Screw this.

Before he could say anything else she hefted herself onto the side of the pool with one graceful push of her arms. And damn if the dress wasn't just as transparent as it had been earlier.

And double damn if his libido wasn't already waking up.

"Let's just forget this ever happened," she said.

He put his hands on the side of the pool and glared up at her. "You think it's going to be that easy? I don't think so, and I bet you don't either."

She stared right back down at him, water dripping from her dress and pooling around her feet.

"You're wrong. I can, and I will." She started to walk away and then stopped. Turned back around to face him. Squatted in front of him. "And just to prove it I'm going to do what the clinic wants and ride on your boat for the regatta."

"I thought that was already decided. And I think you're forgetting something."

"What's that?"

"I have something that belongs to you. Aren't you going to ask for it back?"

She cocked her head. "Ask for what back?"

James reached in his pocket and pulled out her baby blue thong. "This. Unless you want me to run it up the mast as my own personal trophy."

Mila's face turned crimson and she snatched the underwear and got back to her feet. "I bet you think every woman is your personal trophy. Well, guess what, James Rothsberg. Not me. I'm no man's trophy. And especially not yours."

* * *

Dropping Leo off at preschool was one of the hardest things she'd ever done. But one of the agreements she'd made with the judge was that she'd enroll him within the week. The rationale was that he needed to start learning English as soon as possible.

She knew they were right, but she'd still put it off until the very last second. The week was now over and here they both were, in front of the redbrick building that held Leo's well-being in its hands.

Would someone make fun of him? Bully him?

Her throat clenched so hard she thought she might suffocate. She understood that he needed to be in school, but why so soon? Why not wait until after his surgery?

Part of her misgivings had to do with James and what they'd done in the pool a week ago. She'd avoided him as much as she could, concentrating on her LA office, rather than the spiffy new one in The Hollywood Hills Clinic, even though she still needed to paint that damned mural. She figured that by staying away she could just forget he existed.

Not very likely. As much as she'd assured him she could put what they'd done out of her head, it was still there. Right at the surface, ready to rise from its watery grave to taunt her all over again.

How could she have let him have sex with her without protection? She was right in that her cycle wasn't at the optimal time for conception, but stranger things had happened.

Tyler had always taken care of that when they'd been together. And maybe she'd let him because she hadn't been as invested in their relationship as she should have been.

But she certainly would have realized it if he'd made love to her without a condom.

With James, it hadn't even crossed her mind that they hadn't used anything. Until he'd freaked out.

And he had freaked.

All over her. All over her afterglow.

All over any possible child they might have. He'd made his thoughts perfectly clear. Having a baby with her was the end of the world. It should be for her as well.

And yet it wasn't. She'd bought the morning after pill and had sat it on the table in front of her along with a glass of water. She stared at it for the longest time. But she couldn't bring herself to take it.

Shaking herself back to the present, she drummed up her courage to let Leo walk up the path. The school had promised they had a staff member who knew Spanish who would step in if there were any problems.

And she was supposed to place this child in their hands? Yes. Just like every other parent did with their child.

Leo's not yours, Mila.

But he could be.

The whisper was there. Just like it had been for the last two weeks. She tried to suppress it. Chastise it. Curse it. But it was still there.

She took a deep breath and forced herself to smile down at the boy, who stood beside her in his brand-new school clothes.

Only he didn't have shoes on. Just thick socks with protective rubber pads over his damaged feet.

"¿Estás listo?"

"Sí. Listo." He grinned back up at her, showing he was indeed ready to go.

How could he be so cheerful? He'd taken everything in his stride, and the boy had such a wonderful attitude that it brought tears to her eyes at times. He should be furious at the hand he'd been dealt. Terrified at being left alone in a strange place with strange people. Instead, he was fascinated by every new thing that crossed his path.

Like red grapes. And broccoli spears (which he called trees).

A mother and her son walked past them, the mother glancing down at Leo as they strolled by. The woman smiled at her. A genuine smile. And the boy waved at Leo with a mischievous grin.

"Estoy listo." Leo tugged her hand.

He really was ready. Even if Mila was not.

So she trudged up the walkway, following the path that hundreds of other parents had walked at one time or another.

And prayed she was doing the right thing. For her. For James. And most of all for Leo.

CHAPTER EIGHT

JAMES HANDED HER the oversized scissors. She took them, careful not to touch his skin as she did. But she was very aware of his warm scent as it surrounded her. A mixture of aftershave and the ocean. He must have been on his boat the last week, because she hadn't seen him coming or going from his house. Which should have made her sick with relief.

Instead…it just made her sick. Because she'd missed him.

A ridiculous sentiment. Sure, they'd had a quick sexual encounter, but thousands of exes hooked up at least once after their separation.

Well, that had been their once. And now it was over. She didn't have to worry about that kind of tension surrounding them anymore.

Except she still felt it strumming through her like the low throb of the engine on James's boat.

Like now, when he leaned down to murmur in her ear, "Are you going to cut that ribbon or just stare at it all day?"

"Oh. Right." Her mind swung back to the present and the reporters and people grouped around a wide yellow ribbon that covered the main entrance of Bright Hope. Her head tilted when she noticed Avery standing next to Tyler, chatting with him like they were best friends. Was that why the other woman had asked if it was truly over between Mila and the firefighter yesterday? Avery deserved someone like Tyler—and he deserved a woman who could love him unconditionally. And there was no better time than this for new beginnings.

Today was the official opening of the clinic, although they didn't have any patients waiting yet.

There would be, though. Leo was going to be the poster child for the collaboration between the two medical centers. They already had a gorgeous picture that James had snapped of him on the boat, life vest firmly fastened as he stared over the side at the water below. The caption read, "Bright Hope was his life jacket. It can be yours too."

James had come up with the slogan, and Mila had to admit she loved it. The clinic gave the less fortunate members of LA hope and a place to go when no one else cared.

Well, *she* cared. Fiercely.

And she was going to make this work. Even if it meant working with James every day for the rest of her life.

Opening the scissors, she slid them over the ribbon and snapped them back together, severing it in two. The ends fell apart, metaphorically removing the barrier that stood between people and their access to this medical center.

Then people were surrounding her, shaking her hand, sticking microphones in her face and asking her to say a few words.

Maybe James saw the beginnings of panic on her face because he smoothly stepped between her and the throng of reporters and held up his hands. She had no idea what he said as her mind was completely numb, but it must have been enough to satisfy the journalists. They scribbled and filmed and talked to their cameras. And then they were packing up all their gear and heading back to the parking lot, moving on to the next big story.

And this was evidently a big one. There were still some fringe reporters—members of the paparazzi—hovering around the perimeter, hoping to get a shot of something unexpected.

"Come with me." The man she was hoping would leave along with everyone else was still here, holding his hand out for the scissors, which he in turn handed to someone else. A pretty blonde, who hovered nearby and seemed to know him well enough. Maybe a little too well. His assistant? His…what…lover?

He'd had enough of them over the years, according to the tabloids.

Maybe that's why the paparazzi were still here, hoping James would forget himself and give them a hint as to who his current love interest was.

She swallowed hard, trying not to let that thought sink in. It was none of her business. He could sleep with everyone in the western hemisphere and it should mean nothing to her.

Only it did. And she wasn't sure why. Maybe because of what they'd done.

Well, it didn't matter. They'd been over and done for six years. She'd be stupid to let anything start back up. Ha! Anything. Like sleeping with him?

She kept expecting him to check in about her period, to which she would respond that he should mind his own damn business. But he didn't. Nor did he ask her if she'd taken steps to protect them both afterward.

He never said a word about what had happened.

Which was good.

She thought.

Avery and Tyler came over, her assistant giving her a hug and congratulating her, while the firefighter shook James's hand. Her assistant had agreed to work at the new clinic, and Mila would be hiring someone else to take her place at the downtown location. The pair headed toward the parking lot with Avery throwing her a quick wink. Mila smiled back, hoping that meant what she thought it did.

James held the door, letting the blonde from the press conference go in ahead of him. Mila was tempted to just slink away—after all maybe that "Come with me" had been directed at the other woman and not her. Except James threw a glance over his shoulder that told her otherwise. He wasn't really her boss. She could just leave. But his clinic was helping her fulfill a huge dream: to bring the care she'd given in poorer countries to the poor of her own country.

Which meant she needed to suck it up and do whatever it took.

Including sleeping with the man who was instrumental in helping Bright Hope procure a premier spot in his clinic?

Of course not. The pool situation had nothing to do with business and everything to do with hormones and memories. Unfortunately the two had collided at just the wrong moment. Thank heavens she'd been able to separate the guilty duo and put them back in their individual corners. Which meant no more sleeping with this man.

Although the sex had been pretty damned amazing. And she didn't seem to have any real scars that she could see.

Maybe...

Absolutely not!

James was still holding the door, only now one brow was quirked in a silent challenge.

She breezed past him as if she hadn't a care in the world, only to run into Freya just inside. "Hey, I've been looking all over for you two."

The blonde was now nowhere to be seen.

"You have?" Mila had a bad feeling. Her friend had been so busy being in love with Zack that she hadn't seen nearly as much of her as she'd used to. "Why?"

James stopped beside her and tilted his head at his sister. "You could have just called me."

"I texted, but you didn't answer." An impish smile appeared.

"My phone was on silent for the ribbon cutting."

"Mmm-hmm. Sure it was."

What was going on? Freya was acting like there was some kind of inside joke. One that James didn't find particularly amusing.

Mila ignored him. "So you wanted...?"

"Zack and I would like you to be the twins' godmother. We've asked James to be the godfather, but since he'll already be their uncle... Unless, of course, you'd like to make that *aunt* and uncle."

A weird gurgling sound came out before she could stop it. She cleared her throat to cover it. What was Freya talking about? She couldn't be the babies' aunt unless she... Oh, Lord. Unless she married James.

Not going to happen. She'd already tried that once before only to have him back out at the last second.

But she hadn't completely gotten over him. The pool proved that. It also made her realize that what had gone wrong between her and Tyler had probably had a lot to do with James.

In fact, every man she'd ever dated had seemed to fall short, damn them all.

"Mila, are you okay?"

She realized that both James and Freya were staring at her, James with an inscrutable look that made her swallow. He seemed just as unhappy with the prospect of her being involved with his sister's children as she was. As a godparent, she would be invited to all the major events of their lives. Family functions. Baptisms. Special occasions.

Weddings.

Mila cringed at the thought. What if James eventually got married? Would she be forced to attend?

It was on the tip of her tongue to say no, and yet as

Freya stood there, blooming with health and happiness, Mila couldn't find it in her heart to refuse her friend's request. She came forward and caught Freya up in a hug, kissing her on the cheek. "Of course I'll be their godmother. I'd be honored."

Freya gave her a tight squeeze and released her. "I'm so relieved. You can't even imagine. Why don't you and James come over for dinner sometime soon so we can start planning?" She rubbed her belly in tiny circles. "Before I explode would be preferable."

"Oh, I…" She searched her brain for some reason to refuse but came up blank.

James tweaked his sister's chin. "Of course we will. Let us figure out our schedules and get back to you with a date."

"Soon," his sister insisted. Then her face went serious. "Bring Leo as well. When is his surgery, by the way?"

"In a little over a week." How had the time gone by so quickly? The child had been in preschool almost a week and his English vocabulary was already beginning to grow by leaps and bounds.

"Have you taken him sailing yet?" This time the question was directed at James. Why Freya thought her brother was responsible for Leo's care was beyond her. Maybe because they were living on James's property.

"Not yet." His voice had cooled a bit. But why? They'd taken Leo on the boat once already, although it hadn't left its mooring. But that had been to tell her about the regatta. It had been business.

Well, maybe they could make Leo's sailing expedition business as well. They could practice the route they would take for the regatta, getting the timing down. It was now only a week away.

She was already dreading having to get dressed up just to rub shoulders with people she had nothing in common with. But it was all part and parcel of what she'd agreed to. Leo would have his surgery just days after the gala.

She decided to broach the subject of doing something special with the child, not because she wanted to go sailing with James but because it would do Leo good. And it would help her get over having sex with James.

Exactly how was it going to do that?

By giving her a chance to be with him under ordinary circumstances. Besides, Leo would act as a chaperon of sorts. Nothing could happen if they had a child with them.

Ha! Leo had been less than fifty yards away the last time.

"I think maybe we should take him. We could run the regatta route and see how long it takes. Besides, he won't be able to come to the actual event."

They'd decided to ask Rosa to watch him for the fundraiser. Mila didn't want to make any more of a spectacle of him than necessary. The advertising posters were bad enough, she didn't want him exposed to people who might be less than sensitive about his condition.

Thoughts that a mother would have.

Freya laughed. "Exactly. It would be great."

Said by a pregnant woman who would no more board a boat than she would scale a mountain.

"Again, I'll have to check my schedule. I have a medical practice to run," James said, the chill in his voice unmistakable this time.

She decided to ignore it. "I have to check mine as well, but surely we can both juggle some things in order to make this happen for him." She couldn't stop herself from touching his arm. "Nothing in this life is certain. Especially surgery. Please?"

She wasn't sure whether it was the "please" or the comment about the surgery, but the chill left and his face softened. "We'll work something out."

"Okay, my mission is complete. Let me know about dinner." Freya started to turn away and then pivoted around again. "By the way, the mural looks great. When did you have time to finish it?"

Mila glanced behind the reception desk where the painting that matched the one at the LA location graced an entire wall. When? When she'd been avoiding James—that was when. But she couldn't tell Freya that. "I just worked on it a little at a time."

"Well, it looks great. I may have to have you come and do something in the babies' room."

"Anytime," she told her friend.

Freya put her hand on the door. "Did you find a dress?"

Mila blinked. "Excuse me?"

"For the gala, silly."

"Not yet. How about you?"

"You don't want to know." Freya glanced at her midsection. "Not that I'll be able to disguise this."

Mila went over and kissed her on the cheek. "You look beautiful, honey. I bet Zack tells you the same thing every chance he gets."

Her face went pink. "He doesn't exactly—um—*tell* me."

The inference made Mila laugh. "Okay, let's not head into TMI territory."

A muscle in James's cheek jumped. "Too late for that. And on that note I need to head back to my office." He paused to look at Mila. "Let me know your schedule."

Freya cut in again. "Don't forget you have to open the gala with a dance. Together." She threw them a wink and ducked back through the door before anyone could object. And Mila had a whole lot of objecting she wanted to do.

As soon as she was gone, James took a step closer, leaning his head close to her ear. The warmth of his breath sent a shiver through her. "Any more news?"

"News?" The shiver died.

"Yes. On our situation." He stared at a spot just past her shoulder. The fact that he wouldn't quite meet her eyes told her he wasn't talking about the regatta or dances but something else entirely. Still, the word "our" caught her right in the chest.

"Not yet. But, like I said, you're off the hook."

"I don't think so, Mila. I'm very much on the hook. And I plan on staying there until we know something one way or the other."

Two days later, James heard the news he'd been waiting for.

Mila wasn't pregnant.

Even as he feigned relief and did his best "that's great news" impersonation as she'd boarded the boat with Leo, something inside kept sending him withering glances. Which was ridiculous.

He did not want babies. Or any kind of child for that matter.

Even as he thought it, an excited Leo pointed as a sea lion popped its head above the water and looked right at them. And although James did his damnedest to ignore the sheer delight on the boy's face as his small hands clutched one of the chrome rails, he couldn't suppress the stab of joy Leo's happiness brought him. Especially when he ducked his head between the slats to get a closer look.

Mila squatted beside the child, murmuring something. Dressed in a white sundress that looked a little too similar to the one she'd worn in the pool, he found himself stealing glances at her flat stomach and imagining what it would look like if things had been different. But they weren't.

She looked relaxed and happy. Too happy.

Because she was relieved she wasn't pregnant?

Damn it!

He spun the wheel a little to the left to keep the boat headed straight down the coast and to take his mind off things he couldn't control. The trek was meant to take just over a half hour. So far, every second had been excruciating.

Time to do something about it.

From what he'd heard, quite a few of the boats that were to take part in the regatta were planning on decorating their crafts for the event. Whether it was white twinkle lights or elegant paper lanterns, it seemed everyone was planning on going all out. He was pretty sure the board expected him to follow suit with the *Mystic Waters*.

He glanced at Mila. "Maybe Leo would like to help us decorate the boat, since he won't able to come to the party."

Propping her chin on the rail beside Leo's head, he couldn't see her face, but her hand went around the boy's waist and she again said something to him. Leo turned to look at him, eyes wide. *"¿Eso es la verdad?"*

"Yes. I'm telling the truth," he said.

He should be dreading having to spend any more time with Mila and Leo, but today he found himself oddly out of sorts, and he didn't want to examine why.

Instead he focused on the here and now, and found he wanted to decorate the boat. Wanted to see Leo's face as dusk fell and they turned on the lights.

He wanted to see Mila's reaction as well. Speaking of which…

"Freya has been all over me about making sure my tuxedo is ready to go."

She shifted sideways, still holding on to Leo. "She's been asking about my dress color as well. And if we've practiced our dance. I wonder why?"

"Having the clinics join forces has been her pet project. I think she's worried we're going to mess it up somehow."

Mila glanced at him, her lips twisting. "Maybe that's why she's offered to go dress shopping with me. Do you think she guessed about our plans to get off the dance floor as fast as possible?"

"I haven't said a word."

"She knows us pretty well, though." She ruffled Leo's hair. "Maybe we should rethink things, James. I don't want to embarrass her. Or either of our clinics."

"And how do we avoid that?" Mila was a good dancer. A little too good, as she'd always gotten a reaction from him. Then again, she pretty much got a reaction anytime she came within ten feet of him. Even now.

"Maybe we should make it good, rather than bad. Live dangerously."

He had no idea what had gotten into her, but he'd been living dangerously ever since he'd agreed to allow Bright Hope into his clinic.

"Dangerously isn't always the best choice."

Like forgetting to put a condom on before he had sex with someone? He forgot himself around Mila. He always had.

And maybe that's why she suddenly seemed playful and happy. She was glad he hadn't knocked her up.

Yeah? Well, he was glad too. And if the opportunity arose to have sex with her again, he wouldn't turn it down. He'd just be a whole lot smarter about the execution.

And if they danced for real? Would he be able to resist stealing a kiss or two?

Dangerous. Very dangerous.

Yet Mila herself was calling for a little of that very thing. Did that mean she was open to a few kisses too?

"I guess I'd better let her help me find a dress, then." Leaving him to wonder exactly what kind of dress she would choose, she turned back to Leo to point out another sea lion that had joined the first. Their heads bobbed in the water, staring at the boat.

"I think they're begging."

James couldn't blame them. He'd been known to beg for a crumb or two from Mila as well.

"They're out of luck."

Mila explained to Leo why they couldn't feed the pair. Tourists had learned the hard way by getting nipped by some of the more aggressive creatures. Giving them treats only made them bolder.

"We only have about ten more minutes before we get to our destination. Do you want to continue? Or do you want to drop anchor?"

Mila glanced at her watch just as a Jet Ski shot by them, hitting them with a spray of water as the craft turned sharply to the right. Both sea lions ducked beneath the surface.

"Damn it." James shifted to look at Mila and Leo to make sure they were okay before turning back to the idiot who'd cut a little too close to them.

Two people sat aboard the watercraft, and the driver was still hotdogging it, doing circles and zigzags that were more than dangerous. And they were a little farther offshore than he normally saw Jet Skis. It didn't mean they didn't venture out this far but they were almost a mile out.

Even as he thought it, the pair headed back their way, the person on the back lifting a can of something in salute as they raced past and circled James's boat, barely missing the *Mystic Waters*' bow before speeding away again.

They were going to hurt someone if they kept that up. He debated a moment or two about whether to let it go and leave the pair to their stupidity, but decided it wasn't worth the risk. He picked up his radio and turned the frequency to call the coast guard. Suddenly the Jet Ski cut too sharply to the right, sending the craft skittering across the water in a jagged course. It came back on center for a brief second but the driver must have over-corrected because the craft lurched to the other side and in an instant—still going at top speed—it flipped, tossing both of its passengers into the dark waters of the bay.

"Oh, hell!" Kicking off his shoes and yanking his shirt over his head, he yelled at Mila. "Shut the engine down and take the wheel. Radio the coast guard while you're at it."

With that, James dove over the side and into the water.

CHAPTER NINE

WHERE WAS HE?

Mila spotted one of the Jet Ski's passengers floating on the surface, life jacket in place, but the second one was nowhere to be seen. Neither was James.

But she had other things to worry about right now. Like getting the boat anchored so the light wind didn't cause the *Mystic Waters* to drift farther and farther away from where James was. She ran through the steps in her head, using memories of past anchoring to guide her: Point the bow into the wind. Pay out the anchor chain until it hit bottom. Set the anchor.

She wasn't going to worry about the setting part, and thank heavens that Leo's presence had made James decide to use the boat's engine rather than putting up the sails. She wasn't sure she could have gotten those down by herself. Putting Leo into a chair and telling him to stay there, she followed the sequence she'd set up in her head. Glancing back into the water, she still only saw the lone victim.

James was a great swimmer, but the waters off California's coast were chilly and visibility wasn't the best in this area.

The first victim, a woman, was now feebly paddling toward the boat.

"Can you make it?" Mila called out.

She didn't dare jump in the water and leave Leo—still sitting like she'd asked him to, although his eyes were now wide with fear—alone on the boat. She'd radioed a Mayday a minute earlier. The coast guard was on its way.

The person in the water lifted her head and nodded, long hair streaming down her back as she kept swimming toward the boat. Thank God she was able to move under her own power.

Still no sign of James, though. Her heart pumped in her chest at a frantic pace, trying not to think the worst. It had only been a little over two minutes, but it seemed like forever. God, what if something had happened to him? What if he'd gotten turned around underwater? What if…?

Something breached the surface, and she grabbed the rail before realizing it wasn't a porpoise or, worse, a shark but James. And he had the second person with him. He sucked down several gasping breaths before his eyes met hers. Then, arm wrapped around the man's chest in a rescue hold, he swam toward the boat with powerful strokes, saying something to the other person as he crossed in front of her, but not stopping. There was an ominous stillness about the man he towed.

As soon as they came within reach of the loading ramp at the back of the vessel, Mila motioned for Leo to stay in the chair. *"Espera aquí."*

Hoping the boy would wait, like she'd asked him to, she leaned over the side and grabbed the second victim's arms, while James pushed him up from the waist. Within a minute he'd flopped onto the deck. She went into emergency rescue mode, vaguely aware that James had turned and was swimming back toward the woman.

A boat engine rumbled far off in the distance, but she didn't have time to look to see if it was the coast guard. Instead, she put her head to the accident victim's chest and listened. There was a heartbeat but the man wasn't breathing. She turned his head to the left, debating whether to flip him onto his side to give whatever water was in his lungs an easier exit, but the man probably weighed twice as much as she did. She settled for tilting his head to make sure his airway was cleared and then leaning down to start artificial respiration.

Between breaths, she chanced a quick glance at Leo, but he hadn't moved from his spot. And now James was helping the Jet Ski's other passenger onto the *Mystic Waters*, then he was back at her side. "Let me take over. The coast guard is almost here."

Mila didn't argue. Her first duty was to do the best she could for her patient and the best in this situation was to let James do the heavy lifting. She went over to the woman, who had sunk to the deck in a fetal position, softly crying as a cutter with official markings pulled up to the side of the boat.

Mila grabbed the line they tossed her way and tied it off, relaying the situation in brief phrases. "Jet Ski accident with two victims. We're both doctors."

Not waiting for them to come aboard, she checked the woman's vitals, which were surprisingly normal. She coughed up some water, and Mila helped her lean forward and clear her lungs, all the while trying to contain her own emotions.

She shared James's anger. It had been beyond stupid to race around like the pair had. It was a wonder no one had been killed.

Well…she glanced at where James was still working on the man…it was possible someone had been. As if sensing her thoughts, the woman looked up at her. "Is he…?"

Even after hacking up a good amount of water, the woman's breath reeked of alcohol, and Mila had seen her raise a can of something. It hadn't been soda, judging by how reckless the pair had been in circling James's boat. She bit back several responses before settling for something kinder than what she was thinking.

"James is a wonderful doctor. He's doing everything he can."

A choking sob came. "We were just out to have a good time. It was only our second date."

A uniformed man squatted beside them. "Is she stable?"

"For the moment."

The officer nodded and then turned to the woman. "I need your name. Do you have any ID on you?"

Mila let him take over, glad to be able to get back to Leo, who had to be scared out of his mind with the frantic rescue. When she reached him she gripped the boy's small hand. What if he'd wandered off and had gone over the side while her attention had been elsewhere?

Anger pulsed past the relief, followed by concern. James, who was still busy doing mouth-to-mouth, stopped when the other member of the coast guard produced a manual resuscitator. He helped fit it over the man's mouth, and the officer began squeezing the bag while James felt for a pulse.

A minute later the man convulsed. Once. Twice. Then between James and the coast-guard officer they turned him to the side, just as he vomited massive amounts of seawater across the deck, gasping between bouts. But at least he was now breathing and reacting, and not the lifeless figure he'd presented moments earlier.

Once stable, the pair was transferred onto the coast-guard vessel. One of them shook James's hand and then hers, nodding toward the accident victims. "Thank you for your help. I doubt he would have made it without your quick thinking."

Mila shuddered. Undoubtedly. The man would have

sunk to the bottom of the bay without James bravely diving in after him. For a few moments she'd wondered whether he would end up following the man to a watery grave.

But that hadn't happened. She had to remember that.

James's hair was plastered to his head, his strong chest bare. A rush of emotion went through her. A scary familiar feeling that sliced through her midsection.

It was just relief. It had to be. She couldn't let it be anything else. When she jerked her gaze back to his face, she found him watching her.

The coast-guard vessel pulled away with a last wave from one of the men, but still she couldn't pull her eyes from James's face.

Words tumbled out. "I thought you had…" Her eyes closed as another wave of emotion crashed over her. "When you didn't come up…"

She couldn't seem to finish any of her thoughts. Because they were too awful.

Arms came around her and a hand pressed her head against his chest, holding her there for a minute.

"I couldn't find him." His words rumbled low and gruff against her hair. "I knew if I came up for breath, I'd lose my bearings and he'd die."

I thought you *were going to die.*

The sentence rolled through her head, but she didn't dare say it. Leo was still not fluent in English, but she didn't know how much he could or couldn't understand, and she didn't want to upset him more than he already was.

She let her eyes close, her cheek pressed tight against the coolness of James's bare chest, the reassuring beat of his heart beneath her ear.

He hadn't died. And he'd just saved a man's life.

When she finally let her lids part, she realized one of James's hands had reached out to rest on Leo's head and the boy's shoulder was resting against his right leg.

More emotion welled up inside her and suddenly she was crying, trying her damnedest not to sob out loud. But tears leaked and pooled and did all sorts of terrible things to her insides.

"Shh…" Something pressed lightly against her temple. "It's okay."

It was. Despite their past and everything that had happened between them. In this one moment in time the world had righted itself. It might not stay that way but for now she could revel in the fact that James was alive. And here. Holding her and Leo close.

She took a deep breath and let it back out. "Yes. It's okay." Before she could stop herself, she stepped up on tiptoe and kissed him, allowing her mouth to rest against his for several seconds before she finally pulled away. If she could have, she would have done so much more than just kiss him. She wanted him to take her down to that cabin so she could show him how glad she was that he was still here. Still alive.

But with Leo that was impossible.

And at the gala? The tempting thought swirled around and around like a wisp of smoke.

He'd teased her about being dangerous…maybe she should show him just how dangerous she could be. Trying not to let that idea get too firmly entrenched, she used the wide strap of her sundress to mop the moisture from her face. Not very successfully, though.

Not letting go of Leo, James reached over and picked up his discarded shirt and handed it to her. She pressed it to her face, her nostrils catching and holding on to his scent. So achingly familiar.

She wanted another night with him. Just one more. Surely she could do that and then let him go. It wouldn't be an impulsive, crazy dip in the pool but a conscious decision. A reaffirming of life.

As if reading her thoughts, he stared at her for a long time, and then gave Leo's hair a quick ruffle and said, "What do you say we head back and start decorating *Mystic Waters*?"

James knocked on the door to the cottage two days later. Her nerves were twitching and fretting about what he would think when he saw her. Freya had dragged her to almost a dozen stores in search of the perfect dress. And Mila had to admit the red frothy off-the-shoulder confection showed off her figure to its best advantage. Rosa was already camped out in the living room ready to keep Leo for the night. A decision Mila had made on the spur of the moment after reliving their last few minutes on the boat following the Jet Ski accident. Something had passed between them as he'd held her, and Mila wasn't willing to turn her back on it quite yet. Eventually their interactions would cool down to business luncheons and quick nods in the hallway. But Mila— for good or bad—wanted that night with him…would feel cheated if she didn't get it.

She wasn't pregnant, and she already knew where she stood with him. He'd proved his inability to commit during their engagement, and from the various other women he'd been linked to in the tabloids over the years that was still true. And she definitely wasn't going to let Leo get attached to someone he couldn't trust.

He'd already been through too much, his parents' deaths eerily like her own parents' demise. She was going to ask to adopt him if his uncle didn't come forward.

It was the right thing to do. She was convinced of it.

The knock came again, and Mila sucked down a deep breath. Yes, it was the right thing.

And so was this. If James could have meaningless flings, then so could she. With him. Especially with him since there was no fear that he would press her for more, like Tyler had.

She pulled open the door and waited for his reaction.

It didn't take long. His eyes widened and slid slowly down her body.

"Wow." James took her hand and twirled her around in a slow three-hundred-and-sixty-degree turn. "You look beautiful. But, then, you always did."

She smiled. "Thank you. You look pretty good yourself. Then again, you always did."

Clad in a crisp black tuxedo, the man looked good enough to eat. And if she got lucky, she planned on enjoying every single bite.

"Are you ready?" he asked.

"Absolutely."

Something in her voice must have given her away because he glanced at her sideways, a question in his eyes. "What?"

"Nothing." Calling out a goodbye to Rosa, along with her thanks, she went ahead of him out the door. "I'm just planning on enjoying tonight."

He came up close behind her and laid a hand on her bare shoulder, his thumb strumming across her skin. "Enjoying? Or *enjoying*?"

"You'll have to wait and see."

"I'm intrigued. Care to elaborate?"

Despite her outward bravado, when they passed the pool her face sizzled at the memories that crept up. "Not right now. Maybe after the gala."

If she had her way, there would be no crowds, no baby monitors. No one but her and James. On that luxurious boat of his.

As if he'd read her mind, he murmured, "I'm going to hold you to that."

Climbing into his sleek black sports car, Mila settled into

the leather seat, feeling a brief second or two of unease as the door shut behind her.

She pushed it back. She could do this. All of it. The party. The fancy food. The wealthy patrons. It was a price she was willing to pay to help people.

And if she held James out as her reward for sticking it out, she would get through the night just fine.

She was pretty sure James would be willing to go along with that plan. Especially after his last comment. The only question was how long they would last before one of them cracked. The way she was feeling right now, it might very well be her.

He backed the car out of the drive, pausing to tweak one of her auburn curls. "You've let it go natural tonight."

"Freya thought it would go better with the dress than straightening it." When she had been in Brazil she'd tended to let it dry naturally, since she didn't always have access to the straightening iron she used in the States.

"I always did like your curls." One of his brows went up.

Was he remembering how she'd looked straight out of the shower, when they'd had unplanned nights of wild sex? Her curls had been much shorter back then, but he'd used to wind them around his fingers as they'd lain in bed together afterward.

She laughed. "Well, you have a bit of curl to your hair as well." She reached over and rumpled the waves just a bit, making them look wild and untamed. Oh, yeah. James was hot, no matter how his hair was.

"I still have to face my coworkers on Monday morning, you know."

"Don't worry, you can return to your stodgy old style tomorrow."

"Stodgy." He stopped at a light and reached over to slide his fingers over her cheek. "Would you like to take that back?"

"Nope. Always were. Still are."

"I see I'm going to have to work a bit to disabuse you of that notion."

A shiver went through her. They were playing back and forth with their words like they used to in days past, only Mila wasn't quite sure he meant them the way she was taking them. But she hoped the sensual promise hidden in their repartee wasn't just in her imagination.

He might appear cool and polished on the surface, but beneath that sleek playboy veneer James had always been someone to contend with. There was a hard edge to him that excited her. He liked to experiment…and to play. And he'd driven Mila wild with need time and time again. He still did, in fact. Their sex play at the pool had been mild compared to what had gone on between them in the past.

They got to the boat in less than a half hour, and by that time James's hand was resting, warm and heavy, on her thigh, making her squirm.

The way his touch always had.

She was tempted to throw this whole damn party to the wind and just drag him aboard the boat. Except they were scheduled to queue up with other watercraft for the water parade, and it would be pretty conspicuous if the lead boat didn't show up.

A few of the bigger yachts were hosting after-parties. She and James had already received multiple invitations, in fact, which James said he had turned down.

At first she'd wondered if it was because he knew she wasn't fond of all the glitz and glamour or, worse, because he didn't want to spend any extra time with her. But after his touch and words tonight, she hoped it was because he wanted her all to himself. Because she definitely wanted him. And if they hadn't had responsibilities to fulfill for their respective clinics and patients, she would have just chucked it all to the wind and hosted their own little party. A very private one.

But she did have responsibilities. As did James. But that didn't mean they couldn't retreat back to his schooner afterward and spend the rest of the night in that big bed of his. He'd once told her he'd never spent the night on his boat with a woman other than her, and she'd never seen pictures of him there with anyone, so she hoped it was still one of his unspoken rules. She didn't know why that was, other than a glimmer of hope that he considered what they'd once had to be special.

But not special enough to marry her.

She banished that thought, because this time she wasn't looking for marriage. She was looking to spend a single night with a man she was attracted to. A man she'd always been attracted to. And someone she was glad was still alive.

That made it okay. Didn't it? It wasn't like either one of them was hiding something from the other. They both knew the score.

By the time they got on the dinghy that would take them to James's boat, it was dusk and the schooner's white twinkle lights had already been lit. By the boat's caretaker, she assumed.

Since they would once again be powering the boat, using the engine rather than the sails, the lights up the rigging provided a beautiful profile. Someone had also attached white paper lanterns to the railing around the deck. They provided a soft light that made the teakwood glow. A glow she could see even from this distance.

The setting was perfect. More perfect that anything she could imagine.

Maybe she would talk James into mooring the boat out a little way from the rest of the regatta craft and when they were done with the party they could make love on the deck first, before moving below.

After all, they had all night. Something James didn't know. He knew his housekeeper was watching Leo for the duration of the party, but what he wasn't aware of was that Mila had taken her aside and asked her if she could stay the night, in case they got…delayed. The woman had kept a completely straight face and told her she'd be happy to, whether they returned at midnight or the next morning, and for Mila not to worry herself with letting her know one way or the other.

For all she knew, James just assumed they were going home once the gala was over.

Would he accept her suggestion of staying out all night instead?

She hoped so. The disappointment would be crushing if she'd misread his signals.

Maybe she should prepare herself, just in case.

Once James helped her aboard the schooner and went up front to get things ready for the short trip, she did something she hadn't done in ages. She pulled her phone out of the small red clutch she'd brought with her and scrolled through her contacts. She'd added his number not so very long ago, since she knew they'd have to have business meetings, and so on. Finding him, her thumb hovered over the message button. Should she?

Since she wasn't brave enough to ask him outright, she decided to risk it. She quickly typed out the words. And before she lost her nerve, she hit Send.

James had shed his tuxedo jacket and had his back to her, but she could still see the moment he reached his hand into his pocket and pulled something out. His phone. He gazed at the screen for a second. Then he dropped it right back into his pocket without any reaction at all. And without typing anything in return.

What? Oh, no! He wasn't going to respond. Humiliation washed over her in a big wave. Maybe she could jump into the dinghy and take off before he broke the news to her in person.

A second or two later he turned around and his eyes met hers. Too late. All thoughts of running fled.

She swallowed.

He came around the bulkhead, hands in his pockets as he made his way toward her.

Mila's face burned even hotter. She hadn't had the nerve to ask him about his plans for this evening, but he evidently had no problem breaking the bad news to her face-to-face. It would have been so much easier to get the message via text.

No, it wouldn't. But at least then she would have been able to hide her face until she'd composed herself.

And there was always the dinghy.

When he got to her, though, there was no sign of rejection in his eyes. Only some hot emotion that scorched her to the core.

He took a hold of her chin and tipped her head up. "Yes. I do have plans for after the party."

Before she could squirm away from him in renewed mortification, his cheek brushed against hers. "And those plans involve you. And me. And every available surface. Horizontal. Vertical. Upside down."

Her lips parted as realization swept through her. He wasn't rejecting her. He was verifying every thought she'd had.

All that wordplay. All those little touches. He, too, meant this evening to lead to something more.

"I thought you were going to turn me down."

"I've never been able to turn you down."

Oh, yes, he had. She could remember one very specific time. But she'd made up her mind not to dwell on that. Not tonight.

This had nothing to do with their engagement. Or their past relationship. This had to do with want and desire and needing to spend the night with a hot, willing man.

The fact that she'd chosen him and not someone else meant nothing, except the fact that in the end James seemed a whole lot less complicated. He was a master at keeping things light and easy.

She shook off her thoughts. "How long is this party supposed to last?"

"I'm hoping it'll go on all night long."

Another shiver went through her. The man knew exactly the right thing to say.

"I might just hold you to that."

"What about Leo?"

"Rosa said she would stay with him."

He leaned back and a slow smile made the deep groove in the left side of his face come to life. "I see I'm not the only one whose thoughts were running in this direction."

One hand went to the deck railing beside her hip, while the other curled around her back and drew her against his chest. "If we weren't due at this damned event, and if we weren't quite so visible at the moment…" he leaned down until he was right against her ear once again "…I would go ahead and get this little party started."

He already had. Her insides were quivering with anticipation, nerve endings throughout her body going on high alert, waiting for the slightest signal that he was willing to set aside their duties and drag her below deck.

Instead, his arm uncurled from around her. Yes, it was a slow move, but it still had him moving away instead of closing the deal with a kiss.

Before she could draw another breath, though, his eyes met hers again, the soft lighting giving them an amber glow that reminded her of a wolf. "I plan on using the time at that fund-raiser to make you think about what's going to happen the moment we come back aboard. When I have you all to myself."

James had meant to drive Mila crazy with need in little ways. The touch of his fingers as he slid a champagne glass into her hand. The brush of his body against hers as he reached past her for an hors d'oeuvre. Instead, he was driving himself insane. They'd better start up the music for the dancing soon or he was going to drag Mila out onto that floor and make their own special music. One unheard by anyone except them.

He wanted her. Planned on having her. And this time he was prepared for anything. In fact, he'd peppered his whole boat with protection so that it didn't matter where they ended up. He'd done his best to ignore how it reminded him of his disappointment at discovering she wasn't pregnant. He should be glad. Celebrating it from the rooftops, but he wasn't. And he wasn't sure why. Neither was he so vain as to think Mila was a sure thing.

In fact, she was the least sure thing he'd ever come across. Maybe that was part of what drove his crushing need to have her.

He didn't think so.

In fact, if he let himself think too much, he might just come to a conclusion that he didn't want to face. And so he didn't. He let himself dwell on the pleasure that was ahead and dismissed any stray thought that didn't go along with that.

He'd had plenty of women since he'd broken their engagement. He would make this just another meeting of bodies. Only it wasn't, and he knew it. He still didn't bring women aboard his boat. But Mila had already been there during their engagement, so that didn't count. Right?

So why was it that when his phone had buzzed, indicating he'd received a text, his gut had given a knowing twist. And when he'd glanced down at the screen and read the words, his first instinct had been to text her back, jumping back to their former ways of ramping up the heat. In the end, he'd steeled himself against doing so. He hadn't sent a text for six years and he wasn't going to start now. And somehow he knew that if he sent her a message, things would go from a fun, superficial fling to something deeper.

But wasn't it already deeper? He'd slept with the woman once. Planned on doing so again.

His gut churned with a mass of contradictory emotions.

He didn't want to hurt her again. And after that pregnancy scare and with her moving forward with Leo, he was sure he would. So he'd done his damnedest to remind himself this was going to be all about the sex.

If he could just drill that through his thick skull and make himself believe it, he should be fine.

In fact, he knew he would be.

CHAPTER TEN

HE WASN'T FINE.

Over an hour later, there had been toasts and mingling and smiling acknowledgment of patrons as they promised funding for the next year.

James still hadn't danced with her. He'd watched her from across the room, champagne glass in hand, laughing with Abi Thompson and Damien Moore, both doctors who practiced at The Hollywood Hills Clinic. He and Damien had worked together on multiple cases, like Patricia Still-well's, and from what James had heard, Damien and Abi were pretty much inseparable nowadays. Abi, wearing a dark green gown, stood close to him, smiling up at something the other man said.

A spear of some ugly emotion went through him at the obvious affection between them. Damien's hand went around Abi's waist, and she leaned into him for a second. She then held out her left hand, and Mila leaned closer to examine something on it.

Left hand?

His glance went to his friend, who even from this distance looked pretty damned smug about something.

Oh, hell, no. Surely not.

But even as Mila grabbed the woman up in a hug, her face alight with happiness, James felt something in his chest sink.

He'd thrown away something truly good. Something remarkable. No matter what Cindy or his father had done, he could have—and should have—talked it over with Mila. Instead, in trying to protect her from the ugliness of what had happened—the hopeless reality he'd thought he faced— he'd left her with no explanation. No possibility of working toward a solution.

She'd never asked for an explanation.

But then again he'd never offered one.

Maybe he should change that. Give them both the closure they'd been denied. Or it might even be something a little more than that.

Other people from the clinic had gathered around the pair: Flo and Nate, Freya and Zach, Grace and Liam. All couples now. He should be happy for all of them, but the only thing he felt was a pit of emptiness that began in his stomach and spread to the rest of his body.

He decided it was time to go and collect his date, before he let the kernel of jealous longing ruin everything he and Mila had built over the last several hours. Besides, his hands and body were telling him to get a move on. She'd chatted with several other men. None had gotten close enough to touch her, but it had still sent an arrow jetting through his gut each time he'd seen her with someone else. Apart from that firefighter, James hadn't had to deal with the reality that Mila would one day find the man of her dreams. And start that family she'd mentioned long ago.

He would have to see them together day in and day out. Or at least for as long as their two clinics were housed in the same building. And since Freya had asked Mila to be her twins' godmother, it was inevitable that they would see each other over the years.

He wasn't sure he could stomach it. But she deserved all that and more. Deserved so much more than a man who'd broken her heart for reasons that had had nothing to do with her. And everything to do with him and his family.

Or was that just a cop-out he'd told himself over the years to avoid a painful discussion?

One he wasn't going to put off for any longer.

Maybe then he would be able to move forward with his own life. Whether that could ever include Mila was yet to be seen.

So he headed toward her, just as the small crowd that had gathered around Abi and Damien began to disperse. Abi looked relieved. He knew she didn't really care for loud, noisy places, courtesy of the PTSD she'd brought back from the war in Afghanistan. And Damien seemed pretty determined to make sure she was as comfortable as possible, leading her toward a private table a short distance away.

When James reached Mila, he found her staring off into space. But when she saw him, her pensive expression turned into a smile. Relief poured through him.

He let his own lips twitch. "What was that all about?"

"What was what?"

Nodding toward the pair seated at the table, he said, "That?"

Mila slid her hand in his and tugged him a short distance away. "They're engaged. She doesn't want anyone making a big deal over it, though."

"No. She wouldn't. I thought something was brewing between those two."

"Isn't it wonderful? And I think something might be starting up between Avery and Tyler. Did you see them at the ribbon-cutting ceremony?"

"I didn't notice." James looked at her with new eyes. Even with the disillusionment he'd handed her six years ago, she could still find it in her heart to be genuinely happy for others who found love.

Time to think about something else. Something that

would take his mind off the obvious happiness of the newly engaged couple and put it squarely back on the woman in front of him.

"Speaking of wonderful…" He swept an arm around her waist and took her hand in his. "Dance with me."

She laughed. "The music hasn't started yet."

"Then let's change that." He moved over to where the DJ was busy getting things in order and asked him to start the dancing.

The man smiled and then pulled his microphone over, flipping through a chart of some kind. "Let's open up the floor for the first dance of the evening, featuring the heads of the newly merged Bright Hope Clinic and The Hollywood Hills Clinic. Here's to a long and healthy relationship." Probably having no idea of the irony of that statement, the man then held his arm out and a spotlight came up, capturing James and Mila in its glare. "Here to get this show under way is our very own Dr. James Rothsberg and Dr. Mila Brightman."

A round of applause grew and soon became organized into a synchronized rhythm that ended in laughter when James held out his hand, palm uplifted.

Mila obliged by taking it and letting him sweep her onto the dance floor.

They came together, a relearning of things forgotten, although James could swear he'd forgotten nothing about her. One thing he recalled with painful clarity, though: how it felt to have her in his arms. And how he never wanted to let her go.

So he wouldn't. At least not for this dance. Or the next.

Mila settled her hips close to his and laid her cheek on his shoulder. Her scent flooded his nostrils, and he strained to capture it, allowing it to seep into every pore. When she shifted and draped her arms around his neck, everything inside him tightened. He wanted nothing more than to whisk her away and show her how special she was. Show her how much he…

Loved her.

He took a hit to the midsection. Then another.

Why was he so surprised? He'd always loved her. From the moment he'd laid eyes on her he'd known she was someone who would rock his world.

And rock it she had.

The first song went by and soon other couples joined them on the dance floor. He spied Freya across the room, standing next to Zack, one hand on her belly and her other around her husband. She gave a little wave that seemed far too gloating.

Gloating about what? Him dancing with Mila? She'd known they were supposed to have the first dance.

His sister had been furious when he'd walked out on Mila, and rightly so. Maybe this was his chance to make up for past wrongs. He and Mila could surely wind up as friends once all was said and done.

Except he loved her.

Was it possible to love her and be happy with just friendship? He didn't know. But what he did know was that he wanted her in a way he'd never wanted anyone else. And she wanted him. At least that text she'd sent on the boat would seem to indicate she did.

It was worth the risk.

He spun her around, until he couldn't see Freya and Zack anymore. Or Damien and Abi. Or anyone else from the clinic. All he could see was Mila. Along with everything she made him feel.

And suddenly it was enough. At least for tonight. Tomorrow? He had no idea, but he could make those kinds of decisions later.

"Hey," he murmured, allowing his lips to trail over her

ear, suddenly not caring if anyone saw the move. "How much longer do we have to stay?"

Mila shuddered against him, her fingers tightening on his neck. "I'm pretty sure we've fulfilled our duty."

When he moved lower, allowing his teeth to nip at the long lines of her neck, she actually gasped out loud.

He smiled. "I haven't fulfilled anything yet. But I fully intend to."

When she pressed her hips against him, finding the throbbing, aching truth of the matter, he knew he didn't want to wait a moment longer. "Let's go."

Grabbing her hand, he hauled her through the clusters of people, throwing stiff smiles toward a few who got between him and the door and deftly maneuvering around them.

Then they were free. Outside in the cool night air. The second they were in his dinghy, he leaned over her, lips feathering across hers in a kiss that made her moan. Her fingers gripped the sides of the boat.

"That's right, honey. Hang on tight. This is going to be the fastest crossing you've ever made."

A tickly, scratchy sensation ran down one side of her spine. Then back up the other side. Mila squirmed, then groaned and rolled onto her back. The same prickly object flowed between her breasts, down her sternum, over her belly, picking up speed as it headed toward her...

Her breath caught just as her eyes flew open.

"James!" She half laughed, half screamed as she tried to get her bearings.

He looked up at her, his whiskery chin planted just below her belly button, an impish, unapologetic look of need in his eyes.

"I love hearing you say my name." Every word he spoke made those morning bristles scratch across her skin in the most delicious way.

She giggled, her body already heating as memories began flooding over her.

His boat. They were on James's sailboat. And what they'd done last night—well, she'd never forget a single second of it.

She turned her head in a rush to see if they'd actually...

Yes. They evidently had. Both posts of the headboard boasted a coil of rope. Burned into her mind was the exact second he'd released her hands so she could...

He rubbed his chin against her once more, slipping an inch or two farther south. She stopped him with a hand to the back of his head, managing to ask, "What time is it?"

"Still early."

It was? Because she could see light pouring into the cabin. "How early?"

"Just after seven."

Mila relaxed. At least it wasn't ten or eleven. In fact, if it was seven, that meant they'd gone to bed just three hours earlier. No, not gone to bed—because that had been hours ago. They'd finally gone to *sleep* at around four o'clock.

"Still, I have to get back to the house before Rosa worries."

"I called her and told her we'd decided to stay over. It was late and we'd both had a few drinks." He slid to lie beside her, still naked, his taut body making her feel positively drunk. "Besides, I wanted to talk to you for a few minutes before we go back to the real world."

The real world. Where life was not quite as fun and free of complications as it had been last night.

She turned to look at where he lay, his golden head pressing deep into the crisp white pillow. "If it's about...earlier...we used something this time, so we should be good."

"It was definitely good. In fact..."

"Again?" They'd used more than one of those condoms he'd brought.

"Is that a no?"

"No. It's definitely not." James had always been an insatiable lover. And once had never seemed to be enough with him. It made her heart warm in ways she didn't want to think about.

He reached up and wrapped a strand of her hair around his finger and then kissed the tip of her nose. "I have something I want to tell you. Something…" He paused as if trying to find just the right words. "I've been doing some thinking while you slept. I want things to be different between us this time."

This time? Was he saying…?

Maybe it was the same thing she'd been thinking for the last couple of hours.

A bubble of happiness rose to the surface. Maybe the past really could be rewritten. Or, if not rewritten, edited so that what had been a stark, dead ending could be erased, allowing for something better. Sweeter.

So, without waiting for him to say anything else, Mila slid her hands up James's chest until she reached his shoulders and then she gave a light shove, flipping him onto his back on the huge bed. The puzzlement on his face was as plain as the ropes that were still attached to the headboard.

Those cords gave her an idea.

Talking could wait. They had time. Plenty of time.

She took one of his hands and raised it above his head and then straddled his hips, feeling a definite nudge of reaction from somewhere below. Leaning over, she took the length of rope and wound it around his wrist, tying it just tight enough that he wouldn't be able to pull it loose.

"Hey, I'm trying to have a rational conversation here." The protest was halfhearted at best.

"Kind of busy right now."

"What are you doing?" He tugged against the binding, but one side of his mouth quirked.

"Isn't it obvious?" She took his other hand, feeling no resistance this time as she fastened it to the other side of the bed.

The boat rolled slightly to the left.

"And if we sink?" His pupils widened with lust and something a little more profound. Something she didn't want to explore right now. So she bit his lip enough to sting. His breath hissed in and he tried to reach her, but his hands quickly reached the end of their tethers.

"Oh, I'm counting on you sinking, James." She gave a husky laugh. "All the way to the bottom. And I'm going to enjoy every single inch as you do."

CHAPTER ELEVEN

LEO WAS ALREADY out and intubated.

Sitting in the observation room where Adam Walker was preparing to operate, Mila leaned forward, resting her elbows on her knees as she gazed at the scene. "The surgeon said he'll have to wear casts for four months and then braces for probably the next two years."

Adam had told him the same thing when he'd asked. The sad thing was that if Leo had been treated right after birth, while his bones had still been soft and pliable, the doctors might have been able to manipulate his feet into the correct position and held them there using the Ponseti method of casting and bracing. His Achilles tendons might have needed to be lengthened through a quick surgery, and the tendon which was attached to his second toe might have had to be transferred to his third to prevent the foot from re-rotating into the club position, but it was nothing like what the boy was now facing.

As it was, the muscles in his calves would have to be lengthened, as would his tendons to help rotate his feet into the correct position. And Leo would have to learn to walk all over again on his newly corrected feet.

He moved his glance from what was happening in the operating room and put it on Mila, who now had her chin propped in her hands, her muscles tense as she stared at the scene below.

Before he could stop himself, his hand went to her back, his thumb sweeping in gentle circles. He would give anything to take her worry on himself. But he couldn't do that any more than he could ask Adam to operate on him instead of Leo.

And he still hadn't talked to Mila, like he'd promised himself he would. But he needed to, and soon, if he wanted to have a future with her.

He did. Those thoughts had come slowly, but they'd been building with every hour that had passed. They'd spent almost every waking moment together over the last two days, he and Mila and Leo. And for the first time he'd wondered if he actually could have a family. If he could actually be the stand-up guy he hadn't been six years ago.

That would depend on how Mila reacted to what he told her. But first they had to get through this surgery.

Mila drew in a deep breath and blew it back out, then sat up, holding her hand out, palm up, to him. He reached across and gripped it, his other arm wrapping around her shoulders and drawing her against him.

"It's going to be all right." He forced the words from his mouth, more to reassure her than because he really believed them. Oh, he believed that Leo was going to be okay. That he would have a long and happy future. But he and Mila?

Of that he wasn't so sure.

They sat there like that for what seemed like hours, listening as Adam crisply enunciated each step of the surgery into the overhead microphone.

It seemed to take hours. It did, in fact. And yet there was no place James would rather be than sitting here next to Mila.

Finally, the surgeon stood upright and stretched his back. "That's it, ladies and gentlemen. I'm going to close and then we can wake him up."

Just as he took the threaded needle from one of the surgical nurses and leaned over the boy, an alarm went off. Then another.

"Pressure's dropping." The anesthesiologist's voice cut through the celebratory mood like a guillotine.

"What the hell's happening, Ron?" Adam asked the other doctor.

"I have no idea. He was stable a second ago. Give me a minute."

James's muscles went on high alert just as Mila stood and rushed over to the window, pressing her hands against it.

Adam, probably catching the sudden movement, glanced up at them, his jaw tight as he spoke into the microphone that linked the operating room with the observation area. "Get her out of there, James."

There was no way in hell he was going to tell Mila to leave. But if things got really bad, he would carry her out bodily if he had to.

By now the team was on high alert, Leo's feet forgotten as they fought to stabilize his condition.

Damn it!

"What's happening?" He knew Mila didn't expect an answer to her question any more than Adam had expected one from Ron Palmer, head of anesthesia at The Hollywood Hills Clinic.

Sedation was a tricky balance of drugs. Every person was different and the tiniest variation in the way the medication interacted with a patient could have devastating consequences.

Instrument tables were shoved aside and a crash cart wheeled in, just in case.

Hell, he hoped it didn't come to that.

"Let's get him stable, people." The strain in Adam's voice came through loud and clear.

Everyone was already working to do just that, but the alarms continued, unrelenting.

"He's tachy at one-thirty."

Leo's heart was beating too fast. They wouldn't know if it was a reaction to the anesthesia or something else until after they got things back under control.

"V-tach!"

Mila's whole body was now pressed against the glass. "Oh, God!"

If they couldn't get Leo's heart back into normal rhythm, it could spiral down into ventricular fibrillation, the leading cause of cardiac arrest and death.

His eyes burned and his gut was sending up alarm bells of its own. But when he tried to draw Mila away from the window, she shook him off.

"Don't touch me."

Just as suddenly, she spun toward him and wrapped her arms around his waist. "I'm sorry. So sorry. He trusted me. I told him it would be okay."

Mila had trusted James once upon a time, only to have him betray that trust so he didn't try to placate her or reassure her. He just held her and joined his fear to hers and hoped it was enough to ward off whatever was happening in that room.

The alarms switched off just as suddenly as they'd sounded, and everyone seemed to hold their collective breath.

Mila turned back toward the room below, one hand over her mouth.

"And we're back in sinus." The anesthesiologist's voice, full of relief, verified that things were turning around. "It's holding. Pressure's back up to ninety over sixty. Let's get this done."

James tightened his grip on her, kissing the top of her head in relief. If Leo got through this, James was going to spill everything. Tell Mila the truth and ask for a second chance.

Adam worked quickly to suture up the surgical sites and finish his work while Ron kept his eyes glued to the monitors. Ten minutes later the surgeon peeled off his gloves. "Thank God. Let's wake him up."

Mila and James waited with everyone else as Ron eased the sedation. Within a few minutes Leo's eyelids flickered and then opened. The anesthesiologist put his hand on the boy's forehead and said something to him. Leo nodded.

"Thank God." Mila breathed the same words the surgeon had, her whole body sagging as she fell back into one of the plush chairs. "What just happened?"

"I don't know. I'm sure Adam will want to keep an eye on him until the anesthesia has worn off completely."

"I'm going down there." She stood as if she was going to do exactly what she'd said.

"No, Mila. You're not. Not until Adam says you can." They both knew the protocol, and James was not about to break it and risk Leo's life if something happened.

"But—"

He slid an arm around her waist, ignoring all the jabs his conscience was now giving him. "We'll both go. But not until Adam gives us the green light. What we can do is wait for him to come out and talk to us."

So they went down to the waiting area, Mila perched at the very edge of a chair, while James paced in front of her.

After what seemed like hours Adam pushed through the door. "Before either of you says anything, he's stable. He's awake and talking, but I want to give him a half hour before we add more people to the mix."

Meaning he didn't want them in there right now.

"You're sure he's okay?"

"Yes. I'll have the nurse come out as soon as we're ready for you. I want to run a few tests, but I think what you saw in there was a reaction to the anesthesia. It's rare, but it happens."

"We almost lost him." The words were out of his mouth before he could stop them. Mila's head jerked around to look at him, as did Adam's, except the orthopedist, known for his calm demeanor and unflappable nature, barely lifted an eyebrow at his outburst.

"It didn't come to that. My team was on it at the first hint of trouble."

James realized his friend could have taken his words as a criticism. "Your team is top-notch. I appreciate all you've done."

"So do I. Thank you." Mila held out her hand.

Adam gave it a quick squeeze. "Everything we did in there was a success. Leo will need bracing for a while, but he has a great shot at having normal function in both feet. We may need to tweak the tendons and muscles a bit as he grows, but those will be minor procedures under local anesthesia. Nothing like today."

"Thank you, again."

Adam nodded. "Let me get back to him."

We almost lost him. James's words echoed through Mila's skull.

They could have. And when she thought of all the lost years she and James could have had, she felt sick.

Suddenly she had to know.

She turned to him. "You said on the boat you had something to tell me."

"Yes."

"Is it something about the past? Or something about the present?"

His throat moved. "Both."

"Okay. I want to do this now. Before we go back to see him."

He hesitated. "I don't think this is the right time."

"It's the perfect time." She needed to know. Know

whether they were going to be moving forward as a couple or if their lovemaking had been nothing more than passing a few hours. When she faced Leo, she wanted to know the score. Was she doing this on her own? Or did James want to move back into her life? And if she could get past all of their differences, she wanted reassurance that he was there to stay. Which meant she had to understand the past. "Let's start with ancient history. What went wrong six years ago? I want the truth."

The waiting room was empty, but James still pulled her toward the back corner and waited until she sat down. He remained standing, hands pressed deep into his pockets.

"The truth. Okay, my calling things off that day had nothing to do with you. Or my feelings at the time."

She'd avoided the "why" question for years, allowing both her anger and what had happened with her aunt to cloud her thinking. But if it had had nothing to do with how he'd felt about her...

All sorts of alternate scenarios began running through her head. Some of them outrageous. Some of them horrifying.

"So it wasn't because you didn't love me."

"No."

Had he been unfaithful? All those tabloid stories flashed through her head.

She clasped her hands in her lap, suddenly as afraid as she'd been during Leo's surgery. "Okay, then. Tell me why."

James's eyes closed for a second before reopening. "A former girlfriend told me she was pregnant."

The words meant nothing to her for a second or two, then realization dawned. Pain knifed through her abdomen, quickly turning to churning nausea. "You got someone pregnant while we were engaged?"

He knelt down and grabbed her hands. "No. Cindy and I were over a week before you and I danced that first time.

Then things happened so fast, our relationship…everything." He shook his head. "A few weeks before our wedding day she came to me and said she was expecting."

He paused. "I didn't know what to do, knew that a media firestorm would break out as soon as word got out. I waited and waited, hoping some kind of solution would come to me, but there was nothing. So I decided the only thing I could do was break off our engagement, to protect you as best I could from what was about to happen. I'm sorry, Mila. Truly sorry."

The words swirled and danced, looming and receding before her eyes until they were mere pinpoints.

Then something ugly rose as one phrase rang through her ears. "You wanted to protect me? Protect? Me?"

Okay, so she was repeating herself. But it was because the same words were now slamming against her insides like huge lapping waves that threatened to drown her.

Only this time the words were from another source. From her aunt when a sobbing seventeen-year-old Mila had waved a yellowed newspaper in front of her face, the headlines an accusation.

I was just trying to protect you.

What her aunt had done, though, had been to rob her of a chance to see her mom one last time…to say goodbye.

James had robbed her too.

Mila swallowed the bitterness that coated her throat. More than once. Even so, her next words came out as a whisper. "You should have told me the truth."

She wasn't sure if she was talking to James or her aunt's ghost.

"I wasn't thinking straight at the time, and I truly believed she was pregnant. I felt I had…a responsibility toward her, and I didn't want you to have to suffer for it."

I was just trying to protect you.

He didn't say the words this time, but they kept echoing all around her.

"And what about your responsibility toward me? I didn't need protecting. I needed the truth. *Deserved* the truth. Instead, you let me think I wasn't…" She brushed his hands away and stood up. Her skin crawled at the similarities between what her aunt had done and what he had.

"I did what I thought was right at the time."

I just wanted to protect you.

She shook off the words.

"What happened to the baby?" She turned away, not wanting to see his eyes when he told her.

"There was no baby. It was all a lie."

God.

It was. But not just one lie. More like an entire pack of them, circling around lost chances and stolen moments and trapping them inside—only pausing long enough to snap and growl whenever anything got too close.

A mishmash of betrayal, anger, fear and so many other emotions began crowding her mind, all vying for first place in her thoughts. She needed to get away. To think. To breathe. And she couldn't do that with James standing five feet away.

Before she could ask him to leave, though, a nurse headed their way. "You can go back and see Leo. He's asking for you. Both of you."

She did the only thing she could. Without looking to see if James was following, she gritted her teeth to hold back the cry of pain and walked down the long hallway.

Mila was aware of the second Leo opened his eyes and looked at her. Her heart went from the pits of despair to a relief so great that it made her insides contract. She gripped his hand in both of hers, aware of James waiting somewhere behind her. She didn't want to talk to him right now. Maybe never. All her energy had to go toward Leo. Toward making sure he recovered.

Leo's eyes moved from hers to a spot just over her left shoulder. *"Papá, Papá ¿Dónde estás?"*

Mila's throat tightened to breaking point when she realized he wasn't asking where his dead father was but was looking at James.

She glanced back, pleading for him not to hurt Leo. Not now. His mouth moved, but nothing came out, the shock on his face so obvious it might have been funny under different circumstances. Only no one was laughing. Least of all her.

He gave her a long glance before coming forward, the smile he gave Leo as fake as a runway model's. And his posture. It was stiff. His muscles tensed and ready.

Ready to run. Again.

Well, good. She could only hope he did it before she told him to get the hell out of her life.

How dared he look her in the eye six years ago and tell her that he simply couldn't go through with their wedding when all the while he'd been sitting on the real reason.

And somehow his lie was so much worse than her aunt's had been. Because Mila had been an adult, fully capable of dealing with anything he'd handed to her. Only he hadn't given her the chance.

Well, she didn't care. This was about Leo. Not about her. Not about James. He could take his sorry little sack of confessions and saunter right back out of their lives. But not until he helped Leo get through this one last thing.

The child held out his hand and James took it. *"¿Estoy bien?"* Am I okay?

Mila's heart fragmented into a million pieces.

"Yes, Leo." There was a strangled edge to James's voice that she didn't recognize. "You're going to be fine now. I promise."

She took a deep breath. At least this time he'd spoken

the truth. She and Leo would be fine—without James. She would make sure of it, make sure she gave Leo everything he needed. And the thing he needed most was love.

The boy's eyelids fluttered, and Mila leaned down to kiss his brow. "You sleep. I'll be here when you wake up."

When she glanced back at James. There was an anguish in his expression that she recognized all too well. She'd seen it once before. In the church, right before their wedding.

Mila moved away from Leo, hoping James would follow her. She didn't want little ears to hear what she was about to say. She met him by the door.

"Thank you for finally telling me the truth after all these years, but I think you should go. Now, before he wakes up."

Even as she said the words, her heart cried out for him to say something—anything—that would change her mind before she could make the break complete, but he stood there like a stone.

She waited a second or two longer and when there was still nothing she finished the job, bringing down the ax before she lost her courage. "I want you to go, James. And don't come back."

Mila threw herself into her work like never before, flitting between her LA clinic and the new one. James had given her free rein over the hiring of staff, and Avery had helped her in selecting the best candidates and setting up shop.

James had left instructions that no expense should be spared. She had an open checkbook, and he wanted her to use it however she wanted.

Of course he hadn't told her that in person. He'd done as she'd asked. He'd left. In fact, she hadn't seen him in the last two weeks. Someone said he'd taken his sailboat and gone on an extended vacation.

Where?

It didn't matter.

What did matter was that her doubts about the way she'd ended things were beginning to crop up, multiplying like dust bunnies that crouched beneath her bed, hidden from view but there nonetheless.

He'd done what he'd thought best back then.

Had it been the right decision?

No. No more than her aunt had done the right thing by telling her that her parents had died in a car accident.

Had he done it with malicious intent?

No. Of that she had no doubt.

I was trying to protect you.

In truth, nothing could have protected her from the pain of him saying it was over. Or the pain of her parents' deaths. Both things had been devastating losses that she'd never gotten over.

But James had confessed on his own. She hadn't had to wave a newspaper article in his face.

Had she pushed him away too quickly, fearing that if she didn't he would just repeat the mistakes of the past and hurt her again? Well, she'd made sure he never had the chance of doing that.

But if he'd wanted to stay, wouldn't he have fought for her? Or come back later and tried to get her to change her mind? He hadn't done that six years ago, so why did she expect him to do it now?

Besides, she'd basically told him not to bother.

Scrubbing the exam table a little harder than necessary after her last patient of the day, she tried to figure out what exactly she wanted.

She wanted James.

But did he really want her? Oh, he'd made love to her after that gala as if he cared about her. And he'd said that what he wanted to tell her had to do with the past...*and* the present. She'd never given him the chance to tell her anything beyond that awful confession.

But what else could he have wanted to say?

The door opened and Freya poked her head in. In her normal no-nonsense fashion she rounded the corner and braced her back against the wall beside the door, her maternity top skimming over her belly. Her friend glowed with health and happiness. And somehow that made Mila even more miserable. Especially since her cycle had come in with a vengeance, verifying what the pregnancy test had already told her. She wasn't carrying James's child. And if she was, would he have stayed with her just for that reason? He'd mentioned feeling a sense of responsibility toward that Cindy person when he'd thought she'd been pregnant.

More doubts arose, revealing the saddest truth of all.

She missed him. Terribly. Despite everything. As did Leo, who kept asking where Papá was.

That just about killed her.

She tossed her paper towel into the trash and tried to think of something cheery to say to her friend. She came up blank, settling for resting a hip against the exam table and waiting for Freya to spit out whatever it was she was chewing on.

"I know where he is."

A stab of something went through her system. "Where who is?"

Freya gave her a look.

"Okay. I know who you mean. He lied to me, Freya. About everything."

"I know. He told me." Her friend moved as close as she could without her belly touching Mila. "I tried waiting until one of you came to your senses, but since neither of you seems to be heading in that direction, I'm going to tell you something. And then you can decide what you want to do about it."

"Okay." Mila wasn't sure she wanted to hear it, but if it

would help her understand what had happened, maybe she could at least gain closure.

"James said he told you about Cindy. I had no idea. He never said a word. Until I confronted him on the phone a few days ago. Did he also tell you that our father had a habit of getting women pregnant and then paying them off to keep them quiet? Or that he offered to do the same with Cindy?"

"What?" James had said nothing about it. Not that she'd given him a chance.

"It's true. There are probably people walking around out there who have no idea that Michael Rothsberg is their father. Or that they have half-siblings." She paused. "James didn't say it outright, but I think that's why he broke off your engagement. So that he didn't become like our father, unwilling to face the consequences of his actions. If Cindy was pregnant, he wanted that child to know who its father was."

Mila gulped. It all made sense. Had she made a huge mistake?

"You're my friend, Freya. Couldn't you have asked him those questions back then?"

"When? After you'd left for Brazil and said you never wanted to hear James's name again?" Her shoulders twitched. "I was just as angry at him as you were, Mi. Then, after you came back to LA, I thought that bringing up the past would just hurt everyone involved."

She touched Mila's hand. "But now…I think he loves you, Mi. And this time, no matter how hurt you might feel, I don't think you should let him get off quite so easily."

Easily? None of this was easy. Would things have been any different if James had indeed told her the truth six years ago? She searched her heart.

No. Probably not. But now? Was she going to just let

him drop a bombshell about their past and then walk away a second time?

Actually, he hadn't. She'd told him to leave. And he had. If he'd tried to express his undying love for her, she probably would have thrown it back in his face. She hadn't been ready to forgive him.

And now?

"What should I do?"

"Do you love him?"

Mila nodded.

"Can you live with what he did, knowing why he did it?"

Could she? She searched her heart. She hadn't known about his dad. Or about Cindy. But James was a man of integrity, she'd seen that time and time again. He'd been trying to spare her in the best way he knew how.

"Yes. I think I can."

"Then if I were you, I'd hunt the man down and make him grovel. A lot. And then I'd forgive him."

Mila smiled. "I think I'm probably the one who needs to do the groveling. At least this time. I pushed him away, Freya, and didn't even give him a chance to finish explaining."

"Then maybe you should press Rewind and give him that chance."

"Maybe I should." She reached out and grabbed her friend up in a gentle hug. "But first you have to tell me where he is."

"I can do better than that. Zack knows this guy…"

By the time Freya had finished laying out the plan, Mila found something seeping into her heart that hadn't been there for the last six years: hope.

CHAPTER TWELVE

SOMEONE WAS CHASING HIM.

James had just pulled up anchor, not to mention pulling his head out of his ass and finally acknowledging what his heart had known all along. He couldn't live without her. He didn't know exactly how to make this right but he had to at least try.

He wanted it all. And that included Leo.

He'd hurt her twice. Once by leaving her at the altar, and once by sleeping with her before he'd told her the truth about what he'd done all those years ago. He wouldn't blame her if she told him to get the hell off her doorstep—well, technically it was *his* doorstep since she was staying in his guest house. That was if she hadn't already left.

Leo calling him Papá so soon after he'd told Mila the truth had been the last straw. He hadn't earned the right to be called that by anyone, least of all a young boy who'd known pain and fear most of his life. His reaction had been to run, instead of fighting for what he wanted.

But he was done running. Done allowing his life's course to be charted by his father's sins. And by his own past.

James was going to find Mila and tell her exactly what he'd wanted to tell her that day in Leo's hospital room. That he loved her. That he wanted to make this work, and he was willing to do whatever it took to make her forgive him for what he'd done.

He glanced back again. The dinghy was still there, bouncing over the choppy waters and zigzagging to avoid his wake.

What the hell? James was moving under his engine's power. He could just ramp up his speed or set his sails so that they would catch more of the wind and pull away from his pursuer with ease. It wasn't a coast-guard vessel. Maybe it was a member of the paparazzi, looking for more dirt on the Rothsberg family. As if there wasn't enough already.

And if the person decided to follow him farther offshore? They could get themselves into a situation that could turn deadly. He wasn't willing to risk it. It would be better to just cut speed and give the fool a piece of his mind.

Just then his phone pinged, signaling he'd received a text. Perfect.

Suddenly, the normal stab of irritation was replaced by nerves. Or maybe a premonition.

Forgetting about the person behind him for a moment, he glanced at the screen of his cell phone.

Would you mind slowing down so I can catch you?

He blinked and looked closer. Mila's avatar was displayed at the top of the message.

Catch him?

He looked back again to see the person at the wheel was now waving at him like a crazy person.

Damn it!

Mila. What was she…?

He immediately cut the engine and turned the wheel so the bow would face into the wind. By the time the dinghy pulled alongside, he'd dropped anchor and had come over to the side to yell, "Throw me a line."

With hair plastered to her head and soaking wet from head to toe from sea spray, she was still the most beautiful sight he'd ever seen. He'd been heading to LA to try to win her back. And she was here.

And she could have gotten herself killed!

She threw the rope, and James quickly lowered a couple of bumpers down the side of the sailboat to keep the vessels from slamming together in the current. He then tied the dinghy's line to one of the metal cleats on deck. Dropping the rope ladder he kept for swimming outings, he held it steady as Mila grasped the sides and began to climb. When she was close enough, he grabbed her hands and hauled her the rest of the way on board.

"Were you hoping to wind up like those Jet Skiers we ran into a few weeks back? What the hell were you thinking?"

"I was thinking I wasn't going to let the prince turn back into a toad for a second time."

He blinked at her. Maybe that ride out to him had been bumpier than he'd thought. "Come again?"

"Never mind." She took a step closer. "Freya told me what your father did to those women. What he tried to do to you."

Leave it to his sister to interfere. Although this time, maybe she'd been right to.

He swallowed hard. "That is one person I don't want to talk about ever again."

"You don't have to." She reached for his hand. "Let's talk about us instead."

A spark of something came to life in his chest. She'd said "us." As in there might be a chance for him to undo the mess he'd made? "You basically told me there was no us."

"I know. And I'm sorry. I should have heard you out."

"I was just heading back to make you do exactly that. And to ask you to forgive me."

"You were?" Her head tilted as if she was surprised.

"Yes."

She laughed. "Well, I guess I could have saved myself

the trouble of hunting you down, then, couldn't I?" She glanced down at the dinghy.

"Is that thing even licensed?"

"Of course it is. And I caught you, didn't I?"

"You did. You look like you've driven one of those before." He had to admit she'd maneuvered the tiny boat beautifully.

"I have. Many times. In Brazil, while doing my medical missions." Her face turned serious as she gestured at his boat. "I do forgive you, but now that I'm here I have to tell you this scares me a little, James. It always has, even when we were together."

"What does?"

"The fancy boat, expensive fund-raisers, the world-class clinic." She glanced again at the dinghy bouncing far below them. "That little boat…is me. It's what I'm happy with. I believed for six years that I wasn't enough for you, and I'm afraid—"

"Not enough for me?" He grabbed her and hauled her to him. "You were always too much. Too beautiful. Too kind. Too…everything. And I didn't want what I'd done to somehow touch you and destroy everything you are. Just like my dad destroyed the lives of who knows how many women and children."

He kissed her cheek. "I never wanted kids, for that very reason. I'm scared too, Mi. Scared I won't be enough for Leo. For you."

"You are. Of course you are." She reached up and touched his face. "When I saw the way you looked at him…I knew I'd never stopped loving you."

He gulped, a wave of emotion sweeping up from his gut and moving to his lungs. His throat. His mouth. He tried to speak and failed, so he shook his head and then tried again. "You love me?"

"Yes." She wrapped her arms around his neck and pressed a tender kiss against his jaw. "Do you love me?"

"I always have." That one thing he did know. And right now, it was the only thing that was keeping him going.

"Then it's time we both stopped running from the truth and found a way to be together." She lifted her phone. "Text me back."

"What?"

"Freya says you haven't texted anyone in six years." She trailed light fingertips down the side of his temple. "So text me. Tell me you're going to stay with me this time—that you won't keep anything from me ever again. And…I'll believe you."

James tipped up her chin and slid his lips over hers. Once, twice, three times until he was in danger of dragging her down to his cabin and making love to her then and there. But that's not what she wanted. She'd asked him to do something, and he needed to do it. To make them both believe this could work.

Taking her hand, he went over to the steering console and picked up his phone. He slowly depressed the letters on the keypad, and then for several nerve-racking moments stared at the words he'd typed, his thumb hovering over the Send button. He pressed it. Set the cell phone back on the glossy teak surface beside him.

A tiny lion roared from somewhere nearby, ruining the seriousness of the moment. Mila's phone.

Smiling, her eyes on his, she drew the instrument out of her pocket and stared at the screen.

The words he'd typed were seared into his head, he could almost hear them spoken aloud as her eyes skipped across the text.

I love you, Mila. You and Leo. And anyone else who might be tucked inside you in the future. Will you marry me?

We can do the whole damn wedding ceremony through texts, if you want—vows included. Just say you want to be with me.

Moisture rimmed her eyes, one tear sliding down her cheek. "I do. I want to be with you."

"Thank God." He brushed the tear from her face and then took the phone and laid it beside his own. "And now that we've gotten that out of the way, we won't be needing those for a while."

A smile came to her face. "No? And why is that?"

"Because I want any future communication to be up close and personal. Starting now."

With that, James swept her off her feet and headed below deck, where he wouldn't need texts to tell her how he felt. He planned to show her. From this moment and far into the future.

EPILOGUE

HE WAS STILL HERE.

The vows hadn't been texted, they'd been recited. Her wedding veil gently lifted. And he was kissing her. As if he couldn't get enough.

James hadn't run this time. And neither had she.

Clutching the lapels of his tuxedo, and surrounded by their friends from The Hollywood Hills Clinic and Bright Hope, Mila had all she could possibly need.

He finally let her up for air, and clapping erupted from all around them. Freya handed back her bouquet, while Zack passed one of the pair's sleeping twins to his radiant wife. Now a year old, Tobey and Willow Carlton were a sight to behold this beautiful November day.

And Leo…

Mila's eyes sought him out and found him next to Rosa, the woman's arm protectively curled around his shoulders. He was out of his casts and walking with just the help of a crutch. Soon he wouldn't even need that. Adam Walker had performed a second surgery to do some fine-tuning of the tendons in his feet. It had gone wonderfully, and Adam, seated next to Gabriella and Rafael, two other doctors from James's clinic, said Leo would have normal function. An outcome Mila was extremely grateful for.

And soon Leo would be theirs. The adoption papers

were due to be filed next week. His uncle had relinquished all rights and so the barriers were being lifted one by one.

Mila hadn't gotten pregnant during that infamous pool session, but she had a few months later. And this time the missing birth control had been intentional, James's way of physically proving to her that he would be there for her this time. She finally understood why she hadn't been able to make things work with Tyler. It was because she'd never stopped loving James. Thank God they'd both realized it in time.

Mila had also been right about Tyler and Avery. The couple had eloped two weeks ago. Her friend had sent her congratulations through Freya along with a promise to be back at work in a few days. She couldn't be happier.

Taking her hand and lifting it to his mouth, her new husband kissed the ring he'd just placed on her finger. "Don't ever take it off," he murmured.

"I won't."

And then they were running down the aisle of the church, past Flo and Nate, Lola and Jake, Grace and Liam, and so many others who had made their lives richer. The only one who wasn't there was Michael Rothsberg. Mila and James had agreed they weren't going to let him cast a pall over their lives a second time. But James's mom had come—and she'd offered to help Rosa with Leo until they got back from their honeymoon. She'd then kissed Mila's cheek and wished her many happy years. In turn, Mila had hugged her tight and thanked her for making James the man he was today.

"I can't take any credit for that, honey," she'd murmured in that mellow Southern drawl Mila had heard countless times in films. "James is the man he is because that's the man he decided to be."

And the man he'd decided to be was strong yet compassionate. He'd avoided treating children for years, but for the first time he was considering teaming up with Mila for a medical mission. She'd go back to Brazil, where James would do reconstructive surgery on kids who so desperately needed it, while Mila did what she did best, provided health services to at-risk moms and children.

When they exited the church, she wasn't prepared for the flash of cameras everywhere as they ran toward the limousine. But, tucked against James's side, it was a small price to pay for the happiness she'd found.

One of her white high-heeled shoes caught in a crack on the sidewalk and popped off in mid-stride. It flipped end over end before landing on the pavement behind them. Soon it was lost in the sea of paparazzi that closed in on them.

"My shoe!" She hobbled forward a few feet, the difference of the lost inches on one foot slowing her down.

"Leave it." James scooped her up, her wedding dress billowing over his arm while the photographers seemed to eat it up. "Prince Charming might have needed a shoe to find his true love, but I don't. I have you right here. And I never intend to let you go."

With that, they climbed into the sleek black vehicle, and James proceeded to show her the truth of that statement. It was fine by Mila. Because she intended to do the same: to hang on to this man for the rest of her life.

* * * * *